Marzio's Crucifix and Zoroaster by F. Marion Crawford

Francis Marion Crawford was born on August 2nd, 1854 at Bagni di Lucca, Italy. An only son and a nephew to Julia Ward Howe, the American poet and writer of 'The Battle Hymn of the Republic'.

His education began at St Paul's School, Concord, New Hampshire, then to Cambridge University; University of Heidelberg; and the University of Rome.

In 1879 Crawford went to India, to study Sanskrit and then edited The Indian Herald. In 1881 he returned to America to continue his Sanskrit studies at Harvard University.

At this time in Boston he lived at his Aunt Julia house and in the company of his Uncle, Sam Ward. His family was concerned about his employment prospects. After a singing career as a baritone was ruled out, he was encouraged to write.

In December 1882 his first novel, 'Mr Isaacs', was an immediate hit which was amplified by 'Dr Claudius' in 1883.

In October 1884 he married Elizabeth Berdan. They went on to have two sons and two daughters.

Encouraged by his excellent start to a literary career he returned to Italy with Elizabeth to make a permanent home, principally in Sant' Agnello, where he bought the Villa Renzi that then became Villa Crawford.

In the late 1890s, he began to write his historical works: 'Ave Roma Immortalis' (1898), 'Rulers of the South' (1900) and 'Gleanings from Venetian History' (1905). The Saracinesca series is perhaps his best work. 'Saracinesca' was followed by 'Sant' Ilario' in 1889, 'Don Orsino' in 1892 and 'Corleone' in 1897, that being the first major treatment of the Mafia in literature.

Francis Marion Crawford died at Sorrento on Good Friday 1909 at Villa Crawford of a heart attack.

Index of Contents

MARZIO'S CRUCIFIX

CHAPTER I

"The whole of this modern fabric of existence is a living lie!" cried Marzio Pandolfi, striking his little hammer upon the heavy table with an impatient rap. Then he dropped it and turning on his stool rested one elbow upon the board while he clasped his long, nervous fingers together and stared hard at his handsome apprentice. Gianbattista Bordogni looked up from his work without relinquishing his tools, nodded gravely, stared up at the high window, and then went on hammering gently upon his little chisel, guiding the point carefully among the delicate arabesques traced upon the silver.

"Yes," he said quietly, after a few seconds, "it is all a lie. But what do you expect, Maestro Marzio? You might as well talk to a stone wall as preach liberty to these cowards."

"Nevertheless, there are some—there are half a dozen—" muttered Marzio, relapsing into sullen discontent and slowly turning the body of the chalice beneath the cord stretched by the pedal on which he pressed his foot. Having brought under his hand a round boss which was to become the head of a cherub under his chisel, he rubbed his fingers over the smooth silver, mechanically, while he contemplated the red wax model before him. Then there was silence for a space, broken only by the quick, irregular striking of the two little hammers upon the heads of the chisels.

Maestro Marzio Pandolfi was a skilled workman and an artist. He was one of the last of those workers in metals who once sent their masterpieces from Rome to the great cathedrals of the world; one of the last of the artistic descendants of Caradosso, of Benvenuto Cellini, of Claude Ballin, and of all their successors; one of those men of rare talent who unite the imagination of the artist with the executive skill of the practised workman. They are hard to find nowadays. Of all the twenty chisellers of various ages who hammered from morning till night in the rooms outside, one only—Gianbattista Bordogni—had been thought worthy by his master to share the privacy of the inner studio. The lad had talent, said Maestro Marzio, and, what was more, the lad had ideas—ideas about life, about the future of Italy, about the future of the world's society. Marzio found in him a pupil, an artist and a follower of his own political creed.

It was a small room in which they worked together. Plain wooden shelves lined two of the walls from the floor to the ceiling. The third was occupied by tables and a door, and in the fourth high grated windows were situated, from which the clear light fell upon the long bench before which the two men sat upon high stools. Upon the shelves were numerous models in red wax, of chalices, monstrances, marvellous ewers and embossed basins for the ablution of the priests' hands, crucifixes, crowns, palm and olive branches—in a word, models of all those things which pertain to the service and decoration of the church, and upon which it has been the privilege of the silversmith to expend his art and labour from time immemorial until the present day. There were some few casts in plaster, but almost all were of that deep red, strong-smelling wax which is the most fit medium for the temporary expression and study of very fine and intricate designs. There is something in the very colour which, to one acquainted with the art, suggests beautiful fancies. It is the red of the Pompeian walls, and the rich tint seems to call up the matchless traceries of the ancients. Old chisellers say that no one can model anything wholly bad in red wax, and there is truth in the saying. The material is old—the older the better; it has passed under the hand of the artist again and again; it has taken form, served for the model of a lasting work, been kneaded together in a lump, been worked over and over by the boxwood tool. The workman feels that it has absorbed some of the qualities of the master's genius, and touches it with the certainty that its stiff substance will yield new forms of beauty in his fingers, rendering up some of its latent capacity of shape at each pressure and twist of the deftly-handled instrument.

At the extremities of the long bench huge iron vices were fixed by staples that ran into the ground. In one of these was fastened the long curved tool which serves to beat out the bosses of hollow and small-necked vessels. Each of the workmen had a pedal beneath his foot from which a soft cord ascended, passed through the table, and pressed the round object on which he was working upon a thick leather cushion, enabling him to hold it tightly in its place, or by lifting his foot to turn it to a new position. In pots full of sand were stuck hundreds of tiny chisels, so that the workmen could select at a glance the exact form of tool needful for the moment. Two or three half balls of heavy stone stood in leathern collars, their flat surfaces upwards and covered with a brown composition of pitch and beeswax an inch thick, in which small pieces of silver were firmly embedded in position to be chiselled.

The workshop was pervaded by a smell of wax and pitch, mingled with the curious indefinable odour exhaled from steel tools in constant use, and supplemented by the fumes of Marzio's pipe. The red bricks in the portion of the floor where the two men sat were rubbed into hollows, but the dust had been allowed to accumulate freely in the rest of the room, and the dark corners were full of cobwebs which had all the air of being inhabited by spiders of formidable dimensions.

Marzio Pandolfi, who bent over his work and busily plied his little hammer during the interval of silence which followed his apprentice's last remark, was the sole owner and master of the establishment. He was forty years of age, thin and dark. His black hair was turning grey at the temples, and though not long, hung forward over his knitted eyebrows in disorderly locks. He had a strange face. His head, broad enough at the level of the eyes, rose to a high prominence towards the back, while his forehead, which projected forward at the heavy brows, sloped backwards in the direction of the summit. The large black eyes were deep and hollow, and there were broad rings of dark colour around them, so that they seemed strangely thrown into relief above the sunken, colourless cheeks. Marzio's nose was long and pointed, very straight, and descending so suddenly from the forehead as to make an angle with the latter the reverse of the one most common in human faces. Seen in profile, the brows formed the most prominent point, and the line of the head ran back above, while the line of the nose fell inward from the perpendicular down to the small curved nostrils. The short black moustache was thick enough to hide the lips, though deep furrows surrounded the mouth and terminated in a very prominent but pointed chin. The whole face expressed unusual qualities and defects; the gifts of the artist, the tenacity of the workman and the small astuteness of the plebeian were mingled with an appearance of something which was not precisely ideality, but which might easily be fanaticism.

Marzio was tall and very thin. His limbs seemed to move rather by the impulse of a nervous current within than by any development of normal force in the muscles, and his long and slender fingers, naturally yellow and discoloured by the use of tools and the handling of cements, might have been parts of a machine, for they had none of that look of humanity which one seeks in the hand, and by which one instinctively judges the character. He was dressed in a woollen blouse, which hung in odd folds about his emaciated frame, but which betrayed the roundness of his shoulders, and the extreme length of his arms. His apprentice, Gianbattista Bordogni, wore the same costume; but beyond his clothing he bore no trace of any resemblance to his master. He was not a bad type of the young Roman of his class at five-and-twenty years of age. His thick black hair curled all over his head, from his low forehead to the back of his neck, and his head was of a good shape, full and round, broad over the brows and high above the orifice of the ear. His eyes were brown and not over large, but well set, and his nose was slightly aquiline, while his delicate black moustache showed the pleasant curve of his even lips. There was colour in his cheeks, too—that rich colour which dark men sometimes have in their youth. He was of middle height, strong and compactly built, with large, well-made hands that seemed to have more power in them, if less subtle skill, than those of Maestro Marzio.

"Remember what I told you about the second indentation of the acanthus," said the elder workman, without looking round; "a light, light hand—no holes in this work!"

Gianbattista murmured a sort of assent, which showed that the warning was not wanted. He was intent upon the delicate operation he was performing. Again the hammers beat irregularly.

"The more I think of it," said Marzio after the pause, "the more I am beside myself. To think that you and I should be nailed to our stools here, weekdays and feast-days, to finish a piece of work for a scoundrelly priest—"

"A cardinal," suggested Gianbattista.

"Well! What difference is there? He is a priest, I suppose—a creature who dresses himself up like a pulcinella before his altar—to—"

"Softly!" ejaculated the young man, looking round to see whether the door was closed.

"Why softly?" asked the other angrily, though his annoyance did not seem to communicate itself to the chisel he held in his hand, and which continued its work as delicately as though its master were humming a pastoral. "Why softly? An apoplexy on your softness! The papers speak as loudly as they please—why should I hold my tongue? A dog-butcher of a priest!"

"Well," answered Gianbattista in a meditative tone, as he selected another chisel, "he has the money to pay for what he orders. If he had not, we would not work for him, I suppose."

"If we had the money, you mean," retorted Marzio. "Why the devil should he have money rather than we? Why don't you answer? Why should he wear silk stockings—red silk stockings, the animal? Why should he want a silver ewer and basin to wash his hands at his mass? Why would not an earthen one do as well, such as I use? Why don't you answer? Eh?"

"Why should Prince Borghese live in a palace and keep scores of horses?" inquired the young man calmly.

"Ay—why should he? Is there any known reason why he should? Am I not a man as well as he? Are you not a man—you young donkey? I hate to think that we, who are artists, who can work when we are put to it, have to slave for such fellows as that—mumbling priests, bloated princes, a pack of fools who are incapable of an idea! An idea! What am I saying? Who have not the common intelligence of a cabbage-seller in the street! And look at the work we give them—the creation of our minds, the labour of our hands—"

"They give us their money in return," observed Gianbattista. "The ancients, whom you are so fond of talking about, used to get their work done by slaves chained to the bench—"

"Yes! And it has taken us two thousand years to get to the point we have reached! Two thousand years—and what is it? Are we any better than slaves, except that we work better?"

"I doubt whether we work better."

"What is the matter with you this morning?" cried Marzio. "Have you been sneaking into some church on your way here? Pah! You smell of the sacristy! Has Paolo been here? Oh, to think that a brother of mine should be a priest! It is not to be believed!"

"It is the irony of fate. Moreover, he gets you plenty of orders."

"Yes, and no doubt he takes his percentage on the price. He had a new cloak last month, and he asked me to make him a pair of silver buckles for his shoes. Pretty, that—an artist's brother with silver buckles! I told him to go to the devil, his father, for his ornaments. Why does he not steal an old pair from the cardinal, his bondmaster? Not good enough, I suppose—beast!"

Marzio laid aside his hammer and chisel, and lit the earthen pipe with the rough wooden stem that lay beside him. Then he examined the beautiful head of the angel he had been making upon the body of the ewer. He touched it lovingly, loosed the cord, and lifted the piece from the pad, turning it towards the light and searching critically for any defect in the modelling of the little face. He replaced it on the table, and selecting a very fine-pointed punch, laid down his pipe for a moment and set about putting the tiny pupils into the eyes. Two touches were enough. He began smoking again, and contemplated what he had done. It was the body of a large silver ewer of which Gianbattista was ornamenting the neck and mouth, which were of a separate piece. Amongst the intricate arabesques little angels'-heads were embossed, and on one side a group of cherubs was bearing a "monstrance" with the sacred Host through silver clouds. A hackneyed subject on church vessels, but which had taken wonderful beauty under the skilled fingers of the artist, who sat cursing the priest who was to use it, while expending his best talents on its perfections.

"It is not bad," he said rather doubtfully. "Come and look at it, Tista," he added. The young man left his place and came and bent over his master's shoulder, examining the piece with admiration. It was characteristic of Marzio that he asked his apprentice's opinion. He was an artist, and had the chief peculiarities of artists—namely, diffidence concerning what he had done, and impatience of the criticism of others, together with a strong desire to show his work as soon as it was presentable.

"It is a masterpiece!" exclaimed Gianbattista. "What detail! I shall never be able to finish anything like that cherub's face!"

"Do you think it is as good as the one I made last year, Tista?"

"Better," returned the young man confidently. "It is the best you have ever made. I am quite sure of it. You should always work when you are in a bad humour; you are so successful!"

"Bad humour! I am always in a bad humour," grumbled Marzio, rising and walking about the brick floor, while he puffed clouds of acrid smoke from his coarse pipe. "There is enough in this world to keep a man in a bad humour all his life."

"I might say that," answered Gianbattista, turning round on his stool and watching his master's angular movements as he rapidly paced the room. "I might abuse fate—but you! You are rich, married, a father, a great artist!"

"What stuff!" interrupted Marzio, standing still with his long legs apart, and folding his arms as he spoke through his teeth, between which he still held his pipe. "Rich? Yes—able to have a good coat for feast-days, meat when I want it, and my brother's company when I don't want it—for a luxury, you know! Able to take my wife to Frascati on the last Thursday of October as a great holiday. My wife, too! A creature of beads and saints and little books with crosses on them—who would leer at a friar through the grating of a confessional, and who makes the house hideous with her howling if I choose to eat a bit of pork on a Friday! A good wife indeed! A jewel of a wife, and an apoplexy on all such jewels! A nice wife, who has a face like a head from a tombstone in the Campo Varano for her husband, and who has brought up her daughter to believe that her father is condemned to everlasting flames because he hates cod-fish—salt cod-fish soaked in water! A wife who sticks images in the lining of my hat to convert me, and sprinkles holy water on me Then she thinks I am asleep, but I caught her at that the other night—"

"Indeed, they say the devil does not like holy water," remarked Gianbattista, laughing.

"And you want to many my daughter, you young fool," continued Marzio, not heeding the interruption. "You do. I will tell you what she is like. My daughter—yes!—she has fine eyes, but she has the tongue of the—"

"Of her father," suggested Gianbattista, suddenly frowning.

"Yes—of her father, without her father's sense," cried Marzio angrily. "With her eyes, those fine eyes!—those eyes!—you want to marry her. If you wish to take her away, you may, and good riddance. I want no daughter; there are too many women in the world already. They and the priests do all the harm between them, because the priests know how to think too well, and women never think at all. I wish you good luck of your marriage and of your wife. If you were my son you would never have thought of getting married. The mere idea of it made you send your chisel through a cherub's eye last week and cost an hoax's time for repairing. Is that the way to look at the great question of humanity? Ah! if I were only a deputy in the Chambers, I would teach you the philosophy of all that rubbish!"

"I thought you said the other day that you would not have any deputies at all," observed the apprentice, playing with his hammer.

"Such as these are—no! A few of them I would put into the acid bath, as I would a casting, to clean them before chiselling them down. They might be good for something then. You must begin by knocking down, boy, if you want to build up. You must knock down everything, raze the existing system to the ground, and upon the place where it stood shall rise the mighty temple of immortal liberty."

"And who will buy your chalices and monstrances under the new order of things?" inquired Gianbattista coldly.

"The foreign market," returned Marzio. "Italy shall be herself again, as she was in the days of Michael Angelo; of Leonardo, who died in the arms of a king; of Cellini, who shot a prince from the walls of Saint Angelo. Italy shall be great, shall monopolise the trade, the art, the greatness of all creation!"

"A lucrative monopoly!" exclaimed the young man.

"Monopolies! There shall be no monopolies! The free artisan shall sell what he can make and buy what he pleases. The priests shall be turned out in chain gangs and build roads for our convenience, and the superfluous females shall all be deported to the glorious colony of Massowah! If I could but be absolute master of this country for a week I could do much."

"I have no doubt of it," answered Gianbattista, with a quiet smile.

"I should think not," assented Marzio proudly; then catching sight of the expression on the young man's face, he turned sharply upon him. "You are mocking me, you good-for-nothing!" he cried angrily. "You are laughing at me, at your master, you villain you wretch, you sickly hound, you priest-ridden worm! It is intolerable! It is the first time you have ever dared; do you think I am going to allow you to think for yourself after all the pains I have taken to educate you, to teach you my art, you ungrateful reptile?"

"If you were not such a great artist I would have left you long ago," answered the apprentice. "Besides, I believe in your principles. It is your expression of them that makes me laugh now and then; I think you go too far sometimes!"

"As if any one had ever gone far enough" exclaimed Marzio, somewhat pacified, for his moods were very quick. "Since there are still men who are richer than others, it is a sign that we have not gone to the end—to the great end in which we believe. I am sure you believe in it too, Tista, don't you?"

"Oh yes—in the end—certainly. Do not let us quarrel about the means, Maestro Marzio. I must do another leaf before dinner."

"I will get in another cherub's nose," said his master, preparing to relight his pipe for a whiff before going to work again. "Body of a dog, these priests!" he grumbled, as he attacked the next angel on the ewer with matchless dexterity and steadiness. A long pause followed the animated discourse of the chiseller. Both men were intent upon their work, alternately holding their breath for the delicate strokes, and breathing more freely as the chisel reached the end of each tiny curve.

"I think you said a little while ago that I might marry Lucia," observed Gianbattista, without looking up, "that is, if I would take her away!"

"And if you take her away," retorted the other, "where will you get bread?"

"Where I get it now. I could live somewhere else and come here to work; it seems simple enough."

"It seems simple, but it is not," replied Marzio. "Perhaps you could try and get Paolo's commissions away from me, and then set up a studio for yourself; but I doubt whether you could succeed. I am not old yet, nor blind, nor shaky, thank God!"

"I did not catch the last words," said Gianbattista, hiding his smile over his work.

"I said I was not old, nor broken down yet, thanks to my strength," growled the chiseller; "you will not steal my commissions yet awhile. What is the matter with you to-day? You find fault with half I say, and the other half you do not hear at all. You seem to have lost your head, Tista. Be steady over those acanthus leaves; everybody thinks an acanthus leaf is the easiest thing in the world, whereas it is one of the most difficult before you get to figures. Most chisellers seem to copy their acanthus leaves from the cabbage in their soup. They work as though they had never seen the plant growing. When the Greeks began to carve Corinthian capitals, they must have worked from real leaves, as I taught you to model when you were a boy. Few things are harder than a good acanthus leaf."

"I should think women could do the delicate part of our work very well," said the apprentice, returning to the subject from which Marzio was evidently trying to lead him. "Lucia has such very clever fingers."

"Idiot!" muttered Marzio between his teeth, not deigning to make any further answer.

The distant boom of a gun broke upon the silence that followed, and immediately the bells of all the neighbouring churches rang out in quick succession. It was midday.

"I did not expect to finish that nose," said Marzio, rising from his stool. He was a punctual man, who exacted punctuality in others, and in spite of his thin frame and nervous ways, he loved his dinner. In five minutes all the men had left the workshop, and Marzio and his apprentice stood in the street, the former locking the heavy door with a lettered padlock, while the younger man sniffed the fresh spring air that blew from the west out of the square of San Carlo a Catenari down the Via dei Falegnami in which the establishment of the silver-chiseller was situated.

As Marzio fumbled with the fastenings of the door, two women came up and stopped. Marzio had his back turned, and Gianbattista touched his hat in silence. The younger of the two was a stout, black-haired woman of eight-and-thirty years, dressed in a costume of dark green cloth, which fitted very closely to her exuberantly-developed bust, and was somewhat too elaborately trimmed with imitation of jet and black ribands. A high bonnet, decorated with a bunch of purple glass grapes and dark green leaves, surmounted the lady's massive head, and though carefully put on and neatly tied, seemed too small for the wearer. Her ears were adorned by long gold earrings, in each of which were three large garnets, and these trinkets dangled outside and over the riband of the bonnet, which passed under her chin. In her large hands, covered with tight black gloves, she carried a dark red parasol and a somewhat shabby little black leather bag with steel fastenings. The stout lady's face was of the type common among the Roman women of the lower class—very broad and heavy, of a creamy white complexion, the upper lip shaded by a dark fringe of down, and the deep sleepy eyes surmounted by heavy straight eyebrows. Her hair, brought forward from under her bonnet, made smooth waves upon her low forehead and reappeared in thick coils at the back of her neck. Her nose was relatively small, but too thick and broad at the nostrils, although it departed but little from the straight line of the classic model. Altogether the Signora Pandolfi, christened Maria Luisa, and wife to Marzio the silver-chiseller, was a portly and pompous-looking person, who wore an air of knowing her position, and of being sure to maintain it. Nevertheless, there was a kindly expression in her fat face, and if her eyes looked sleepy they did not look dishonest.

Signora Pandolfi's companion was her old maid-of-all-work, Assunta, commonly called Suntarella, without whom she rarely stirred abroad—a little old woman, in neat but dingy-coloured garments, with a grey woollen shawl drawn over her head like a cowl, instead of a bonnet.

Marzio finished fastening the door, and then turned round. On seeing his wife he remained silent for a moment, looking at her with an expression of dissatisfied inquiry. He had not expected her.

"Well?" he ejaculated at last.

"It is dinner time," remarked the stout lady.

"Yes, I heard the gun," answered Marzio drily. "It is the same as if you had told me," he added ironically, as he turned and led the way across the street.

"A pretty answer!" exclaimed Maria Luisa, tossing her large head as she followed her lord and master to the door of their house. Meanwhile Assunta, the old servant, glanced at Gianbattista, rolled up her eyes with an air of resignation, and spread out her withered hands for a moment with a gesture of despair, instantly drawing them in again beneath the folds of her grey woollen shawl.

"Gadding!" muttered Marzio, as he entered the narrow door from which the dark steps led abruptly upwards. "Gadding—always gadding! And who minds the soup-kettle when you are gadding, I should like to know? The cat, I suppose! Oh, these women and their priests! These priests and these women!"

"Lucia is minding the soup-kettle," gasped Maria Luisa, as she puffed up stairs behind her thin and active husband.

"Lucia!" cried Marzio angrily, a flight of steps higher. "I suppose you will bring her up to be woman of all work? Well, she could earn her living then, which is more than you do! After all, it is better to mind a soup-kettle than to thump a piano and to squeal so that I can hear her in the shop opposite, and it is better than hanging about the church all the morning, or listening to Paolo's drivelling talk. By all means keep her in the kitchen."

It was hard to say whether Signora Pandolfi was puffing or sighing as she paused for breath upon the landing, but there was probably something of both in the labour of her lungs. She was used to Marzio. She had lived with him for twenty years, and she knew his moods and his ways, and detected the coming storm from afar. Unfortunately, or perhaps fortunately, for her, there was little variety in the sequence of his ideas. She was accustomed to his beginning at the grumbling stage before dinner, and proceeding by a crescendo movement to the pitch of rage, which was rarely reached until he had finished his meal, when he generally seized his hat and dragged Gianbattista away with him, declaring loudly that women were not fit for human society. The daily excitement of this comedy had long lost its power to elicit anything more than a sigh from the stout Maria Luisa, who generally bore Marzio's unreasonable anger with considerable equanimity, waiting for his departure to eat her boiled beef and salad in peace with Lucia, while old Assunta sat by the table with the cat in her lap, putting in a word of commiseration alternately with a word of gossip about the lodgers on the other side of the landing. The latter were a young and happy pair: the husband, a chorus singer at the Apollo, who worked at glove cleaning during the day time; his wife, a sempstress, who did repairs upon the costumes of the theatre. Their apartments consisted of two rooms and a kitchen, while Marzio and his family occupied the rest of the floor, and entered their lodging by the opposite door.

Maria Luisa envied the couple in her sleepy fashion. Her husband was indeed comparatively rich, and though economical in his domestic arrangements, he had money in the bank enough to keep him comfortably for the rest of his days. His violence did not extend beyond words and black looks, and he was not miserly about a few francs for dress, or a dinner at the Falcone two or three times a year. But in the matter of domestic peace his conduct left much to be desired. He was a sober man, but his hours were irregular, for he attended the meetings of a certain club which Maria Luisa held in abhorrence, and brought back opinions which made her cross herself with her fat fingers, shuddering at the things he said. As for Gianbattista Bordogni, who lived with them, and consequently received most of his wages in the shape of board and lodging, he loved Lucia Pandolfi, his master's daughter, and though he shared Marzio's opinions, he held his tongue in the house. He understood how necessary to him the mother's sympathy must be, and, with subtle intelligence, he knew how to create a contrast between himself and his master by being reticent at the right moment.

Lucia opened the door in answer to the bell her father had rung, and stood aside in the narrow way to let members of the household pass by, one by one. Lucia was seventeen years old, and probably resembled her mother as the latter had looked at the same age. She was slight, and tall, and dark, with a quantity of glossy black hair coiled behind her head. Her black eyes had not yet acquired that sleepy look which advancing life and stoutness had put into her mother's, as a sort of sign of the difficulty of quick motion. Her figure was lithe, though she was not a very active girl, and one might have predicted that at forty she, too, would pay her debt to time in pounds of flesh. There are thin people who look as though they could never grow stout, and there are others whose leisurely motion and deliberate step foretells increase of weight. But Gianbattista had not studied these matters of physiological horoscopy. It sufficed him that Lucia Pandolfi was at present a very pretty girl, even beautiful, according to some standards. Her thick hair, low forehead, straight classic features, and severe mouth fascinated the handsome apprentice, and the intimacy which had developed between the two during the years of his residence under Marzio's roof, from the time when Lucia was a little girl to the present day, had rendered the transition from friendship to love almost imperceptible to them both. Gianbattista was the last of the party to enter the lodging, and as he paused to shut the door, Lucia was still lingering at the threshold.

"Hist! They will see!" she protested under her breath.

"What do I care!" whispered the apprentice, as he kissed her cheek in the dusky passage. Then they followed the rest.

CHAPTER II

That evening Marzio finished the last cherub's head on the ewer before he left the shop. He had sent Gianbattista home, and had dismissed the men who were working at a huge gilded grating ordered by a Roman prince for a church he was decorating. Marzio worked on by the light of a strong lamp until the features were all finished and he had indicated the pupils of the eyes with the fine-pointed punch. Then he sat some time at his bench with the beautiful piece of workmanship under his fingers, looking hard at it and straining his eyes to find imperfections that did not exist. At last he laid it down tenderly upon the stuffed leather pad and stared at the green shade of the lamp, deep in thought.

The man's nature was in eternal conflict with itself, and he felt as though he were the battle-ground of forces he could neither understand nor control. A true artist in feeling, in the profound cultivation of his tastes, in the laborious patience with which he executed his designs, there was an element in his character and mind which was in direct contradiction with the essence of what art is. If art can be said to depend upon anything except itself, that something is religion. The arts began in religious surroundings, in treating religious subjects, and the history of the world from the time of the early Egyptians has shown that where genius has lost faith in the supernatural, its efforts to produce great works of lasting beauty in the sensual and material atmosphere of another century have produced comparatively insignificant results. The science of silver-chiselling began, so far as this age is concerned, in the church. The tastes of Francis the First directed the attention of the masters of the art to the making of ornaments for his mistresses, and for a time the men who had made chalices for the Vatican succeeded in making jewelry for Madame de Chateaubriand, Madame d'Etampes, and Diane de Poitiers. But the art itself remained in the church, and the marvels of repoussé gold and silver to be seen in the church of Notre Dame des Victoires, the masterpieces of Ossani of Rome, could not have been produced by any goldsmith who made jewelry for a living.

Marzio Pandolfi knew all this better than any one, and he could no more have separated himself from his passion for making chalices and crucifixes than he could have changed the height of his stature or the colour of his eyes. But at the same time he hated the church, the priests, and every one who was to use the beautiful things over which he spent so much time and labour. Had he been indifferent, a careless, good-natured sceptic, he would have been a bad artist. As it was, the very violence of his hatred lent spirit and vigour to his eye and hand. He was willing to work upon the figure, perfecting every detail of expression, until he fancied he could feel and see the silver limbs of the dead Christ suffering upon the cross under the diabolical skill of his long fingers. The monstrous horror of the thought made him work marvels, and the fancied realisation of an idea that would startle even a hardened unbeliever, lent a feverish impulse to this strange man's genius.

As for the angels on the chalices, he did not hate them; on the contrary, he saw in them the reflection of those vague images of loveliness and innocence which haunt every artist's soul at times, and the mere manual skill necessary to produce expression in things so minute, fascinated a mind accustomed to cope with difficulties, and so inured to them as almost to love them.

Nevertheless, when a man is constantly a prey to strong emotions, his nature cannot long remain unchanged. The conviction had been growing in Marzio's mind that it was his duty, for the sake of consistency, to abandon his trade. The thought saddened him, but the conclusion seemed inevitable. It was absurd, he repeated to himself, that one who hated the priests should work for them. Marzio was a fanatic in his theories, but he had something of the artist's simplicity in his idea of the way they should be carried out. He would have thought it no harm to kill a priest, but it seemed to him contemptible to receive a priest's money for providing the church with vessels which were to serve in a worship he despised.

Moreover, he was not poor. Indeed, he was richer than any one knew, and the large sums paid for his matchless work went straight from the workshop to the bank, while Marzio continued to live in the simple lodgings to which he had first brought home his wife, eighteen years before, when he was but a young partner in the establishment he now owned. As he sat at the bench, looking from his silver ewer to the green lampshade, he was asking himself whether he should not give up this life of working for people he hated and launch into that larger work of political agitation, for which he fancied himself so well fitted. He looked forward into an imaginary future, and saw himself declaiming in the Chambers against all that existed, rousing the passions of a multitude to acts of destruction—of justice, as he called it in his thoughts—and leading a vast army of angry men up the steps of the Capitol to proclaim himself the champion of the rights of man against the rights of kings. His eyelids contracted and the concentrated light of his eyes was reduced to two tiny bright specks in the midst of the pupils; his nervous hand went out and the fingers clutched the jaws of the iron vice beside him as he would have wished to grapple with the jaws of the beast oppression, which in his dreams seemed ever tormenting the poor world in which he lived.

There was something lacking in his face, even in that moment of secret rage as he sat alone in his workroom before the lamp. There was the frenzy of the fanatic, the exaltation of the dreamer, clearly expressed upon his features, but there was something wanting. There was everything there except the force to accomplish, the initiative which oversteps the bank of words, threats, and angry thoughts, and plunges boldly into the stream, ready to sacrifice itself to lead others. The look of power, of stern determination, which is never absent from the faces of men who change their times, was not visible in the thin dark countenance of the silver-chiseller. Marzio was destined never to rise above the common howling mob which he aspired to lead.

This fact asserted itself outwardly as he sat there. After a few minutes the features relaxed, a smile that was almost weak—the smile that shows that a man lacks absolute confidence—passed quickly over his face, the light in his eyes went out, and he rose from his stool with a short, dissatisfied sigh, which was repeated once or twice as he put away his work and arranged his tools. He made the rounds of the workshop, looked to the fastenings of the windows, lighted a taper, and then extinguished the lamp. He threw a loose overcoat over his shoulders without passing his arms through the sleeves, and went out into the street. Glancing up at the windows of his house opposite, he saw that the lights were burning brightly, and he guessed that his wife and daughter were waiting for him before sitting down to supper.

"Let them wait," he muttered with a surly grin, as he put out the taper and went down the street in the opposite direction.

He turned the street corner by the dark Palazzo Antici Mattei, and threaded the narrow streets towards the Pantheon and the Piazza Sant' Eustachio. The weather had changed, and the damp south-east wind was blowing fiercely behind him. The pavement was wet and slippery with the strange thin coating of greasy mud which sometimes appears suddenly in Rome even when it has not rained. The insufficient gas lamps flickered in the wind as though they would go out, and the few pedestrians who hurried along clung closely to the wall as though it offered them some protection from the moist scirocco. The great doors of the palaces were most of them closed, but here and there a little red light announced a wine-shop, and as Marzio passed by he could see through the dirty panes of glass dark figures sitting in a murky atmosphere over bottles of coarse wine. The streets were foul with the nauseous smell of decaying vegetables and damp walls which the south-east wind brings out of the older parts of Rome, and while few voices were heard in the thick air, the clatter of horses' hoofs on the wet stones rattled loudly from the thoroughfares which lead to the theatres. It was a dismal night, but Marzio Pandolfi felt that his temper was in tune with the weather as he tramped along towards the Pantheon.

The streets widened as he neared his destination, and he drew his overcoat more closely about his neck. Presently he reached a small door close to Sant' Eustachio, one of the several entrances to the ancient Falcone, an inn which has existed for centuries upon the same spot, in the same house, and which affords a rather singular variety of accommodation. Down stairs, upon the square, is a modern restaurant with plate-glass windows, marble floor, Vienna cane chairs, and a general appearance of luxury. A flight of steps leads to an upper story, where there are numerous rooms of every shape and dimension, furnished with old-fashioned Italian simplicity, though with considerable cleanliness. Thither resort the large companies of regular guests who have eaten their meals there during most of their lives. But there is much more room in the house than appears. The vast kitchen on the ground floor terminates in a large space, heavily vaulted and lighted by oil lamps, where rougher tables are set and spread, and where you may see the well-to-do wine-carter eating his supper after his journey across the Campagna, in company with some of his city acquaintances of a similar class. In dark corners huge wine-casks present their round dusty faces to the doubtful light, the smell of the kitchen pervades everything, tempered by the smell of wine from the neighbouring cellars; the floor is of rough stone worn by generations of cooks, potboys, and guests. Beyond this again a short flight of steps leads to a narrow doorway, passing through which one enters the last and most retired chamber of the huge inn. Here there is barely room for a dozen persons, and when all the places are full the bottles and dishes are passed from the door by the guests themselves over each other's heads, for there is no room to move about in the narrow space. The walls are whitewashed and the tables are as plain as the chairs, but the food and drink that are consumed there are the best that the house affords, and the society, from the point of view of Marzio Pandolfi and his friends, is of the most agreeable.

The chiseller took his favourite seat in the corner furthest from the window. Two or three men of widely different types were already at the table, and Marzio exchanged a friendly nod with each. One was a florid man of large proportions, dressed in the height of the fashion and with scrupulous neatness. He was a jeweller. Another, a lawyer with a keen and anxious face, wore a tightly-buttoned frock coat and a black tie. Immense starched cuffs covered his bony hands and part of his fingers. He was supping on a salad, into which he from time to time poured an additional dose of vinegar. A third man, with a round hat on one side of his head, and who wore a very light-coloured overcoat, displaying a purple scarf with a showy pin at the neck, held a newspaper in one hand and a fork in the other, with which he slowly ate mouthfuls of a ragout of wild boar. He was a journalist on the staff of an advanced radical paper.

"Halloa, Sor Marzio!" cried this last guest, suddenly looking up from the sheet he was reading, "here is news of your brother."

"What?" asked Marzio briefly, but as though the matter were utterly indifferent to him. "Has he killed anybody, the assassin?" The journalist laughed hoarsely at the jest.

"Not so bad as that," he answered. "He is getting advancement. They are going to make him a canon of Santa Maria Maggiore. It is in the Osservatore Romano of this evening."

"He is good for nothing else," growled Marzio. "It is just like him not to have told me anything about it."

"With the sympathy which exists between you, I am surprised," said the journalist. "After all, you might convert him, and then he would be useful. He will be an archdeacon next, and then a bishop—who knows?—perhaps a cardinal!"

"You might as well talk of converting the horses on Monte Cavallo as of making Paolo change his mind," replied Pandolfi, beginning to sip the white wine he had ordered. "You don't know him—he is an angel, my brother! Oh, quite an angel! I wish somebody would send him to heaven, where he is so anxious to be!"

"Look out, Marzio!" exclaimed the lawyer, glancing from the vinegar cruet towards the door and then at his friend.

"No such luck," returned the chiseller. "Nothing ever happens to those black-birds. When we get as far as hanging them, my dear brother will happen to be in Paris instead of in Rome. You might as well try to catch a street cat by calling to it micio, micio! as try and catch a priest. You may as well expect to kill a mule by kicking it as one of those animals, Burn the Vatican over their heads and think you have destroyed them like a wasps' nest, they will write you a letter from Berlin the next day saying that they are alive and well, and that Prince Bismarck protests against your proceedings."

"Bravo, Sor Marzio!" cried the journalist. "I will put that in the paper to-morrow—it is a fine fulmination. You always refresh my ideas—why will you not write an article for us in that strain? I will publish it as coming from a priest who has given up his orders, married, and opened a wine-shop in Naples. What an effect! Magnificent! Do go on!"

Marzio did not need a second invitation to proceed upon his favourite topic. He was soon launched, and as the little room filled, his pale and sunken cheeks grew red with excitement, his tongue was unloosed, and he poured out a continuous stream of blasphemous ribaldry such as would have shocked the ears of a revolutionist of the year '89 or of a pétroleuse of the nineteenth century. It seemed as though the spring once opened would never dry. His eyes flashed, his fingers writhed convulsively on the table, and his voice rang out, ironical and cutting, with strange intonations that roused strange feelings in his hearers. It was the old subject, but he found something new to say upon it at each meeting with his friends, and they wondered where he got the imagination to construct his telling phrases and specious, virulent arguments.

We have all wondered at such men. They are the outcome of this age and of no previous time, as it is also to be hoped that their like may not arise hereafter. They are found everywhere, these agitators, with their excited faces, their nervous utterances, and their furious hatred of all that is. They find their way into the parliaments of the world, into the dining-rooms of the rich, into the wine-shops of the working men, into the press even, and some of their works are published by great houses and read by great ladies, if not by great men. Suddenly, when we least expect it, a flaming advertisement announces a fiery tirade against all that the great mass of mankind hold in honour, if not in reverence. Curiosity drives thousands to read what is an insult to humanity, and even though the many are disgusted, some few are found to admire a rhetoric which exalts their own ignorance to the right of judging God. And still the few increase and grow to be a root and send out shoots and creepers like an evil plant, so that grave men say among themselves that if there is to be a universal war in our times or hereafter it will be fought by Christians of all denominations defending themselves against those who are not Christians.

Marzio sat long at his table, and his modest pint of wine was enough to moisten his throat throughout the time during which he held forth. When the liquor was finished he rose, took down his overcoat from the peg on which it hung, pushed his soft hat over his eyes, and with a sort of triumphant wave of the hand, saluted his friends and left the room. He was a perfectly sober man, and no power would have induced him to overstep the narrow limit he allowed to his taste. Indeed, he did not care for wine itself, and still less for any excitement it produced in his brain. He ordered his half-litre as a matter of respect for the house, as he called it, and it served to wet his throat while he was talking. Water would have done as well. Consumed by the intensity of his hatred for the things he attacked, he needed no stimulant to increase his exaltation.

When he was gone, there was silence in the room for some few minutes. Then the journalist burst into a loud laugh.

"If we only had half a dozen fellows like that in the Chambers, all talking at once!" he cried.

"They would be kicked into the middle of Montecitorio in a quarter of an hour," answered the thin voice of the lawyer. "Our friend Marzio is slightly mad, but he is a good fellow in theory. In practice that sort of thing must be dropped into public life a little at a time, as one drops vinegar into a salad, on each leaf. If you don't, all the vinegar goes to the bottom together, and smells horribly sour."

While Marzio was holding forth to his friends, the family circle in the Via dei Falegnami was enjoying a very pleasant evening in his absence. The Signora Pandolfi presided at supper in a costume which lacked elegance, but ensured comfort—the traditional skirt and white cotton jacket of the Italian housewife. Lucia wore the same kind of dress, but with less direful effects upon her appearance. Gianbattista, as usual after working hours, was arrayed in clothes of fashionable cut, aiming at a distant imitation of the imaginary but traditional English tourist. A murderous collar supported his round young chin, and a very stiffly-constructed pasteboard-lined tie was adorned by an exquisite silver pin of his own workmanship—the only artistic thing about him.

Besides these members of the family, there was a fourth person at supper, the person whom, of all others, Marzio detested, Paolo Pandolfi, his brother the priest, commonly called Don Paolo. He deserves a word of description, for there was in his face a fleeting resemblance to Marzio, which might easily have led a stranger to believe that there was a similarity between their characters. Tall, like his brother, the priest was a little less thin, and evidently far less nervous. The expression of his face was thoughtful, and the deep, heavily-ringed eyes were like Marzio's, but the forehead was broader, and the breadth ascended higher in the skull, which was clearly defined by the short, closely-cropped hair and the smooth tonsure at the back. The nose was larger and of more noble shape, and Paolo's complexion was less yellow than his brother's; the features were not surrounded by furrows or lines, and the leanness of the priest's face threw them into relief. The clean shaven upper lip showed a kind and quiet mouth, which smiled easily and betrayed a sense of humour, but was entirely free from any suggestion of cruelty. Don Paolo was scrupulous of his appearance, and his cassock and mantle were carefully brushed, and his white collar was immaculately clean. His hands were of the student type—white, square at the tips, lean, and somewhat knotty.

Marzio, in his ill-humour, had no doubt flattered himself that his family would wait for him for supper. But his family had studied him and knew his ways. When he was not punctual, he seldom came at all, and a quarter of an hour was considered sufficient to decide the matter.

"What are we waiting to do?" exclaimed Maria Luisa, in the odd Italian idiom. "Marzio is in his humours—he must have gone to his friends. Ah! those friends of his!" she sighed. "Let us sit down to supper," she added; and, from her tone, the idea of supper seemed to console her for her husband's absence.

"Perhaps he guessed that I was coming," remarked Don Paolo, with a smile. "In that case he will be a little nervous with me when he comes back. With your leave, Maria Luisa," he added, by way of announcing that he would say grace. He gave the short Latin benediction, during which Gianbattista never looked away from Lucia's face. The boy fancied she was never so beautiful as when she stood with her hands folded and her eyes cast down.

"Marzio does not know what I have come for," began Don Paolo again, as they all sat down to the square table in the little room. "If he knew, perhaps he might have been here—though perhaps he would not care very much after all. You all ask what it is? Yes; I will tell you. His Eminence has obtained for me the canonry that was vacant at Santa Maria Maggiore—"

At this announcement everybody sprang up and embraced Don Paolo, and overwhelmed him with congratulations, reproaching him at the same time for having kept the news so long to himself.

"Of course, I shall continue to work with the Cardinal," said the priest, when the family gave him time to speak. "But it is a great honour. I have other news for Marzio—"

"I imagine that you did not count upon the canonry as a means of pleasing him," remarked the Signora, Pandolfi, with a smile.

"No, indeed," laughed Lucia. "Poor papa—he would rather see you sent to be a curate in Città Lavinia!"

"Dear me! I fear so," answered Don Paolo, with a shade of sadness. "But I have a commission for him. The Cardinal has ordered another crucifix, which he desires should be Marzio's masterpiece—silver, of course, and large. It must be altogether the finest thing he has ever made, when it is finished."

"I daresay he will be very much pleased," said Maria Luisa, smiling comfortably.

"I wish he could make the figure solid, cast and chiselled, instead of repoussé," remarked Gianbattista, whose powerful hands craved heavy work by instinct.

"It would be a pity to waste so much silver; and besides, the effects are never so light," said Lucia, who, like most artists' daughters, knew something of her father's work.

"What is a little silver, more or less, to the Cardinal?" asked Gianbattista, with a little scorn; but as he met the priest's eye his expression instantly became grave.

The apprentice was very young; he was not beyond that age at which, to certain natures, it seems a fine thing to be numbered among such men as Marzio's friends. But at the same time he was not old enough, nor independent enough, to exhibit his feelings on all occasions. Don Paolo exercised a dominant influence in the Pandolfi household. He had the advantage of being calm, grave, and thoroughly in earnest, not easily ruffled nor roused to anger, any more than he was easily hurt. By character sensitive, he bore all small attacks upon himself with the equanimity of a man who believes his cause to be above the need of defence against little enemies. The result was that he dominated his brother's family, and even Marzio himself was not free from a certain subjection which he felt, and which was one of the most bitter elements in his existence. Don Paolo imposed respect by his quiet dignity, while Marzio asserted himself by speaking loudly and working himself voluntarily into a state of half-assumed anger. In the contest between quiet force and noisy self-assertion the issue is never doubtful. Marzio lacked real power, and he felt it. He could command attention among the circle of his associates who already sympathised with his views, but in the presence of Paolo he was conscious of struggling against a superior and incomprehensible obstacle, against the cool and unresentful disapprobation of a man stronger than himself. It was many years since he had ventured to talk before his brother as he talked when he was alone with Gianbattista, and the latter saw the change that came over his master's manner before the priest, and guessed that Marzio was morally afraid. The somewhat scornful allusion to the Cardinal's supposed wealth certainly did not constitute an attack upon Don Paolo, but Gianbattista nevertheless felt that he had said something rather foolish, and made haste to ignore his words. The influence could not be escaped.

It was this subtle power that Marzio resented, for he saw that it was exerted continually, both upon himself and the members of his household. The chiseller acknowledged to himself that in a great emergency his wife, his daughter, and even Gianbattista Bordogni, would most likely follow the advice of Don Paolo, in spite of his own protests and arguments to the contrary. He fancied that he himself alone was a free agent. He doubted Gianbattista, and began to think that the boy's character would turn out a failure. This was the reason why he no longer encouraged the idea of a marriage between his daughter and his apprentice, a scheme which, somewhat earlier, had been freely discussed. It had seemed an admirable arrangement. The young man promised to turn out a freethinker after Marzio's own heart, and showed a talent for his profession which left nothing to be desired. Some one must be ready to take Marzio's place in the direction of the establishment, and no one could be better fitted to undertake the task than Gianbattista. Lucia would inherit her father's money as the capital for the business, and her husband should inherit the workshop with all the stock-in-trade. Latterly, however, Marzio had changed his mind, and the idea no longer seemed so satisfactory to him as at first. Gianbattista was evidently falling under the influence of Don Paolo, and that was a sufficient reason for breaking off the match. Marzio hardly realised that as far as his outward deportment in the presence of the priest was concerned, the apprentice was only following his master's example.

Marzio had been looking about him for another husband for his daughter, and he had actually selected one from among his most intimate friends. His choice had fallen upon the thin lawyer—by name Gasparo Carnesecchi—who, according to the chiseller's views, was in all respects a most excellent match. A true freethinker, a practising lawyer with a considerable acquaintance in the world of politics, a discreet man not far from forty years of age, it seemed as though nothing more were required to make a model husband. Marzio knew very well that Lucia's dowry would alone have sufficed to decide the lawyer to marry her, and an interview with Carnesecchi had almost decided the matter. Of course, he had not been able to allude to the affair this evening at the inn, when so many others were present, but the preliminaries were nearly settled, and Marzio had made up his mind to announce his intention to his family at once. He knew well enough what a storm he would raise, and, like many men who are always trying to seem stronger than they really are, he had determined to choose a moment for making the disclosure when he should be in a thoroughly bad humour. As he walked homewards from the old inn he felt that this moment had arrived. The slimy pavement, the moist wind driving through the streets and round every corner, penetrating to the very joints, contributed to make him feel thoroughly vicious and disagreeable; and the tirade in which he had been indulging before his audience of friends had loosed his tongue, until he was conscious of being able to face any domestic disturbance or opposition.

The little party had adjourned from supper, and had been sitting for some time in the small room which served as a place of meeting. Gianbattista was smoking a cigarette, which he judged to be more in keeping with his appearance than a pipe when he was dressed in civilised garments, and he was drawing an elaborate ornament of arabesques upon a broad sheet of paper fixed on a board. Lucia seated at the table was watching the work, while Don Paolo sat in a straight-backed chair, his white hands folded on his knee, from time to time addressing a remark to Maria Luisa. The latter, being too stout to recline in the deep easy-chair near the empty fireplace, sat bolt upright, with her feet upon the edge of a footstool, which was covered by a tapestry of worsted-work, displaying an impossible nosegay upon a vivid green ground.

They had discussed the priest's canonry, and the order for the crucifix. They had talked about the weather. They had made some remarks upon Marzio's probable disposition of mind when he should come home, and the conversation was exhausted so far as the two older members were concerned. Gianbattista and Lucia conversed in a low tone, in short, enigmatic phrases.

"Do you know?" said the apprentice.

"What?" inquired Lucia.

"I have spoken of it to-day." Both glanced at the Signora Pandolfi. She was sitting up as straight as ever, but her heavy head was slowly bending forward.

"Well?" asked the young girl

"He was in a diabolical humour. He said I might take you away." Gianbattista smiled as he spoke, and looked into Lucia's eyes. She returned his gaze rather sadly, and only shook her head and shrugged her shoulders for a reply.

"If we took him at his word," suggested Gianbattista.

"Just so—it would be a fine affair!" exclaimed Lucia ironically.

"After all, he said so," argued the young man. "What does it matter whether he meant it?"

"Things are going badly for us," sighed his companion. "It was different a year ago. You must have done something to displease him, Tista. I wish I knew!" Her dark eyes suddenly assumed an angry expression, and she drew in her red lips.

"Wish you knew what?" inquired the apprentice, in a colder tone.

"Why he does not think about it as he used to. He never made any objections until lately. It was almost settled."

Gianbattista glanced significantly at Don Paolo, shrugged his shoulders, and went on drawing.

"What has that to do with it?" asked Lucia impatiently.

"It is enough for your father that it would please his brother. He would hate a dog that Don Paolo liked."

"What nonsense!" exclaimed the girl. "It is something else. Papa sees something—something that I do not see. He knows his own affairs, and perhaps he knows yours too, Tista. I have not forgotten the other evening."

"I!" ejaculated the young man, looking up angrily.

"You know very well where I was—at the Circolo Artistico. How do you dare to think—"

"Why are you so angry if there is no one else in the case?" asked Lucia, with a sudden sweetness, which belied the jealous glitter in her eyes.

"It seems to me that I have a right to be angry. That you should suspect me after all these years! How many times have I sworn to you that I went nowhere else?"

"What is the use of your swearing? You do not believe in anything—why should you swear? Why should I believe you?"

"Oh—if you talk like that, I have finished!" answered Gianbattista. "But there—you are only teasing me. You believe me, just as I believe you. Besides, as for swearing and believing in something besides you— who knows? I love you—is not that enough?"

Lucia's eyes softened as they rested on the young man's face. She knew he loved her. She only wanted to be told so once more.

"There is Marzio," said Don Paolo, as a key rattled in the latch of the outer door.

"At this hour!" exclaimed the Signora Pandolfi, suddenly waking up and rubbing her eyes with her fat fingers.

CHAPTER III

Marzio, having divested himself of his heavy coat and hat, appeared at the door of the sitting-room.

Everybody looked at him, as though to discern the signs of his temper, and no one was perceptibly reassured by the sight of his white face and frowning forehead.

"Well, most reverend canon," he began, addressing Don Paolo, "I am in time to congratulate you, it seems. It was natural that I should be the last to hear of your advancement, through the papers."

"Thank you," answered Don Paolo quietly. "I came to tell you the news."

"You are very considerate," returned Marzio. "I have news also; for you all." He paused a moment, as though to give greater effect to the statement he was about to make. "I refer," he continued very slowly, "to the question of Lucia's marriage."

"Indeed!" exclaimed the priest. "I am glad if it is to be arranged at last."

The other persons in the room held their breath. The young girl blushed deeply under her white skin, and Gianbattista grew pale as he laid aside his pencil and shaded his eyes with his hands. The Signora Pandolfi panted with excitement and trembled visibly as she looked at her husband. His dark figure stood out strongly from the background of the shabby blue wall paper, and the petroleum lamp cast deep shadows in the hollows of his face.

"Yes," he continued, "I talked yesterday with Gasparo Carnesecchi—you know, he is the lawyer I always consult. He is a clever fellow and understands these matters. We talked of the contract; I thought it better to consult him, you see, and he thinks the affair can be arranged in a couple of weeks. He is so intelligent. A marvel of astuteness; we discussed the whole matter, I say, and it is to be concluded as soon as possible. So now, my children—"

Gianbattista and Lucia, seated side by side at the table, were looking into each other's eyes, and as Marzio fixed his gaze upon them, their hands joined upon the drawing-board, and an expression of happy surprise overspread their faces. Marzio smiled too, as he paused before completing the sentence.

"So that now, my children," he continued, speaking very slowly, "you may as well leave each other's hands and have done with all this nonsense."

The lovers looked up suddenly with a puzzled air, supposing that Marzio was jesting.

"I am in earnest," he went on. "You see, Tista, that it will not be proper for you to sit and hold Lucia's hand when she is called Signora Carnesecchi, so you may as well get used to it."

For a moment there was a dead silence in the room. Then Lucia and Gianbattista both sprang to their feet.

"What!" screamed the young girl in an agony of terror. "Carnesecchi! what do you mean?"

"Infame! Wretch!" shouted Gianbattista, beside himself with rage as he sprang forward to grasp Marzio in his hands.

But the priest had risen too, and placed himself between the young man and Marzio to prevent any struggle. "No violence!" he cried in a tone that dominated the angry voices and the hysterical weeping of Maria Luisa, who sat rocking herself in her chair. Gianbattista stepped back and leaned against the wall, choking with anger. Lucia fell back into her seat and covered her face with her hands.

"Violence? Who wants violence?" asked Marzio in contemptuous tones. "Do you suppose I am afraid of Tista? Let him alone, Paolo; let us see whether he will strike me."

The priest now turned his back on the apprentice, and confronted Marzio. He was not pale like the rest, for he was not afraid of the chiseller, and the generous flush of a righteous indignation mounted to his calm face.

"You are mad," he said, meeting his brother's gaze fearlessly.

"Not in the least," returned Marzio. "Lucia shall marry Gasparo Carnesecchi at once, or she shall not marry any one; what am I saying? She shall have no choice. She must and she shall marry the man I have chosen. What have you to do with it? Have you come here to put yourself between me and my family? I advise you to be careful. The law protects me from such interference, and fellows of your cloth are not very popular at present."

"The law," answered the priest, controlling his wrath, "protects children against their parents. The law which you invoke provides that a father shall not force his daughter to marry against her will, and I believe that considerable penalties are incurred in such cases."

"What do you know of law, except how to elude it?" inquired Marzio defiantly.

Not half an hour had elapsed since he had been haranguing the admiring company of his friends, and his words came easily. Moreover, it was a long time since he had broken through the constraint he felt in Don Paolo's presence, and the opportunity having presented itself was not to be lost.

"Who are you that should teach me?" he repeated, raising his voice to a strained key and gesticulating fiercely. "You, your very existence is a lie, and you are the server of lies, and you and your fellow liars would have created them if they didn't already exist, you love them so. You live by a fraud, and you want to drag everybody into the comedy you play every day in your churches, everybody who is fool enough to drop a coin into your greedy palm! What right have you to talk to men? Do you work? Do you buy? Do you sell? You are worse than those fine gentlemen who do nothing because their fathers stole our money, for you live by stealing it yourselves! And you set yourselves up as judges over an honest man to tell him what he is to do with his daughter? You fool, you thing in petticoats, you deceiver of women, you charlatan, you mountebank, go! Go and perform your antics before your altars, and leave hardworking men like me to manage their families as they can, and to marry their daughters to whom they will!"

Marzio had rolled off his string of invective in such a tone, and so rapidly, that it had been impossible to interrupt him. The two women were sobbing bitterly. Gianbattista, pale and breathing hard, looked as though he would throttle Marzio if he could reach him, and Don Paolo faced the angry artist, with reddening forehead, folding his arms and straining his muscles to control himself. When Marzio paused for breath, the priest answered him with an effort.

"You may insult me if it pleases you," he said, "it is nothing to me. I cannot prevent your uttering your senseless blasphemies. I speak to you of the matter in hand. I tell you simply that in treating these two, who love each other, as you are treating them, you are doing a thing unworthy of a man. Moreover, the law protects your daughter, and I will see that the law does its duty."

"Oh, to think that I should have such a monster for a husband," groaned the fat Signora Pandolfi, still rocking herself in her chair, and hardly able to speak through her sobs.

"You will do a bad day's work for yourself and your art when you try to separate us," said Gianbattista between his teeth.

Marzio laughed hoarsely, and turned his back on the rest, beginning to fill his pipe at the chimney-piece. Don Paolo heard the apprentice's words, and understood their meaning. He went and laid his hand on the young man's shoulder.

"Do not let us have any threats, Tista," he said quietly. "Sor Marzio will never do this thing—believe me, he cannot if he would."

"Go on," cried Marzio, striking a match. "Go on—sow the seeds of discord, teach them all to disobey me. I am listening, my dear Paolo."

"All the better, if you are," answered the priest, "for I assure you I am in earnest. You will have time to consider this thing. I have a matter of business with you, Marzio. That is what I came for this evening. If you have done, we will speak of it."

"Business?" exclaimed Marzio in loud ironical tones. "This is a good time for talking of business—as good as any other! What is it?"

"The Cardinal wants another piece of work done, a very fine piece of work."

"The Cardinal? I will not make any more chalices for your cardinals. I am sick of chalices, and monstrances, and such stuff."

"It is none of those," answered Don Paolo quietly. "The Cardinal wants a magnificent silver crucifix. Will you undertake it? It must be your greatest work, if you do it at all."

"A crucifix?" repeated Marzio, in a changed tone. The angry gleam faded from his eyes, and a dreamy look came into them as he let the heavy lids droop a little, and remained silent, apparently lost in thought. The women ceased sobbing, and watched his altered face, while Gianbattista sank down into a chair and absently fingered the pencil that had fallen across the drawing-board.

"Will you do it?" asked Don Paolo, at last.

"A crucifix," mused the artist. "Yes, I will make a crucifix. I have made many, but I have never made one to my mind. Yes, tell the Cardinal that I will make it for him, if he will give me time."

"I do not think he will need it in less than three or four months," answered Don Paolo.

"Four months—that is not a long time for such a work. But I will try."

Thereupon Marzio, whose manner had completely changed, puffed at his pipe until it burned freely, and then approached the table, glancing at Gianbattista and Lucia as though nothing had happened. He drew the drawing-board which the apprentice had been using towards him, and, taking the pencil from the hand of the young man, began sketching heads on one corner of the paper.

Don Paolo looked at him gravely. After the words Marzio had spoken, it had gone against the priest's nature to communicate to him the commission for the sacred object. He had hesitated a moment, asking himself whether it was right that such a man should be allowed to do such work. Then the urgency of the situation, and his knowledge of his brother's character, had told him that the diversion might avert some worse catastrophe, and he had quickly made up his mind. Even now he asked himself whether he had done right. It was a question of theology, which it would have taken long to analyse, and Don Paolo had other matters to think of in the present, so he dismissed it from his mind. He wanted to be gone, and he only stayed a few minutes to see whether Marzio's mind would change again. He knew his brother well, and he was sure that no violence was to be feared from him, except in his speech. Such scenes as he had just witnessed were not uncommon in the Pandolfi household, and Don Paolo did not believe that any consequence was to be expected after he had left the house. He only felt that Marzio had been more than usually unreasonable, and that the artist could not possibly mean seriously what he had proposed that evening.

The priest did not indeed think that Gianbattista was altogether good enough for Lucia. The boy was occasionally a little wild in his speech, and though he was too much in awe of Don Paolo to repeat before him any of the opinions he had learned from his master, his manner showed occasionally that he was inclined to take the side of the latter in most questions that arose. But the habit of controlling his feelings in order not to offend the man of the church, and especially in order not to hurt Lucia's sensitive nature, had begun gradually to change and modify the young man's character. From having been a devoted admirer of Marzio's political creed and extreme free thought, Gianbattista had fallen, into the way of asking questions of the chiseller, to see how he would answer them; and the answers had not always satisfied him. Side by side with his increasing skill in his art, which led him to compare himself with his teacher, there had grown up in the apprentice the habit of comparing himself with Marzio from the intellectual point of view as well as from the artistic. The comparison did not appear to him advantageous to the elder man, as he discovered, in his way of thinking, a lack of logic on the one hand, and a love of frantic exaggeration on the other, which tended to throw a doubt upon the whole system of ideas which had produced these defects. The result was that the young man's mental position was unbalanced, and he was inclined to return to a more normal condition of thought. Don Paolo did not know all this, but he saw that Gianbattista had grown more quiet during the last year, and he hoped that his marriage with Lucia would complete the change. To see her thrown into the arms of a man like Gasparo Carnesecchi was more than the priest's affection for his niece could bear. He hardly believed that Marzio would seriously think again of the scheme, and he entertained a hope that the subject would not even be broached for some time to come.

Marzio continued to draw in silence, and after a few minutes, Don Paolo rose to take his leave. The chiseller did not look up from his pencil.

"Good-night, Marzio—let it be a good piece of work," said Paolo.

"Good-night," growled the artist, his eyes still fixed on the paper. His brother saluted the rest and left the room to go home to his lonely lodgings at the top of an old palace, in the first floor of which dwelt the Cardinal, whom he served as secretary. When he was gone, Lucia rose silently and went to her room, leaving her father and mother with Gianbattista. The Signora Pandolfi hesitated as to whether she should follow her daughter or stay with the two men. Her woman's nature feared further trouble, and visions of drawn knives rose before her swollen eyes, so that, after making as though she would rise twice, she finally remained in her seat, her fat hands resting idly upon her knees, staring at her husband and Gianbattista. The latter sat gloomily watching the paper on which his master was drawing.

"Marzio, you do not mean it?" said Maria Luisa, after a long interval of silence. The good woman did not possess the gift of tact.

"Do you not see that I have an idea?" asked her husband crossly, by way of an answer, as he bent his head over his work.

"I beg your pardon," said the Signora Pandolfi, in a humble tone, looking piteously at Gianbattista. The apprentice shook his head, as though he meant that nothing could be done for the present. Then she rose slowly, and with a word of good-night as she turned to the door, she left the room. The two men were alone.

"Now that nobody hears us, Sor Marzio, what do you mean to do?" asked Gianbattista in a low voice. Marzio shrugged his shoulders.

"What I told you," he answered, after a few seconds. "Do you suppose that rascally priest of a brother has made me change my mind?"

"No, I did not expect that, but I am not a priest; nor am I a boy to be turned round your fingers and put off in this way—sent to the wash like dirty linen. You must answer to me for what you said this evening."

"Oh, I will answer as much as you please," replied the artist, with an evil smile.

"Very well. Why do you want to turn me out, after promising for years that I should marry Lucia with your full consent when she was old enough?"

"Why? because you have turned yourself out, to begin with. Secondly, because Carnesecchi is a better match for my daughter than a beggarly chiseller. Thirdly, because I please; and fourthly, because I do not care a fig whether you like it or not. Are those reasons sufficient or not?"

"They may satisfy you," answered Gianbattista. "They leave something to be desired in the way of logic, in my humble opinion."

"Since I have told you that I do not care for your opinion—"

"I will probably find means to make you care for it," retorted the young man. "Don Paolo is quite right, in the first place, when he tells you that the thing is simply impossible. Fathers do not compel their daughters to marry in this century. Will you do me the favour to explain your first remark a little more clearly? You said I had turned myself out—how?"

"You have changed, Tista," said Marzio, leaning back to sharpen his pencil, and staring at the wall. "You change every day. You are not at all what you used to be, and you know it. You are going back to the priests. You fawn on my brother like a dog."

"You are joking," answered the apprentice. "Of course I would not want to make trouble in your house by quarrelling with Don Paolo, even if I disliked him. I do not dislike him. This evening he showed that he is a much better man than you."

"Dear Gianbattista," returned Marzio in sour tones, "every word you say convinces me that I have done right. Besides, I am busy—you see—you disturb my ideas. If you do not like my house, you can leave it. I will not keep you. I daresay I can educate another artist before I die. You are really only fit to swing a censer behind Paolo, or at the heels of some such animal."

"Perhaps it would be better to do that than to serve the mass you sing over your work-bench every day," said Gianbattista. "You are going too far, Sor Marzio. One may trifle with women and their feelings. You had better not attempt it with men."

"Such as you and Paolo? There was once a mule in the Pescheria Vecchia; when he got half-way through he did not like the smell of the fish, and he said to his leader, 'I will turn back.' The driver pulled him along. Then said the mule, 'Do not trifle with me. I will turn round and kick you.' But there is not room for a mule to turn round in the Pescheria Vecchia. The mule found it out, and followed the man through the fish market after all. I hope that is clear? It means that you are a fool."

"What is the use of bandying words?" cried the apprentice angrily. "I will offer you a bargain, Sor Marzio. I will give you your choice. Either I will leave the house, and in that case I will carry off Lucia and marry her in spite of you. Or else I will stay here—but if Lucia marries any one else, I will cut your throat. Is that a fair bargain?"

"Perfectly fair, though I cannot see wherein the bargain consists," answered Marzio, with a rough laugh. "I prefer that you should stay here. I will run the risk of being murdered by you, any day, and you may ran the risk of being sent to the galleys for life, if you choose. You will be well cared for there, and you can try your chisel on paving-stones for a change from silver chalices."

"Never mind what becomes of me afterwards, in that case," said the young man. "If Lucia is married to some one else, I do not care what happens. So you have got your warning!"

"Thank you. If you had remained what you used to be, you might have married her without further difficulty. But to have you and Lucia and Maria Luisa and Paolo all conspiring against me from morning till night is more than I can bear. Good-night, and the devil be with you, you fool!"

"Et cum spiritu tuo," answered Gianbattista as he left the room.

When Marzio was alone he returned to the head he was drawing—a head of wonderful beauty, inclined downwards and towards one side, bearing a crown of thorns, the eyelids drooped and shaded in death. He glanced at it with a bitter smile and threw aside the pencil without making another stroke upon the paper.

He leaned back, lighted another pipe, and began to reflect upon the events of the evening. He was glad it was over, for a strange weakness in his violent nature made it hard for him to face such scenes unless he were thoroughly roused. Now, however, he was satisfied. For a long time he had seen with growing distrust the change in Gianbattista's manner, and in the last words he had spoken to the apprentice he had uttered what was really in his heart. He was afraid of being altogether overwhelmed by the majority against him in his own house. He hated Paolo with his whole soul, and he had hated him all his life. This calm, obliging brother of his stood between him and all peace of mind. It was not the least of his grievances that he received most of his commissions through the priest who was constantly in relation with the cardinal and rich prelates who were the patrons of his art. The sense of obligation which he felt was often almost unbearable, and he longed to throw it off. The man whom he hated for his own sake and despised for his connection with the church, was daily in his house; at every turn he met with Paolo's tacit disapprobation or outspoken resistance. For a long time Paolo had doubted whether the marriage between the two young people would turn out well, and while he expressed his doubts Marzio had remained stubborn in his determination. Latterly, and doubtless owing to the change in Gianbattista's character, Paolo had always spoken of the marriage with favour. This sufficed at first to rouse Marzio's suspicions, and ultimately led to his opposing with all his might what he had so long and so vigorously defended; he resolved to be done with what he considered a sort of slavery, and at one stroke to free himself from his brother's influence, and to assure Lucia's future. During several weeks he had planned the scene which had taken place that evening, waiting for his opportunity, trying to make sure of being strong enough to make it effective, and revolving the probable answers he might expect from the different persons concerned. It had come, and he was satisfied with the result.

Marzio Pandolfi's intelligence lacked logic. In its place he possessed furious enthusiasm, an exaggerated estimate of the value of his social doctrines, and a whole vocabulary of terms by which to describe the ideal state after which he hankered. But though he did not possess a logic of his own, his life was itself the logical result of the circumstances he had created. As, in the diagram called the parallelogram of forces, various conflicting powers are seen to act at a point, producing an inevitable resultant in a fixed line, so in the plan of Marzio's life, a number of different tendencies all acted at a centre, in his overstrained intelligence, and continued to push him in a direction he had not expected to follow, and of which even now he was far from suspecting the ultimate termination.

He had never loved his brother, but he had loved his wife with all his heart. He had begun to love Lucia when she was a child. He had felt a sort of admiring fondness for Gianbattista Bordogni, and a decided pride in the progress and the talent of the apprentice. By degrees, as the prime mover, his hatred for Paolo, gained force, it had absorbed his affection for Maria Luisa, who, after eighteen years of irreproachable wifehood, seemed to Marzio to be nothing better than an accomplice and a spy of his brother's in the domestic warfare. Next, the lingering love for his child had been eaten up in the same way, and Marzio said to himself that the girl had joined the enemy, and was no longer worthy of his confidence. Lastly, the change in Gianbattista's character and ideas seemed to destroy the last link which bound the chiseller to his family. Henceforth, his hand was against each one of his household, and he fancied that they were all banded together against himself.

Every step had followed as the inevitable consequence of what had gone before. The brooding and suspicious nature of the artist had persisted in seeing in each change in himself the blackest treachery in those who surrounded him. His wife was an implacable enemy, his daughter a spy, his apprentice a traitor, and as for Paolo himself, Marzio considered him the blackest of villains. For all this chain of hatreds led backwards, and was concentrated with tenfold virulence in his great hatred for his brother. Paolo, in his estimation, was the author of all the evil, the sole ultimate cause of domestic discord, the arch enemy of the future, the representative, in Marzio's sweeping condemnation, not only of the church and of religion, but of that whole fabric of existing society which the chiseller longed to tear down.

Marzio's socialism, for so he called it, had one good feature. It was sincere of its kind, and disinterested. He was not of the common herd, a lazy vagabond, incapable of continuous work, or of perseverance in any productive occupation, desiring only to be enriched by impoverishing others, one of the endless rank and file of Italian republicans, to whom the word "republic" means nothing but bread without work, and the liberty which consists in howling blasphemies by day and night in the public streets. His position was as different from that of a private in the blackguard battalion as his artistic gifts and his industry were superior to those of the throng. He had money, he had talent, and he had been very successful in his occupation. He had nothing to gain by the revolutions he dreamed of, and he might lose much by any upsetting of the existing laws of property. He was, therefore, perfectly sincere, so far as his convictions went, and disinterested to a remarkable degree. These conditions are often found in the social position of the true fanatic, who is the more ready to run to the greatest length, because he entertains no desire to better his own state. Marzio's real weakness lay in the limited scope of his views, and in a certain timid prudence which destroyed his power of initiative. He was an economical man, who distrusted the future; and though such a disposition produces a good effect in causing a man to save money against the day of misfortune, it is incompatible with the career of the true enthusiast, who must be ready to risk everything at any moment. The man who would move other men, and begin great changes, must have an enormous belief in himself, an unbounded confidence in his cause, and a large faith in the future, amounting to the absolute scorn of consequence.

These greater qualities Marzio did not possess, and through lack of them the stupendous results of which he was fond of talking had diminished to a series of domestic quarrels, in which he was not always victorious. His hatred of the church was practically reduced to the detestation of his brother, and to an unreasoning jealousy of his brother's influence in his home. His horror of social distinctions, which speculated freely upon the destruction of the monarchy, amounted in practice to nothing more offensive than a somewhat studious rudeness towards the few strangers of high position who from time to time visited the workshop in the Via dei Falegnami. In the back room of his inn, Marzio could find loud and cutting words in which to denounce the Government, the monarchy, the church, and the superiority of the aristocracy. In real fact, Marzio took off his hat when he met the king in the street, paid his taxes with a laudable regularity, and increased the small fortune he had saved by selling sacred vessels to the priests against whom he inveighed. Instead of burning the Vatican and hanging the College of Cardinals to the pillars of the Colonnade, Marzio Pandolfi felt a very unpleasant sense of constraint in the presence of the only priest with whom he ever conversed, his brother Paolo. When, on very rare occasions, he broke out into angry invective, and ventured to heap abuse upon the calm individual who excited his wrath, he soon experienced the counter-shock in the shape of a strong conviction that he had injured his position rather than bettered it, and the melancholy conclusion forced itself upon him that by abusing Paolo he himself lost influence in his own house, and not unfrequently called forth the contempt of those he had sought to terrify.

The position was galling in the extreme; for, like many artists who are really remarkable in their profession, Marzio was very vain of his intellectual superiority in other branches. It may be a question whether vanity is not essential to any one who is forced to compete in excellence with other gifted men. Vanity means emptiness, and in the case of the artist it means that emptiness which craves to be filled with praise. The artist may doubt his own work, but he is bitterly disappointed if other people doubt it also. Marzio had his full share of this kind of vanity, which, as in most cases, extended beyond the sphere of his art. How often does one hear two or three painters or sculptors who are gathered together in a studio, laying down the law concerning Government, society, and the distribution of wealth. And yet, though they make excellent statues and paint wonderful pictures, there are very few instances on record of artists having borne any important part in the political history of their times. Not from any want of a desire to do so, in many cases, but from the real want of the power; and yet many of them believe themselves far more able to solve political and social questions than the men who represent them in the Parliament of their country, or the persons who by innate superiority of tact have made themselves the arbiters of society.

Marzio's vanity suffered terribly, for he realised the wide difference that existed between his aims and the result actually produced. For this reason he had determined to bring matters to a point of contention in his household, in order to assert once and for all the despotic authority which he believed to be his right. He knew well enough that in proposing the marriage of Lucia with Carnesecchi, he had hit upon a plan which Paolo would oppose with all his might. It seemed as though he could not have selected a question more certain to produce a hot contention. He had brought forward his proposal boldly, and had not hesitated to make a most virulent personal attack on his brother when the latter had shown signs of opposition. And yet, as he sat over his drawing board, staring at the clouds of smoke that rose from his pipe, he was unpleasantly conscious that he had not been altogether victorious, that he had not played the part of the despot to the end, as he had intended to do, that he had suddenly felt his inferiority to Paolo's calmness, and that upon hearing of the proposition concerning the crucifix he had acted as though he had received a bribe to be quiet. He bit his thin lips as he reflected that all the family must have supposed his silence from that moment to have been the effect of the important commission which Paolo had communicated to him; for it seemed impossible that they should understand the current of his thoughts.

As he glanced at the head he had drawn he understood himself better than others had understood him, for he saw on the corner of the paper the masterly sketch of an ideal Christ he had sought after for years without ever reaching it. He knew that that ideal had presented itself to his mind at the very moment when Paolo had proposed the work to him—the result perhaps, of the excitement under which he laboured at the moment. From that instant he had been able to think of nothing. He had been impelled to draw, and the expression of his thought had driven everything else out of his mind. Paolo had gained a fancied victory by means of a fancied bribe. Marzio determined to revenge himself for the unfair advantage his brother had then taken, by showing himself inflexible in his resolution concerning the marriage. It was but a small satisfaction to have braved Gianbattista's boyish threats, after having seemed to accept the bribe of a priest.

CHAPTER IV

On the following morning, Marzio left the house earlier than usual Gianbattista had not finished his black coffee, and was not in a humour to make advances to his master, after the scene of the previous evening. So he did not move from the table when the chiseller left the room, nor did he make any remark upon the hour. The door that led to the stairs had hardly closed after Marzio, when Lucia put her head into the room where Gianbattista was seated.

"He is gone," said the young man; "come in, we can talk a few minutes."

"Tista," began, Lucia, coming forward and laying her fingers on his curly hair, "what did all that mean last night? Have you understood?"

"Who understands that lunatic!" exclaimed Gianbattista, passing his arm round the girl's waist, and drawing her to him. "I only understand one thing, we must be married as soon as possible and be done with it. Is it not true, Lucia?"

"I hope so," answered his companion, with a blush and a sigh. "But I am so much afraid."

"Do not be afraid, leave it all to me, I will protect you, my darling," replied the young man, tapping his breast with the ready gesture of an Italian, as though to prove his courage.

"Oh, I am sure of that! But how can it be managed? Of course he cannot force me to marry Carnesecchi, as Uncle Paolo explained to him. But he will try, and he is so bad!"

"Let him try, let him try," repeated Gianbattista. "I made a bargain with him last night after you had gone to bed. Do you know what I told him? I told him that I would stay with him, but that if you married any one but me, I would cut his throat—Sor Marzio's throat, do you understand?"

"Oh, Tista!" cried Lucia. "How did you ever have the courage to tell him such a thing? Besides, you know, you would not do it, would you?"

"Do not trouble yourself, he saw I was in earnest, and he will think twice about it. Besides, he said yesterday that I might have you if I would take you away."

"A nice thing for a father to say of his daughter!" exclaimed the girl angrily. "And what did you answer him then, my love?"

"Oh! I said that I had not the slightest objection to the proceeding. And then he tried to prove to me that we should starve without him, and then he swore at me like a Turk. What did it matter? He said I was changed. By Diana! Any man would change, just for the sake of not being like him!"

"How do you mean that you are changed, dear?" asked Lucia anxiously.

"Who knows? He said I fawned on Don Paolo like a dog, instead of hating the priests as I used to do. What do you think, love?"

"I think Uncle Paolo would laugh at the idea," answered the girl, smiling herself, but rather sadly. "I am afraid you are as bad as ever, in that way."

"I am not bad, Lucia. I begin to think I like Don Paolo. He was splendid last night. Did you see how he stared your father out of countenance, and then turned him into a lamb with the order for the crucifix? Don Paolo has a much stronger will than Sor Marzio, and a great deal more sense. He will make your father change his mind."

"Of course it would be for the better if we could be married without any objection, and I am very glad you are growing fond of Uncle Paolo. But I have seen it for some time. He is so good!"

"Yes. That is the truth," answered Gianbattista in meditative tone. "He is too good. It is not natural. And then he has a way of making me feel it. Now, I would have strangled Sor Marzio last night if your uncle had not been there, but he prevented me. Of course he was right. Those people always are. But one hates to be set right by a priest. It is humiliating!"

"Well, it is better than not to be set right at all," said Lucia. "You see, if you had strangled poor papa, it would have been dreadful! Oh, Tista, promise me that you will not do anything violent! Of course he is very unkind, I know. But it would be terrible if you were to be angry and hurt him. You will not, Tista? Tell me you will not?"

"We shall see; we shall see, my love!"

"You do not love me if you will not promise."

"Oh, if that is all, my love, I will promise never to lay a finger on him until you are actually married to some one else. But then—" Gianbattista made the gesture which means driving the knife into an enemy.

"Then you may do anything you please," answered Lucia, with a laugh. "He will never make me marry any one but you. You know that, my heart!"

"In that case we ought to be married very soon," argued the young man. "We need not live here, you know. Indeed, it would be out of the question. We will take one of those pretty little places in the new quarter—"

"That is so far away," interrupted the girl.

"Yes, but there is the tramway, and there are omnibuses. It only takes a quarter of an hour."

"But you would be so far from me all day, my love. I could not run into the studio at all hours, and you would not come home for dinner. Oh! I could not bear it!"

"Very well, we will try and find something near here," said Gianbattista, yielding the point. "We will get a little apartment near the Minerva, where there is sun."

"And we will have a terrace on the top of the house, with pots of carnations."

"And red curtains on rings, that we can draw; it is such a pretty light when the sun shines through them."

"And green wall paper with blue furniture," suggested Lucia. "It is so gay."

"Or perhaps the furniture of the same colour as the paper—you know they have it so in all fashionable houses."

"Well, if it is really the fashion, I suppose we must," assented the girl rather regretfully.

"Yes, it is the fashion, my heart, and you must have everything in the fashion. But I must be going," added the young man, rising from his seat.

"Already? It is early, Tista—" she hesitated, "Dear Tista," she began again, her dark eyes resting anxiously on his face, "what will you say to him in the workshop? You will tell him that I would rather die than marry Carnesecchi, that we are solemnly promised, that nothing shall part us! You will make him see reason, Tista, will you not? I cannot go to him, or I would; and mamma, poor mamma, is so afraid of him when he is in his humours. There are only you and Uncle Paolo to manage him; and after the way he insulted Uncle Paolo last night, it will be all the harder. Think of it, Tista, while you are at work, and bring me word when you come to dinner."

"Never fear, love," replied Gianbattista confidently; "what else should I think of while I am hammering away all day? A little kiss, to give me courage."

In a moment he was gone, and his quick step resounded on the stairs as he ran down, leaving Lucia at the door above, to catch the last good-bye he called up to her when he reached the bottom. His fresh voice came up to her mingled with the rattle of the lumbering carts in the street. She answered the cry and went in.

Just then the sleepy Signora Pandolfi emerged from her chamber, clad in the inevitable skirt and white cotton jacket, her heavy black hair coiled in an irregular mass on the top of her head, and held in place by hair-pins that seemed to be on the point of dropping out.

"Ah, Lucia, my darling! Such a night as I have passed!" she moaned, sinking into a chair beside the table, on which the coffee-pot and the empty cups were still standing. "Such a night, my dear! I have not closed an eye. I am sure it is the last judgment! And this scirocco, too, it is enough to kill one!"

"Courage, mamma," answered Lucia gaily. "Things are never so bad as they seem."

"Oh, that monster, that monster!" groaned the fat lady. "He would make an angel lose his patience! Imagine, my dear, he insists that you shall be married in a fortnight, and he has left me money to go and buy things for your outfit! Oh dear! What are we to do? I shall go mad, my dear, and you will all have to take me to Santo Spirito! Oh dear! Oh dear! This scirocco!"

"I think papa will go mad first," said Lucia. "I never heard of such an insane proposition in my life. All in a moment too—I think I am to marry Tista—papa gets into a rage and—patatunfate! a new husband—like a conjuror's trick, such a comedy! I expected to see the door open at every minute, Pulcinella walk in and beat everybody with a blown bladder! But Uncle Paolo did quite as well."

"Oh, my head!" complained the Signora Pandolfi. "I have not slept a wink!"

"And then it was shameful to see the way papa grew quiet and submissive when Uncle Paolo gave him the order for the crucifix! If it had been anybody but papa, I should have said that a miracle had been performed. But poor papa! No—the miracle of the soldi—that is the truth. I would like to catch sight of the saint who could work a miracle on papa! Capers, what a saint he would have to be!"

"Bacchus!" ejaculated Maria Luisa, "San Filippo Neri would be nowhere! The Holy Father would have to make a saint on purpose to convert that monster! A saint who should have nothing else to do. Oh, how hot it is! My head is splitting. What are we to do, Lucia, my heart? Tell me a little what we are to do— two poor women—all alone—oh dear!"

"In the first place, it needs courage, mamma," answered Lucia, "and a cup of coffee. It is still hot, and you have not had any—"

"Coffee! Who thinks of coffee?" cried the Signora Pandolfi, taking the cup from her daughter's hands, and drinking the liquid with more calmness than might have been anticipated.

"That is right," continued the girl. "Drink, mamma, it will do you good. And then, and then—let me see. And then you must talk to Suntarella about the dinner. That old woman has no head—"

"Dinner!" cried the mother, "who thinks of dinner at such a time? And he left me the money for the outfit, too! Lucia, my love, I have the fever—I will go to bed."

"Eh! What do you suppose? That is a way out of all difficulties," answered Lucia philosophically.

"But you cannot go out alone—"

"I will stay at home in that case."

"And then he will come to dinner, and ask to see the things—"

"There will be no things to show him," returned the young girl.

"Well? And then where should we be?" inquired the Signora Pandolfi. "I see him, my husband, coming back and finding that nothing has been done! He would tear his hair! He would kill us! He would bring his broomstick of a lawyer here to marry you this very afternoon, and what should we have gained then? It needs judgment, Lucia, my heart—judgment, judgment!" repeated the fat lady, tapping her forehead.

"Eh! If you have not enough for two, mamma, I do not know what we shall do."

"At the same time, something must be done," mused Maria Luisa. "My head is positively bursting! We might go out and buy half a dozen handkerchiefs, just to show him that we have begun. Do you think a few handkerchiefs would quiet him, my love? You could always use them afterwards—a dozen would be too many—"

"Bacchus!" exclaimed Lucia, "I have only one nose."

"It is a pity," answered her mother rather irrelevantly. "After all, handkerchiefs are the cheapest things, and if we spread them out, all six, on the green sofa, they will make a certain effect—these men! One must deceive them, my child."

"Suppose we did another thing," began Lucia, looking out of the window. "We might get some things—in earnest, good things. They will always do for the wedding with Tista. Meanwhile, papa will of course have to change his mind, and then it will be all right."

"What genius!" cried the Signora Pandolfi. "Oh, Lucia! You have found it! And then we can just step into the workshop on our way—that will reassure your father."

"Perhaps, after all, it would be better to go and tell him the truth," said Lucia, beginning to walk slowly up and down the room. "He must know it, sooner or later."

"Are you mad, Lucia?" exclaimed her mother, holding up her hands in horror. "Just think how he would act if you went and faced him!"

"Then why not go and find Uncle Paolo?" suggested the girl. "He will know what is best to be done, and will help us, you may be sure. Of course, he expected to see us before anything was done in the matter. But I am not afraid to face papa all alone. Besides, Tista is talking to him at this very minute. I told him all he was to say, and he has so much courage!"

"I wish I had as much," moaned the Signora Pandolfi, lapsing into hesitation.

"Come, mamma, I will decide for you," said Lucia. "We will go and find Uncle Paolo, and we will do exactly as he advises."

"After all, that is best," assented her mother, rising slowly from her seat.

Half an hour later they left the house upon their errand, but they did not enter the workshop on their way. Indeed, if they had, they would have been surprised to find that Marzio was not there, and that Gianbattista was consequently not talking to him as Lucia had supposed.

When Gianbattista reached the workshop, he was told that Marzio had only remained five minutes, and had gone away so soon as everybody was at work. He hesitated a moment, wondering whether he might not go home again and spend another hour in Lucia's company; but it was not possible to foretell whether Marzio would be absent during the whole morning, and Gianbattista decided to remain. Moreover, the peculiar smell of the studio brought with it the idea of work, and with the idea came the love of the art, not equal, perhaps, to the love of the woman but more familiar from the force of habit.

All men feel such impressions, and most of all those who follow a fixed calling, and are accustomed to do their work in a certain place every day. Théophile Gautier confessed in his latter days that he could not work except in the office of the Moniteur—elsewhere, he said, he missed the smell of the printers' ink, which brought him ideas. Artists know well the effect of the atmosphere of the studio. Five minutes of that paint-laden air suffice to make the outer world a mere dream, and to recall the reality of work. There was an old dressing-gown to which Thackeray was attached as to a friend, and which he believed indispensable to composition. Balzac had his oval writing-room, when he grew rich, and the creamy white colour of the tapestries played a great part in his thoughts. The blacksmith loves the smoke of the forge and the fumes of hot iron on the anvil, and the chiseller's fingers burn to handle the tools that are strewn on the wooden bench.

Gianbattista stood at the door of the studio, and had he been master instead of apprentice, he could not have resisted the desire to go to his place and take up the work he had left on the previous evening. In a few minutes he was hammering away as busily as though there were no such thing as marriage in the world, and nothing worth living for but the chiselling of beautiful arabesques on a silver ewer. His head was bent over his hands, his eyes followed intently the smallest movements of the tool he held, he forgot everything else, and became wholly absorbed in his occupation.

Nevertheless, much of a chiseller's work is mechanical, and as the smooth iron ran in and out of the tiny curves under the gentle tap of the hammer, the young man's thoughts went back to the girl he had left at the top of the stairs a quarter of an hour earlier; he thought of her, as he did daily, as his promised wife, and he fell to wondering when it would be, and how it would be. They often talked of the place in which they would live, as they had done that morning; and as neither of them was very imaginative, there was a considerable similarity between the speculations they indulged in at one time and at another. It was always to be a snug home, high up, with a terrace, pots of carnations, and red curtains. Their only difference of opinion concerned the colour of the walls and furniture. Like most Italians, they had very little sense of colour, and thought only of having everything gay, as they called it; that is to say, the upholstery was to be chosen of the most vivid hues, probably of those horrible tints known as aniline. Italians, as a rule, and especially those who belong to the same class as the Pandolfi family, have a strong dislike for the darker and softer tones. To them anything which is not vivid is sad, melancholy, and depressing to the senses. Gianbattista saw in his mind's eye a little apartment after his own heart, and was happy in the idea. But, as he followed the train of thought, it led him to the comparison of the home to which he proposed to take his wife with the one in which they now lived under her father's roof, and suddenly the scene of the previous evening rose clearly in the young man's imagination. He dropped his hammer, and stared up at the grated windows.

He went over the whole incident, and perhaps for the first time realised its true importance, and all the danger there might be in the future should Marzio attempt to pursue his plan to the end. Gianbattista had only once seen the lawyer who was thus suddenly thrust into his place. He remembered a thin, cadaverous man, in a long and gloomy black coat, but that was all. He did not recall his voice, nor the expression of his face; he had only seen him once, and had thought little enough of the meeting. It seemed altogether impossible, and beyond the bounds of anything rational, that this stranger should ever really be brought forward to be Lucia's husband.

For a moment the whole thing looked like an evil dream, and Gianbattista smiled as he looked down again at his work. Then the reality of the occurrence rose up again and confronted him stubbornly. He was not mistaken, Marzio had actually pronounced those words, and Don Paolo had sprung forward to prevent Gianbattista from attacking his master then and there. The young man looked at his work, holding his tools in his hands, but hesitating to lay the point of the chisel on the silver, as he hesitated to believe the evidence of his memory.

CHAPTER V

Marzio had risen early that morning, as has been said, and had left the house before any one but Gianbattista was up. He was in reality far from inclined to drink his coffee in the company of his apprentice, and would have avoided it, if possible. Nor did he care to meet Lucia until he had found time and occasion to refresh his anger. His wife was too sleepy to quarrel, and hardly seemed to understand him when he gave her money and bade her look to Lucia's outfit, adding that the wedding was to take place immediately.

"Will you not let me sleep in peace, even in the morning?" she groaned.

"Magari! I wish you would sleep, and for ever!" growled Marzio, as he left the room.

He drank his coffee in silence, and went out. After looking into the workshop he walked slowly away in the direction of the Capitol. The damp morning air was pleasant to him, and the gloomy streets through which he passed were agreeable to his state of feeling. He wished Home might always wear such a dismal veil of dampness, scirocco, and cloud.

A man in a bad humour will go out of his way to be rained upon and blown against by the weather. We would all like to change our surroundings with our moods, to fill the world with sunshine when we are happy, and with clouds when we have stumbled in the labyrinths of life. Lovers wish that the whole earth might be one garden, crossed and recrossed by silent moonlit paths; and when love has taken the one and left the other, he who stays behind would have his garden changed to an angry ocean, and the sweet moss banks to storm-beaten rocks, that he may drown in the depths, or be dashed to pieces by the waves, before he has had time to know all that he has lost.

As we grow older, life becomes the expression of a mood, according to the way we have lived. He who seeks peace will find that with advancing age the peaceful moment, that once came so seldom, returns more readily, and that at last the moments unite to make hours, and the hours to build up days and years. He who stoops to petty strife will find that the oft-recurring quarrel has power to perpetuate the discontented weakness out of which it springs, and that it can make all life a hell. He who rejoices in action will learn that activity becomes a habit, and at last excludes the possibility of rest, and the desire for it; and his lot is the best, for the momentary gladness in a great deed well done is worth a millennium of sinless, nerveless tranquillity. The positive good is as much better than the negative "non-bad," as it is better to save a life than not to destroy a life. But whatever temper of mind we choose will surely become chronic in time, and will be known to those among whom we live as our temper, our own particular temper, as distinguished from the tempers of other people.

Marzio had begun life in a bad humour. He delighted in his imaginary grievances, and inflicted his anger on all who came near him, only varying the manifestation of it to suit the position in which he chanced to find himself. With his wife he was overbearing; with his brother he was insolent; with his apprentice he was sullen; and with his associates at the old Falcone he played the demagogue. The reason of these phases was very simple. His wife could not oppose him, Don Paolo would not wrangle with him, Gianbattista imposed upon him by his superior calm and strength of character, and, lastly, his socialist friends applauded him and nattered his vanity. It is impossible for a weak man to appear always the same, and his weakness is made the more noticeable when he affects strength. The sinews of goodness are courage, moral and physical, a fact which places all really good men and women beyond the reach of ridicule and above the high-water mark of the world's contempt.

Marzio lacked courage, and his virulence boiled most hotly when he had least to fear for his personal safety. It was owing to this innate weakness that such a combination of artistic sensitiveness and spasmodic arrogance was possible. The man's excitable imagination apprehended opposition where there was none, and his timidity made him fear a struggle, and hate himself for fearing it. As soon as he was alone, however, his thoughts generally returned to his art, and found expression in the delicate execution of the most exquisite fancies. Under other circumstances his character might have developed in a widely different way; his talent would still have been the same. There is a sort of nervous irritability which acts as a stimulant upon the faculties, and makes them work faster. With Marzio this unnatural state was chronic, and had become so because he had given himself up to it. It is a common disease in cities, where a man is forced to associate with his fellow-men, and to compete with them, whether he is naturally inclined to do so or not. If Marzio could have exercised his art while living as a hermit on the top of a lonely mountain he might have been a much better man.

He almost understood this himself as he walked slowly through the Via delle Botteghe Oscure—"the street of dark shops"—in the early morning. He was thinking of the crucifix he was to make, and the interest he felt in it made him dread the consequences of the previous night's domestic wrangling. He wanted to be alone, and at the same time he wanted to see places and things which should suggest thoughts to him. He did not care whither he went so long as he kept out of the new Rome. When he reached the little garden in front of San Marco he paused, looked at the deep doorway of the church, remembered the barbarous mosaics within, and turned impatiently into a narrow street on the right—the beginning of the Via di Marforio.

The network of by-ways in this place is full of old-time memories. Here is the Via Giulio Romano, where the painter himself once lived; here is the Macel dei Corvi, where Michael Angelo once lodged; hard by stood the statue of Marforio, christened by the mediæval Romans after Martis Forum, and famous as the interlocutor of Pasquino. The place was a centre of artists and scholars in those days. Many a simple question was framed here, to fit the two-edged biting answer, repeated from mouth to mouth, and carefully written down among Pasquino's epigrams. First of all the low-born Roman hates all that is, and his next thought is to express his hatred in a stinging satire without being found out.

Like every real Roman, Marzio thought of old Marforio as he strolled up the narrow street towards the Capitol, and regretted the lawless days of conspiracy and treacherous deeds when every man's hand was against his fellow. He wandered on, his eyes cast down, and his head bent. Some one jostled against him, walking quickly in the opposite direction. He looked up and recognised Gasparo Carnesecchi's sallow face and long nose.

"Eh! Sor Marzio—is it you?" asked the lawyer.

"I think so," answered the artist. "Excuse me, I was thinking of something."

"No matter. Of what were you thinking, then? Of Pasquino?"

"Why not? But I was thinking of something else. You are in a hurry, I am sure. Otherwise we would speak of that affair."

"I am never in a hurry when there is business to be treated," replied Carnesecchi, looking down the street and preparing to listen.

"You know what I mean," Marzio began. "The matter we spoke of two days ago—my plans for my daughter."

The lawyer glanced quickly at his friend and assumed an indifferent expression. He was aware that his position, was socially superior to that of the silver-chiseller, in spite of Marzio's great talent. But he knew also that Lucia was to have a dowry, and that she would ultimately inherit all her father possessed. A dowry covers a multitude of sins in the eyes of a man to whom money is the chief object in life. Carnesecchi, therefore, meant to extract as many thousands of francs from Marzio as should be possible, and prepared himself to bargain. The matter was by no means settled, in spite of the chiseller's instructions to his wife concerning the outfit.

"We must talk," said Carnesecchi. "Not that I should be altogether averse to coming easily to an understanding, you know. Bat there are many things to be considered. Let us see."

"Yes, let us see," assented the other. "My daughter has education. She is also sufficiently well instructed. She could make a fine marriage. But then, you see, I desire a serious person for my son-in-law. What would you have? One must be prudent."

It is not easy to define exactly what a Roman means by the word "serious." In some measure it is the opposite of gay, and especially of what is young and unsettled. The German use of the word Philistine expresses it very nearly. A certain sober, straitlaced way of looking at life, which was considered to represent morality in Rome fifty years ago; a kind of melancholy superiority over all sorts of amusements, joined with a considerable asceticism and the most rigid economy in the household—that is what was meant by the word "serious." To-day its signification has been slightly modified, but a serious man—un uomo serio—still represents to the middle-class father the ideal of the correct son-in-law.

"Eh, without prudence!" exclaimed Carnesecchi, elliptically, as though to ask where he himself would have been had he not possessed prudence in abundance.

"Exactly," answered Marzio, biting off the end of a common cigar and fixing his eyes on the lawyer's thin, keen face. "Precisely. I think—of course I do not know—but I think that you are a serious man. But then, I may be mistaken."

"Well, it is human to err, Sor Marzio. But then, I am no longer of that age—what shall I say? Everybody knows I am serious. Do I lead the life of the café? Do I wear out my shoes in Piazza Colonna? Capers! I am a serious man."

"Yes," answered Marzio, though with some hesitation, as though he were prepared to argue even this point with the sallow-faced lawyer. He struck a match on the gaudy little paper box he carried and began to smoke thoughtfully. "Let us make a couple of steps," he said at last.

Both men moved slowly on for a few seconds, and then stopped again. In Italy "a couple of steps" is taken literally.

"Let us see," said Carnesecchi. "Let us look at things as they are. In these days there are many excellent opportunities for investing money."

"Hum!" grunted Marzio, pulling a long face and looking up under his eyebrows. "I know that is your opinion, Sor Gasparo. I am sorry that you should put so much faith in the stability of things. So you, too, have got the malady of speculation. I suppose you are thinking of building a Palazzo Carnesecchi out at Sant' Agnese in eight floors and thirty-two apartments."

"Yes, I am mad," answered the lawyer ironically.

"Who knows?" returned the other. "I tell you they are building a Pompeii in those new quarters. When you and I are old men, crazy Englishmen will pay two francs to be allowed to wander about the ruins."

"It may be. I am not thinking of building. In tine first place I have not the soldi."

"And if you had?" inquired Marzio.

"What nonsense! Besides, no one has. It is all done on credit, and the devil take the hindmost. But if I really had a million—eh! I know what I would do."

"Let us hear. I also know what I would do. Besta! What is the use of building castles in the air?"

"In the air, or not in the air, if I had a million, I know what I would do."

"I would have a newspaper," said Marzio. "Whew! how it would sting!"

"It would sting you, and bleed you into the bargain," returned the lawyer with some contempt. "No one makes mosey out of newspapers in these times. If I had money, I would be a deputy. With prudence there is much to be earned in the Chambers, and petitioners know that they must pay cash."

"It is certainly a career," assented the artist "But, as you say, it needs money for the first investment."

"Not so much as a million, though. With a good opening, and some knowledge of the law, a small sum would be enough."

"It is a career, as I said," repeated Marzio. "But five thousand francs would not give you an introduction to it."

"Five thousand francs!" exclaimed Carnesecchi, with a scornful laugh. "With five thousand francs you had better play at the lottery. After all, if you lose, it is nothing."

"It is a great deal of money, Sor Gasparo," replied the chiseller. "When you have made it little by little—then you know what it means."

"Perhaps. But we have been standing here more than a quarter of an hour, and I have a client waiting for me about a big affair, an affair of millions."

"Bacchus!" ejaculated Marzio. "You are not in a hurry about the matter. Well, we can always talk, and I will not keep you."

"We might walk together, and say what we have to say."

"I am going to the Capitol," Marzio said, for he had been walking in that direction when they met.

"That is my way, too," answered the lawyer, forgetting that he had run into Marzio as he came down the street.

"Eh! That is lucky," remarked the artist with an almost imperceptible smile. "As I was saying," he continued, "five thousand francs is not the National Bank, but it is a very pretty little sum, especially when there is something more to be expected in the future."

"That depends on the future. But I do not call it a sum. Nothing under twenty thousand is a sum, properly speaking."

"Who has twenty thousand francs?" laughed Marzio, shrugging his shoulders with an incredulous look.

"You talk as though Rome were an asylum for paupers," returned Carnesecchi. "Who has twenty thousand francs? Why, everybody has. You have, I have. One must be a beggar not to have that much. After all, we are talking about business, Sor Marzio. Why should I not say it? I have always said that I would not marry with less than that for a dowry. Why should one throw away one's opportunities? To please some one? It is not my business to try and please everybody. One must be just."

"Of course. What? Am I not just? But if justice were done, where would some people be? I say it, too. If you marry my daughter, you will expect a dowry. Have I denied it? And then, five thousand is not so little. There is the outfit, too; I have to pay for that."

"That is not my affair," laughed the lawyer. "That is the business of the woman. But five thousand francs is not my affair either. Think of the responsibilities a man incurs when he marries! Five thousand! It is not even a cup of coffee! You are talking to a galantuomo, an honest man, Sor Marzio. Reflect a little."

"I reflect—yes! I reflect that you ask a great deal of money, Signer Carnesecchi," replied Marzio with some irritation.

"I never heard that anybody gave money unless it was asked for."

"It will not be for lack of asking if you do not get it," retorted the artist.

"What do you mean, Signor Pandolfi?" inquired Carnesecchi, drawing himself up to his full height and then striking his hollow chest with his lean hand. "Do you mean that I am begging money of you? Do you mean to insult an honest man, a galantuomo? By heaven, Signor Pandolfi, I would have you know that Gasparo Carnesecchi never asked a favour of any man! Do you understand? Let us speak clearly."

"Who has said anything?" asked Marzio. "Why do you heat yourself in this way? And then, after all, we shall arrange this affair. You wish it. I wish it. Why should it not be arranged? If five thousand does not suit you, name a sum. We are Christians—we will doubtless arrange. But we must talk. How much should you think, Sor Gasparo?"

"I have said it. As I told you just now, I have always said that I would not marry with less than eighteen thousand francs of dowry. What is the use of repeating? Words are not roasted chestnuts."

"Nor eighteen thousand francs either," answered the other. "Magari! I wish they were. You should have them in a moment. But a franc is a franc."

"I did not say it was a cabbage," observed Carnesecchi. "After all, why should I marry?"

"Perhaps you will not," suggested Marzio, who was encouraged to continue the negotiations, however, by the diminution in the lawyer's demands.

"Why not?" asked the latter sharply, "Do you think nobody else has daughters?"'

"If it comes to that, why have you not married before?"

"Because I did not choose to marry," answered Carnesecchi, beginning to walk more briskly, as though to push the matter to a conclusion.

Marzio said nothing in reply. He saw that his friend was pressing him, and understood that, to do so, the lawyer must be anxious to marry Lucia. The chiseller therefore feigned indifference, and was silent for some minutes. At the foot of the steps of the Capitol he stopped again.

"You know, Sor Gasparo," he said, "the reason why I did not arrange about Lucia's marriage a long time ago, was because I was not particularly in a hurry to have her married at all. And I am not in a hurry now, either. We shall have plenty of opportunities of discussing the matter hereafter. Good-bye, Sor Gasparo. I have business up there, and that client of yours is perhaps impatient about his millions."

"Good-bye," answered Carnesecchi. "There is plenty of time, as you say. Perhaps we may meet this evening at the Falcone."

"Perhaps," said Marab drily, and turned away.

He had a good understanding of his friend's character, and though in his present mood he would have been glad to fix the wedding day, and sign the marriage contract at once, he had no intention of yielding to Carnesecchi's exorbitant demands. The lawyer was in need of money, Marzio thought, and as he himself was the possessor of what the other coveted, there could be little doubt as to the side on which the advantage would ultimately be taken. Marzio went half-way up the steps of the Capitol, and then stopped to look at the two wretched wolves which the Roman municipality thinks it incumbent on the descendants of Romulus to support. He thought one of them very like Carnesecchi. He watched the poor beasts a moment or two as they tramped and swung and pressed their lean sides against the bars of their narrow cage.

"What a sympathetic animal it is!" he exclaimed aloud. A passer-by stared at him and then went on hurriedly, fearing that he might be mad. Indeed, there was a sort of family likeness between the lawyer, the chiseller, and the wolves.

Other thoughts, however, occupied Marzio's attention; and as soon as he was sure that his friend was out of the way, he descended the steps. He did not care whither he went, but he had no especial reason for climbing the steep ascent to the Capitol. The crucifix his brother had ordered from him on the previous evening engaged his attention, and it was as much for the sake of being alone and of thinking about the work that he had taken his solitary morning walk, as with the hope of finding in some church a suggestion or inspiration which might serve him. He knew what was to be found in Roman churches well enough; the Crucifixion in the Trinità dei Pellegrini and the one in San Lorenzo in Lucina—both by Guido Reni, and both eminently unsympathetic to his conception of the subject—he had often looked at them, and did not care to see them again. At last he entered the Church of the Gesù, and sat down upon a chair in a corner.

He did not look up. The interior of the building was as familiar to him as the outside. He sat in profound thought, occasionally twisting his soft hat in his hands, and then again remaining quite motionless. He did not know how long he stayed there. The perfect silence was pleasant to him, and when he rose he felt that the idea he had sought was found, and could be readily expressed. With a sort of sigh of satisfaction he went out again into the air and walked quickly towards his workshop.

The men told him that Gianbattista was busy within, and after glancing sharply at the work which was proceeding, Marzio opened the inner door and entered the studio. He strode up to the table and took up the body of the ewer, which lay on its pad where he had left it the night before. He held it in his hands for a moment, and then, pushing the leather cushion towards Gianbattista, laid it down.

"Finish it," he said shortly; "I have something else to do."

The apprentice looked up in astonishment, as though he suspected that Marzio was jesting.

"I am afraid—" he answered with hesitation.

"It makes no difference; finish it as best you can; I am sick of it; you will do it well enough. If it is bad, I will take the responsibility."

"Do you mean me really to finish it—altogether?"

"Yes; I tell you I have a great work on hand. I cannot waste my time over such toys as acanthus leaves and cherubs' eyes!" He bent down and examined the thing carefully. "You had better lay aside the neck and take up the body just where I left it, Tista," he continued. "The scirocco is in your favour. If it turns cold to-morrow the cement may shrink, and you will have to melt it out again."

Marzio spoke to him as though there had not been the least difference between them, as though Gianbattista had not proposed to cut his throat the night before, as though he himself had not proposed to marry Carnesecchi to Lucia.

"Take my place," he said. "The cord is the right length for you, as it is too short for me. I am going to model."

Without more words Marzio went and took a large and heavy slate from the corner, washed it carefully, and dried it with his handkerchief. Then he provided himself with a bowl full of twisted lengths of red wax, and with a couple of tools he sat down to his work. Gianbattista, having changed his seat, looked over the tools his master had been using, with a workman's keen glance, and, taking up his own hammer, attacked the task given him. For some time neither of the men spoke.

"I have been to church," remarked Marzio at last, as he softened a piece of wax between his fingers before laying it on the slate. The news was so astounding that Gianbattista uttered an exclamation of surprise.

"You need not be frightened," answered the artist. "I only went to look at a picture, and I did not look at it after all. I shall go to a great many more churches before I have finished this piece of work. You ought to go to the churches and study, Tista. Everything is useful in our art—pictures, statues, mosaics, metal-work. Now I believe there is not a really good crucifix, nor a crucifixion, in Rome. It is strange, too, I have dreamed of one all my life."

Gianbattista did not find any answer ready in reply to the statement. The words sounded so strangely in Marzio's mouth this morning, that the apprentice was confused. And yet the two had often discussed the subject before.

"You do not seem to believe me," continued Marzio quietly. "I assure you it is a fact. The other things of the kind are not much better either. Works of art, perhaps, but not satisfactory. Even Michael Angelo's Pietà in Saint Peter's does not please me. They say it did not please the people of his time either—he was too young to do anything of that sort—he was younger than you, Tista, only twenty-four years old when he made that statue."

"Yes," answered Gianbattista, "I have heard you say so." He bent over his work, wondering what his master meant by this declaration of taste. It seemed as though Marzio felt the awkwardness of the situation and was exerting himself to make conversation. The idea was so strange that the apprentice could almost have laughed. Marzio continued to soften the wax between his fingers, and to lay the pieces of it on the slate, pressing them roughly into the shape of a figure.

"Has Paolo been here?" asked the master after another long pause.

Gianbattista merely shook his head to express a negative.

"Then he will come," continued Marzio. "He will not leave me in peace all day, you may be sure."

"What should he come for? He never comes," said the young man.

"He will be afraid that I will have Lucia married before supper time. I know him—and he knows me."

"If he thinks that, he does not know you at all," answered Gianbattista quietly.

"Indeed?" exclaimed Marzio, raising his voice to the ironical tone he usually affected when any one contradicted him. "To-day, to-morrow, or the next day, what does it matter? I told you last night that I had made up my mind."

"And I told you that I had made up mine."

"Oh yes—boy's threats! I am not the man to be intimidated by that sort of thing. Look here, Tista, I am in earnest. I have considered this matter a long time; I have determined that I will not be browbeaten any longer by two women and a priest—certainly not by you. If things go on as they are going, I shall soon not be master in my own house."

"You would be the only loser," retorted Gianbattista.

"Have done with this, Tista!" exclaimed Marzio angrily. "I am tired of your miserable jokes. You have gone over to the enemy, you are Paolo's man, and if I tolerate you here any longer it is merely because I have taught you something, and you are worth your wages. As for the way I have treated you during all these years, I cannot imagine how I could have been such a fool. I should think anybody might see through your hypocritical ways."

"Go on," said Gianbattista calmly. "You know our bargain of last night"

"I will risk that. If I see any signs of your amiable temper I will have you arrested for threatening my life. I am not afraid of you, my boy, but I do not care to die just at present. You have all had your way long enough, I mean to have mine now."

"Let us talk reasonably, Sor Marzio. You say we have had our way. You talk as though you had been in slavery in your own house. I do not think that is the opinion of your wife, nor of your daughter. As for me, I have done nothing but execute your orders for years, and if I have learnt something, it has not been by trying to overrule you or by disregarding your advice. Two years ago, you almost suggested to me that I should marry Lucia. Of course, I asked nothing better, and we agreed to wait until she was old enough. We discussed the matter a thousand times. We settled the details. I agreed to go on working for the same small wages instead of leaving you, as I might have done, to seek my fortune elsewhere. You see I am calm, I acknowledge that I was grateful to you for having taught me so much, and I am grateful still. You have just given me another proof of your confidence in putting this work into my hands to finish. I am grateful for that. Well, we have talked of the marriage often; I have lived in your house; I have seen Lucia every day, for you have let us be together as much as we pleased; the result is that I not only am more anxious to marry her than I was before—I love her; I am not ashamed to say so. I know you laugh at women and say they are no better than monkeys with parrots' heads. I differ from you. Lucia is an angel, and I love her as she loves me. What happens? One day you take an unreasonable dislike for me, without even warning me of the fact, and then, suddenly, last night, you come home and say she is to marry the Avvocato Gasparo Carnesecchi. Now, for a man who has taught me that there is no God but reason, all this strikes me as very unreasonable. Honestly, Sor Marzio, do you not think so yourself?"

Marzio looked at his apprentice and frowned, as though hesitating whether to lose his temper and launch into the invective style, or to answer Gianbattista reasonably. Apparently he decided in favour of the more peaceable course.

"It is unworthy of a man who follows reason to lose his self-control and indulge in vain threats," he answered, assuming a grand didactic air. "You attempt to argue with me. I will show you what argument really means, and whither it leads. Now answer me some questions, Tista, and I will prove that you are altogether in the wrong. When a man is devoted to a great and glorious cause, should he not do everything in his power to promote its success against those who oppose it?"

"Undoubtedly," assented Gianbattista.

"And should not a man be willing to sacrifice his individual preferences in order to support and to further the great end of his life?"

"Bacchus! I believe it!"

"Then how much the more easy must it be for a man to support his cause when there are no individual preferences in the way!" said Marzio triumphantly. "That is true reason, my boy. That is the inevitable logic of the great system."

"I do not understand the allegory," answered Gianbattista.

"It is as simple as roasted chestnuts," returned Marzio. "Even if I liked you, it would be my duty to prevent you from marrying Lucia. As I do not like you—you understand?"

"I understand that," replied the young man. "For some reason or other you hate me. But, apart from the individual preferences, which you say it is your duty to overcome, I do not see why you are morally obliged to hinder our marriage, after having felt morally obliged to promote it?"

"Because you are a traitor to the cause," cried Marzio, with sudden fierceness. "Because you are a friend of Paolo. Is not that enough?"

"Poor Don Paolo seems to stick in your throat," observed Gianbattista. "I do not see what he has done, except that he prevented me from killing you last night!"

"Paolo! Paolo is a snake, a venomous viper! It is his business, his only aim in life, to destroy my peace, to pervert my daughter from the wholesome views I have tried to teach her, to turn you aside from the narrow path of austere Italian virtue, to draw you away from following in the footsteps of Brutus, of Cassius, of the great Romans, of me, your teacher and master! That is all Paolo cares for, and it is enough—more than enough! And he shall pay me for his presumptuous interference, the villain!"

Marzio's voice sank into a hissing whisper as he bent over the wax he was twisting and pressing. Gianbattista glanced at his pale face, and inwardly wondered at the strange mixture of artistic genius, of bombastic rhetoric and relentless hatred, all combined in the strange man whom destiny had given him for a master. He wondered, too, how he had ever been able to admire the contrasts of virulence and weakness, of petty hatred and impossible aspirations which had of late revealed themselves to him in a new light. Have we not most of us assisted at the breaking of the Image of Baal, at the destruction of an imaginary representative of an illogical ideal?

"Well, Sor Marzio," said Gianbattista after a pause, "if I were to return to my worship of you and your principles—what would you do? Would you take me back to your friendship and give me your daughter?"

Marzio looked up suddenly, and stared at the apprentice in surprise. But the fresh young face gave no sign. Gianbattista had spoken quietly, and was again intent upon his work.

"If you gave me a proof of your sincerity," answered Marzio, in low tones, "I would do much for you. Yes, I would give you Lucia—and the business too, when I am too old to work. But it must be a serious proof—no child's play."

"What do you call a serious proof? A profession of faith?"

"Yes—sealed with the red wax that is a little thicker than water," answered Marzio grimly, his eyes still fixed on Gianbattista's face.

"In blood," said the young man calmly. "Whose blood would you like, Sor Marzio?"

"Paolo's!"

The chiseller spoke in a scarcely audible whisper, and bent low over his slate, modelling hard at the figure under his fingers.

"I thought so," muttered Gianbattista between his teeth. Then he raised his voice a little and continued: "And have you the courage, Sor Marzio, to sit there and bargain with me to kill your brother, bribing me with the offer of your daughter's hand? Why do you not kill him yourself, since you talk of such things?"

"Nonsense, my dear Tista—I was only jesting," said the other nervously. "It is just like your folly to take me in earnest." The anger had died out of Marzio's voice and he spoke almost persuasively.

"I do not know," answered the young man. "I think you were in earnest for a moment. I would not advise you to talk in that way before any one else. People might interpret your meaning seriously."

"After all, you yourself were threatening to cut my throat last night," said Marzio, with a forced laugh. "It is the same thing. My life is as valuable as Paolo's. I only suggested that you should transfer your tender attentions from me to my brother."

"It is one thing to threaten a man to his face. It is quite another to offer a man a serious inducement to commit murder. Since you have been so very frank with me, Sor Marzio, I will confess that if the choice lay between killing you, or killing Don Paolo, under the present circumstances I would not hesitate a moment."

"And which would you—"

"Neither," replied the young man, with a cool laugh. "Don Paolo is too good to be killed, and you are not good enough. Come and look at the cherub's head I have made."

CHAPTER VI

Lucia's cheerfulness was not genuine, and any one possessing greater penetration than her mother would have understood that she was, in reality, more frightened than she was willing to show. The girl had a large proportion of common sense, combined with a quicker perception than the stout Signora Pandolfi. She did not think that she knew anything about logic, and she had always shown a certain inconsistency in her affection for Gianbattista, but she had nevertheless a very clear idea of what was reasonable, a quality which is of immense value in difficulties, though it is very often despised in every-day life by people who believe themselves blessed by the inspirations of genius.

It seems very hard to make people of other nationalities understand that the Italians of the present day are not an imaginative people. It is nevertheless true, and it is only necessary to notice that they produce few, if any, works of imagination. They have no writers of fiction, no poets, few composers of merit and few artists who rank with those of other nations. They possessed the creative faculty once; they have lost it in our day, and it does not appear that they are likely to regain it. On the other hand, the Italians are remarkable engineers, first-rate mathematicians, clever, if unscrupulous, diplomatists. Though they overrate their power and influence, they have shown a capacity for organisation which is creditable on the whole. If they fail to obtain the position they seek in Europe, their failure will have been due to their inordinate vanity and over-governing, if I may coin the word, rather than to an innate want of intelligence.

The qualities and defects of the Italian nation all existed in the Pandolfi family. Marzio possessed more imagination than most of his countrymen, and he had, besides, that extraordinary skill in his manual execution of his work, which Italians have often exhibited on a large scale. On the other hand, he was full of bombastic talk about principles which he called great. His views concerning society, government, and the future of his country, were entirely without balance, and betrayed an amazing ignorance of the laws which, direct the destinies of mankind. He suffered in a remarkable degree from that mental disease which afflicts Italians—the worship of the fetish—of words which mean little, and are supposed to mean much, of names in history which have been exalted by the rhetoric of demagogues from the obscurity to which they had been wisely consigned by the judgment of scholars. He was alternately weak and despotic, cunning about small things which concerned his own fortunes, and amazingly foolish about the set of ideas which he loosely defined as politics.

Lucia's nature illustrated another phase of the Italian character, and one which, if it is less remarkable, is much more agreeable. She possessed the character which looks at everything from the point of view of daily life. Without imagination, she regarded only the practical side of existence. Her vanity was confined to a modest wish to make the best of her appearance, while her ambition went no further than the strictest possibility, in the shape of a marriage with Gianbattista Bordogni, and a simple little apartment with a terrace and pots of pinks. Had she known how much richer her father was than she suspected him of being, the enlargement of her views for the future would have been marked by a descent, from the fourth story of the house which was to be her imaginary home, to the third story. It could never have entered her head that Gianbattista ought to give up his profession until he was too old to work any longer. In her estimation, the mere possession of money could not justify a change of social position. She had been accustomed from her childhood to hear her father air his views in regard to the world in general, but his preaching had produced but little impression upon her. When he thought she was listening in profound attention to his discourse, she was usually wishing that he could be made to see the absurdity of his theories. She wished also that he would sacrifice some of his enthusiasm for the sake of a little more quiet in the house, for she saw that his talking distressed her mother. Further than this she cared little what he said, and not at all for what he thought. Her mind was generally occupied with the one subject which absorbed her thoughts, and which had grown to be by far the most important part of her nature, her love for Gianbattista Bordogni.

Upon that point she was inflexible. Her Uncle Paolo might have led her to change her mind in regard to many things, for she was open to persuasion where her common sense was concerned. But in her love for Gianbattista she was fixed and determined. It would have been more easy to turn her father from his ideas than to make Lucia give up the man she loved. When Marzio had suddenly declared that she should marry the lawyer, her first feeling had been one of ungovernable anger which had soon found vent in tears. During the night she had thought the matter over, and had come to the conclusion that it was only an evil jest, invented by Marzio to give her pain. But in the morning it seemed to her as though on the far horizon a black cloud of possible trouble were gathering; she had admitted to herself that her father might be in earnest, and she had felt something like the anticipation of the great struggle of her life. Then she felt that she would die rather than submit.

She had no theatrical desire to swear a fearful oath with Gianbattista that they should drown themselves at the Ponte Quattro Capi rather than be separated. Her nature was not dramatic, any more than his. The young girl dressed herself quickly, and made up her mind that if any pressure were brought to bear upon her she would not yield, but that, until then, there was no use in making phrases, and it would be better to be as cheerful as possible under the circumstances. But for Lucia's reassuring manner, the Signora Pandolfi would have doubtless succumbed to her feelings and gone to bed. Lucia, however, had no intention of allowing her mother any such weakness, and accordingly alternately comforted her and suggested means of escape from the position, as though she were herself the mother and Maria Luisa were her child.

They found Don Paolo in his small lodging, and he bid them enter, that they might all talk the matter over.

"In the first place," said the priest, "it is wrong. In the second place it is impossible. Thirdly, Marzio will not attempt to carry out his threat."

"Dear me! How simple you make it seem!" acclaimed the Signora Pandolfi, reviving at his first words, like a tired horse when he sees the top of the hill.

"But if papa should try and force me to it—what then?" asked Lucia, who was not so easily satisfied.

"He cannot force you to it, my child—the law will not allow him to do so. I told you so last night"

"But the law is so far off—and he is so violent" answered the young girl.

"Never fear," said Don Paolo, reassuring her. "I will manage it all. These will be a struggle, perhaps; but I will make him see reason. He had been with his friends last night, and his mind was excited; he was not himself. He will have thought differently of it this morning;"

"On the contrary," put in the Signora Pandolfi, "he waked me up at daylight and gave me a quantity of money to go and buy Lucia's outfit. And he will come home at midday and ask to see the things I have brought, and so I thought perhaps we had better buy something just to show him—half a dozen handkerchiefs—something to make a figure, you understand?"

Don Paolo smiled, and Lucia looked sympathetically from him to her mother.

"I am afraid that half a dozen handkerchiefs would have a bad effect," said the priest. "Either he would see that you are not in earnest, and then he would be very angry, or else he would be deceived and would think that you were really buying the outfit. In that case you would have done harm. This thing must not go any further. The idea must be got out of his head as soon as possible."

"But if I do nothing at all before dinner he will be furious—he will cry out that we are all banded together against him—"

"So we are," said Don Paolo simply.

"Oh dear, oh dear!" moaned the Signora Pandolfi, looking for her handkerchief in the anticipation of fresh tears.

"Do not cry, mamma. It is of no use," said Lucia.

"No, it is of no use to cry," assented the priest. "There is nothing to be done but to go and face Marzio, and not leave him until he has changed his mind. You are afraid to meet him at midday. I will go now to the workshop and find him."

"Oh, you are an angel, Paolo!" cried Maria Luisa, regaining her composure and replacing her handkerchief in her pocket. "Then we need not buy anything? What a relief!"

"I told you Uncle Paolo would know what to do," said Lucia. "He is so good—and so courageous. I would not like to face papa this morning. Will you really go, Uncle Paolo?" The young girl went and took down his cloak and hat from a peg on the wall, and brought them to him.

"Of course I will go, and at once," he answered. "But I must give you a word of advice."

"We will do everything you tell us," said the two women together.

"You must not ask him any questions, nor refer to the matter at all when he comes home."

"Diana! I would as soon speak of death!" exclaimed the Signora Pandolfi.

"And if he begins to talk about it you must not answer him, nor irritate him in any way."

"Be easy about that," answered the fat lady. "Never meddle with sleeping dogs—I know."

"If he grows very angry you must refer him to me."

"Oh, but that is another matter! I would rather offer pepper to a cat than talk to him of you. You would see how he would curse and swear and call you by bad names."

"Well, you must not do anything to make him swear, because that would be a sin; but if he only abuses me, I do not mind. He will do that when I talk to him. Perhaps after all, if he mentions the matter, you had better remain silent."

"Eh! that will be easy. He talks so much, and he talks so fast, never waiting for an answer. But are you not afraid for yourself, dear Paolo?"

"Oh, he will not hurt me—I am not afraid of him," answered the priest. "He will talk a little, he will use some big words, and then it will be finished. You see, it is not a great thing, after all. Take courage, Maria Luisa, it will be a matter of half an hour."

"Heaven grant it may be only that!" murmured Marzio's wife, turning up her eyes, and rising from her chair.

Lucia, who, as has been said, had a very keen appreciation of facts, did not believe that things would go so smoothly.

"You had better come back with him to our house when it is all over," she said, "just to give us a sign that it is settled, you know, Uncle Paolo."

Don Paolo himself had his doubts about the issue, although he put such a brave face on it, and in spite of the Signora Pandolfi. That good lady was by nature very sincere, but she always seemed to bring an irrelevant and comic element into the proceedings.

The result of the interview was that, in half an hour, Don Paolo knocked at the door of the workshop in the Via dei Falegnami, where Marzio and Gianbattista were at work. The chiseller's voice bade him enter.

Don Paolo had not found much time to collect his thoughts before he reached the scene of battle, but his opinion of the matter in hand was well formed. He loved his niece, and he had begun to like Gianbattista. He knew the lawyer, Carnesecchi, by reputation, and what he had heard of him did not prejudice him in the man's favour. It would have been the same had Marzio chosen any one else. In the priest's estimation, Gianbattista had a right to expect the fulfilment of the many promises which had been made to him. To break those promises for no ostensible reason, just as Gianbattista seemed to be growing up to be a sensible man, was an act of injustice which Don Paolo would not permit if he could help it. Gianbattista was not, perhaps, a model man, but, by contrast with Marzio, he seemed almost saintly. He had a good disposition and no vices; married to Lucia and devoted to his art, much might be expected of him. On the other hand, Gasparo Carnesecchi represented the devil in person. He was known to be an advanced freethinker, a radical, and, perhaps, worse than a radical—a socialist. He was certainly not very rich, and Lucia's dowry would be an object to him; he would doubtless spend the last copper of the money in attempting to be elected to the Chambers. If he succeeded, he would represent another unit in that ill-guided minority which has for its sole end the subversion of the existing state of things. He would probably succeed in getting back the money he had spent, and more also, by illicit means. If he failed, the money would be lost, and he would go from bad to worse, intriguing and mixing himself up with the despicable radical press, in the hope of getting a hearing and a place.

There is a scale in the meaning of the word socialist. In France it means about the same thing as a communist, when one uses plain language. When one uses the language of Monsieur Dramont, it means a Jew. In England a socialist is equal to a French conservative republican. In America it means a thief. In Germany it means an ingenious individual of restricted financial resources, who generally fails to blow up some important personage with wet dynamite. In Italy a socialist is an anarchist pure and simple, who wishes to destroy everything existing for the sake of dividing a wealth which does not exist at all. It also means a young man who orders a glass of water and a toothpick at a café, and is able to talk politics for a considerable time on this slender nourishment. Signor Succi and Signor Merlatti have discovered nothing new. Their miracles of fasting may be observed by the curious at any time in a Roman café.

Don Paolo regarded the mere idea of an alliance with Gasparo Carnesecchi as an outrage upon common sense, and when he entered Marzio's workshop he was determined to say so. Marzio looked up with an air of inquiry, and Gianbattista foresaw what was coming. He nodded to the priest, and brought forward the old straw chair from the corner; then he returned to his work in silence.

"You will have guessed my errand," Don Paolo began, by way of introducing his subject.

"No," answered Marzio doggedly. "Something about the crucifix, I suppose."

"Not at all," returned the priest, folding his hands over the handle of his umbrella. "A much more delicate matter. You suggested last night an improbable scheme for marrying Lucia."

"You had better say that I told you plainly what I mean to do. If you have come to talk about that, you had better talk to the workmen outside. They may answer you. I will not!"

Don Paolo was not to be so easily put off. He waited a moment as though to give Marzio time to change his mind, and then proceeded.

"There are three reasons why this marriage will not take place," he said. "In the first place, it is wrong—that is my point of view. In the second place, it is impossible—and that is the view the law takes of it. Thirdly, it will not take place because you will not attempt to push it. What do you say of my reasons, Marzio?"

"They are worthy of you," answered the artist. "In the first place, I do not care a fig for what you think is wrong, or right either. Secondly, I will take the law into my own hands. Thirdly, I will bring it about and finish it in a fortnight; and fourthly, you may go to the devil! What do you think of my reasons, Paolo? They are better than yours, and much more likely to prevail."

"My dear Marzio," returned the priest quietly, "you may say anything you please, I believe, in these days of liberty. But the law will not permit you to act upon your words. If you can persuade your daughter to marry Gasparo Carnesecchi of her own free will, well and good. If you cannot, there is a statute, I am quite sure, which forbids your dragging her up the steps of the Capitol, and making her sign her name by force or violence in the presence of the authorities. You may take my word for it; and so you had better dismiss the matter from your mind at once, and think no more about it."

"I remember that you told her so last night," growled Marzio, growing pale with anger.

"Certainly."

"You—you—you priest!" cried the chiseller, unable in his rage to find an epithet which he judged more degrading. Don Paolo smiled.

"Yes, I am a priest," he answered calmly.

"Yea, you are a priest," yelled Marzio, "and what is to become of paternal authority in a household where such fellows as you are listening at the keyholes? Is a man to have no more rights? Are we to be ruled by women and creatures in petticoats? Viper! Poisoning my household, teaching my daughter to disobey me, my wife to despise me, my paid workmen to—"

"Silence!" cried Gianbattista in ringing tones, and with the word he sprang to his feet and clapped his hand on Marzio's mouth.

The effect was sudden and unexpected. Marzio was utterly taken by surprise. It was incredible to him that any one should dare to forcibly prevent him from indulging in the language he had used with impunity for so many years. He leaned back pale and astonished, and momentarily dumb with amazement. Gianbattista stood over him, his young cheeks flushed with anger, and his broad fist clenched.

"If you dare to talk in that way to Don Paolo, I will kill you with my hands!" he said, his voice sinking lower with concentrated determination. "I have had enough of your foul talk. He is a better man than you, as I told you last night, and I repeat it now—take care—"

Marzio made a movement as though he would rise, and at the same instant Gianbattista seized the long, fine-pointed punch, which served for the eyes of the cherubs—a dangerous weapon in a determined hand.

Don Paolo had risen from his chair, and was trying to push himself between the two. But Gianbattista would not let him.

"For heaven's sake," cried the priest in great distress, "no violence, Tista—I will call the men—"

"Never fear," answered the apprentice quietly; "the man is a coward."

"To me—you dare to say that to me!" exclaimed Marzio, drawing back at the same time.

"Yes—it is quite true. But do not suppose that I think any the worse of you on that account, Sor Marzio."

With this taunt, delivered in a voice that expressed the most profound contempt, Gianbattista went back to his seat and took up his hammer as though nothing had happened. Don Paolo drew a long breath of relief. As for Marzio, his teeth chattered with rage. His weakness had been betrayed at last, and by Gianbattista. All his life he had succeeded in concealing the physical fear which his words belied. He had cultivated the habit of offering to face danger, speaking of it in a quiet way, as he had observed that brave men did. He had found it good policy to tell people that he was not afraid of them, and his bearing had hitherto saved him from physical violence. Now he felt as though all his nerves had been drawn out of his body. He had been terrified, and he knew that he had shown it. Gianbattista's words stung in his ears like the sting of wasps.

"You shall never enter this room again," he hissed out between his teeth. The young man shrugged his shoulders as though he did not care. Don Paolo sat down again and grasped his umbrella.

"Gianbattista," said the priest, "I am grateful to you for your friendship, my boy. But it is very wrong to be violent—"

"It is one of the seven deadly sins!" cried Marzio, finding his voice at last, and by a strange accident venting his feelings in a sentence which might have been spoken by a confessor to a penitent.

Gianbattista could not help laughing, but he shook his head as though to explain that it was not his fault if he was violent with such a man.

"It is very wrong to threaten people, Tista," repeated Don Paolo; "and besides it does not hurt me, what Marzio says. Let us all be calm. Marzio, let us discuss this matter reasonably. Tista, do not be angry at anything that is said. There is nothing to be done but to look at the question quietly."

"It is very well for you to talk like that," grumbled Marzio, pretending to busy himself over his model in order to cover his agitation.

"It is of no use to talk in any other way," answered the priest "I return to the subject. I only want to convince you that you will find it impossible to carry out your determination by force. You have only to ask the very man you have hit upon, the Avvocato Garnesecchi, and he will tell you the same thing. He knows the law better than you or I. He will refuse to be a party to such an attempt. Ask him, if you do not believe me."

"Yes; a pretty position you want to put me in, by the body of a dog! To ask a man to marry my daughter by force! A fine opinion he would conceive of my domestic authority! Perhaps you will take upon yourself to go and tell him—won't you, dear Paolo? It would save me the trouble."

"I think that is your affair," answered Don Paolo, taking him in earnest. "Nevertheless, if you wish it—"

"Oh, this is too much!" cried Marzio, his anger rising again. "It is not enough that you thwart me at every turn, but you come here to mock me, to make a figure of me! Take care, Paolo, take care! You may go too far."

"I would not advise you to go too far, Sor Marzio," put in Gianbattista, turning half round on his stool.

"Cannot I speak without being interrupted? Go on with your work, Tista, and let us talk this matter out. I tell you, Paolo, that I do not want your advice, and that I have had far too much of your interference. I will inquire into this matter, so far as it concerns the law, and I will show you that I am right, in spite of all your surmises and prophecies. A man is master in his own house and must remain so, whatever laws are made. There is no law which can force a man to submit to the dictation of his brother—even if his brother is a priest."

Marzio spoke more calmly than he had done hitherto, in spite of the sneer in the last sentence. He had broken down, and he felt that Paolo and Gianbattista were too much for him. He desired no repetition of the scene which had passed, and he thought the best thing to be done was to temporise for a while.

"I am glad you are willing to look into the matter," answered Don Paolo. "I am quite sure you will soon be convinced."

Marzio was silent, and it was evident that the interview was at an end. Don Paolo was tolerably well satisfied, for he had gained at least one point in forcing his brother to examine the question. He remained a moment in his seat, reviewing the situation, and asking himself whether there was anything more to be said. He wished indeed that he could produce some deeper impression on the artist. It was not enough, from the moral point of view, that Marzio should be made to see the impossibility of his scheme, although it was as much as could be expected. The good man wished with all his heart that Marzio could be softened a little, that he might be made to consider his daughter's feelings, to betray some sign of an affection which seemed wholly dead, to show some more human side of his character. But the situation at present forbade Don Paolo from making any further effort. The presence of Gianbattista, who had suddenly constituted himself the priest's defender, was a constraint. Alone with his brother, Marzio might possibly have exhibited some sensibility, but while the young man who had violently silenced him a few moments earlier was looking on, the chiseller would continue to be angry, and would not forget the humiliation he had suffered. There was nothing more to be done at present, and Don Paolo prepared to take his departure, gathering his cloak around him, and smoothing the felt of his three-cornered hat while he held his green umbrella under his arm.

"Are you going already, Don Paolo?" asked Gianbattista, rising to open the door.

"Yes, I must go. Good-bye, Marzio. Bear me no ill-will for pressing you to be cautious. Good-bye, Tista." He pressed the young man's hand warmly, as though to thank him for his courageous defence, and then left the workshop. Marzio paid no attention to his departure. When the door was closed, and as Gianbattista was returning to his bench, the artist dropped his modelling tools and faced his apprentice.

"You may go too," he said in a low tone, as though he were choking. "I mean you may go for good. I do not need you any longer."

He felt in his pocket for his purse, opened it, and took out some small notes.

"I give you an hour to take your things from my house," he continued. "There are your wages—you shall not tell the priest that I cheated you."

Gianbattista stood still in the middle of the room while Marzio held out the money to him. A hot flush rose to his young forehead, and he seemed on the point of speaking, but the words did not pass his lips. With a quick step he came forward, took the notes from Marzio's hand, and crumpling them in his fingers, threw them in his face with all his might. Then he turned on his heel, spat on the floor of the room, and went out before Marzio could find words to resent the fresh insult.

The door fell back on the latch and Marzio was alone. He was very pale, and for a moment his features worked angrily. Then a cruel smile passed over his face. He stooped down, picked up the crumpled notes, counted them, and replaced them in his purse. The economical instinct never forsook him, and he did the thing mechanically. Glancing at the bench his eyes fell on the pointed punch which Gianbattista had taken up in his anger. He felt it carefully, handled it, looked at it, smiled again and put it into his pocket.

"It is not a bad one," he muttered. "How many cherubs' eyes I have made with that thing!"

He turned to the slate and examined the rough model he had made in wax, flat still, and only indicated by vigorous touches, the red material smeared on the black surface all around it by his fingers. There was force in the figure, even in its first state, and there was a strange pathos in the bent head, the only part as yet in high relief. But Marzio looked at it angrily. He turned it to the light, closed his eyes a moment, looked at it again, and then, with an incoherent oath, his long, discoloured hand descended on the model, and, with a heavy pressure and one strong push, flattened out what he had done, and smeared it into a shapeless mass upon the dark stone.

"I shall never do it," he said in a low voice. "They have destroyed my idea."

For some minutes he rested his head in his hand in deep thought. At last he rose and went to a corner of the workshop in which stood a heavily ironed box. Marzio fumbled in his pocket till he found a key, bright from always being carried about with him, and contrasting oddly with the rusty lock into which he thrust it. It turned with difficulty in his nervous fingers, and he raised the heavy lid. The coffer was full of packages wrapped in brown paper. He removed one after another till he came to a wooden case which filled the whole length and breadth of the safe. He lifted it out carefully and laid it on the end of the bench. The cover was fastened down by screws, and he undid them one by one until it moved and came off in his hands. The contents were wrapped carefully in a fine towel, which had once been white, but which had long grown yellow with age. Marzio unfolded the covering with a delicate touch as though he feared to hurt what was within. He took out a large silver crucifix, raising it carefully, and taking care not to touch the figure. He stood it upon the bench before him, and sat down to examine it.

It was a work of rare beauty, which he had made more than ten years before. With the strange reticent instinct which artists sometimes feel about their finest works, he had finished it in secret, working at night alone, and when it was done he had put it away. It was his greatest feat, he had said to himself, and, as from time to time he took it out and looked at it, he gradually grew less and less inclined to show it to any one, resolving to leave it in its case, until it should be found after his death. It had seemed priceless to him, and he would not sell it. With a fantastic eccentricity of reasoning he regarded it as a sacred thing, to part with which would be a desecration. So he kept it. Then, taking it out again, it had seemed less good to him, as his mind became occupied with other things, and he had fancied he should do better yet. At last he screwed it up in a wooden case and put it at the bottom of his strong box, resolving never to look at it again. Many years had passed since he had laid eyes upon it.

The idea which had come to him when Paolo had communicated the order to him on the previous evening, had seemed absolutely new. It had appeared to him as a glorification of the work he had executed in secret so long ago. Time, and the habit of dissatisfaction had effaced from his mind the precise image of the work of the past, and the emotions of the present had seemed something new to him. He had drawn and modelled during many hours, and yet he was utterly disappointed with the new result. He felt the innate consciousness of having done it before, and of having done it better.

And now the wonderful masterpiece of his earlier years stood before him—the tall and massive ebony cross, bearing the marvellous figure of the dead Saviour. A ray of sunlight fell through the grated window upon the dying head, illuminating the points of the thorns in the crown, the falling locks of hair, the tortured hands, and casting a shadow of death beneath the half-closed eyes.

For several minutes Marzio sat motionless on his stool, realising the whole strength and beauty of what he had done ten years before. Then he wanted to get a better view of it. It was not high enough above him, for it was meant to stand upon an altar. He could not see the face. He looked about for something upon which to make it stand, but nothing was near. He pushed away his stool, and turning the cross a little, so that the sunlight should strike it at a better angle, he kneeled down on the floor, his hands resting on the edge of the bench, and he looked up at the image of the dead Christ.

CHAPTER VII

When Don Paolo left the workshop, he immediately crossed over and entered the street door of Marzio's house, intending to tell Maria Luisa and Lucia the result of the interview. He had not got to the top of the first flight of stairs when he heard Gianbattista's step behind him, and turning he saw the young man's angry face.

"What is the matter, Tista?" asked the priest, stopping on the steps and laying his hand on the iron railing.

"I am discharged, turned out, insulted by that animal!" answered the apprentice hotly. "He is like a piece of wood! You might as well talk to a wall! You had only just closed the door when he pulled out his purse, counted my wages, and told me to take my things from his house in an hour. I threw the money in his face—the beast!"

"Hush, Tista," said Don Paolo. "Do not be angry—we will arrange it all before night. He cannot do without you, and after all it is my fault. Calm yourself, Tista, my boy—we will soon set that straight."

"Yes—in an hour I will have left the house. Then it will be straight enough, as you call it. Oh! I would like to strangle him! Dear Don Paolo, nobody but you can arrange this affair—"

"Hush, hush, Tista. I cannot hear you talk in this way. Come, we will go back to Marzio. He will listen to reason—"

"Do you know what he said to me not a quarter of an hour before you came in?" asked Gianbattista quickly, laying his hand on the priest's arm. "He said I might have Lucia and welcome if I would kill you! Do you understand? I wish you could have seen the look in his eyes!"

"No, no, my boy—he was angry. He did not mean it."

"Mean it! Bacchus! He would kill you himself if he were not such a dastardly coward!"

Don Paolo shook his head with an incredulous smile, and looked kindly into the young man's eyes.

"You have all lost your heads over this unfortunate affair, Tista. You are all talking of killing each other and yourselves as though it were as simple as 'good-morning.' It is very wrong to talk of such things, and besides, you know, it is not really worth while—"

"It seems simple enough to me," answered the young man, frowning and clenching his hand.

"Come with me," urged the other, making as though he would descend the steps. "Come back to the workshop, and we will talk it all over."

"Wait a minute, Don Paolo. There is one thing—one favour I want to ask of you." Gianbattista lowered his voice. "You can do it for us—I am sure you will. I will call Lucia, and we will go with you—"

"Where?" asked the priest, not understanding the look of the young man.

"To church, of course. You can marry us in ten minutes, and the thing will be all over. Then we can laugh at Sor Marzio."

Don Paolo smiled.

"My dear boy," he answered, "those things are not done in a moment like roasting chestnuts. There are banns to be published. There is a civil marriage at the Capitol—"

"I should be quite satisfied with your benediction—a Pater Noster, an Oremus properly said—eh? Would it not be all right?"

"Really, Tista!" exclaimed the good man, holding up his hands in horror. "I had no idea that your religious education had been so neglected! My dear child, marriage is a very solemn thing."

"By Diana! I should think so! But that need not make it such a long ceremony. A man dies in a moment—paff!—the light is out!—you are dead. It is very solemn. The same thing for marriage. The priest looks at you, says Oremus—paff! You are married, and it cannot be undone! I know it is very serious, but it is only the affair of a moment."

Don Paolo did not know whether to laugh or to look grave at this exposition of Gianbattista's views of death and matrimony. He put it down to the boy's excitement.

"There is another reason, Tista. The law does not allow a girl of seventeen to be married without her father's consent."

"The law again!" exclaimed Gianbattista in disgust. "I thought the law protected Lucia from her father. You said so last night, and you repeated it this morning."

"Certainly, my boy. But the law also protects parents against any rashness their children may meditate. It would be no marriage if Lucia had not Marzio's consent."

"I wish there were no laws," grumbled the young man. "How do you come to know so much about marriage, Don Paolo?"

"It is my profession. Come along; we will talk to Marzio."

"What can we say to him? You do not suppose I will go and beg to be taken back?"

"You must be forgiving—"

"I believe in forgiveness when the other side begins," said Gianbattista.

"Perhaps Marzio will forgive too," argued the priest.

"He has nothing to forgive," answered the young man. The reasoning seemed to him beyond refutation.

"But if he says he has no objection, if he begs you to come back, I think you might make some advance on your side, Tista. Besides, you were very rough with him this morning."

"He turned me out like a dog—after all these years," said Gianbattista. "I will go back and work for him on one condition. He must give me Lucia at once."

"I am afraid that as a basis of negotiations that plan leaves much to be desired," replied Don Paolo, in a meditative tone. "Of course, we are all determined that you shall marry her in the end; but unless Providence is pleased to change Marzio's state of mind, you may have to wait until she is of age. He will never consent at present."

"In that case I had better go and take my things away from his house," returned the apprentice. "And say good-bye to Lucia—for a day or two," he added in a low voice.

"Of course, if you will not agree to be conciliatory it is of no use for you to come with me," said Don Paolo rather sadly. "Dear me! Here comes Maria Luisa with Suntarella!"

"Ah, dear Paolo, dear Paolo!" cried the stout lady, puffing up the stairs with the old woman close behind her. "How good you are! And what did he say? We asked if you had gone at the workshop, and they said you had, so Lucia went in to ask her father whether he would have the chickens boiled or roasted. Well, well, tell me all about it. These stairs! Suntarella, run up and open the door while I get my breath! Dear Paolo, you are an angel of goodness!"

"Softly, Maria Luisa," answered the priest. "There is good and bad. He has admitted that he will have to consider the matter because he cannot make Lucia marry without her consent. But on the other hand— poor Tista—" he looked at the young man and hesitated.

"He has turned me out," said Gianbattista. "He has given me an hour to leave his house. I believe a good part of the hour has passed already—"

"And Tista says he will not go back at any price," put in Don Paolo. The Signora Pandolfi gasped for breath.

"Oh! oh! I shall faint!" she sobbed, pressing the handle of her parasol against her breast with both hands. "Oh, what shall we do? We are lost! Paolo, your arm—I shall die!"

"Courage, courage, Maria Luisa," said the priest kindly. "We will find a remedy. For the present Tista can come to my house. There is the little room Where the man-servant sleeps, who is gone to see his sick wife in the country. The Cardinal will not mind."

"But you are not going like tins?" cried the stout lady, grasping Gianbattista's arm and looking into his face with an expression of forlorn bewilderment. "You cannot go to-day—it is impossible, Tista—your shirts are not even ironed! Oh dear I oh dear! And I had anticipated a feast because I was sure that Marzio would see reason before midday, and there are chickens for dinner—with rice, Tista, just as you like them—oh, you cannot go, Tista, I cannot let you go!"

"Courage, Maria Luisa," exhorted Don Paolo. "It is not a question of chickens."

"Dear Sora Luisa, you are too good," said Gianbattista. "Let us go upstairs first, to begin with—you will catch cold here on the steps. Come, come, courage, Sora Luisa!"

He took the good woman's arm and led her upwards. But Don Paolo stayed behind. He believed it to be his duty to return to the workshop, and to try and undo the harm Gianbattista had done himself by the part he had played in the proceedings of the morning. The Signora Pandolfi suffered herself to be led upstairs, panting and sobbing as she went, and protesting still that Gianbattista could not possibly be allowed to leave the house.

When Don Paolo had parted from the two women an hour earlier, they had not gone home as he had supposed, but, chancing to meet old Assunta near the house, the three had gone together to make certain necessary purchases. On their return they had inquired for Paolo at the workshop, as Maria Luisa had explained, and Lucia had entered in the confident expectation of finding that the position of things had mended considerably since the early morning. Moreover, since the announcement of the previous evening, the young girl had not seen her father alone. She wanted to talk to him on her own account, in order to sound the depth of his determination. She was not afraid of him. The fact that for a long time he had regarded favourably the project of her marriage with Gianbattista had given her a confidence which was not to be destroyed in a moment, even by Marzio's strange conduct. She passed through the outer rooms, nodding to the workmen, who touched their caps to the master's daughter. A little passage separated the large workshop from the inner studio. The door at the end was not quite closed. Lucia went up to it, and looked through the opening to see whether Gianbattista were with her father. The sight she saw was so surprising that she leaned against the door-post for support. She could not believe her eyes.

There was her father in his woollen blouse, kneeling, on the brick floor of the room, before a crucifix, his back turned towards her, his hands raised, and, as it seemed from the position of the arms, folded in prayer. The sunlight fell upon the silver figure, and upon the dark tangled hair of the artist who remained motionless, as though absorbed in devotion, while his daughter watched him through the half-open door. The scene was one which would have struck any one; the impression it made on Lucia was altogether extraordinary. She easily fancied that Marzio, after his interview with Don Paolo, had felt a great and sudden revulsion of sentiment. She knew that the priest had not left the studio many minutes before, and she saw her father apparently praying before a crucifix. A wonderful conversion had been effected, and the result was there manifest to the girl's eyes.

She held her breath, and remained at the door, determined not to move until Marzio should have risen from his knees. To interrupt him at such a moment would have been almost a sacrilege; it might produce the most fatal results; it would be an intrusion upon the privacy of a repentant man. She stood watching and waiting to see what would happen.

Presently Marzio moved. Lucia thought he was going to rise from his knees, but she was surprised to see that he only changed the position of the crucifix with one hand. He approached his head so near the lower part of it that Lucia fancied he was in the act of pressing his lips upon the crossed feet of the silver Christ. Then he drew back a little, turned his head to one side, and touched the figure with his right hand. It was evident, now, that he was no longer praying, but that something about the workmanship had attracted his attention.

How natural, the girl said to herself, that this man, even in such a supreme moment, should not forget his art—that, even in prayer, his eyes should mechanically detect an error of the chisel, a flaw in the metal, or some such detail familiar to his daily life. She did not think the worse of him for it. He was an artist! The habit of his whole existence could not cease to influence him—he could as soon have ceased to breathe. Lucia watched him and felt something like love for her father. Her sympathy was with him in both actions; in his silent prayer, in the inner privacy of his working-room, as well as in the inherent love of his art, from which he could not escape even when he was doing something contrary to the whole tenor of his life. Lucia thought how Don Paolo's face would light up when she should tell him of what she had seen. Then she wondered, with a delicate sense of respect for her father's secret feelings, whether she would have the right to tell any one what she had accidentally seen through the half-closed door of the studio.

Marzio moved again, and this time he rose to his feet and remained standing, so that the crucifix was completely hidden from her view. She knocked at the door. Her father turned suddenly round, and faced the entrance, still hiding the crucifix by his figure.

"Who is it?" he asked in a tone that sounded as though he were startled.

"Lucia," answered the girl timidly. "May I come in, papa?"

"Wait a minute," he answered. She drew back, and, still watching him, saw that he laid the cross down upon the table, and covered it with a towel—the same one in which it had been wrapped.

"Come in," he called out "What is the matter?"

"I only came for a moment, papa," answered Lucia, entering the room and glancing about her as she came forward. "Mamma sent me in to ask you about the chickens—there are chickens for dinner—she wanted to know whether you would like them roasted or boiled with rice."

"Roasted," replied Marzio, taking up a chisel and pretending to be busy. "It is Gianbattista who likes them boiled."

"Thank you, I will go home and tell her. Papa—" the girl hesitated.

"What is the matter?"

"Papa, you are not angry any more as you were last night?"

"Angry? No. What makes you ask such a question? I was not angry last night, and I am not angry now. Who put the idea into your head?"

"I am so glad," answered Lucia. "Not with me, not with Tista? I am so glad! Where is Tista, papa?"

"I have not the slightest idea. You will probably not see Tista any more, nor Gianbattista, nor his excellency the Signorino Bordogni"

Lucia turned suddenly pale, and rested her hand upon the old straw chair on which Don Paolo had sat during his visit.

"What is this? What do you tell me? Not see Tista?" she asked quickly.

"Gianbattista had the bad taste to attack me this morning—here—in my own studio," said Marzio, turning round and facing his daughter. "He put his hands upon my face, do you understand? He would have stabbed me with a chisel if Paolo had not interfered. Do you understand that? Out of deference for your affections I did not kill him, as I might have done. I dismissed him from my service, and gave him an hour to take his effects out of my house. Is that clear? I offered him his money. He threw it in my face and spat at me as he went out. Is that enough? If I find him at home when I come to dinner I will have him turned out by the police. You see, you are not likely to set eyes on him for a day or two. You may go home and tell your mother the news, if she has not heard it already. It will be sauce for her chickens."

Lucia leaned upon the chair during this speech, her black eyes growing wider and wider, and her face turning whiter at every word. To her it seemed, in this first moment, like a hopeless separation from the man she loved. With a sudden movement she sprang forward, and fell on her knees at Marzio's feet.

"Oh, my father, I beseech you, in the name of heaven," she cried wildly.

"It is not of the slightest use," answered Marzio, drawing back. Lucia knelt for one moment before him, with upturned face, an expression of imploring despair on her features. Then she sank down in a heap upon the floor against the three-legged stool, which tottered, lost its balance under her weight, and fell over upon the bricks with a loud crash. The poor girl had fainted away.

Marzio was startled by the sight and the sound, and then, seeing what had happened, he was very much frightened. He knelt down beside his daughter's prostrate body and bent over her face. He raised her up in his long, nervous arms, and lifted her to the old chair till she sat upon it, and he supported her head and body, kneeling on the floor beside her. A sharp pain shot through his heart, the faint indication of a love not wholly extinguished.

"Lucia, dear Lucia!" he said, in a voice so tender that it sounded strangely in his own ears. But the gill gave no sign. Her head would have fallen forward if he had not supported it with his hands.

"My daughter! Little Lucia! You are not dead—tell me you are not dead!" he cried. In his fright and sudden affection he pressed his lips to her face, kissing her again and again. "I did not mean to hurt you, darling child," he repeated, as though she could hear him speak.

At last her eyes opened. A shiver ran through her body and she raised her head. She was very pale as she leaned back in the chair. Marzio took her hands and robbed them between his dark fingers, still looking into her eyes.

"Ah!" she gasped, "I thought I was dead." Then, as Marzio seemed about to speak, she added faintly: "Don't say it again!"

"Lucia—dear Lucia! I knew you were not dead I knew you would come back to me," he said, still in very tender tones. "Forgive me, child—I did not mean to hurt you."

"No? Oh, papa! Then why did you say it?" she cried, suddenly bursting into tears and weeping upon his shoulder. "Tell me it is not true—tell me so!" she sobbed.

Marzio was almost as much disconcerted by Lucia's return to consciousness as he had been by her fainting away. His nature had unbent, momentarily, under the influence of his strong fear for his daughter's life. Now that she had recovered so quickly, he remembered Gianbattista's violence and scornful words, and he seemed to feel the young man's strong hand upon his mouth, stifling his speech. He hesitated, rose to his feet, and began to pace the floor. Lucia watched him with intense anxiety. There was a conflict in his mind between the resentment which was not half an hour old, and the love for his child, which had been so quickly roused during the last five minutes.

"Well—Lucia, my dear—I do not know—" he stopped short in his walk and looked at her. She leaned forward as though to catch his words.

"Do you think you could not—that you would be so very unhappy, I mean, if he lived out of the house—I mean to say, if he had lodgings, somewhere, and came back to work?"

"Oh, papa—I should faint away again—and I should die. I am quite sure of it."

Marzio looked anxiously at her, as though he expected to see her fall to the ground a second time. It went against the grain of his nature to take Gianbattista back, although he had discharged him hastily in the anger of the moment. He turned away and glanced at the bench. There were the young man's tools, the hammer as he had left it, the piece of work on the leathern pad. The old impulse of foresight for the future acted in Marzio's mind. He could never find such another workman. In the uncertainty of the moment, as often happens, details rose to his remembrance and produced their effect. He recollected the particular way in which Gianbattista used to hold the blunt chisel in first tracing over the drawing on a silver plate. He had never seen any one do it in the same way.

"Well, Lucia—don't faint away. If you can make him stay, I will take him back. But I am afraid you will have hard work. He will make difficulties. He threw the money in my face, Lucia—in your father's face, girl! Think of that. Well, well, do what you like. He is a good workman. Go away, child, and leave me to myself. What will you say to him?"

Lucia threw her arms round her father's neck and kissed him in her sudden joy. Then she stood a moment in thought.

"Give me his money," she said. "If he will take the money he will come back."

Marzio hesitated, slowly drew out his purse, and began to take out the notes.

"Well—if you will have it so," he grumbled. "After all, as he threw it away, I do not see that he has much right to it. There it is. If he says anything about that ten-franc note being torn, tell him he tore it himself. Go home, Lucia, and manage things as you can."

Lucia put the money in her glove, and busied herself for a moment in brushing the dust from her clothes. Mechanically, her father helped her.

"You are quite sure you did not hurt yourself?" he asked. The whole occurrence seemed indistinct, as though some one had told something which he had not understood—as we sometimes listen to a person reading aloud, and, missing by inattention the verb of the sentence, remain confused, and ask ourselves what the words mean.

"No—not at all. It is nothing," answered Lucia, and in a moment she was at the door.

Opening it to go out, she saw the tall figure of Don Paolo at the other end of the passage coming rapidly towards her. She raised her finger to her lips and nodded, as though to explain that everything was settled, and that the priest should not speak to Marzio. She, of course, did not know that he had been talking with Gianbattista and her mother, nor that he knew anything about the apprentice's dismissal. She only feared fresh trouble, now that the prospect looked so much clearer, in case Don Paolo should again attack her father upon the subject of the marriage. But her uncle came forward and made as though he would enter the workshop.

"It is all settled," she said quietly. Don Paolo looked at her in astonishment. At that moment Marzio caught sight of him over the girl's shoulder, in the dusky entrance.

"Come in, Paolo," he called out "I have something to show you. Go home, Lucia, my child."

Not knowing what to expect, and marvelling at the softened tone of his brother's voice, Don Paolo entered the room, waited till Lucia was out of the passage, and then closed the door behind him. He stood in the middle of the floor, grasping his umbrella in his hand and wondering upon what new phase the business was entering.

"I have something to show you," Marzio repeated, as though to check any question which the priest might be going to put to him. "You asked me for a crucifix last night. I have one here. Will it do! Look at it."

While speaking, Marzio had uncovered the cross and lifted it up, so that it stood on the bench where he had at first placed it to examine it himself. Then he stepped back and made way for Don Paolo. The priest stood for a moment speechless before the masterpiece, erect, his hands folded before him. Then, as though recollecting himself, he took off his hat, which he had forgotten to remove on entering the workshop.

"What a miracle!" he exclaimed, in a low voice.

Marzio stood a little behind him, his hands in the pockets of his woollen blouse. A long silence followed. Don Paolo could not find words to express his admiration, and his wonder was mixed with a profound feeling of devotion. The amazing reality of the figure, clothed at the same time in a sort of divine glory, impressed itself upon him as he gazed, and roused that mystical train of religious contemplation which is both familiar and dear to devout persons. He lost himself in his thoughts, and his refined features showed as in a mirror the current of his meditation. The agony of the Saviour of mankind was renewed before him, culminating in the sacrifice upon the cross. Involuntarily Paolo bent his head and repeated in low tones the words of the Creed, "Qui propter nos homines et propter nostram, salutem descendit de coelis," and then, "Crucifixus etiam pro nobis."

Marzio stood looking on, his hands in his pockets. His fingers grasped the long sharp punch he had taken from the table after Gianbattista's departure. His eyes fixed themselves upon the smooth tonsure at the back of Paolo's head, and slowly his right hand issued from his pocket with the sharp instrument firmly clenched in it. He raised it to the level of his head, just above that smooth shaven circle in the dark hair. His eyes dilated and his mouth worked nervously as the pale lips stretched themselves across the yellow teeth.

Don Paolo moved, and turned to speak to his brother concerning the work of art. Seeing Marzio's attitude, he started with a short cry and stretched out his arm as though to parry a blow.

"Marzio!"

The artist had quickly brought his hand to his forehead, and the ghastly affectation of a smile wreathed about his white lips. His voice was thick.

"I was only shading my eyes from the sun. Don't you see how it dazzles me, reflected from the silver? What did you imagine, Paolo? You look frightened."

"Oh, nothing," answered the priest bravely. "Perhaps I am a little nervous to-day."

"Bacchus! It looks like it," said Marzio, with an attempt to laugh. Then he tossed the tool upon the table among the rest with an impatient gesture. "What do you think of the crucifix?"

"It is very wonderful," said Paolo, controlling himself by an effort. "When did you make it, Marzio? You have not had time—"

"I made it years ago," answered the chiseller, turning his face away to hide his pallor. "I made it for myself. I never meant to show it, but I believe I cannot do anything better. Will it do for your cardinal? Look at the work. It is as fine as anything of the kind in the world, though I say it. Yes—it is cast. Of course, you do not understand the art, Paolo, but I will explain it all to you in a few minutes—"

Marzio talked very fast, almost incoherently, and he was evidently struggling with an emotion. Paolo, standing back a little from the bench, nodded his head from time to time.

"It is all very simple," continued the artist, as though he dared not pause for breath. "You see one sometimes makes little figures of real repoussé, half and half, done in cement and then soldered together so that they look like one piece, but it is impossible to do them well unless you have dies to press the plate into the first shape—and the die always makes the same figure, though you can vary the face and twist the arms and legs about. Cheap silver crucifixes and angels and those things are all made in that way, and with care a great deal can be done, of course, to give them an artistic look."

"Of course," assented Don Paolo, in a low voice. He thought he understood the cause of his brother's eloquence.

"Yes, of course," continued Marzio, as rapidly as before. "But to make a really good thing like this, is a different matter. A very different matter. Here you must model your figure in wax, and make moulds of the parts of it, and chisel each part separately, copying the model. And then you must join all the parts together with silver-soldering, and go over the lines carefully. It needs the most delicate handling, for although the casting is very heavy it is not like working on a chalice that is filled with cement and all arranged for you, that can be put in the fire, melted out, softened, cooled, and worked over as often as you please. There is no putting in the fire here—not more than once after you have joined the pieces. Do you understand me? Why do you look at me in that way, Paolo? You look as though you did not follow me."

"On the contrary," said the priest, "I think I understand it very well—as well as an outsider can understand such a process. No—I merely look at the finished work. It is superb, Marzio—magnificent! I have never seen anything like it."

"Well, you may have it to-night," said Marzio, turning away, and walking about the room. "I will touch it over. I can improve it a little. I have learned something in ten years. I will work all to-day, and I will bring it home this evening to show Maria Luisa. Then you may take it away."

"And the price? I must be able to tell the Cardinal."

"Oh, never mind the price. I will be content to take whatever he gives me, since it is going. No price would represent the labour. Indeed, Paolo, if it were any one but you, I would not let it go. Nothing but my affection for you would make me give it to you. It is the gem of my studio. Ah, how I worked at it ten years ago!"

"Thank you. I think I understand," answered the priest. "I am very much obliged to you, Marzio, and I assure you it will be appreciated. I must be going. Thank you for showing it to me. I will come and get it to-night."

"Well, good-bye, Paolo," said Marzio. "Here is your umbrella."

As Don Paolo turned away to leave the room, the artist looked curiously at the tonsure on his head, and his eyes followed it until Paolo had covered it with his hat. Then he closed the door and went back to the bench.

CHAPTER VIII

Lucia hastened homewards with the good news she bore. Her young nature was elastic, and, in the sudden happiness of having secured Gianbattista's recall, she quickly recovered from the shock she had received. She did not reflect very much, for she had not the time. It had all happened so quickly that her senses were confused, and she only knew that the man she loved must be in despair, and that the sooner she reached him the sooner she would be able to relieve him from what he must be suffering. Her breath came fast as she reached the top of the stairs, and she panted as she rang the bell of the lodging. Apparently she had rung so loud in her excitement as to rouse the suspicions of old Assunta, who cautiously peered through the little square that opened behind a grating in the door, before she raised the latch. On seeing Lucia she began to laugh, and opened quickly.

"So loud!" chuckled the old thing. "I thought it was the police or Sor Marzio in a rage."

Lucia did not heed her, but ran quickly on to the sitting-room, where the Signora Pandolfi was alone, seated on her straight chair and holding her bonnet in her hand, the bonnet with the purple glass grapes; she was the picture of despair. Lucia made haste to comfort her.

"Do not cry, mamma," she said quickly. "I have arranged it all. I have seen papa. I have brought Tista's money. Papa wants him to stay after all. Yes—I know you cannot guess how it all happened. I went in to ask about the chickens, and then I asked about Tista, and he told me that I should not see him any more, and then—then I felt this passion—here in the chest, and everything went round and round and round like a whirligig at the Termini, and I fell right down, mamma, down upon the bricks—I know, my frock is all dusty still, here, look, and here, but what does it matter? Patience! I fell down like a sack of flour— pata tunfate!"

"T-t-t-t!" exclaimed the Signora Pandolfi, holding up her hands and drawing in her breath as she clacked her tongue against the roof of her mouth. "T-t-t-t! What a pity!"

"And when I came to my senses—I had fainted, you understand—I was sitting on the old straw chair and papa was holding my hands in his and calling me his angel! Capperi! But it was worth while. You can imagine the situation when he called me an angel! It is the first time I have ever fainted, mamma—you have no idea—it was so curious!"

"Ah, my dear, it must have softened his heart!" cried Maria Luisa. "If I could only faint away like that once in a while! Who knows? He might be converted. But what would you have?" The signora glanced down sadly at her figure, which certainly suggested no such weakness as she seemed to desire. "Well, Lucia," she continued, "and then?"

"Yes, I talked to him, I implored him, I told him I should probably faint again, and, indeed, I felt like it. So he said I might have my way, and he told me to come home and tell Tista at once. Where is Tista?"

"Eh! He is in his room, packing up his things. I will go and call him. Oh dear! What a wonderful day this is, my child! To think that it is not yet eleven o'clock, and all that has happened! It is enough to make a woman crazy, fit to send to Santo Spirito. First you are to be married, and then you are not to be married! Then Gianbattista is sent away—after all these years, and such a good boy! And then he is taken back! And then—but the chickens, Lucia, you forgot to ask about the chickens—"

"Not a bit of it," answered the young girl. "I asked first, before he told me. Afterwards, I don't know—I should not have had the strength to speak of chickens. He said roasted, mamma. Poor Tista! He likes them with rice. Well, one cannot have everything in this world."

The Signora Pandolfi had reached the door, and called out at the top of her voice to the young man.

"Tista! Tista!" She could have been heard in the street.

"Eh, Sora Luisa! We are not in the Piazza Navona," said Gianbattista, appearing at the door of his little room. "What has happened?"

"Go and talk to Lucia," answered the good lady, hurrying off in search of Assunta to tell her the decision concerning the dinner.

Gianbattista entered the sitting-room, and, from the young girl's radiant expression, he guessed that some favourable change had taken place in his position, or in the positions of them both. Lucia began to tell him what had passed, and gave much the same account as she had given to her mother, though some of the intonations were softer, and accompanied by looks which told her happiness. When she had explained the situation she paused for an answer. Gianbattista stood beside her and held her hand, but he looked out of the window, as though uncertain what to say.

"Here is the money," said Lucia. "You will take it, won't you? Then it will be all settled. What is the matter, Tista? Are you not glad?"

"I do not trust him," answered the young man. "It is not like him to change his mind like that, all in a minute. He means some mischief."

"What can he do?"

"I do not know. I feel as if some evil were coming. Patience! Who knows? You are an angel, Lucia, darling."

"Everybody is telling me so to-day," answered the young girl. "Papa, you—"

"Of course. It is quite true, my heart, and so every one repeats it. What do you think? Will he come home to dinner? It is only eleven o'clock—perhaps I ought to go back and work at the ewer. Somehow I do not want to see him just now—"

"Stay with me, Tista. Besides, you were packing up your belongings to go away. You have a right to take an hour to unpack them. Tell me, what is this idea you have that papa is not in earnest? I want to understand it. He was quite in earnest just now—so good, so good, like sugar! Is it because you are still angry with him, that you do not want to see him?"

"No—why should I still be angry? He has made reparation. After all, I took a certain liberty with him."

"That is all the more reason. If he is willing to forget it—but I could tell you something, Tista, something that would persuade you."

"What is it, my treasure?" asked Gianbattista with a smile, bending down to look into her eyes.

"Oh, something very wonderful, something of which you would never dream. I could scarcely believe my eyes. Imagine, when I went to find him just now, the door was open. I looked through before I went in, to see if you were there. Do you know what papa was doing? He was kneeling on the floor before a beautiful crucifix, such a beautiful one. I think he was saying prayers, but I could not see his face. He stayed a long time, and then when I knocked he covered it up, was not that strange? That is the reason why I persuaded him so easily to change his mind."

Gianbattista smiled incredulously. He had often seen Marzio kneel on the floor to get a different view of a large piece of work.

"He was only looking at the work," he answered. "I have seen him do it very often. He would laugh if he could hear you, Lucia. Do you imagine he is such a man as that? Perhaps it would not do him any harm—a little praying. But it is a kind of medicine he does not relish. No, Lucia, you have been deceived, believe me."

The girl's expression changed. She had quite persuaded herself that a great moral change had taken place in her father that morning, and had built many hopes upon it. To her sanguine imagination it seemed as though his whole nature must have changed. She had seen visions of him as she had always wished he might be, and the visions had seemed likely to be realised. She had doubted whether she should tell any one the story of what she regarded as Marzio's conversion, but she had made an exception in favour of Gianbattista. Gianbattista simply laughed, and explained the matter away in half a dozen words. Lucia was more deeply disappointed than any one, listening to her light talk, could have believed possible. Her face expressed the pain she felt, and she protested against the apprentice's explanation.

"It is too bad of you, Tista," she said in hurt tones. "But I do not think you are right. You have no idea how quietly he knelt, and his hands were folded on the bench. He bent his head once, and I believe he kissed the feet—I wish you could have seen it, you would not doubt me. You think I have invented a silly tale, I am sure you do."

The tears filled her eyes as she turned away and stared vacantly out of the window at the dark houses opposite. The sun, which had been shining until that moment, disappeared behind a mass of driving clouds, and a few drops of rain began to beat against the panes of glass. The world seemed suddenly more dreary to Lucia. Gianbattista, who was sensitive where she was concerned, looked at her, and understood that he had destroyed something in which she had wished to believe.

"Well, well, my heart, perhaps you are right," he said softly, putting his arm round her.

"No, you do not believe it," she answered.

"For you, I will believe in anything, in everything—even in Sor Marzio's devotions," he said, pressing her to his side. "Only—you see, darling, he was talking in such a way a few moments before—that it seemed impossible—"

"Nothing is quite impossible," replied Lucia. "The heart beats fast. There may be a whole world between one beat and the next."

"Yes, my love," assented Gianbattista, looking tenderly into her eyes. "But do you think that between all the beatings of our two hearts there could ever be a world of change?"

"Ah—that is different, Tista. Why should we change? We could only change for worse if we began to love each other less, and that is impossible. But papa! Why should he not change for the better? Who can tell you, Tista, dear, that in a moment, in a second, after you were gone, he was not sorry for all he had done? It may have been in an instant. Why not?"

"Things done so very quickly are not done well," answered the young man. "I know that from my art. You may stamp a thing in a moment with the die—it is rough, unfinished. It takes weeks to chisel it—"

"The good God is not a chiseller, Tista."

The words fell very simply from the young girl's lips, and the expression of her face did not change. Only the tone of her voice was grave and quiet, and there was a depth of conviction in it which struck Gianbattista forcibly. In a short sentence she had defined the difference between his mode of thought and her own. To her mind omnipotence was a reality. To him, it was an inconceivable power, the absurdity of which he sought to demonstrate by comparing the magnitude claimed for it with the capacities of man. He remained silent for a moment, as though seeking an answer. He found none, and what he said expressed an aspiration and not a retort.

"I sometimes wish that I could believe as you do," he said. "I am sure I could do much greater things, make much more beautiful angels, if I were quite sure that they existed."

"Of course you could," answered Lucia. Then, with a tact beyond her years, she changed the subject of their talk. She would not endanger the durability of his aspiration by discussing it. "To go back to what we were speaking of," she said, "you will go to the workshop this afternoon, Tista, won't you?"

"Yes," he said mechanically. "What else should I do? Oh, Lucia, my darling, I cannot bear this uncertainty," he cried, suddenly giving vent to his feelings. "Where will it end? He may have changed, he may be all you say he is to-day, all that he was not yesterday, but do you really believe he has given up his wild idea? It is not all as it should be, and that is not his nature. It will come upon us suddenly with something we do not expect. He will do something—I cannot tell what, but I know him better than you do. He is cruel, he plots over his work, and then, when all seems calm, the storm breaks. It will not end well."

"We must love each other, Tista. Then all will end well. Who can divide us?"

"No one," answered the young maid firmly. "But many things may happen before we are united for ever."

He was not subject to presentiments, and his self-confident nature abhorred the prospect of trouble. He had arrived at his conclusion by a logical process, and there seemed no escape from it. As he had told Lucia, he knew the character of the chiseller better than the women of the household could know it, for he had been his constant companion for years, and was not to be deceived in his estimate of Marzio's temper. A man's natural disposition shows itself most clearly when he is in his natural element, at his work, busied in the ordinary occupations of his life. To such a man as Marzio, the workshop is more sympathetic than the house. Disagreeing on most points with his family, obliged to be absent during the whole day, wholly absorbed in the production of works which the women of his household could not thoroughly appreciate, because they did not thoroughly understand the ideas which originated them, nor the methods employed in their execution—under these combined circumstances it was to be expected that the artist's real feelings would find expression at the work-bench rather than in the society of his wife and daughter. Seated by Marzio's side, and learning from him all that could be learned, Gianbattista had acquired at the same time a thorough knowledge of his instincts and emotions, which neither Maria Luisa nor Lucia was able to comprehend.

Marzio was tenacious of his ideas and of his schemes. Deficient in power of initiative and in physical courage, he was obstinate beyond all belief in his adherence to his theories. That he should suddenly yield to a devotional impulse, fall upon his knees before a crucifix and cry meâ culpâ over his whole past life, was altogether out of the question. In Gianbattista's opinion it was almost as impossible that he should abandon in a moment the plan which he had announced with so much resolution on the previous evening. It was certain that before declaring his determination to marry his daughter to the lawyer he must have ruminated and planned during many days, as it was his habit to do in all the matters of his life, without consulting any one, or giving the slightest hint of his intention. Some part of his remarkable talent depended upon this faculty of thoroughly considering a resolution before proceeding to carry it out; and it is a part of every really great talent in every branch of creative art, for it is the result of a great continuity in the action of the mind combined with the power of concentration and the virtue of reticence. Many a work has appeared to the world to be the spontaneous creation of transcendent genius, which has, in reality, been conceived, studied, and elaborated during years of silence. Reticence, concentration, and continuity, are characteristics which cannot influence one part of a man's life without influencing the rest as well. The habit of studying before proceeding is co-existent with the necessity of considering before acting; and a man who is reticent concerning one half of his thoughts is not communicative about the other half. Nature does not do things by halves, and the nerves which animate the gesture at the table are the same which guide the chisel at the work-bench.

Gianbattista understood Marzio's character, and in his mind tried to construct the future out of the present. He endeavoured to follow out what he supposed to be the chiseller's train of thought to its inevitable conclusion, and the more he reflected on the situation the more certain he became that Lucia's hypothesis was untenable. It was not conceivable, under any circumstances whatever, that

Marzio should suddenly turn into a gentle, forgiving creature, anxious only for the welfare of others, and willing to sacrifice his own inclinations and schemes to that laudable end.

At twelve o'clock, Marzio appeared, cold, silent, and preoccupied. His manner did not encourage the idea entertained by Lucia, though the girl explained it to herself on the ground that her father was ashamed of having yielded so easily, and was unwilling to have it thought that he was too good-natured. There was truth in her idea, and it showed a good deal of common sense and appreciation of character. But it was not the whole truth. Marzio not only felt humiliated at having suffered himself to be overcome by his daughter's entreaties; he regretted it, and wished he could undo what he had done. It was too late, however. To change his mind a second time would be to show such weakness as his family had never witnessed in his actions.

He ate his food in silence, and the rest of the party ventured but few remarks. They inwardly congratulated themselves upon the favourable issue of the affair, in so far as it could be said to have reached a conclusion, and they all dreaded equally some fresh outburst of anger, should Marzio's temper be ruffled. Gianbattista himself set the example of discretion. As for the Signora Pandolfi, she had ready in her pocket the money her husband had given her in the morning for the purchase of Lucia's outfit, and she hoped at every moment that Marzio would ask for it, which would have been a sign that he had abandoned the idea of the marriage with Carnesecchi. But Marzio never mentioned the subject. He ate as quickly as he could, swallowed a draught of weak wine and water, and rose from the table without a word. With a significant nod to Maria Luisa and Lucia, Gianbattista left his seat and followed the artist towards the door. Marzio looked round sharply as he heard the steps behind him.

"Lucia told me," said the young man simply. "If you wish it, I will come and work."

Marzio hesitated a moment, beating his soft felt hat over his arm to remove the dust.

"You can go with the men and put up the prince's grating," he said at last. "The right hand side is ready fitted. If you work hard you can finish it before night."

"Very well," answered Gianbattista. "I will see to it. I have the keys here. In fire minutes I will come across."

Marzio nodded and went out. Gianbattista returned to the room where the women were finishing their dinner.

"It is all right," he said. "I am to put up the grating this afternoon. Will you come and see it, Sora Luisa?" He spoke to the mother, but he included the daughter by his look.

"It is very far," objected the Signora Pandolfi, "and we have been walking so much this morning. I think this day will never end!"

"Courage, mamma," said Lucia, "it will do you good to walk. Besides, there is the omnibus. What did he say, Tista? Am I not right?"

"Who knows? He is very quiet," replied the apprentice.

"What is it? What are you right about, my heart?" asked Maria Luisa.

"She thinks Sor Marzio has suddenly turned into a sugar doll," answered Gianbattista, with a laugh. "It may be. They say they make sugar out of all sorts of things nowadays."

"Capperi! It would be hard!" exclaimed Maria Luisa. "If there is enough sugar in him to sweeten a teaspoonful of coffee, write to me," she added ironically.

"Well—I shall be at the church in an hour, but it will be time enough if you come at twenty-three o'clock—between twenty-two and twenty-three." This means between one hour and two hours before sunset. "The light is good then, for there is a big west window," added Gianbattista in explanation.

"We will come before that," said Lucia. "Good-bye, Tista, and take care not to catch cold in that damp place."

"And you too," he answered, "cover yourselves carefully."

With this injunction, and a parting wave of the hand, he left the house, affecting a gay humour he did not really feel. His invitation to the two women to join him in the church had another object besides that of showing them the magnificent gilded grating which was to be put in place. Gianbattista feared that Marzio had sent him upon this business for the sake of getting him out of the way, and he did not know what might happen in his absence. The artist might perhaps choose that time for going in search of Gasparo Carnesecchi in order to bring him to the house and precipitate the catastrophe which the apprentice still feared, in spite of the last events of the morning. It was not unusual for Maria Luisa and her daughter to accompany him and Marzio when a finished work was to be set up, and Gianbattista knew that there could be no reasonable objection to such, a proceeding.

With an anxious heart he left the house and crossed the street to the workshop where the men were already waiting for the carts which were to convey the heavy grating to its destination. The pieces were standing against the walls, wrapped in tow and brown paper, and immense parcels lay tied up upon the benches. It was a great piece of work of the decorative kind, but of the sort for which Marzio cared little. Great brass castings were chiselled and finished according to his designs without his touching them with his hands. Huge twining arabesques of solid metal were prepared in pieces and fitted together with screws that ran easily in the thread, and then were taken apart again. Then came the laborious work of gilding by the mercury process, smearing every piece very carefully with an amalgam of mercury and gold, and putting it into a gentle, steady fire, until the mercury had evaporated, tearing only the dull gold in an even deposit on the surfaces. Then the finishing, the burnishing of the high lights, and the cleaning of the portions which were to remain dull. Sometimes the gilding of a piece failed, and had to be begun again, and there was endless trouble in saving the gold, as well as in preventing the workmen from stealing the amalgam. It was slow and troublesome work, and Marzio cared little for it, though his artistic instinct restrained him from allowing it to leave the workshop until it had been perfected to the highest degree.

At present the artist stood in the outer room among the wrapped pieces, his pipe in his mouth and his hands in his pockets. A moment after Gianhattista had entered, two carts rolled up to the door and the loading began.

"Take the drills and some screws to spare," said Marzio, looking into the bag of tools the foreman had prepared. "One can never tell in these monstrous things."

"It will be the first time, if we have to drill a new hole after you have fitted a piece of work, Maestro Marzio," answered the foreman, who had an unlimited admiration for his master's genius and foresight.

"Never mind; do as I tell you. We may all make mistakes in this world," returned the artist, giving utterance to a moral sentiment which did not influence him beyond the precincts of the workshop. The workman obeyed, and added the requisite instruments to the furnishing of his leather bag.

"And be careful, Tista," added Marzio, turning to the apprentice. "Look to the sockets in the marble when you place the large pieces. Measure them with your compass, you know; if they are too loose you have the thin plates of brass to pack them; if they are tight, file away, but finish and smooth it well Don't leave anything rough."

Gianbattista nodded as he lent a helping hand to the workmen who were carrying the heavy pieces to the carts.

"Will you come to the church before night?" he asked.

"Perhaps. I cannot tell. I am very busy."

In ten minutes the pieces were all piled upon the two vehicles, and Gianbattista strode away on foot with the workmen. He had not thought of changing his dress, and had merely thrown an old overcoat over his grey woollen blouse. For the time, he was an artisan at work. When working hours were over, and on Sundays, he loved to put on the stiff high collar and the cheeked clothes which suggested the garments of the English tourist. He was then a different person, and, in accordance with the change, he would smoke a cigarette and pull his cuffs over his hands, like a real gentleman, adjusting the angle of his hat from time to time, and glancing at his reflection in the shop windows as he passed along. But work was work; it was a pity to spoil good clothes with handling tools and castings, and jostling against the men, and, moreover, the change affected his nature. He could not handle a hammer or a chisel when he felt like a real gentleman, and when he felt like an artisan he must enjoy the liberty of being able to tuck up his sleeves and work with a will. At the present moment, too, he was proud of being in sole charge of the work, and he could not help thinking what a fine thing it would be to be married to Lucia and to be the master of the workshop. With the sanguine enthusiasm of a very young man who loves his occupation, he put his whole soul into what he was to do, assured that every skilful stroke of the hammer, every difficulty overcome, brought him nearer to the woman he loved.

Marzio entered the inner studio when Gianbattista was gone, leaving a boy who was learning to cut little files—the preliminary to the chiseller's profession—in charge of the outer workshop. The artist shut himself in and bolted the door, glad to be alone with the prospect of not being disturbed during the whole afternoon. He seemed not to hesitate about the work he intended to do, for he immediately took in hand the crucifix, laid it upon the table, and began to study it, using a lens from time to time as he scrutinised each detail. His rough hair fell forward over his forehead, and his shoulders rounded themselves till he looked almost deformed.

He had suffered very strong emotions during the last twenty-four hours—enough to have destroyed the steadiness of an ordinary man's hand; but with Marzio manual skill was the first habit of nature, and it would have been hard to find a mental impression which could shake his physical nerves. His mind, however, worked rapidly and almost fiercely, while his eyes searched the minute lines of the work he was examining.

Uppermost in his thoughts was a confused sense of humiliation and of exasperation against his brother. The anger he felt had nearly been expressed in a murderous deed not more than two or three hours earlier, and the wish to strike was still present in his mind. He twisted his lips into an ugly smile as he recalled the scene in every detail; but the determination was different from the reality and more in accordance with his feelings. He realised again that moment during which he had held the sharp instrument over his brother's head, and the thought which had then passed so rapidly through his brain recurred again with increased clearness. He remembered that beneath the iron-bound box in the corner there was a trap-door which descended to the unused cellar, for his workshop had in former times been a wine-shop, and he had hired the cellar with it. One sharp blow would have done the business. A few quick movements and Paolo's body would have been thrown down the dark steps beneath, the trap closed again, the safe replaced in its position. It was eleven o'clock then, or thereabouts. He would have sent the workmen to their dinner, and would have returned to the inner studio. They would have supposed afterwards that Don Paolo had left the place with him. He would have gone home and would have said that Paolo had left him—or, no—he would have said that Paolo had not been there, for some one might see him leave the workshop alone. In the night he would have returned, his family thinking he had gone to meet his friends, as he often did. When the streets were quiet he would have carried the body away upon the hand-cart that stood in the entry of the outer room. It was not far—scarcely three hundred yards, allowing for the turnings—to the place where the Via Montella ends in a mud bank by the dark river. A deserted neighbourhood, too—a turn to the left, the low trees of the Piazza de' Branca, the dark, short, straight street to the water. At one o'clock after midnight who was stirring? It would all have been so simple, so terribly effectual.

And then there would have been no more Paolo, no more domestic annoyances, no more of the priest's smooth-faced disapprobation and perpetual opposition in the house. He would have soon brought Maria Luisa and Lucia to reason. What could they do without the support of Paolo? They were only women after all. As for Gianbattista, if once the poisonous influence of Paolo were removed—and how surely removed!—Marzio's lips twisted as though he were tasting the sourness of failure, like an acid fruit—if once the priest were gone, Gianbattista would come back to his old ways, to his old scorn of priests in general, of churches, of oppression, of everything that Marzio hated. He might marry Lucia then, and be welcome. After all, he was a finer fellow for the pretty girl than Gasparo Carnesecchi, with his claw fingers and his vinegar salad. That was only a farce, that proposal about the lawyer—the real thing was to get rid of Paolo. There could be no healthy liberty of thought in the house while this fellow was sneaking in and out at all hours. Tumble Paolo into a quiet grave—into the river with a sackful of old castings at his neck—there would be peace then, and freedom. Marzio ground his teeth as he thought how nearly he had done the thing, and how miserably he had failed. It had been the inspiration of the moment, and the details had appeared clear at once to his mind. Going over them he found that he had not been mistaken. If Paolo came again, and he had the chance, he would do it. It was perhaps all the better that he had found time to weigh the matter.

But would Paolo come again? Would he ever trust himself alone in the workshop? Had he guessed, when he turned so suddenly and saw the weapon in the air, that the blow was on the very point of descending? Or had he been deceived by the clumsy excuse Marzio had made about the sum shining in his eyes?

He had remained calm, or Marzio tried to think so. But the artist himself had been so much moved during the minutes that followed that he could hardly feel sure of Paolo's behaviour. It was a chilling thought, that Paolo might have understood and might have gone away feeling that his life had been saved almost by a miracle. He would not come back, the cunning priest, in that case; he would not risk his precious skin in such company. It was not to be expected—a priest was only human, after all, like any other man. Marzio cursed his ill luck again as he bent over his work. What a moment this would be if Paolo would take it into his head to make another visit! Even the men were gone. He would send the one boy who remained to the church where Gianbattista was working, with a message. They would be alone then, he and Paolo. The priest might scream and call for help—the thick walls would not let any sound through them. It would be even better than in the morning, when he had lost his opportunity by a moment, by the twinkling of an eye.

"They say hell is paved with good intentions—or lost opportunities," muttered Marzio. "I will send Paolo with the next opportunity to help in the paving."

He laughed softly at his grim joke, and bent lower over the crucifix. By this time he had determined what to do, for his reflections had not interfered with his occupation. Removing two tiny silver screws which fitted with the utmost exactness in the threads, he loosened the figure from the cross, removed the latter to a shelf on the wall, and returning laid the statue on a soft leathern pad, surrounding it with sand-bags till it was propped securely in the position he required. Then he took a very small chisel, adjusted it with the greatest care, and tapped upon it with the round wooden handle of his little hammer. At each touch he examined the surface with his lens to assure himself that he was making the improvement he contemplated. It was very delicate work, and as he did it he felt a certain pride in the reflection that he could not have detected the place where improvement was possible when he had worked upon the piece ten years ago. He found it now, in the infinitesimal touches upon the expression of the face, in the minute increase in the depressions and accentuated lines in the anatomy of the figure. As he went over each portion he became more and more certain that though he could not at present do better in the way of idea and general execution, he had nevertheless gained in subtle knowledge of effects and in skill of handling the chisel upon very delicate points. The certainty gave him the real satisfaction of legitimate pride. He knew that he had reached the zenith of his capacities. His old wish to keep the crucifix for himself began to return.

If he disposed of Paolo he might keep his work. Only Paolo had seen it. The absurd want of logic in the conclusion did not strike him. He had not pledged himself to his brother to give this particular crucifix to the Cardinal, and if he had, he could easily have found a reason for keeping it back. But he was too much accustomed to think that Paolo was always in the way of his wishes, to look at so simple a matter in such a simple light.

"It is strange," he said to himself. "The smallest things seem to point to it. If he would only come!"

Again his mind returned to the contemplation of the deed, and again he reviewed all the circumstances necessary for its safe execution. What an inspiration, he thought, and what a pity it had not found shape in fact at the very moment when it had presented itself! He considered why he had never thought of it before, in all the years, as a means of freeing himself effectually from the despotism he detested. It was a despotism, he reflected, and no other word expressed it. He recalled many scenes in his home, in which Paolo had interfered. He remembered how one Sunday, in the afternoon, they had all been together before going to walk in the Corso, and how he had undertaken to demonstrate to Maria Luisa and Lucia the folly of wasting time in going to church on Sundays. He had argued gently and reasonably, he thought. But suddenly Paolo had interrupted him, saying that he would not allow Marzio to compare a church to a circus, nor priests to mountebanks and tight-rope dancers. Why not? Then the women had begun to scream and cry, and to talk of his blasphemous language until he could not hear himself speak. It was Paolo's fault. If Paolo had not been there the women would have listened patiently enough, and would doubtless have reaped some good from his reasonable discourse. On another occasion Marzio had declared that Lucia should never be taught anything about Christianity, that the definition of God was reason, that Garibaldi had baptized one child in the name of Reason and that he, Marzio, could baptize another quite as effectually. Paolo had interfered, and Maria Luisa had screamed. The contest had lasted nearly a month, at the end of which tune, Marzio had been obliged to abandon the uneven contest, vowing vengeance in some shape for the future.

Many and many such scenes rose to his memory, and in every one Paolo was the opposer, the enemy of his peace, the champion of all that he hated and despised. In great things and small his brother had been his antagonist from his early manhood, through eighteen years of married life to the present day. And yet, without Paolo, he could hardly have hoped to find himself in his present state of fortune.

This was one of the chief sources of his humiliation in his own eyes. With such a character as his, it is eminently true that it is harder to forgive a benefit than an injury. He might have felt less bitterly against his brother if he had not received at his hands the orders and commissions which had turned into solid money in the bank. It was hard to face Paolo, knowing that he owed two-thirds of his fortune to such a source. If he could get rid of the priest he would be relieved at once from the burden of this annoyance, of this financial subjection, as well as of all that embittered his life. He pictured to himself his wife and daughter listening respectfully to his harangues and beginning to practise his principles, Gianbattista, an eloquent member of the society in the inner room of the old inn, reformed, purged from his sneaking fondness for Paolo—since Paolo would not be in the world any longer—and ultimately married to Lucia, the father of children who should all be baptized in the name of Reason, and the worthy successor of himself, Marzio Pandolfi.

Scrutinising the statue under his lens, he detected a slight imperfection in the place where one of the sharp thorns touched the silver forehead of the beautiful, tortured head. He looked about for a tool fine enough for the work, but none suited his wants. He took up the long fine-pointed punch he had thrown back upon the table after the scene in the morning. It was too long, and over sharp, but by turning it sideways it would do the work under his dexterous fingers.

"Strange!" he muttered, as he tapped upon the tool. "It is like a consecration!"

When he had made the stroke he dropped the instrument into the pocket of his blouse, as though fearing to lose it. He had no occasion to use it again, though he went on with his work during several hours.

The thoughts which had passed through his brain recurred, and did not diminish in clearness. On the contrary, it was as though the passing impulse of the morning had grown during those short hours into a settled and unchangeable resolution. Once he rose from his stool, and going to the corner, dragged away the iron-bound safe from its place. A rusty ring lay flat in a little hollow in the surface of the trap-door. Marzio bent over it with a pale face and gleaming eyes. It seemed to him as though, if he looked round, he should see Paolo's body lying on the floor, ready to be dropped into the space below. He raised the wood and set the trap back against the wall, peering down into the black depths. A damp smell came up to his nostrils from the moist staircase. He struck a match, and held it into the opening, to see in what direction the stairs led down.

Something moved behind him and made a little noise. With a short cry of horror Marzio sprang back from the opening and looked round. It was as though the body of the murdered man had stirred upon the floor. His overstrained imagination terrified him, and his eyes started from his head. He examined the bench and saw the cause of the sound in a moment. The silver Christ, unsteadily propped in the position in which he had just placed it, had fallen upon one side of the pad by its own weight.

Marzio's heart still beat desperately as he went back to the hole and carefully reclosed the trap-door, dragging the heavy safe to its position over the ring. Trembling violently, he sat down upon his stool and wiped the cold perspiration from his forehead. Then, as he laid the figure upon the cushion, he glanced uneasily behind him and at the corner.

CHAPTER IX

When Don Paolo had shut the door of the studio and found himself once more in the open street, he felt a strangely unpleasant sensation about the heart, and for a few moments he was very pale. He had suffered a shock, and in spite of his best efforts to explain away what had occurred, he knew that he had been in danger. Any one who, being himself defenceless, has suddenly seen a pistol pointed at him in earnest, or a sharp weapon raised in the air to strike him, knows the feeling well enough. Probably he has afterwards tried to reason upon what he felt in that moment, and has failed to come to any conclusion except the very simple one, that he was badly frightened. Hector was no coward, but he let Achilles chase him three times round Troy before he could make up his mind to stand and fight, and but for Athena he might have run even further. And yet Hector was armed at all points for battle. He was badly frightened, brave man as he was.

But when the first impression was gone, and Paolo was walking quickly in the direction of the palace where the Cardinal lived, he stoutly denied to himself that Marzio had meant to harm him. In the first place, he could find no adequate reason for such an attempt upon his life. It was true that his relations with his brother had not been very amicable for some time; but between quarrelling and doing murder, Paolo saw a gulf too wide to be easily overstepped, even by such a person as Marzio. Then, too, the good man was unwilling to suspect any one of bad intentions, still less of meditating a crime. This consideration, however, was not, logically speaking, in Marzio's favour; for since Paolo was less suspicious than other men, it must necessarily have needed a severe shock to shake his faith in his brother's innocence. He had seem the weapon in the air, and had seen also the murderous look in the artist's eyes.

"I had better not think anything more about it," he said to himself, fearing lest he should think anything unjust.

So he went on his way towards the palace, and tried to think about Gianbattista and Lucia, their marriage and their future life. The two young faces came up before him as he walked, and he smiled calmly, forgetting what he had so recently passed through, in the pleasant contemplation of a happiness not his own. He reached his rooms, high up at the top of the ancient building, and he sighed with a sense of relief as he sat down upon the battered old chair before his writing-table.

Presently the Cardinal sent for him. Don Paolo rose and carefully brushed the dust from his cassock and mantle, and smoothed the long silk nap of his hat. He was a very neat man and scrupulous as to his appearance. Moreover, he regarded the Cardinal with a certain awe, as being far removed beyond the sphere of ordinary humanity, even though he had known him intimately for years. This idea of the great importance of the princes of the Church is inherent in the Roman mind. There is no particular reason why it should be eradicated, since it exists, and does no harm to any one, but it is a singular fact and worthy of remark. It is one of those many relics of old times, which no amount of outward change has been able to obliterate. A cardinal in Rome occupies a position wholly distinct from that of any other dignitary or hereditary noble. It is not so elsewhere, except perhaps in some parts of the south. The Piedmontese scoffs at cardinals, because he scoffs at the church and at all religion in general. The Florentine shrugs his shoulders because cardinals represent Rome, and Rome, with all that is in it, is hateful to Florence, and always was. But the true Roman, even when he has adopted the ideas of the new school, still feels an unaccountable reverence for the scarlet mantle. There is a dignity—often, now, very far from magnificent—about the household of a cardinal, which is not found elsewhere. The servants are more grave and tread more softly, the rooms are darker and more severe, the atmosphere is more still and the silence more intense, than in the houses of lay princes. A man feels in the very air the presence of a far-reaching power, noiselessly working to produce great results.

Don Paolo descended the stairs and entered the apartments through the usual green baize door, which swung upon its hinges by its own weight behind him. He passed through several large halls, scantily and sombrely furnished, in the last of which stood the throne chair, turned to the wall, beneath a red canopy. Beyond this great reception-chamber, and communicating with it by a low masked door, was the Cardinal's study, a small room, very high and lighted by a single tall window which opened upon an inner court of the palace. The furniture was very simple, consisting of a large writing-table, a few high-backed chairs, and the Cardinal's own easy-chair, covered with dingy leather and well worn by use. On the dark green walls hung two engravings, one a portrait of Pius IX., the other a likeness of Leo XIII. The Cardinal himself sat in the arm-chair, holding a newspaper spread out upon his knees.

"Good-day, Don Paolo," he said, in a pleasant, but not very musical voice.

His Eminence was a man about sixty years of age, hale and strong in appearance, but below the middle height and somewhat inclining to stoutness. His face was round, and the complexion very clear, which, with his small and bright brown eyes, gave him a look of cheerful vitality. Short white hair fringed his head where it was not covered by the small scarlet skull-cap. He wore a purple cassock with scarlet buttons and a scarlet silk mantle, which fell in graceful folds over one arm of the chair.

"Good-day, Eminence," answered Don Paolo, touching the great ruby ring with his lips. Then, in obedience to a gesture, the priest sat down upon one of the high-backed chairs.

"What weather have we to-day?" asked the Cardinal after a pause.

"Scirocco, Eminence."

"Ah, I thought so—especially this morning, very early. It is very disagreeable. Since Padre Secchi found that the scirocco really brings the sand of the desert with it, I dislike it more than ever. And what have you been doing, Don Paolo? Have you been to see about the crucifix?"

"I spoke to my brother about it last night, Eminence. He said he would do his best to make it in the time, but that he would have preferred to have a little longer."

"He is a good artist, your brother," said the Cardinal, nodding his head slowly and joining his hands, while the newspaper slipped to the floor.

"A good artist," repeated Don Paolo, stooping to pick up the sheet. "I have just seen his best work—a crucifix such as your Eminence wishes. Indeed, he proposed that you should take it, for he says he can make nothing better."

"Let us see, let us see," answered the prelate, in a tone which showed that he did not altogether like the proposal. "You say he has it already made. Tell me, has your brother much work to do just now?"

"Not much, Eminence. He has just finished the grating of a chapel for some church or other. I think I saw a silver ewer begun upon his table."

"I thought that perhaps he had not time for my crucifix."

"But he is an artist, my brother!" cried the priest, who resented the idea that Marzio might wish to palm off an ill-made object in order to save time. "He is a good artist, he loves the work, he always does his best! When he says he can do nothing better than what he has already finished, I believe him."

"So much the better," replied the Cardinal. "But we must see the work before deciding. You seem to have great faith in your brother's good intentions, Don Paolo. Is it not true? Dear me! You were almost angry with me for suggesting that he might be too busy to undertake my commission."

"Angry! I angry? Your Eminence is unjust. Marzio puts much conscience into his work. That is all."

"Ah, he is a man of conscience? I did not know. But, being your brother, he should be, Don Paolo." The prelate's bright brown eyes twinkled.

Paolo was silent, though he bowed his head in acknowledgment of the indirect praise.

"You do not say anything," observed the Cardinal, looking at his secretary with a smile.

"He is a man of convictions," answered Paolo, at last.

"That is better than nothing, better than being lukewarm. 'Because thou art lukewarm,' you know the rest."

"Incipiam te evomere," replied the priest mechanically. "Marzio is not lukewarm."

"Frigidusne?" asked the Cardinal.

"Hardly that."

"An calidus?"

"Not very, Eminence. That is, not exactly."

"But then, in heaven's name, what is he?" laughed the prelate. "If he is not cold, nor hot, nor lukewarm, what is he? He interests me. He is a singular case."

"He is a man who has his opinions," answered Don Paolo. "What shall I say? He is so good an artist that he is a little crazy about other things."

"His opinions are not ours, I suppose. I have sometimes thought as much from the way you speak of him. Well, well—he is not old; his opinions will change. You are very much attached to your brother, Don Paolo, are you not?"

"We are brothers, Eminence."

"So were Cain and Abel, if I am not mistaken," observed the Cardinal. Paolo looked about the room uneasily. "I only mean to say," continued the prelate, "that men may be brothers and yet not love each other."

"Come si fà? What can one do about it?" ejaculated Paolo.

"You must try and influence him. You must do your best to make him change his views. You must make an effort to bring him to a better state of mind."

"Eh! I know," answered the priest. "I do my best, but I do not succeed. He thinks I interfere. I am not San Filippo Neri. Why should I conceal the matter? Marzio is not a bad man, but he is crazy about what he calls politics. He believes in a new state of things. He thinks that everything is bad and ought to be destroyed. Then he and his friends would build up the ideal state."

"There would soon be nothing but equality to eat—fried, roast and boiled. I have heard that there are socialists even here in Rome. I cannot imagine what they want."

"They want to divide the wealth of the country among themselves," answered Don Paolo. "What strange ideas men have!"

"To divide the wealth of the country they have only to subtract a paper currency from an inflated national debt. There would be more unrighteousness than mammon left after such a proceeding. It reminds me of a story I heard last year. A deputation of socialists waited upon a high personage in Vienna. Who knows what for? But they went. They told him that it was his duty to divide his wealth amongst the inhabitants of the city. And he said they were quite right. 'Look here,' said he, 'I possess about seven hundred thousand florins. It chances that Vienna has about seven hundred thousand inhabitants. Here, you have each one florin. It is your share. Good-morning.' You see he was quite just. So, perhaps, if your brother had his way, and destroyed everything, and divided the proceeds equally, he would have less afterwards than he had before. What do you think?"

"It is quite true, Eminence. But I am afraid he will never understand that. He has very unchangeable opinions."

"They will change all the more suddenly when he is tired of them. Those ideas are morbid, like the ravings of a man in a fever. When the fever has worn itself out, there comes a great sense of lassitude, and a desire for peace."

"Provided it ever really does wear itself out," said Don Paolo, sadly.

"Eh! it will, some day. With such political ideas, I suppose your brother is an atheist, is he not?"

"I hope he believes in something," replied the priest evasively.

"And yet he makes a good living by manufacturing vessels for the service of the Church," continued the Cardinal, with a smile. "Why did you never tell me about your brother's peculiar views, Don Paolo?"

"Why should I trouble you with such matters? I am sorry I have said so much, for no one can understand exactly what Marzio is, who does not know him. It is an injury to him to let your Eminence know that he is a freethinker. And yet he is not a bad man, I believe. He has no vices that I know of, except a sharp tongue. He is sober and works hard. That is much in these days. Though he is mistaken, he will doubtless come to his senses, as you say. I do not hate him; I would not injure him."

"Why do you think it can harm him to let me about him? Do you think that I, or others, would not employ him if we knew all about him?"

"It would seem natural that your Eminence should hesitate to do so."

"Let us see, Don Paolo. There are some bad priests in the world, I suppose; are there not?"

"It is to be feared—"

"Yes, there are. There are bad priests in all forms of religion. Yet they say mass. Of course, very often the people know that they are bad. Do you think that the mass is less efficacious for the salvation of those who attend it, provided that they themselves pray with the same earnestness?"

"No; certainly not. For otherwise it would be necessary that the people should ascertain whether the priest is in a state of grace every time he celebrates; and since their salvation would then, depend upon that, they would be committing a sin if they did not examine the relative morality of different priests and select the most saintly one."

"Well then, so much the more is it indifferent whether the inanimate vessels we use are chiselled by a saint or an unbeliever. Their use sanctifies them, not the moral goodness of the artist. For, by your own argument, we should otherwise he committing a sin if we did not find out the most saintly men and set them to silver-chiselling instead of ordaining them bishops and archbishops. It would take a long time to build a church if you only employed masons who were in a state of grace."

"Well, but would you not prefer that the artist should be a good man?"

"For his own sake, Don Paolo, for his own sake. The thing he makes is not at all less worthy if he is bad. Are there not in many of our churches pillars that stood in Roman temples? Is not the canopy over the high altar in Saint Peter's made of the bronze roof of the Pantheon? And besides, what is goodness? We are all bad, but some are worse than others. It is not our business to judge, or to distribute commissions for works of art to those whom we think the best among men, as one gives medals and prizes to industrious and well-behaved children."

"That is very clear, and very true," answered the priest.

He did not really want to discuss the question of Marzio's belief or unbelief. Perhaps, if he had not been disturbed in mind by the events of the morning he would have avoided the subject, as he had often done before when the Cardinal had questioned him. But to-day he was not quite himself, and being unable to tell a falsehood of any kind he had spoken more of idle truth than he had wished. He felt that he had perhaps been unjust to his brother. He looked ill at ease, and the Cardinal noticed it, for he was a kindly man and very fond of his secretary.

"You must not let the matter trouble you," said the prelate, after a pause. "I am an inquisitive old man, as you know, and I like to be acquainted with my friends' affairs. But I am afraid I have annoyed you—"

"Oh! Your Eminence could never—"

"Never intentionally," interrupted the Cardinal. "But it is human to err, and it is especially human to bore one's fellow-creatures with inquisitive questions. We all have our troubles, Don Paolo, and I am yours. Some day, perhaps, you will be a cardinal yourself—who knows? I hope so. And then you will have an excellent secretary, who will be much too good, even for you, and whom you can torture by the hour together with inquiries about his relations. Well, if it is only for your sake, Sor Marzio shall never have any fewer commissions, even if he turn out more in earnest with his socialism than most of those fellows."

"You are too kind," said Paolo simply.

He was very grateful for the kindly words, for he knew that they were meant and not said merely in jest. The idea that he had perhaps injured Marzio in the Cardinal's estimation was very painful to him, in spite of what he had felt that morning. Moreover, the prelate's plain, common-sense view of the case reassured him, and removed a doubt that had long ago disturbed his peace of mind. On reflection it seemed true enough, and altogether reasonable, but Paolo knew in his heart what a sensation of repulsion, not to say loathing, he would experience if he should ever be called upon to use in the sacred services a vessel of his brother's making. The thought that those long, cruel fingers of Marzio's had hammered and worked out the delicate design would pursue him and disturb his thoughts. The sound of Marzio's voice, mocking at all the priest held holy, would be in his ears and would mingle with the very words of the canon.

But then, provided that he himself were not obliged to use his brother's chalices, what could it matter? The Cardinal did not know the artist, and whatever picture he might make to himself of the man would be shadowy and indistinct. The feeling, then, was his own and quite personal. It would be the height of superstitious folly to suppose that any evil principle could be attached to the silver and gold because they were chiselled by impious hands. A simple matter this, but one which had many a time distressed Don Paolo.

There was a long pause after the priest's last words, during which the prelate looked at him from time to time, examined his own white hands, and turned his great ruby ring round his finger.

"Let us go to work," he said at length, as though dismissing the subject of the conversation from his mind.

Paolo fetched a large portfolio of papers and established himself at the writing-table, while the Cardinal examined the documents one by one, and dictated what he had to say about them to his secretary. During two hours or more the two men remained steadily at their task. When the last paper was read and the last note upon it written out, the Cardinal rose from his arm-chair and went to the window. There was no sound in the room but that of the sand rattling upon the stiff surface, as Paolo poured it over the wet ink in the old-fashioned way, shook it about and returned it to the little sandbox by the inkstand. Suddenly the old churchman turned round and faced the priest.

"One of these days, when you and I are asleep out there at San Lorenzo, there will be a fight, my friend," he said.

"About what, Eminence?" asked the other.

"About silver chalices, perhaps. About many things. It will be a great fight, such as the world has never seen before."

"I do not understand," said Don Paolo.

"Your brother represents an idea," answered the Cardinal. "That idea is the subversion of all social principle. It is an idea which must spread, because there is an enormous number of depraved men in the world who have a very great interest in the destruction of law. The watchword of that party will always be 'there is no God,' because God is order, and they desire disorder. They will, it is true, always be a minority, because the greater part of mankind are determined that order shall not be destroyed. But those fellows will fight to the death, because they know that in that battle there will be no quarter for the vanquished. It will be a mighty struggle and will last long, but it will be decisive, and will perhaps never be revived when it is once over. Men will kill each other where-ever they meet, during months and years, before the end comes, for all men who say that there is a God in Heaven will be upon the one side, and all those who say there is no God will be upon the other."

"May we not be alive to see anything so dreadful!" exclaimed Don Paolo devoutly.

"No, you and I shall not see it. But those little children who are playing with chestnuts down there in the court—they will see it. The world is uneasy and dreads the very name of war, lest war should become universal if it once breaks out. Tell your brother that."

"It is what he longs for. He is always speaking of it."

"Then it is inevitable. When many millions like him have determined that there shall be evil done, it cannot long be warded off. Their blood be on their own heads."

When Don Paolo had climbed again to his lonely lodging, half an hour later, he pondered long upon what the Cardinal had said to him, and the longer he thought of it, the more truth there seemed to be in the prediction.

Gianbattista reached the church in which he was to do his work, and superintended the unloading of the carts. It was but a little after one o'clock, and he expected to succeed in putting up the grating before night. The pieces were carefully carried to the chapel where they were to be placed, and laid down in the order in which they would be needed. It took a long time to arrange them, and the apprentice was glad he had advised Maria Luisa and Lucia to come late. It would have wearied them, he reflected, to assist at the endless fitting and screwing of the joints, and they would have had no impression of the whole until they were tired of looking at the details.

For hours he laboured with the men, not allowing anything to be done without his supervision, and doing more himself than any of the workmen. He grew hot and interested as the time went on, and he began to doubt whether the work could be finished before sunset. The workmen themselves, who preferred a job of this kind to the regular occupation of the studio, seemed in no hurry, though they did what was expected of them quietly and methodically. Each one of them was calculating, as nearly as possible, the length of time needed to drive a screw, to lift a piece into position, to finish off a shank till it fitted closely in the prepared socket. Half an hour wasted by driblets to-day, would ensure them for the morrow the diversion of an hour or two in coming to the church and returning from it.

From time to time Gianbattista glanced towards the door, and as the hours advanced his look took the same direction more often. At last, as the rays of the evening sun fell through the western window, he heard steps, and was presently rewarded by the appearance of the Signora Pandolfi, followed closely by Lucia. They greeted Gianbattista from a distance, for the church being under repairs was closed to the public, and had not been in use for years, so that the sound of voices did not seem unnatural nor irreverent.

"It is not finished," said Gianbattista, coming forward to meet them; "but you can see what it will be like. Another hour will be enough."

At that moment Don Paolo suddenly appeared, walking fast up the aisle in pursuit of the two women. They all greeted him with an exclamation of surprise.

"Eh!" he exclaimed, "you are astonished to see me? I was passing and saw you go in, and as I knew about the grating, I guessed what you came for and followed you. Is Marzio here?"

"No," answered Gianbattista. "He said he might perhaps come, but I doubt it. I fancy he wants to be alone."

"Yes," replied Don Paolo thoughtfully, "I daresay he wants to be alone."

"He has had a good many emotions to-day," remarked Gianbattista. "We shall see how he will be this evening. Of course, you have heard the news, Don Paolo? Besides, you see I am at work, so that the first great difference has been settled. Lucia managed it—she has an eloquence, that young lady! She could preach better than you, Don Paolo."

"She is a little angel," exclaimed the priest, tapping his niece's dark cheek with his white hand.

"That is four to-day!" cried Lucia, laughing. "First mamma, then papa—figure to yourself papa!—then Tista, and now Uncle Paolo. Eh! if the wings don't grow before the Ave Maria—"

She broke off with a pretty motion of her shoulders, showing her white teeth and turning to look at Gianbattista. Then the young man took them to see the grating. A good portion of it was put up, and it produced a good effect. The whole thing was about ten or twelve feet high, consisting of widely-set gilt bars, between which were fastened large arabesques and scrolls. On each side of the gate, in the middle, an angel supported a metal drapery, of which the folds were in reality of separate pieces, but which, as it now appeared, all screwed together in its place, had a very free and light effect. It was work of a conventional kind and of a conventional school, but even here Marzio's great talent had shown itself in his rare knowledge of effects and free modelling; the high lights were carefully chosen and followed out, and the deep shadows of the folds in dull gold gave a richness to the drapery not often found in this species of decoration. The figures of the angels, too, were done by an artist's hand— conventional, like the rest, but free from heaviness or anatomical defects.

"It is not bad," said Don Paolo, in a tone which surprised every one. He was not often slow to praise his brother's work.

"How, not bad? Is that all you say?" asked Gianbattista, in considerable astonishment. He felt, too, that as Marzio and he worked together, he deserved acme part of the credit. "It is church decoration of course, and not a 'piece,' as we say, but I would like to see anybody do better."

"Well, well, Tista, forgive me," he answered, "The fact is, Marzio showed me something to-day so wonderful, that I see no beauty in anything else—or, at least, not so much beauty as I ought to see. I went in to find him again, you know, just as Lucia was leaving, and he showed me a crucifix—a marvel, a wonder!—he said he had had it a long time, put away in a box."

"I never saw it," said Tista.

"I did!" exclaimed Lucia. She regretted the words as soon as she had spoken them, and bit her lip. She had not told her mother what she had told Gianbattista.

"When did you see it? Is it so very beautiful?" asked the Signora Pandolfi.

"Oh, I only saw it through the door, when I went," she answered quickly. "The door was open, but I knocked and I saw him hide it. But I think it was very fine—splendid! What did you talk about, Uncle Paolo? You have not told us about your visit. I whispered to you that everything was settled, but you looked as though you did not understand. What did you say to each other?"

"Oh, nothing—nothing of any importance," said Don Paolo in some embarrassment. He suddenly recollected that, owing to his brother's strange conduct, he had left the studio without saying a word about the errand which had brought him. "Nothing," he repeated. "We talked about the crucifix, and Marzio gave a very long explanation of the way it was made. Besides, as Lucia says, she had told me that everything was settled, and Marzio spoke very quietly."

This was literally true. Marzio's words had been gentle enough. It was his action that had at first startled Don Paolo, and had afterwards set him thinking and reflecting on the events of those few minutes. But he would not for anything in the world have allowed any of his three companions to know what had happened. He was himself not sure. Marzio had excused the position of his hand by saying that the sun was in his eyes. There was something else in his eyes, thought Paolo; a look of hatred and of eager desire for blood which it was horrible to remember. Perhaps he ought not to remember it, for he might, be mistaken, after all, and it was a great sin to suspect any one of wishing to commit such a crime; but nevertheless; and in spite of his desire that it might not have been true, Don Paolo was conscious of having received the impression, and he was sure that it had not been the result of any foolish fright. He was not a cowardly, man, and although his physical courage had rarely been put to the test, no one who knew him would have charged him with the contemptible timidity which imagines danger gratuitously, and is afraid where no fear is. He was of a better temper than Marzio, who had been startled so terribly by a slight noise when his back was turned. And yet he had been profoundly affected by the scene of the morning, and had not yet entirely recovered his serenity.

Lucia noticed the tone of his answer, and suspected that something had happened, though her suspicion took a direction exactly opposed to the fact. She remembered what she had seen herself, and recalling the fact that Paolo had entered the workshop just as she was leaving it, she saw nothing unnatural in the supposition that her father's conversation with her uncle had taken a religious tone. She used the word religion to express to herself what she meant. She thought it quite possible that after Marzio had been so suddenly softened, and evidently affected, by her own fainting fit, and after having been absorbed in some sort of devotional meditation, he might have spoken of his feelings to Don Paolo, who in his turn would have seized the opportunity for working upon his brother's mind. Paolo, she thought, would naturally not care to speak lightly of such an occurrence, and his somewhat constrained manner at the present moment might be attributed to this cause. To prevent any further questions from her mother or Gianbattista, Lucia interposed.

"Yes," she said, "he seemed very quiet. He hardly spoke at dinner. But Tista says he may perhaps be here before long, and then we shall know."

It was not very clear what was to be known, and Lucia hastened to direct their attention to the new grating. Gianbattista returned to work with the men, and the two women and Don Paolo stood looking on, occasionally shifting their position to get a better view of the work. Gianbattista was mounted upon a ladder which leaned against one of the marble pillars at the entrance of the side chapel closed by the grating. A heavy piece of arabesque work had just been got into its place, and was tied with cords while the young man ran a screw through the prepared holes to fasten one side of the fragment to the bar. He was awkwardly placed, but he had sent the men to uncover and clean the last pieces, at a little distance from where he was at work. The three visitors observed him with interest, probably remarking to themselves that it must need good nerves to maintain one's self in such a position. Don Paolo, especially, was more nervous than the rest, owing, perhaps, to what had occurred in the morning. All at once, as he watched Gianbattista's twisted attitude, as the apprentice strained himself and turned so as to drive the screw effectually, the foot of the ladder seemed to move a little on the smooth marble pavement. With a quick movement Don Paolo stepped forward, with the intention of grasping the ladder.

Hearing the sound of rapid steps, Gianbattista turned his head and a part of his body to see what had happened. The sudden movement shifted the weight, and definitely destroyed the balance of the ladder. With a sharp screech, like that of a bad pencil scratching on a slate, the lower ends of the uprights slipped outward from the pillar. Gianbattista clutched at the metal bars desperately, but the long screw-driver in his hands impeded him, and he missed his hold.

Don Paolo, the sound of whose step had at first made the young man turn, and had thus probably precipitated the accident, sprang forward, threw himself under the falling ladder, and grasped it with all his might. But it was too late. Gianbattista was heavy, and the whole ladder with his weight upon it had gained too much impetus to be easily stopped by one man. With a loud crash he fell with the wooden frame upon the smooth marble floor. Rolling to one side, Gianbattista leapt to his feet, dazed but apparently unhurt.

The priest lay motionless in a distorted position under the ladder, his head bent almost beneath his body, and one arm projecting upon the pavement, seemingly twisted in its socket, the palm upwards. The long white fingers twitched convulsively once or twice, and then were still. It was all the affair of a moment. Maria Luisa screamed and leaned against the pillar for support, while Lucia ran forward and knelt beside the injured man. Gianbattista, whose life had probably been saved by Don Paolo's quick action, was dragging away the great ladder, and the workmen came running up in confusion to see what had happened.

It seemed as though Marzio's wish had been accomplished without his agency. A deadly livid colour overspread the priest's refined features, and as they lifted him his limp limbs hung down as though the vitality would never return to them—all except the left arm, which was turned stiffly out and seemed to refuse to hang down with the rest. It was dislocated at the shoulder.

A scene of indescribable confusion followed, in which Gianbattista alone seemed to maintain some semblance of coolness. The rest all spoke and cried at once. Maria Luisa and Lucia knelt beside the body where they had laid it on the steps of the high altar, crying aloud, kissing the white hands and beating their breasts, praying, sobbing, and calling upon Paolo to speak to them, all in a breath.

"He is dead as a stone," said one of the workmen in a low voice.

"Eh! He is in Paradise," said another, kneeling at the priest's feet and rubbing them.

"Take him to the hospital, Sor Tista—"

"Better take him home—"

"I will run and call Sor Marzio—"

"There is an apothecary in the next street."

"A doctor is better—apothecaries are all murderers."

Gianbattista, very pale, but collected and steady, pushed the men gently away from the body.

"Cari miei, my dear fellows," he said, "he may be alive. One of you run and get a carriage to the side door of the sacristy. The rest of you put the things together and be careful to leave nothing where it can fall. We will take him to Sor Marzio's house and get the best doctor."

"There is not even a drop of holy water in the basins," moaned Maria Luisa.

"He will go to Heaven without holy water," sobbed Lucia. "Oh, how good he was—"

Gianbattista kneeled down in his turn and tried to find the pulse in the poor limp wrist. Then he listened for the heart. He fancied he could hear a faint flutter in the breast. He looked up and a little colour came to his pale face.

"I think he is alive," he said to the two women, and then bent down again and listened. "Yes," he continued joyfully. "The heart beats. Gently—help me to carry him to the sacristy; get his hat one of you. So—carefully—do not twist that arm. I think I see colour in his cheeks—"

With four other men Gianbattista raised the body and bore it carefully to the sacristy. The cab was already at the door, and in a few minutes poor Don Paolo was placed in it. The hood was raised, and Maria Luisa got in and sat supporting the drooping head upon her broad bosom. Lucia took the little seat in front, and Gianbattista mounted to the box, after directing the four men to follow in a second cab as fast as they could, to help to carry the priest upstairs. He sent another in search of a surgeon.

"Do not tell Sor Marzio—do not go to the workshop," he said in a last injunction. He knew that Marzio would be of no use in such an emergency, and he hoped that Don Paolo might be pronounced out of danger before the chiseller knew anything of the accident.

In half an hour the injured man was lying in Gianbattista's bed. It was now evident that he was alive, for he breathed heavily and regularly. But the half-closed eyes had no intelligence in them, and the slight flush in the hollow cheeks was not natural to see. The twisted arm still stuck out of the bed-coverings in a painfully distorted attitude. The two women and Gianbattista stood by the bedside in silence, waiting for the arrival of the surgeon.

He came at last, a quiet-looking man of middle age, with grizzled hair and a face deeply pitted with the smallpox. He seemed to know what he was about, for he asked for a detailed account of the accident from Gianbattista while he examined the patient. The young man, who was beginning to feel the effects of the fall, now that the first excitement had subsided, sat down while he told the story. The surgeon urged the two women to leave the room.

"The left arm is dislocated at the shoulder, without fracture," said the surgeon. "Lend me a hand, will you? Hold his body firmly—here and here—with all your might, while I pull the joint into place. If his head or spine are not injured the pain may bring him to consciousness. That will be a good thing. Now, ready—one, two, three, pull!"

The two men gave a vigorous jerk, and to Gianbattista's surprise the arm fell back in a natural position; but the injured priest's features expressed no pain. He was evidently quite unconscious. A further examination led the surgeon to believe that the harm was more serious. There was a bad bruise on one side of the head, and more than one upon other parts of the body.

"Will he live?" asked Gianbattista faintly, as he sank back into his chair.

"Oh yes—probably. He is likely to have a brain fever; One cannot tell. How old is he?"

He asked one or two other questions, arranging the patient's position with skilful hands while he talked Then he asked for paper and wrote a prescription.

"Nothing more can be done for the present," he said. "You should put some ice on his head, and if he recovers consciousness, so as to speak before I come back, observe what he says. He may be in a delirium, or he may talk quite rationally. One cannot tell Send for this medicine and give it to him if he is conscious. Otherwise, only keep his head cool. I will come back early in the evening. You are not hurt yourself?" he inquired, looking at Gianbattista curiously.

"No; I am badly shaken, and my hands are a little cut—that is all," answered the young man.

"What a beautiful thing youth is!" observed the surgeon philosophically, as he went away.

Gianbattista remained alone in the sick-room, seated upon his chair by the head of the bed. With anxious interest and attention he watched the expressionless face as the heavy breath came and went between the parted lips. In the distance he could hear the sobbing and incoherent talk of the two women, as the doctor explained to them Paolo's condition, but he was now too much dazed to give any thought to them. It seemed to him that Don Paolo had sacrificed his life for him, and that he had no other duty than to sit beside the bed and watch his friend. All the impressions of the afternoon were very much confused, and the shock of the fall had told upon his nerves far more severely than he had at first realised. His limbs ached and his hands pained him; at the same time he felt dizzy, and the outline of Don Paolo's face grew indistinct as he watched it. He was roused by the entry of Lucia, who had hastily laid aside her hat. Her face was pale, and her dark eyes were swollen with tears; her hair was in disorder and was falling about her neck. Gianbattista instinctively rose and put his arm about the girl's waist as they stood together and looked at the sick man. He felt that it was his duty to comfort her.

"The doctor thinks he may get well," he said.

"Who knows," she answered tearfully, and shook her head, "Oh, Tista, he was our best friend!"

"It was in trying to save me—" said the young fellow. But he got no further. The words stuck in his throat.

"If he lives I will be a son to him!" he added presently. "I will never leave him. But perhaps—perhaps he is too good to live, Lucia!"

"He must not die. I will take care of him," answered Lucia. "You must pray for him, Tista, and I will—we all will!"

"Eh! I will try, but I don't understand that kind of thing as well as you," said Gianbattista dolefully. "If you think it is of any use—"

"Of course it is of use, my heart; do not doubt it," replied the young girl gravely. Then her features suddenly quivered, she turned away, and, hiding her face on the pillow beside the priest's unconscious, head, she sobbed as though her heart would break. Gianbattista knelt down at her side and put his arm round her neck, whispering lovingly in her ear.

The day was fading, and the last glow of the sun in the south-western sky came through the small window at the other end of the narrow room, illuminating the simple furniture, the white bed coverings, the upturned face of the injured man, and the two young figures that knelt at the bedside. It was

Gianbattista's room, and there was little enough in it. The bare bricks, with only a narrow bit of green drugget by the bed, the plain deal table before the window, the tiny round mirror set in lead, at which the apprentice shaved himself, the crazy old chest of drawers—that was all. The whitewashed walls were relieved by two or three drawings of chalices and other church vessels, the colour of the gold or silver, and of the gems, washed into one half of the design and the other side left in black and white. A little black cross hung above the bedstead, with a bit of an olive branch nailed over it—a reminiscence of the last Palm Sunday. There were two nails in another part of the room, on which some old clothes were hung—that was all. But the deep light of the failing day shed a peaceful halo aver everything, and touched the coarse details of a hardworking existence with the divine light of Heaven.

Lucia's sobbing ceased after a while, and, as the sunset faded into twilight and dusk, the silence grew more profound; the sick man's breathing became lighter, as though in his unconsciousness he were beginning to rest after the day in which he had endured so much. From the sitting-room beyond the short passage the sound of Maria Luisa's voice, moaning in concert with old Assunta, gradually diminished till they were heard only at intervals, and at last ceased altogether. The household of Marzio Pandolfi was hushed in the presence of a great sorrow, and awed by the anticipation of a great misfortune.

CHAPTER XI

Marzio, in ignorance of all that was happening at the church, continued to work in the solitude of his studio, and the current of his thoughts flowed on in the same channel. He tried to force his attention upon the details of the design he meditated against his brother's life, and for some time he succeeded. But another influence had begun to work upon his brain, since the moment when he had been frightened by the sound behind him while he was examining the hole beneath the strong box. He would not own to himself that such a senseless fear could have produced a permanent impression on him, and yet he felt disturbed and unsettled, unaccountably discomposed, and altogether uncomfortable. He could not help looking round from time to time at the door, and more than once his eyes rested for several seconds upon the safe, while a slight shiver ran through his body and seemed to chill his fingers.

But he worked on in spite of all this. The habit of the chisel was not to be destroyed by the fancied scare of a moment, and though his eyes wandered now and then, they came back to the silver statue as keen as ever. A little touch with the steel at one point, a little burnishing at another, the accentuation of a line, the deepening of a shadow—he studied every detail with a minute and scrupulous care which betrayed his love for the work he was doing.

And yet the uneasiness grew upon him. He felt somehow as though Paolo were present in the room with him, watching him over his shoulder, suggesting improvements to be made, in that voice of his which now rang distinctly in the artist's ear. His imagination worked morbidly, and he thought of Paolo standing beside him, ordering him to do this or that against his will, until he began to doubt his own judgment in regard to what he was doing. He wondered whether he should feel the same thing when Paolo was dead. Again he looked behind him, and the idea that he was not alone gained force. Nevertheless the room was bright, brighter indeed in the afternoon than it ever was in the morning, for the window was towards the south, and though the first rays of the sun reached it at about eleven in the morning, the buildings afterwards darkened it again until the sun was in the west. Moreover to-day, the weather had been changeable, and it had rained a little about noon. Now the air was again clear, and the workshop was lit up so that the light penetrated even to the ancient cobwebs in the corners, and touched the wax models and casts on the shelves, and gilded the old wood of the door opposite with rich brown gold. Marzio had a curtain of dusty grey linen which he drew across the lower part of the window to keep the sunshine off his work.

He was impatient with himself, and annoyed by the persistency of the impression that Paolo was in some way present in the place. As though to escape from it by braving it he set himself resolutely to consider the expediency of destroying his brother. The first quick impulse in the morning had developed to a purpose in the afternoon. He had constructed the probable occurrences out of the materials of his imagination, and had done it so vividly as to frighten himself. The fright had in some measure cooled his intention, and had been now replaced by a new element in his thoughts, by the apprehension for the future if the deed were accomplished. He began to speculate upon what would happen afterwards, wondering whether by any means the murder could be discovered, and if in that case it could ever be traced to him.

At the first faint suggestion that such a thing as he was devising could possibly have another issue than he had supposed, Marzio felt a cold sensation in his heart, and his thoughts took a different direction. It was all simple enough. To get Paolo into the workshop alone—a blow—the concealment of the dead body until night—then the short three hundred yards with the hand-cart—it seemed very practicable. Yes, but if by any chance he should meet a policeman under those low trees in the Piazza de' Branca, what would happen? A man with a hand-cart, and with something shapeless upon the hand-cart, in the dark, hurrying towards the river—such a man would excite the suspicions of a policeman. Marzio might be stopped and asked what he was taking away. He would answer—what would he answer in such a case? The hand-cart would be examined and found to contain a dead priest. Besides, he reflected that the wheels would make a terrible clatter in the silent streets at night. Of course he might go out and walk down to the river first and see if there was anybody in the way, but even then he could not be sure of finding no one when he returned with his burden.

But there was the cellar, after all. He could go down in the night and bury his brother's body there. No one ever went down, not even he himself. Who would suspect the place? It would be a ghastly job, the chiseller thought. He fancied how it would be in the cold, damp vault with a lantern—the white face of the murdered man. No, he shrank from thinking of it. It was too horrible to be thought of until it should be absolutely necessary. But the place was a good one.

And then when Paolo was buried deep under the damp stones, who would be the first to ask for him? For two or three days no one would be much surprised if he did not come to the house. Marzio would say that he had met him in the street, and that Paolo had excused himself for not coming, on the ground of extreme pressure of work. But the Cardinal, whom he served as secretary, would ask for the missing man. He would be the first. The Cardinal would be told that Paolo had not slept at home, in his lodging high up in the old palace, and he would send at once to Marzio's house to know where his secretary was. Well, he might send, Marzio would answer that he did not know, and the matter would end there.

It would be hard to sit calmly at the bench all day with Gianbattista at his side. He would probably look very often at the iron-bound box. Gianbattista would notice that, and in time he would grow curious, and perhaps explore the cellar. It would be a miserable ending to such a drama to betray himself by his own weakness after it was all done, and Paolo was gone for ever—a termination unworthy of Marzio, the strong-minded freethinker. To kill a priest, and then be as nervous and conscious as a boy in a scrape! The chiseller tried to laugh aloud in his old way, but the effort was ineffectual, and ended in a painful twisting of the lips, accompanied by a glance at the corner. It would not do; he was weak, and was forced to submit to the humiliation of acknowledging the fact to himself. With a bitter scorn of his incapacity, he began to wonder whether he could ever get so far as to kill Paolo in the first instance. He foresaw that if he did kill him, he could never get rid of him afterwards.

Where do people go when they die? The question rose suddenly in the mind of the unbeliever, and seemed to demand an answer. He had answered often enough over a pint of wine at the inn, with Gaspare Carnesecchi the lawyer and the rest of his friends. Nowhere. That was the answer, clear enough. When a man dies he goes to the ground, as a slaughtered ox to the butcher's stall, or a dead horse to the knacker's. That is the end of him, and it is of no use asking any more questions. You might as well ask what becomes of the pins that are lost by myriads of millions, to the weight of many tons in a year. You might as well inquire what becomes of anything that is old, or worn out, or broken. A man is like anything else, an agglomeration of matter, capable of a few more tricks than a monkey, and capable of a few less than a priest. He dies, and is swallowed up by the earth and gives no more trouble. These were the answers Marzio was accustomed to give to the question, "Where do people go to when they die?" Hitherto they had satisfied him, as they appear to satisfy a very small minority of idiots.

But what would became of Paolo when Marzio had killed him? Well, in time his body would become earth, that was all. There was something else, however. Marzio was conscious to certainty that Paolo would in some way or other be at his elbow ever afterwards, just as he seemed to feel his presence this afternoon in the workshop. What sort of presence would it be? Marzio could not tell, but he knew he should feel it. It did not matter whether it were real to others or not, it would be too real to him. He could never get rid of the sensation; it would haunt him and oppress him for the rest of his life, and he should have no peace.

How could it, if it were not a real thing? Even the priests said that the spirits of dead men did not come back to earth; how much more impossible must it be in Marzio's view, since he denied that man had a soul. It would then only be the effect of his imagination recalling constantly the past deed, and a thing which only existed in imagination did not exist at all. If it did not exist, it could not be feared by a sensible man. Consequently there was nothing to fear.

The conclusion contradicted the given facts from which he had argued, and the chiseller was puzzled. For the first time his method of reasoning did not satisfy him, and he tried to find out the cause. Was it, he asked to himself, because there lingered in his mind some early tradition of the wickedness of doing murder? Since there was no soul, there was no absolute right and wrong, and everything must be decided by the standard of expediency. It was a mistake to allow people to murder each other openly, of course, because people of less intellectual capacity would take upon themselves to judge such cases in their own way. But provided that public morality, the darling of the real freethinker, were not scandalised, there would be no inherent wrong in doing away with Paolo. On the contrary, his death would be a benefit to the community at large, and an advantage to Marzio in particular. Not a pecuniary advantage either, for in Marzio's strange system there would have been an immorality in murdering Paolo for his money if he had ever had any, though it seemed right enough to kill him for an idea. That is, to a great extent, the code of those persons who believe in nothing but what they call great ideas. The individuals who murdered the Czar would doubtless have scrupled to rob a gentleman in the street of ten francs. The same reasoning developed itself in Marzio's brain. If his brothel had been rich, it would have been a crime to murder him for his wealth. It was no crime to murder him for an idea. Marzio said to himself that to get rid of Paolo would be to emancipate himself and his family from the rule and interference of a priest, and that such a proceeding was only the illustration on a small scale of what he desired for his country; consequently it was just, and therefore it ought to be done.

Unfortunately for his logic, the continuity of his deductions was blocked by a consideration which he had not anticipated. That consideration could only be described as fear for the future, and it had been forcibly thrust upon him by the fright he had received while he was examining the hole in the floor. In order to neutralise it, Marzio had tried the experiment of braving what he considered to be a momentary terror by obstinately studying the details of the plan he intended to execute. To his surprise he found that he returned to the same conclusion as before. He came back to that unaccountable fear of the future as surely as a body thrown upwards falls again to the earth. He went over it all in his mind again, twice, three times, twenty times. As often as he reached the stage at which he imagined Paolo dead, hidden, and buried in a cellar, the same shiver passed through him as he glanced involuntarily behind him. Why? What power could a dead body possibly exercise over a living man in the full possession of his senses?

Here was something which Marzio could not understand, but of which he was made aware by his own feelings. The difficulty only increased in magnitude as he faced it, considered it, and tried to view it from all its horrible aspects. But he could not overcome it. He might laugh at the existence of the soul and jest about the future state after death; he could not escape from the future in this life if he did the deed he contemplated. He should see the dead man's face by day and night as long as he lived.

This forced conclusion was in logical accordance with his original nature and developed character, for it was the result of that economical, cautious disposition which foresees the consequences of action and guides itself accordingly. Even in the moment when he had nearly killed Paolo that morning he had not been free from this tendency. In the instant when he had raised the tool to strike he had thought of the means of disposing of the body and of hindering suspicion. The panorama of coming circumstances had presented itself to his mind with the rapidity of a flash of lightning, but in that infinitesimal duration of time Paolo had turned round, and the opportunity was gone. His mind had worked quickly, but it had not gone to the end of its reasoning. Now in the solitude of his studio he had found leisure to follow out the results to the last link of the chain. He saw clearly that even if he eluded discovery after the crime, he could never escape from the horror of his dead brother's presence.

He laid the silver figure of the Christ straight before him upon the leathern pad, and looked intently at it, while his hands played idly with the tools upon the table. His deep-set, heavy eyes gazed fixedly at the wonderful face, with an expression which had not yet been there. There was no longer any smile upon his thin lips, and his dark emaciated features were restful and quiet, almost solemn in their repose.

"I am glad I did not do it," he said aloud after some minutes.

Still he gazed at his work, and the impression stole over him that but for a slight thing he might yet have killed his brother. If he had left the figure more securely propped upon the pad, it could not have slipped upon the bench; it could not have made that small distinct sound just as he was examining the place which was to have been his brother's grave; he would not have been suddenly frightened; he would not have gone over the matter in his mind as he had done, from the point of view of a future fear; he would have waited anxiously for another opportunity, and when it presented itself he would have struck the blow, and Paolo would have been dead, if not to-day, to-morrow. There would have been a search which might or might not have resulted in the discovery of the body. Then there would have been, the heartrending grief of his wife, of Lucia, and the black suspicious looks of Gianbattista. The young man had heard him express a wish that Paolo might disappear. His home would have been a hell, instead of being emancipated from tyranny as he had at first imagined. Discovery and conviction would have come at last, the galleys for life for himself, dishonour and contempt for his family.

He remembered Paolo's words as he stood contemplating the crucifix just before that moment which had nearly been his last. Qui propter nos homines et propter nostram salutem—"Who for us men and for our salvation came down from Heaven." In a strange revulsion of feeling Marzio applied the words to himself, with an odd simplicity that was at once pathetic and startling.

"If Christ had not died," he said to himself, "I should not have made this crucifix. If I had not made it, it would not have frightened me. I should have killed my brother. It has saved me. 'For us men and for our salvation'—those are the words—for my salvation, it is very strange. Poor Paolo! If he knew to what he owed his life he would be pleased. Who can believe such things? Who would have believed this if I had told it? And yet it is true."

For some minutes still he gazed at the figure. Then he shook himself as though to rouse his mind from a trance, and took up his tools. He did not glance behind him again, and, for the time at least, his nervous dislike of the box in the corner seemed to have ceased. He laboured with patient care, touching and re-touching, believing that each tap of the hammer should be the last, and yet not wholly satisfied.

The light waned, and he took down the curtain to admit the last glows of the evening. He could do no more, art itself could have done no more to beautify and perfect the masterpiece that lay upon the cushion before him. The many hours he had spent in putting the last finish upon the work had produced their result. His hand had imparted something to the features of the dying head which had not been there before, and as he stood over the bench he knew that he had surpassed his greatest work. He went and fetched the black cross from the shelf, and polished its smooth surface carefully with a piece of silk. Then he took the figure tenderly in his hands and laid it in its position. The small screws turned evenly in the threads, fitting closely into their well-concealed places, and the work was finished. Marzio placed the whole crucifix upon the bench and sat down to look at it.

It made a strong impression upon him, this thing of his own hands, and again he remained a long time resting his chin upon his folded fingers and gazing up at the drooping lids. The shadows lay softly on the modelled silver, so softly that the metal itself seemed to tremble and move, and in his reverie Marzio could almost have expected the divine eyes to open and look into his face. And gradually the shadows deepened more and more, and gathered into gloom till in the dark the black arms of the cross scarcely stood out from the darkness, and in the last lingering twilight he could see only the clear outline of the white head and outstretched hands, that seemed to emit a soft radiance gathered from the brightness of the departed day.

Marzio struck a match and lit his lamp. His thoughts were so wholly absorbed that he had not remembered the workmen, nor wondered why they had not come back. After all, most of them lived in the direction of the church, and if they had finished their work late they would very probably go home without returning to the shop. The chiseller wrapped the crucifix in the old white cloth, and laid it in its plain wooden box, but he did not screw the cover down, merely putting it on loosely so that it could be removed in a moment. He laid his tools in order, mechanically, as he did every evening, and then he extinguished the light and made his way to the door, carrying the box under his arm.

The boy who alone had remained at work had lighted a tallow candle, and was sitting dangling his heels from his stool as Marzio came out.

"Still here!" exclaimed the artist.

"Eh! You did not tell me to go," answered the lad.

Marzio locked the heavy outer door and crossed over to his house, while the boy went whistling down the street in the dusk. Slowly the artist mounted the stairs, pondering, as he went, on the many emotions of the day, and at last repeating his conclusion, that he was glad that he had not killed Paolo.

By a change of feeling which he did not wholly realise, he felt for the first time in many years that he would be glad to see his brother alive and well. He had that day so often fancied him dead, lying on the floor of the workshop, or buried in a dark corner of the cellar, that the idea of meeting him, calm and well as ever, had something refreshing in it. It was like the waking from a hideous dream of evil to find that the harm is still undone, to experience that sense of unutterable relief which every one knows when the dawn suddenly touches the outlines of familiar objects in the room, and dispels in an instant the visions of the night.

Paolo might not come that evening, but at least Maria Luisa and Lucia would speak of him, and it would be a comfort to hear his name spoken aloud. Marzio's step quickened with the thought, and in another moment he was at the door. To his surprise it was opened before he could ring, and old Assunta came forward with her wrinkled fingers raised to her lips.

"Hist! hist!" she whispered. "It goes a little better—or at least—"

"What? Who?" asked Marzio, instinctively whispering also.

"Eh! You have not heard? Don Paolo—they have killed him!"

"Paolo!" exclaimed Marzio, staggering and leaning against the door-post.

"He is not dead—not dead yet at least," went on the old woman in low, excited tones. "He was in the church with Tista—a ladder—"

Marzio did not stop to hear more, but pushed past Assunta with his burden under his arm, and entered the passage. The door at the end was open, and he saw his wife standing in the bright light in the sitting-room, anxiously looking towards him as though she had heard his coming.

"For God's sake, Gigia," he said, addressing her by her old pet name, "tell me quickly what has happened!"

The Signora Pandolfi explained as well as she could, frequently giving way to her grief in passionate sobs. She was incoherent, but the facts were so simple that Marzio understood them. He was standing by the table, his hand resting upon the wooden case he had brought, and his face was very pale.

"Let me understand," he said at last. "Tista was on the ladder. The ladder slipped, Paolo ran to catch it, and it fell on him. He is badly hurt, but not dead; is that it, Gigia?"

Maria Luisa nodded in the midst of a fit of weeping.

"The surgeon has been, you say? Yes. And where is Paolo lying?"

"In Tista's room," sobbed his wife. "They are with him now."

Marzio stood still and hesitated. He was under the influence of the most violent emotion, and his face betrayed something of what he felt. The idea of Paolo's death had played a tremendous part in his thoughts during the whole day, and he had firmly believed that he had got rid of that idea, and was to realise in meeting his brother that it had all been a dream. The news he now heard filled him with horror. It seemed as if the intense wish for Paolo's death had in some way produced a material result without his knowledge; it was as though he had killed his brother by a thought—as though he had had a real share in his death.

He could hardly bear to go and see the wounded man, so strong was the impression that gained possession of him. His fancy called up pictures of Paolo lying wounded in bed, and he dreaded to face the sight. He turned away from the table and began to walk up and down the little room. In a corner his foot struck against something—the drawing board on which he had begun to sketch the night before. Marzio took it up and brought it to the light. Maria Luisa stared at him sorrowfully, as though reproaching him with indifference in the general calamity. But Marzio looked intently at the drawing. It was only a sketch, but it was very beautifully done. He saw that his ideal was still the same, and that upon the piece of paper he had only reproduced the features he had chiselled ten years ago, with an added beauty of expression, with just those additions which to-day he had made upon the original. The moment he was sure of the fact he laid aside the board and opened the wooden case.

Maria Luisa, who was very far from guessing what an intimate connection existed between the crucifix and Paolo in her husband's mind, looked on with increasing astonishment as he took out the beautiful object and Bet it upon the table in the light. But when she saw it her admiration overcame her sorrow for one moment.

"Dio mio! What a miracle!" she exclaimed.

"A miracle?" repeated her husband, with a strange expression. "Who knows? Perhaps!"

At that moment Gianbattista and Lucia entered through the open door, and stood together watching the scene without understanding what was passing. The young girl recognised the crucifix at once. She supposed that her father did not realise Paolo's condition, and was merely showing the masterpiece to her mother.

"That is the one I saw," she whispered to Gianbattista. The young man said nothing, but fixed his eyes upon the cross.

"Papa," said Lucia timidly, "do you know?"

"Yes. Is he alone?" asked Marzio in a tone which was not like his own.

"There is Assunta," answered the young girl.

"I will go to him," said the artist, and without further words he lifted the crucifix from the table and went out. His face was very grave, and his features had something in them that none of the three had seen before—something almost of grandeur. Gianbattista and Lucia followed him.

"I will be alone with him," said Marzio, looking back at the pair as he reached the door of the sick chamber. He entered and a moment afterwards old Assunta came out and shuffled away, holding her apron to her eyes.

Marzio went in. There was a small shaded lamp on the deal table, which illuminated the room with a soft light. Marzio felt that he could not trust himself at first to look at his brother's face. He set the crucifix upon the old chest of drawers, and put the lamp near it. Then he remained standing before it with his back to the bed, and his hands in the pockets of his blouse. He could hear the regular breathing which told that Paolo was still alive. For a long time he could not turn round; it was as though an unseen power held him motionless in his position. He looked at the crucifix.

"If he wakes," he thought, "he will see it. It will comfort him if he is going to die!"

With his back still turned towards the bed, he moved to one side, until he thought that Paolo could see what he had brought, if consciousness returned. Very slowly, as though fearing some horrible sight, he changed his position and looked timidly in the direction of the sick man. At last he saw the pale upturned face, and was amazed that such an accident should have produced so little change in the features. He came and stood beside the bed.

Paolo had not moved since the surgeon had left; he was lying on his back, propped by pillows so that his face was towards the light. He was pale now, for the flush that had been in his cheeks had subsided; his eyelids, which had been half open, had dropped and closed, so that he seemed to be sleeping peacefully, ready to wake at the slightest sound.

Marzio stood and looked at him. This was the man he had hated through so many years of boyhood and manhood—the man who had faced him and opposed him at every step—who had stood up boldly before him in his own house to defend what he believed to be right. This was Paolo, whom he had nearly killed that morning. Marzio's right hand felt the iron tool in the pocket of his blouse, and his fingers trembled as he touched it, while his long arms twitched nervously from the shoulder to the elbow. He took it out, looked at it, and at the sick man's face. He asked himself whether he could think of using it as he had meant to, and then he let it fall upon the bit of green drugget by the bedside.

That was Paolo—it would not need any sharpened weapon to kill him now. A little pressure on the throat, a pillow held over his face for a few moments, and it would all be over. And what for? To be pursued for ever by that same white face? No. It was not worth while, it had never been worth while, even were that all. But there was something else to be considered. Paolo might now die of his accident, in his bed. There would be no murder done in that case, no haunting horror of a presence, no discovery to be feared, since there would have been no evil. Let him die, if he was dying!

But that was not all either. What would it be when Paolo should be dead? Well, he had his ideas, of course. They were mistaken ideas. Were they? Perhaps, who could tell? But he was not a bad man, this Paolo. He had never tried to wring money out of Marzio, as some people did. On the contrary, Marzio still felt a sense of humiliation when he thought how much he owed to the kindness of this man, his brother, lying here injured to death, and powerless to help himself or to save himself. Powerless? yes—utterly so. How easy it would be, after all, to press a pillow on the unconscious face. There would probably not even be a struggle. Who should save him, or who could know of it? And yet Marzio did not want to do it, as he had wished to a few hours ago. As he looked down on the pale head he realised that he did not want Paolo to die. Standing on the sharp edge of the precipice where life ends and breaks off, close upon the unfathomable depths of eternity, himself firmly standing and fearing no fall, but seeing his brother slipping over the brink, he would put out his hand to save him, to draw him back. He would not have Paolo die.

He gazed upon the calm features, and he knew that he feared lest they should be still for ever. The breath came more softly, more and more faintly. Marzio thought. He bent down low and tried to feel the warm air as it issued from the lips. His fears grew to terror as the life seemed to ebb away from the white face. In the agony of his apprehension, Marzio inadvertently laid his hand upon the injured shoulder, unconsciously pressing his weight upon the place.

With a faint sigh the priest's eyes opened and seemed to gaze for a moment on the crucifix standing in the bright light of the lamp. An expression of wonderful gentleness and calm overspread the refined features.

"Qui propter nos homines et propter nostram salutem descendit de coelis."

The words came faintly from the dying man's lips, the last syllables scarcely audible in the intense stillness. A deathly pallor crept quickly over the smooth forehead and thin cheeks. Marzio looked for one instant more, and then with a loud cry fell upon his knees by the bedside, his long arms extended across his brother's body. The strong hot tears fell upon the bed coverings, and his breast heaved with passionate sobbing.

He did not see that Paolo opened his eyes at the sound. He did not notice the rush of feet in the passage without, as Maria Luisa and Lucia and Gianbattista ran to the door, followed by old Assunta holding up her apron to her eyes.

"Courage, Sor Marzio," said Gianbattista, drawing the artist back from the bed. "You will disturb him. Do you not see that he is conscious at last?"

Lucia was arranging the pillows under Paolo's head, and Maria Luisa was crying with joy. Marzio sprang to his feet and stared as though he could not believe what he saw. Paolo turned his head and looked kindly at his brother.

"Courage, Marzio," he said, "I have been asleep, I believe—what has happened to me? Why are you all crying?"

Marzio's tears broke out again, mingled with incoherent words of joy. In his sudden happiness he clasped the two persons nearest to him, and hugged them and kissed them. These two chanced to be Lucia and Gianbattista. Paolo smiled, but the effort of speaking had tired him.

"Well," said Marzio at last, with a kinder smile than had been on his face for many a day—"very well, children. For Paolo's sake you shall have your own way."

Half an hour later the surgeon made his visit and assured them all that there was no serious injury, nor any further danger to be feared. The patient had been very badly stunned, that was all. Marzio remained by his brother's side.

"You see, Tista," said Lucia when they were in the sitting-room, "I was quite right about the crucifix and the rest."

"Of course," assented the Signora Pandolfi, though she did not understand the allusion in the least. "Of course you are all of you right. But what a day this has been, cari miei! What a day! Dear, dear!" She spread out her fat hands upon her knees, looking the picture of solid contentment.

ZOROASTER

To My Beloved Wife
I DEDICATE THIS DRAMA

ZOROASTER

CHAPTER I

The hall of the banquets was made ready for the feast in the palace of Babylon. That night Belshazzar the king would drink wine with a thousand of his lords, and be merry before them; and everything was made ready.

From end to end of the mighty nave, the tables of wood, overlaid with gold and silver, stood spread with those things which the heart of man can desire; with cups of gold and of glass and of jade; with great dishes heaped high with rare fruits and rarer flowers; and over all, the last purple rays of the great southern sun came floating through the open colonnades of the porch, glancing on the polished marbles, tingeing with a softer hue the smooth red plaster of the walls, and lingering lovingly on the golden features and the red-gold draperies of the vast statue that sat on high and overlooked the scene.

On his head the head-dress of thrice royal supremacy, in his right hand and his left the sceptre of power and the winged wheel of immortality and life, beneath his feet the bowed necks of prostrate captives;— so sat the kingly presence of great Nebuchadnezzar, as waiting to see what should come to pass upon his son; and the perfume of the flowers and the fruits and the rich wine came up to his mighty nostrils, and he seemed to smile there in the evening sunlight, half in satisfaction, half in scorn.

On each side of the great building, in the aisles and wings, among the polished pillars of marble thronged the serving-men, bearing ever fresh spices and flowers and fruits, wherewith to deck the feast, whispering together in a dozen Indian, Persian and Egyptian dialects, or in the rich speech of those nobler captives whose pale faces and eagle eyes stood forth everywhere in strong contrast with the coarser features and duskier skins of their fellows in servitude,—the race not born to dominate, but born to endure even to the end. These all mingled together in the strange and broken reflections of the evening light, and here and there the purple dye of the sun tinged the white tunic of some poor slave to as fair a colour as a king's son might wear.

On this side and on that of the tables that were spread for the feast, stood great candlesticks, as tall as the height of two men, tapering from the thickness and heavy carving below to the fineness and delicate tracery above, and bearing upon them cups of bronze, each having its wick steeped in fine oil mixed with wax. Moreover, in the midst of the hall, where the seat of the king was put upon a raised floor, the pillars stood apart for a space, so that there was a chamber, as it were, from the wall on the right to the wall on the left, roofed with great carved rafters; and the colour of the walls was red,—a deep and glorious red that seemed to make of the smooth plaster a sheet of precious marble. Beyond, beneath the pillars, the panels of the aisles were pictured and made many-coloured with the story of Nebuchadnezzar the king, his conquests and his feasts, his captives and his courtiers, in endless train upon the splendid wall. But where the king should sit in the midst of the hall there were neither pillars nor paintings; only the broad blaze of the royal colour, rich and even. Beside the table also stood a great lamp, taller and more cunningly wrought than the rest,—the foot of rare marble and chiselled bronze and the lamp above of pure gold from southern Ophir. But it was not yet kindled, for the sun was not set and the hour for the feast was not fully come.

At the upper end of the hall, before the gigantic statue of wrought gold, there was an open space, unencumbered by tables, where the smooth, polished marble floor came to view in all its rich design and colour. Two persons, entering the hall with slow steps, came to this place and stood together, looking up at the face of the golden king.

Between the two there was the gulf of a lifetime. The one was already beyond the common limit of age, while he who stood beside him was but a fair boy of fourteen summers.

The old man was erect still, and his snowy hair and beard grew like a lion's mane about his massive brow and masterful face. The deep lines of thought, graven deeper by age, followed the noble shaping of his brows in even course, and his dark eyes still shot fire, as piercing the bleared thickness of time to gaze boldly on the eternity beyond. His left hand gathered the folds of a snow-white robe around him, while in his right he grasped a straight staff of ebony and ivory, of fine workmanship, marvellously polished, whereon were wrought strange sayings in the Israelitish manner of writing. The old man stood up to his noble height, and looked from the burnished face of the king's image to the eyes of the boy beside him, in silence, as though urging his young companion to speak for him the thoughts that filled the hearts of both.

The youth spoke not, nor gave any sign, but stood with folded hands and gazed up to the great features of Nebuchadnezzar.

He was but fourteen years of age, tall and delicately made, full of the promise of a graceful and elastic power, fine of skin, and instinct with the nervous strength of a noble and untainted race. His face was fair and white, tinged with faint colour, and his heavy golden hair fell in long curls upon his shoulders, thick and soft with the silken fineness of early youth. His delicate features were straight and noble, northern rather than Oriental in their type—supremely calm and thoughtful, almost godlike in their young restfulness. The deep blue eyes were turned upward with a touch of sadness, but the broad forehead was as marble, and the straight marking of the brows bounded it and divided it from the face. He wore the straight white tunic, edged about with fine embroideries of gold and gathered at the waist with a rich belt, while his legs were covered with wide Persian trousers wrought in many colours of silk upon fine linen. He wore also a small cap of linen, stiffened to a point and worked with a cunning design in gold and silver. But the old man's head was covered only by the thick masses of his snowy hair, and his wide white mantle hid the details of his dress from view.

Again he glanced from the statue to his companion's eyes, and at last he spoke, in a deep smooth voice, in the Hebrew tongue.

"Nebuchadnezzar the king is gathered to his fathers, and his son also, and Nabonnedon Belshazzar reigns in his stead, yet have I endured to this day, in Babylon, these threescore and seven years, since Nebuchadnezzar the king destroyed our place upon the earth and led us away captive. Unto this day, Zoroaster, have I endured, and yet a little longer shall I stand and bear witness for Israel."

The old man's eyes flashed, and his strong aquiline features assumed an expression of intense vitality and life. Zoroaster turned to him and spoke softly, almost sadly:

"Say, O Daniel, prophet and priest of the Lord, why does the golden image seem to smile to-day? Are the times accomplished of thy vision which thou sawest in Shushan, in the palace, and is the dead king glad? I think his face was never so gentle before to look upon,—surely he rejoices at the feast, and the countenance of his image is gladdened."

"Nay, rather then should his face be sorrowful for the destruction of his seed and of his kingdom," answered the prophet somewhat scornfully. "Verily the end is at hand, and the stones of Babylon shall no longer cry out for the burden of the sins of Belshazzar, and the people call upon Bel to restore unto life the King Nebuchadnezzar; nay, or to send hither a Persian or a Mede to be a just ruler in the land."

"Hast thou read it in the stars, or have thine eyes seen these things in the visions of the night, my master?" The boy came nearer to the aged prophet and spoke in low earnest tones. But Daniel only bent his head, till his brow touched his ebony staff, and so he remained, deep in thought.

"For I also have dreamed,"—continued Zoroaster, after a short pause,—"and my dream took hold of me, and I am sorry and full of great weariness. Now this is the manner of my dreaming." He stopped and glanced down the great nave of the hall through the open porch at the other end. The full glory of the red sun, just touching the western plain, streamed upon his face and made the tables, the preparations and the crowd of busy serving-men look like black shadows between him and the light. But Daniel leaned upon his staff and spoke no word, nor moved from his position.

"I saw in my dream," said Zoroaster, "and there was darkness; and upon the winds of the night arose the sound of war, and the cry and the clash of battle, mighty men striving one with another for the mastery and the victory, which should be to the stronger. And I saw again, and behold it was morning, and the people were led away captive, by tens, and by hundreds, and by thousands, and the maidens also and young women into a far country. And I looked, and the face of one of the maidens was as the face of the fairest among the daughters of thy people. Then my heart yearned for her, and I would have followed after into the captivity; but darkness came upon me, and I saw her no more. Therefore am I troubled and go heavily all the day."

He ceased and the cadence of the boy's voice trembled and was sad. The sun set out of sight beneath the plain, and from far off a great sound of music came in upon the evening breeze.

Daniel raised his snowy head and gazed keenly on his young companion, and there was disappointment in his look.

"Wouldst thou be a prophet?" he asked, "thou that dreamest of fair maidens and art disquieted for the love of a woman? Thinkest thou, boy, that a woman shall help thee when thou art grown to be a man, or that the word of the Lord dwelleth in vanity? Prophesy, and interpret thy vision, if so be that thou art able to interpret it. Come, let us depart, for the king is at hand, and the night shall be given over for a space to the rioters and the mirth-makers, with whom our portion is not. Verily I also have dreamed a dream. Let us depart."

The venerable prophet stood up to his height, and grasping his staff in his right hand, began to lead the way from the hall. Zoroaster laid hold of him by the arm, as though entreating him to remain.

"Speak, master," he cried earnestly, "and declare to me thy dream, and see whether it accords with mine, and whether there shall be darkness and rumour of war in the land."

But Daniel the prophet would not stay to speak, but went out of the hall, and Zoroaster the Persian youth went with him, pondering deeply on the present and on the future, and on the nature of the vision he had seen; and made fearful by the silence of his friend and teacher.

The darkness fell upon the twilight, and within the hall the lamps and candlesticks were kindled and gave out warm light and rare perfumes. All down the endless rows of tables, the preparations for the feast were ready; and from the gardens without, strains of music came up ever stronger and nearer, so that the winged sounds seemed to come into the vast building and hover above the tables and seats of honour, preparing the way for the guests. Nearer and nearer came the harps and the pipes and the trumpets and the heavy reed-toned bagpipes, and above all the strong rich chorus of the singers chanting high the evening hymn of praise to Bel, god of sunlight, honoured in his departing, as in his coming, with the music of the youngest and most tuneful voices in Shinar.

First came the priests of Bel, two and two, robed in their white tunics, loose white garments on their legs, the white mitre of the priestly order on their heads, and their great beards curled smooth and glossy as silk. In their midst, with stately dignity, walked their chief, his eyes upon the ground, his hands crossed upon his breast, his face like dark marble in the twilight. On either side, those who had officiated at the sacrifice, bore the implements of their service,—the knife, the axe, the cord, and the fire in its dish; and their hands were red with the blood of the victim lately slain. Grand, great men, mighty of body and broad of brow, were these priests of Bel,—strong with the meat and the wine of the offerings that were their daily portion, and confident in the faith of their ancient wisdom.

After the priests the musicians, one hundred chosen men of skill, making strange deep harmonies in a noble and measured rhythm, marching ten and ten abreast, in ten ranks; and as they came on, the light streaming from the porch of the palace caught their silver ornaments and the strange shapes of their instruments in broken reflections between the twilight and the glare of the lamps.

Behind these came the singers,—of young boys two hundred, of youths a hundred, and of bearded men also a hundred; the most famous of all that sang praises to Bel in the land of Assur. Ten and ten they marched, with ordered ranks and step in time to the massive beat of the long-drawn measure.

"Mighty to rule the day, great in his glory and the pride of his heat,

Shooting great bolts of light into the dark earth, turning death into life,
Making the seed to grow, strongly and fairly, high in furrow and field,
Making the heart of man glad with his gladness, rideth over the dawn
Bel, the prince, the king of kings.

"Hotly his flaming hair, streaming with brightness, and the locks of his beard
Curl'd into clouds of heat, sweeping the heavens, spread all over the sky:
Who shall abide his face, fearful and deadly, when he devours the land,
Angry with man and beast, horribly raging, hungry for sacrifice?
Bel, the prince, the king of kings.

"Striding his three great strides, out of the morning through the noon to the night,
Cometh he down at last, ready for feasting, ready for sacrifice:
Then doth he tread the wine, purple and golden, foaming deep in the west;
Shinar is spread for him, spread as a table, Assur shall be his seat:
Bel, the prince, the king of kings.

"Bring him the fresh-slain flesh, roast it with fire, with the savour of salt,
Pour him the strength of wine, chalice and goblet, trodden for him alone:
Raise him the song of songs, cry out in praises, cry out and supplicate
That he may drink delight, tasting our off'ring, hearing our evening song:
Bel, the prince, the king of kings.

"So, in the gentle night, when he is resting, peace descendeth on earth;
High in the firmament, where his steps led him, gleam the tracks of his way:
Where the day felt his touch, there the night also breaketh forth into stars,
These are the flowers of heaven, garlands of blossoms, growing to weave his crown:
Bel, the prince, the king of kings.

"Hail! thou king of the earth, hail! Belteshazzar, hail! and for ever live!
Born of the gods on high, prince of the nations, ruling over the world:
Thou art the son of Bel, full of his glory, king over death and life;
Let all the people bow, tremble and worship, bow them down and adore
The prince of Bel, the king of kings."

As the musicians played and the singers sang, they divided their ranks and came and stood on each side of the broad marble staircase; and the priests had done so before them, but the chief priest stood alone on the lowest step.

Then, between the files of those who stood, advanced the royal procession, like a river of gold and purple and precious stones flowing between banks of pure white. Ten and ten, a thousand lords of Babylon marched in stately throng, and in their midst rode Belshazzar the king, high upon his coal-black steed, crowned with the great tiara of white linen and gold and jewels, the golden sceptre of the kingdom in his right hand. And after the lords and the king came a long procession of litters borne by stalwart slaves, wherein reclined the fairest women of all Assyria, bidden to the great feast. Last of all, the spearmen of the guard in armour all chased with gold, their mantles embroidered with the royal cognisance, and their beards trimmed and curled in the close soldier fashion, brought up the rear; a goodly company of men of war.

As the rich voices of the singers intoned the grand plain chant of the last stanza in the hymn, the king was in the middle of the open space at the foot of the staircase; there he drew rein and sat motionless on his horse, awaiting the end. As the ripe corn bends in its furrows to the wind, so the royal host around turned to the monarch, and fell upon their faces as the music died away at the signal of the high priest. With one consent the lords, the priests, the singers and the spearmen bowed and prostrated themselves on the ground; the bearers of the litters set down their burden while they did homage; and each of those beautiful women bent far forward, kneeling in her litter, and hid her head beneath her veil.

Only the king sat erect and motionless upon his steed, in the midst of the adoring throng. The light from the palace played strangely on his face, making the sneering smile more scornful upon his pale lips, and shading his sunken eyes with a darker shadow.

While you might count a score there was silence, and the faint evening breeze wafted the sweet smell of the roses from the gardens to the king's nostrils, as though even the earth would bring incense of adoration to acknowledge his tremendous power.

Then the host rose again and fell back on either side while the king rode to the staircase and dismounted, leading the way to the banquet; and the high priest followed him and all the ranks of the lords and princes and the ladies of Babylon, in their beauty and magnificence, went up the marble steps and under the marble porch, spreading then like a river, about the endless tables, almost to the feet of the golden image of Nebuchadnezzar. And presently, from beneath the colonnades a sound of sweet music stole out again and filled the air; the serving-men hurried hither and thither, the black slaves plied their palm-leaf fans behind each guest, and the banquet was begun.

Surely, a most glorious feast, wherein the hearts of the courtiers waxed merry, and the dark eyes of the Assyrian women shot glances sweeter than the sweetmeats of Egypt and stronger than the wine of the south to move the spirit of man. Even the dark king, wasted and hollow-eyed with too much pleasure-seeking, smiled and laughed,—sourly enough at first, it is true, but in time growing careless and merry by reason of his deep draughts. His hand trembled less weakly as the wine gave him back his lost strength, and more than once his fingers toyed playfully with the raven locks and the heavy earrings of the magnificent princess at his elbow. Some word of hers roused a thought in his whirling brain.

"Is not this day the feast of victories?" he cried in sudden animation; and there was silence to catch the king's words. "Is not this the day wherein my sire brought home the wealth of the Israelites, kept holy with feasting for ever? Bring me the vessels of the unbelievers' temple, that I may drink and pour out wine this night to Bel, the god of gods!"

The keeper of the treasure had anticipated the king's desire and had caused everything to be made ready; for scarcely had Belshazzar spoken when a long train of serving-men entered the hall of the banquet and came and stood before the royal presence, their white garments and the rich vessels they bore aloft standing vividly out against the deep even red of the opposite wall.

"Let the vessels be distributed among us," cried the king,—"to every man a cup or a goblet till all are served."

And so it was done, and the royal cup-bearer came and filled the huge chalice that the king held, and the serving-men hastened to fill all the cups and the small basins; while the lords and princes laughed at the strange shapes, and eyed greedily enough the thickness and the good workmanship of the gold and silver. And so each man and each woman had a vessel from the temple of Jerusalem wherein to drink to the glory of Bel the god and of Belshazzar his prince. And when all was ready, the king took his chalice in his two hands and stood up, and all that company of courtiers stood up with him, while a mighty strain of music burst through the perfumed air, and the serving-men showered flowers and sprinkled sweet odours on the tables.

Without stood the Angel of Death, whetting his sword upon the stones of Babylon. But Belshazzar held the chalice and spoke with a loud voice to the princes and the lords and the fair women that stood about the tables in the great hall:

"I, Belshazzar the king, standing in the hall of my fathers, do pour and drink this wine to the mighty majesty of Bel the great god, who lives for ever and ever; before whom the gods of the north and of the west and of the east and of the south are as the sand of the desert in the blast; at whose sight the vain deities of Egypt crumbled into pieces, and the God of the Israelites trembled and was made little in the days of Nebuchadnezzar my sire. And I command you, lords and princes of Babylon, you and your wives and your fair women, that ye also do pour wine and drink it, doing this homage to Bel our god, and to me, Belshazzar the king."

And so saying, he turned about to one side and spilled a few drops of wine upon the marble floor, and set the cup to his lips, facing the great throng of his guests; and he drank. But from all the banquet went up a great shout.

"Hail! king, live for ever! Hail! prince of Bel, live for ever! Hail! king of kings, live for ever!" Long and loud was the cry, ringing and surging through the pillars and up to the great carved rafters till the very walls seemed to rock and tremble with the din of the king's praise.

Slowly Belshazzar drained the cup to the dregs, while with half-closed eyes he listened to the uproar, and perhaps sneered to himself behind the chalice, as was his wont. Then he set the vessel down and looked up. But as he looked he staggered and turned pale, and would have fallen; he grasped the ivory chair behind him and stood trembling in every joint, and his knees knocking together, while his eyes seemed starting from his head, and all his face was changed and distorted with dreadful fear.

Upon the red plaster of the wall, over against the candlestick which shed its strong rays upon the fearful sight, the fingers of a vast hand moved and traced letters. Only the fingers could be seen, colossal and of dazzling brightness, and as they slowly did their work, huge characters of fire blazed out upon the dark red surface, and their lambent angry flame dazzled those who beheld, and the terror of terrors fell upon all the great throng; for they stood before Him whose shadow is immortality and death.

In a silence that could be felt, the dread hand completed its message and vanished out of sight, but the strange fire burned bright in the horrid characters of the writing that remained upon the wall.

This was the inscription in Chaldean letters:

SUTMM

IPKNN

NRLAA

Then at last the king found speech and shrieked aloud wildly, and he commanded that they should bring in all the astrologers, the Chaldeans and the diviners, for he was in great terror and he dreaded some fearful and imminent catastrophe.

"Whoever shall read this writing," he cried, his voice changed and broken, "and declare to me the meaning of it, shall be clothed in purple, and shall have a chain of gold about his neck and shall rule as the third in the kingdom."

Amidst the mighty confusion of fear, the wise men were brought in before the king.

CHAPTER II

In Ecbatana of Media Daniel dwelt in his extreme old age. There he built himself a tower within the seven-fold walls of the royal fortress, upon the summit of the hill, looking northward towards the forests of the mountains, and southward over the plain, and eastward to the river, and westward to Mount Zagros. His life was spent, and he was well-nigh a hundred years old. Seventeen years had passed since he had interpreted the fatal writing on the wall of the banquet-hall in Babylon in the night when Nabonnedon Belshazzar was slain, and the kingdom of the Assyrians destroyed for ever. Again and again invested with power and with the governorship of provinces, he had toiled unceasingly in the reigns of Cyrus and Cambyses, and though he was on the very boundary of possible lifetime, his brain was unclouded, and his eye keen and undimmed still. Only his grand figure was more bent and his step slower than before.

He dwelt in Ecbatana of the north, in the tower he had built for himself. In the midst of the royal palaces of the stronghold he had laid the foundations duly to the north and south, and story upon story had risen, row upon row of columns, balcony upon balcony of black marble, sculptured richly from basement to turret, and so smooth and hard, that its polished corners and sides and ornaments glittered like black diamonds in the hot sun of the noonday, and cast back the moonbeams at night in a darkly brilliant reflection.

Far down below, in the gorgeous dwellings that filled the interior of the fortress, dwelt the kinsfolk of the aged prophet, and the families of the two Levites who had remained with Daniel and had chosen to follow him to his new home in Media rather than to return to Jerusalem under Zerubbabel, when Cyrus issued the writ for the rebuilding of the temple. There lived also in the palace Zoroaster, the Persian prince, being now in the thirty-first year of his age, and captain of the city and of the stronghold. And there, too, surrounded by her handmaidens and slaves, in a wing of the palace apart from the rest, and more beautiful for its gardens and marvellous adornment, lived Nehushta, the last of the descendants of Jehoiakim the king remaining in Media; she was the fairest of all the women in Media, of royal blood and of more than royal beauty.

She was born in that year when Babylon was overthrown, and Daniel had brought her with him to Shushan when he had quitted Assyria, and thence to Ecbatana. In the care of the prophet's kinswomen the little maid had thriven and grown fair in the stranger's land. Her soft child's eyes had lost their wondering look and had turned very proud and dark, and the long black lashes that fringed the heavy lids drooped to her cheek when she looked down. Her features were noble and almost straight in outline, but in the slight bend, at the beginning of the nose, in the wide curved nostrils, the strong full lips, and in the pale olive skin, where the blood ebbed and flowed so generously, the signs of the Jewish race were all present and unmistakable.

Nehushta, the high-born lady of Judah, was a princess in every movement, in every action, in every word she uttered. The turn of her proud head was sovereign in its expression of approval or contempt, and Zoroaster himself bowed to the simple gesture of her hand as obediently as he would have done before the Great King in all his glory. Even the venerable prophet, sitting in his lofty tower high above the city and the fortress, absorbed in the contemplation of that other life which was so very near to him, smiled tenderly and stretched out his old hands to greet Nehushta when she mounted to his chamber at sunset, attended by her maidens and her slaves. She was the youngest of all his kinsfolk—fatherless and motherless, the last direct descendant of King Jehoiakim remaining in Media, and the aged prophet and governor cherished her and loved her for her royalty, as well as for her beauty and her kinship to himself. Assyrian in his education, Persian in his adherence to the conquering dynasty and in his long and faithful service of the Persians, Daniel was yet in his heart, as in his belief, a true son of Judah; proud of his race and tender of its young branches, as though he were himself the father of his country and the king of his people.

The last red glow of the departed day faded and sank above the black Zagros mountains to westward. The opposite sky was cold and gray, and all the green plain turned to a dull soft hue as the twilight crept over it, ever darker and more misty. In the gardens of the palace the birds in thousands sang together in chorus, as only Eastern birds do sing at sunrise and at nightfall, and their voices sounded like one strong, sweet, high chord, unbroken and drawn out.

Nehushta wandered in the broad paths alone. The dry warm air of the summer's evening had no chill in it, and though a fine woven mantle of purple from Srinagur hung loosely from her shoulders, she needed not to draw it about her. The delicate folds of her upper tunic fell closely around her to her knees, and were gathered at the waist by a magnificent belt of wrought gold and pearls; the long sleeves, drawn in at the wrist by clasps of pearls, almost covered her slender hands; and as she walked her delicate feet moved daintily in rich embroidered sandals with high golden heels, below the folds of the wide trousers of white and gold embroidery, gathered in at the ankle. Upon her head the stiff linen tiara of spotless white sat proudly as a royal crown, the folds of it held by a single pearl of price, and from beneath it her magnificent hair rolled down below her waist in dark smooth waves.

There was a terrace that looked eastward from the gardens. Thither Nehushta bent her steps, slowly, as though in deep thought, and when she reached the smooth marble balustrade, she leaned over it and let her dark eyes rest on the quiet landscape. The peace of the evening descended upon her; the birds of the day ceased singing with the growing darkness; and slowly, out of the plain, the yellow moon soared up and touched the river and the meadows with mystic light; while far off, in the rose-thickets of the gardens, the first notes of a single nightingale floated upon the scented breeze, swelling and trilling, quivering and falling again, in a glory of angelic song. The faint air fanned her cheek, the odours of the box and the myrtle and the roses intoxicated her senses, and as the splendid shield of the rising moon cast its broad light into her dreaming eyes, her heart overflowed, and Nehushta the princess lifted up her voice and sang an ancient song of love, in the tongue of her people, to a soft minor melody, that sounded like a sigh from the southern desert.

"Come unto me, my beloved, in the warmth of the darkness, come—
Rise, and hasten thy footsteps, to be with me at night-time, come!

"I wait in the darkness for him, and the sand of the desert whirling
Is blown at the door of my tent which is open toward the desert.

"My ear in the darkness listeth for the sound of his coming nearer,
Mine eyes watch for him and rest not, for I would not he found me sleeping.

"For when my beloved cometh, he is like the beam of the morning;
Ev'n as the dawn in a strange land to the sight of a man journeying.

"Yea, when my beloved cometh, as dew that descendeth from heaven,
No man can hear when it falleth, but as rain it refresheth all things.

"In his hand bringeth he lilies, in his right hand are many flowers,
Roses hath he on his forehead, he is crowned with roses from Shinar.

"The night-winds make sweet songs for him, even in the darkness soft music;
Whithersoever he goeth, there his sweetness goeth before him."

Her young voice died away in a soft murmuring cadence, and the nightingale alone poured out her heartful of lore to the ancient moon. But as Nehushta rested immovable by the marble balustrade of the terrace, there was a rustle among the myrtles and a quick step on the pavement. The dark maiden started at the sound, and a happy smile parted her lips. But she did not turn to look; only her hand stole out behind her on the marble where she knew her lover's would meet it. There was in the movement all the certainty of conquest and yet all the tenderness of love. The Persian trod quickly and laid his hand on hers, and bent to her, trying to meet her eyes: for one moment still she gazed out straight before her, then turned and faced him suddenly, as though she had withheld her welcome as long as she could and then given it all at once.

"I did not call you," she said, covering him with her eyes in the moonlight, but making as though she would withdraw herself a little from him, as he drew her with his hand, and with his arm, and with his eyes.

"And yet I heard you call me, my beloved," answered Zoroaster. "I heard your voice singing very sweet things in your own language—and so I came, for you did call me."

"But did you pride yourself it was for you?" laughed Nehushta. "I sang of the desert, and of tents, and of whirling sand—there is none of these things here."

"You said that your beloved brought roses in his hand—and so I do. I will crown you with them. May I? No—I shall spoil your head-dress. Take them and do as you will with them."

"I will take them—and—I always do as I will."

"Then will to take the giver also," answered Zoroaster, letting his arm steal about her, as he half sat upon the balustrade. Nehushta looked at him again, for he was good to see, and perhaps she loved his straight calm features the better in that his face was fair, and not dark like hers.

"Methinks I have taken the giver already," she answered.

"Not yet—not all," said Zoroaster in a low voice, and a shadow of sadness crossed his noble face that looked white in the moonlight. Nehushta sighed softly and presently she laid her cheek upon his shoulder where the folding of his purple mantle made a pillow between her face and the polished golden scales of his breastplate.

"I have strange news to tell you, beloved," said Zoroaster presently. Nehushta started and looked up, for his voice was sad. "Nay, fear not!" he continued, "there is no harm in it, I trust; but there are great changes in the kingdom, and there will be greater changes yet. The seven princes have slain Smerdis in Shushan, and Darius is chosen king, the son of Gushtasp, whom the Greeks call Hystaspes."

"He who came hither last year?" asked Nehushta quickly. "He is not fair, this new king."

"Not fair," replied the Persian, "but a brave man and a good. He has, moreover, sent for me to go to Shushan—"

"For you!" cried Nehushta, suddenly laying her two hands on Zoroaster's shoulders and gazing into his eyes. His face was to the moonlight, while hers was in the dark, and she could see every shade of expression. He smiled. "You laugh at me!" she cried indignantly. "You mock me—you are going away and you are glad!"

She would have turned away from him, but he held her two hands.

"Not alone," he answered. "The Great King has sent an order that I shall bring to Shushan the kinsfolk of Jehoiakim, saving only Daniel, our master, for he is so old that he cannot perform the journey. The king would honour the royal seed of Judah, and to that end he sends for you, most noble and most beloved princess."

Nehushta was silent and thoughtful; her hand slipped from Zoroaster's grasp, and her eyes looked dreamily out at the river, on which the beams of the now fully-risen moon glanced, as on the scales of a silver serpent.

"Are you glad, my beloved?" asked Zoroaster. He stood with his back to the balustrade, leaning on one elbow, and his right hand played carelessly with the heavy gold tassels of his cloak. He had come up from the fortress in his armour, as he was, to bring the news to Nehushta and to Daniel; his gilded harness was on his back, half-hidden by the ample purple cloak, his sword was by his side, and on his head he wore the pointed helmet, richly inlaid with gold, bearing in front the winged wheel which the sovereigns of the Persian empire had assumed after the conquest of Assyria. His very tall and graceful body seemed planned to combine the greatest possible strength with the most surpassing activity, and in his whole presence there breathed the consciousness of ready and elastic power, the graceful elasticity of a steel bow always bent, the inexpressible ease of motion and the matchless swiftness that men had when the world was young—that wholeness of harmonious proportion which alone makes rest graceful, and the inactivity of idleness itself like a mode of perfect motion. As they stood there together, the princess of Judah and the noble Persian, they were wholly beautiful and yet wholly contrasted—the Semite and the Aryan, the dark race of the south, on which the hot air of the desert had breathed for generations in the bondage of Egypt, and left its warm sign-manual of southern sunshine,—and the fair man of the people whose faces were already set northwards, on whom the north breathed already its icy fairness, and magnificent coldness of steely strength.

"Are you glad, my beloved?" asked Zoroaster again, looking up and laying his right hand on the princess's arm. She had given no answer to his question, but only gazed dreamily out over the river.

She seemed about to speak, then paused again, then hesitated and answered his question by another.

"Zoroaster—you love me," again she paused, and, as he passionately seized her hands and pressed his lips to them, she said softly, turning her head away, "What is love?"

He, too, waited one moment before he answered, and, standing to his lordly height, took her head between his hands and pressed it to his breast; then, with one arm around her, he stood looking eastward and spoke:

"Listen, my beloved, and I, who love you, will tell you what love is. In the far-off dawn of the soul-life, in the ethereal distance of the outer firmament, in the mist of the star-dust, our spirits were quickened with the spirit of God, and found one another, and met. Before earth was for us, we were one; before time was for us, we were one—even as we shall be one when there is no time for us any more. Then Ahura Mazda, the all-wise God, took our two souls from among the stars, and set them in the earth, clothed for a time with mortal bodies. But we know each other, that we were together from the first, although these earthly things obscure our immortal vision, and we see each other less clearly. Yet is our love none the less—rather, it seems every day greater, for our bodies can feel joy and sorrow, even as our spirits do; so that I am able to suffer for you, in which I rejoice, and I would that I might be chosen to lay down my life for you, that you might know how I love you; for often you doubt me, and sometimes you doubt yourself. There should be no doubt in love. Love is from the first, and will be to the end, and beyond the end; love is so eternal, so great, so whole, that this mortal life of ours is but as a tiny instant, a moment of pausing in our journey from one star-world to another along the endless paths of heavenly glory we shall tread, together—it is nothing, this worldly life of ours. Before it shall seem long that we have loved, this earth we stand on, these things we touch, these bodies of ours that we think so strong and fair, will be forgotten and dissolved into their elements in the trackless and undiscoverable waste of past mortality, while we ourselves are ever young, and ever fair, and for ever living in our immortal love."

Nehushta looked up wonderingly into her lover's eyes, then let her head rest on his shoulder. The high daring of his thoughts seemed ever trying to scale heaven itself, seeking to draw her to some wondrous region of mystic beauty and strange spirit life. She was awed for a moment, then she, too, spoke in her own fashion.

"I love life," she said, "I love you because you live, not because you are a spirit chained and tied down for a time. I love this soft sweet earth, the dawn of it, and the twilight of it; I love the sun in his rising and in his setting; I love the moon in her fulness and in her waning; I love the smell of the box and of the myrtle, of the roses and of the violets; I love the glorious light of day, the splendour of heat and greenness, the song of the birds of the air and the song of the labourer in the field, the hum of the locust, and the soft buzzing of the bee; I love the brightness of gold and the richness of fine purple, the tramp of your splendid guards and the ring of their trumpets clanging in the fresh morning, as they march through the marble courts of the palace. I love the gloom of night for its softness, the song of the nightingale in the ivory moonlight, the rustle of the breeze in the dark rose-thickets, and the odour of the sleeping flowers in my gardens; I love even the cry of the owl from the prophet's tower, and the soft thick sound of the bat's wings, as he flits past the netting of my window. I love it all, for the whole earth is rich and young and good to touch, and most sweet to live in. And I love you because you are more beautiful than other men, fairer and stronger and braver, and because you love me, and will let no other love me but yourself, if you were to die for it. Ah, my beloved, I would that I had all the sweet voices of the earth, all the tuneful tongues of the air, to tell you how I love you!"

"There is no lack of sweetness, nor of eloquence, my princess," said Zoroaster; "there is no need of any voice sweeter than yours, nor of any tongue more tuneful. You love in your way, I in mine; the two together must surely be the perfect whole. Is it not so? Nay—seal the deed once again—and again—so! 'Love is stronger than death,' says your preacher."

"'And jealousy is as cruel as the grave,' he says, too," added Nehushta, her eyes flashing fire as her lips met his. "You must never make me jealous, Zoroaster, never, never! I would be so cruel—you cannot dream how cruel I would be!"

Zoroaster laughed under his silken beard, a deep, joyous, ringing laugh that startled the moonlit stillness.

"By Nabon and Bel, there is small cause for your jealousy here," he said.

"Swear not by your false gods!" laughed Nehushta. "You know not how little it would need to rouse me."

"I will not give you that little," answered the Persian. "And as for the false gods, they are well enough for a man to swear by in these days. But I will swear by any one you command me, or by anything!"

"Swear not, or you will say again that the oath has need of sealing," replied Nehushta, drawing her mantle around her, so as to cover half her face. "Tell me, when are we to begin our journey? We have talked much and have said little, as it ever is. Shall we go at once, or are we to wait for another order? Is Darius safe upon the throne? Who is to be chiefest at the court—one of the seven princes, I suppose, or his old father? Come, do you know anything of all these changes? Why have you never told me what was going to happen—you who are high in power and know everything?"

"Your questions flock upon me like doves to a maiden who feeds them from her hand," said Zoroaster, with a smile, "and I know not which shall be fed first. As for the king, I know that he will be great, and will hold securely the throne, for he has already the love of the people from the Western sea to the wild Eastern mountains. But it seemed as though the seven princes would have divided the empire amongst them, until this news came. I think he will more likely take one of your people for his close friend than trust to the princes. As for our journey, we must depart betimes, or the king will have gone before us from Shushan to Stakhar in the south, where they say he will build himself a royal dwelling and stay in the coming winter time. Prepare yourself for the journey, therefore, my princess, lest anything be forgotten and you should be deprived of what you need for any time."

"I am never deprived of what I need," said Nehushta, half in pride and half in jest.

"Nor I, when I am with my beloved!" answered the Persian. "And now the moon is high, and I must bear this news to our master, the prophet."

"So soon?" said Nehushta reproachfully, and she turned her head away.

"I would there were no partings, my beloved, even for the space of an hour," answered Zoroaster, tenderly drawing her to him; but she resisted a little and would not look at him.

"Farewell now—good-night, my princess—light of my soul;" he kissed her dark cheek passionately. "Good-night!"

He trod swiftly across the terrace.

"Zoroaster! prince!" Nehushta called aloud, but without turning. He came back. She threw her arms about his neck and kissed him almost desperately. Then she pushed him gently away from her.

"Go—my love—only that," she murmured, and he left her standing by the marble balustrade, while the yellow moon turned slowly pale as she rose in the heavens, and the song of the lorn nightingale re-echoed in the still night, from the gardens to the towers, in long sweet cries of burning love, and soft, complaining, silvery notes of mingled sorrow and joy.

CHAPTER III

In the prophet's chamber, also, the moonbeams fell upon the marble floor; but a seven-beaked Hebrew lamp of bronze shed a warmer light around, soft and mellow, yet strong enough to illuminate the scroll that lay open upon the old man's knee. His brows were knit together, and the furrows on his face were shaded deeply by the high light, as he sat propped among many cushions and wrapped in his ample purple cloak that was thickly lined with fur and drawn together over his snowy beard; for the years of his life were nearly accomplished, and the warmth of his body was even then leaving him.

Zoroaster raised the heavy curtain of carpet that hung before the low square door, and came and bowed himself before the teacher of his youth and the friend of his manhood. The prophet looked up keenly, and something like a smile crossed his stern features as his eyes rested on the young officer in his magnificent armour; Zoroaster held his helmet in his hand, and his fair hair fell like a glory to his shoulders, mingling with his silky beard upon his breastplate. His dark blue eyes met his master's fearlessly.

"Hail! and live for ever, chosen of the Lord!" he said in salutation. "I bring tidings of great moment and importance. If it be thy pleasure, I will speak; but if not, I will come at another season."

"Sit upon my right hand, Zoroaster, and tell me all that thou hast to tell. Art thou not my beloved son, whom the Lord hath given me to comfort mine old age?"

"I am thy servant and the servant of thine house, my father," answered Zoroaster, seating himself upon a carved chair at a little distance from the prophet.

"Speak, my son,—what tidings hast thou?"

"There is a messenger come in haste from Shushan, bearing tidings and letters. The seven princes have slain Smerdis in his house, and have chosen Darius the son of Gushtasp to be king."

"Praise be to the Lord who hath chosen a just man!" exclaimed the prophet devoutly. "So may good come out of evil, and salvation by the shedding of blood."

"Even so, my master," answered Zoroaster. "It is also written that Darius, may he live for ever, will establish himself very surely upon the throne of the Medes and Persians. There are letters by the hand of the same messenger, sealed with the signet of the Great King, wherein I am bidden to bring the kinsfolk of Jehoiakim, who was king over Judah, to Shushan without delay, that the Great King may do them honour as is meet and right; but what that honour may be that he would do to them, I know not."

"What is this that thou sayest?" asked Daniel, starting forward from his reclining position, and fixing his dark eyes on Zoroaster. "Will the king take away from me the children of my old age? Art not thou as my son? And is not Nehushta as my daughter? As for the rest, I care not if they go. But Nehushta is as the apple of my eye! She is as a fair flower growing in the desert of my years! What is this that the king hath done to me? Whither will he take her from me?"

"Let not my lord be troubled," said Zoroaster, earnestly, for he was moved by the sudden grief of the prophet. "Let not my lord be troubled. It is but for a space, for a few weeks; and thy kinsfolk will be with thee again, and I also."

"A space, a few weeks! What is a space to thee, child, or a week that thou shouldest regard it? But I am old and full of years. It may be, if now thou takest my daughter Nehushta from me, that I shall see her face no more, neither thine, before I go hence and return not. Go to! Thou art young, but I am now nigh unto a hundred years old."

"Nevertheless, if it be the will of the Great King, I must accomplish this thing," answered the young man. "But I will swear by thy head and by mine that there shall no harm happen to the young princess; and if anything happen to her that is evil, may the Lord do so to me and more also. Behold, I have sworn; let not my lord be troubled any more."

But the prophet bowed his head and covered his face with his hands. Aged and childless, Zoroaster and Nehushta were to him children, and he loved them with his whole soul. Moreover, he knew the Persian Court, and he knew that if once they were taken into the whirl and eddy of its intrigue and stirring life, they would not return to Ecbatana; or returning, they would be changed and seem no more the same. He was bitterly grieved and hurt at the thought of such a separation, and in the grand simplicity of his greatness he felt no shame at shedding tears for them. Zoroaster himself, in the pride of his brilliant youth, was overcome with pain at the thought of quitting the sage who had been a father to him for thirty years. He had never been separated from Daniel save for a few months at a time during the wars of Cambyses; at six-and-twenty years of age he had been appointed to the high position of captain of the fortress of Ecbatana; since which time he had enjoyed the closest intercourse with the prophet, his master.

Zoroaster was a soldier by force of circumstances, and he wore his gorgeous arms with matchless grace, but there were two things that, with him, went before his military profession, and completely eclipsed it in importance.

From his earliest youth he had been the pupil of Daniel, who had inspired him with his own love of the mystic lore to which the prophet owed so much of his singular success in the service of the Assyrian and Persian monarchs. The boy's poetical mind, strengthened and developed by the study of the art of reasoning, and of the profound mathematical knowledge of the Chaldean astronomers, easily grasped the highest subjects, and showed from the first a capacity and lucidity that delighted his master. To attain by a life of rigid ascetic practice to the intuitive comprehension of knowledge, to the understanding of natural laws not discernible to the senses alone, and to the merging of the soul and higher intelligence in the one universal and divine essence, were the objects Daniel proposed to his willing pupil. The noble boy, by his very nature, scorned and despised the pleasures of sense, and yearned ever for the realising of an ideal wherein a sublime wisdom of transcendent things should direct a sublime courage in things earthly to the doing of great deeds.

Year after year the young Persian grew up in the splendid surroundings of the court, distinguished before all those of his age for his courage and fearless honesty, for his marvellous beauty, and for his profound understanding of all subjects, great and small, that came within the sphere of his activity; most of all remarkable, perhaps, for the fact that he cared nothing for the society of women, and had never been known to love any woman. He was a favourite with Cyrus; and even Cambyses, steeped in degrading vice, and surrounded by flatterers, panderers, and priests of the Magians, from the time when he began to suspect his brother, the real Smerdis, of designs upon the throne, recognised the exceptional merits and gifts of the young noble, and promoted him to his position in Echatana, at the time when he permitted Daniel to build his great tower in that ancient fortress. The dissipated king may have understood that the presence of such men as Daniel and Zoroaster would be of greater advantage in an outlying district where justice and moderation would have a good effect upon the population, than in his immediate neighbourhood, where the purity and temperance of their lives contrasted too strongly with the degrading spectacle his own vices afforded to the court.

Here, in the splendid retirement of a royal palace, the prophet had given himself up completely to the contemplation of those subjects which, through all his life, had engrossed his leisure time, and of which the knowledge had so directly contributed to his singular career; and in the many hours of leisure which Zoroaster's position allowed him, Daniel sought to bring the intelligence of the soldier-philosopher to the perfection of its final development. Living, as he did, entirely in his tower, save when, at rare intervals, he caused himself to be carried down to the gardens, the prophet knew little of what went on in the palace below, so that he sometimes marvelled that his pupil's attention wandered, and that his language betrayed occasionally a keener interest in his future, and in the possible vicissitudes of his military life, than he had formerly been wont to show.

For a new element had entered into the current of Zoroaster's thoughts. For years he had seen the lovely child Nehushta growing up. As a boy of twenty summers he had rocked her on his knee; later he had taught her and played with her, and seen the little child turn to the slender girl, haughty and royal in her young ways, and dominating her playfellows as a little lioness might rule a herd of tamer creatures; and at last her sixteenth year had brought with it the bloom of early southern womanhood, and Zoroaster, laughing with her among the roses in the gardens, on a summer's day, had felt his heart leap and sink within him, and his own fair cheek grow hot and cold for the ring of her voice and the touch of her soft hand.

He who knew so much of mankind, who had lived so long at the court, and had coldly studied every stage of human nature, where unbridled human nature ever ruled the hour, knew what he felt; and it was as though he had received a sharp wound that thrust him through, body and heart and soul, and cleft his cold pride in two. For days he wandered beneath the pines and the rhododendron trees alone, lamenting for the fabric of mighty philosophy he had built himself, in which no woman was ever to set foot; and which a woman's hand, a woman's eyes had shattered in a day. It seemed as if his whole life were blasted and destroyed, so that he was become even as other men, to suffer love and eat his heart out for a girl's fair word. He would have escaped from meeting the dark young princess again; but one evening, as he stood alone upon the terrace of the gardens, sorrowing for the change in himself, she found him, and there they looked into each other's eyes and saw a new light, and loved each other fiercely from that day, as only the untainted children of godlike races could love. But neither of them dared to tell the prophet, nor to let those of the palace know that they had pledged each other their troth, down there upon the moonlit terrace, behind the myrtles. Instinctively they dreaded lest the knowledge of their love should raise a storm of anger in Daniel's breast at the idea that his chosen philosopher should abandon the paths of mystic learning and reduce himself to the level of common mankind by marriage; and Zoroaster guessed how painful to the true Israelite would be the thought that a daughter and a princess of Judah should be united in wedlock with one who, however noble and true and wise, was, after all, a stranger and an unbeliever. For Zoroaster, while devoting himself heart and soul to the study of Daniel's philosophy, and of the wisdom the latter had acquired from the Chaldeans, had nevertheless firmly maintained his independence of thought. He was not an Israelite, nor would he ever wish to become one; but he was not an idolater nor a Magian, nor a follower of Gomata, the half-Indian Brahmin, who had endeavoured to pass himself off as Smerdis the son of Cyrus.

Either of these causes alone would have sufficed to raise a serious obstacle to the marriage. Together they seemed insurmountable. During the disorder and anarchy that prevailed in the seven months of the reign of Pseudo-Smerdis, it would have been madness to have married, trusting to the favour of the wretched semi-monarch for fortune and advancement; nor could Nehushta have married and maintained her state as a princess of Judah without the consent of Daniel, who was her guardian, and whose influence was paramount in Media, and very great even at court. Zoroaster was therefore driven to conceal his passion as best he could, trusting to the turn of future events for the accomplishment of his dearest wish. In the meanwhile, he and the princess met daily in public, and Zoroaster's position as captain of the fortress gave him numerous opportunities of meeting Nehushta in the solitude of the gardens, which were jealously guarded and set apart exclusively for the use of Nehushta and her household.

But now that the moment had come when it seemed as though a change were to take place in the destinies of the lovers, they felt constrained. Beyond a few simple questions and answers, they had not discussed the matter of the journey when they were together; for Nehushta was so much surprised and delighted at the idea of again seeing the magnificence of the court at Shushan, which she so well remembered from the period of her childhood, that she feared to let Zoroaster see how glad she was to leave Ecbatana, which, but for him, would have been to her little better than a prison. He, on the contrary, thinking that he foresaw an immediate removal of all obstacle and delay through the favor of Darius, was, nevertheless, too gentle and delicate of tact to bring suddenly before Nehushta's mind the prospect of marrying which presented itself so vividly to his own fancy. But he felt no less disturbed in his heart when face to face with the old prophet's sorrow at losing his foster-daughter; and, for the first time in his life, he felt guilty when he reflected that Daniel was grieved at his own departure almost as deeply as on account of Nehushta. He experienced what is so common with persons of cold and even temperament when brought into close relation with more expansive and affectionate natures; he was overcome with the sense that his old master gave him more love and more thought than he could possibly give in return, and that he was therefore ungrateful; and the knowledge he alone possessed, that he surely intended to marry the princess in spite of the prophet, and by the help of the king, added painfully to his mental suffering.

The silence lasted some minutes, till the old man suddenly lifted his head and leaned back among his cushions, gazing at his companion's face.

"Hast thou no sorrow, nor any regret?" he asked sadly.

"Nay, my lord doth me injustice," answered Zoroaster, his brows contracting in his perplexity. "I should be ungrateful if I repented not leaving thee even for the space of a day. But let my lord be comforted; this parting is not for long, and before the flocks come down from Zagros to take shelter from the winter, we will be with thee."

"Swear to me, then, that thou wilt return before the winter," insisted the prophet half-scornfully.

"I cannot swear," answered Zoroaster. "Behold, I am in the hands of the Great King. I cannot swear."

"Say rather that thou art in the hand of the Lord, and that therefore thou canst not swear. For I say thou wilt not return, and I shall see thy face no more. The winter cometh, and the birds of the air fly towards the south, and I am alone in the land of snow and frost; and the spring cometh also, and I am yet alone, and my time is at hand; for thou comest not any more, neither my daughter Nehushta, neither any of my kinsfolk. And behold, I go down to the grave alone."

The yellow light of the hanging lamp above shone upon the old man's eyes, and there was a dull fire in them. His face was drawn and haggard, and every line and furrow traced by the struggles of his hundred years stood out dark and rugged and tremendous in power. Zoroaster shuddered as he looked on him, and, though he would have spoken, he was awed to silence.

"Go forth, my son," cried the prophet in deep tones, and as he spoke he slowly raised his body till he sat rigidly erect, and his wan and ancient fingers were stretched out towards the young soldier. "Go forth and do thy part, for thou art in the hand of the Lord, and some things that thou wilt do shall be good, and some things evil. For thou hast departed from the path of crystal that leadeth among the stars, and thou hast fallen away from the ladder whereby the angels ascend and descend upon the earth, and thou art gone after the love of a woman which endureth not. And for a season thou shalt be led astray, and for a time thou shalt suffer great things; and after a time thou shalt return into the way; and again a time, and thou shalt perish in thine own imaginations, because thou hast not known the darkness from the light, nor the good from the evil. By a woman shalt thou go astray, and from a woman shalt thou return; yet thou shalt perish. But because there is some good in thee, it shall endure, and thy name also, for generations; and though the evil that besetteth thee shall undo thee, yet at the last thy soul shall live."

Zoroaster buried his face in his hands, overcome by the majesty of the mighty prophet and by the terror of his words.

"Rise and go forth, for the hand of the Lord is upon thee, and no man can hinder that thou doest. Thou shalt look upon the sun and shalt delight in him; and again thou shalt look and the light of the air shall be as darkness. Thou shalt boast in thy strength and in thine armour that there is none like thee, and again thou shalt cast thy glory from thee and say, 'This also is vanity.' The king delighteth in thee, and thou shalt stand before the queen in armour of gold and in fine raiment; and the end is near, for the hand of the Lord is upon thee. If the Lord will work great things by thee, what is that to me? Go forth quickly, and rest not by the way, lest the woman tempt thee and thou perish. And as for me, I go also—not with thee, but before thee. See that thou follow after—for I go. Yea, I see even now light in the darkness of the world, and the glory of the triumph of heaven is over me, triumphing greatly in the majesty of light."

Zoroaster looked up and fell to the ground upon his knees in wonder and amazement at Daniel's feet, while his heavy helmet rolled clanging on the marble pavement. The prophet stood erect as a giant oak, stretching his withered hands to heaven, all the mass of his snow-white hair and beard falling about him to his waist. His face was illuminated as from within with a strange light, and his dark eyes turned upward seemed to receive and absorb the brightness of an open heaven. His voice rang again with the strength of youth, and his whole figure was clothed as with the majesty of another world. Again he spoke:

"Behold, the voice of the ages is in me, and the Lord my God hath taken me up. My days are ended; I am taken up and shall no more be cast down. The earth departeth and the glory of the Lord is come which hath no end for ever."

"The Lord cometh—He cometh quickly. In His right hand are the ages, and the days and the nights are under His feet. His ranks of the Cherubim are beside Him, and the armies of the Seraphim are dreadful. The stars of heaven tremble, and the voice of their moaning is as the voice of the uttermost fear. The arch of the outer firmament is shivered like a broken bow, and the curtain of the sky is rent in pieces as a veil in the tempest. The sun and the moon shriek aloud, and the sea crieth horribly before the Lord."

"The nations are extinct as the ashes of a fire that is gone out, and the princes of the earth are no more. He hath bruised the earth in a mortar, and the dust of it is scattered abroad in the heavens. The stars in their might hath He pounded to pieces, and the foundations of the ages to fine powder. There is nothing of them left, and their voices are dead. There are dim shapes in the horror of emptiness."

"But out of the north ariseth a fair glory with brightness, and the breath of the Lord breatheth life into all things. The beam of the dawn is risen, and there shall again be times and seasons, and the Being of the majesty of God is made manifest in form. From the dust of the earth is the earth made again, and of the beams of His glory shall He make new stars."

"Send up the voices of praise, O ye things that are; cry out in exultation with mighty music! Praise the Lord in whom is Life, and in whom all things have Being! Praise Him and glorify Him that is risen with the wings of the morning of heaven; in whose breath the stars breathe, in whose brightness also the firmament is lightened! Praise Him who maketh the wheels of the spheres to run their courses; who maketh the flowers to bloom in the spring, and the little flowers of the field to give forth their sweetness! Praise Him, winter and summer; praise Him, cold and heat! Praise Him, stars of heaven; praise Him, men and women in the earth! Praise and glory and honour be unto the Most High Jehovah, who sitteth upon the Throne for ever, and ever, and ever...."

The prophet's voice rang out with tremendous force and majestic clearness as he uttered the last words. Throwing up his arms to their height, he stood one moment longer, immovable, his face radiantly illuminated with an unearthly glory. One instant he stood there, and then fell back, straight and rigid, to his length upon the cushioned floor—dead!

Zoroaster started to his feet in amazement and horror, and stood staring at the body of his master and friend lying stiff and stark beneath the yellow light of the hanging lamp. Then suddenly he sprang forward and kneeled again beside the pale noble head that looked so grand in death. He took one of the hands and chafed it, he listened for the beating of the heart that beat no more, and sought for the stirring of the least faint breath of lingering life. But he sought in vain; and there, in the upper chamber of the tower, the young warrior fell upon his face and wept alone by the side of the mighty dead.

CHAPTER IV

Thus died Daniel, and for seven days the women sat apart upon the ground and mourned him, while the men embalmed his body and made it ready for burial. They wrapped him in much fine linen and poured out very precious spices and ointments from the store-houses of the palaces. Round about his body they burned frankincense and myrrh and amber, and the gums of the Indian benzoe and of the Persian fir, and great candles of pure wax; for all the seven days the mourners from the city made a great mourning, ceasing not to sing the praises of the prophet and to cry aloud by day and night that the best and the worthiest and the greatest of all men was dead.

Thus they watched and mourned, and sang his great deeds. And in the lower chamber of the tower the women sat upon the floor, with Nehushta in their midst, and sorrowed greatly, fasting and mourning in raiment of sackcloth, and strewing ashes upon the floor and upon themselves. Nehushta's face grew thin and very pale and her lips white in that time, and she let her heavy hair hang neglected about her. Many of the men shaved their heads and went barefooted, and the fortress and the palaces were filled with the sound of weeping and grief. The Hebrews who were there mourned their chief, and the two Levites sat beside the dead man and read long chapters from their scriptures. The Medes mourned their great and just governor, under the Assyrian name of Belteshazzar, given first to Daniel by Nebuchadnezzar; and from all the town the noise of their weeping and mourning came up, like the mighty groan of a nation, to the ears of those that dwelt in the fortress and the palace.

On the eighth day they buried him, with pomp and state, in a tomb in the garden which they had built during the week of mourning. The two Levites and a young Hebrew and Zoroaster himself, clad in sackcloth and barefooted, raised up the prophet's body upon a bier and bore him upon their shoulders down the broad staircase of the tower and out into the garden to his tomb. The mourners went before, many hundreds of Median women with dishevelled hair, rending their dresses of sackcloth and scattering ashes upon their path and upon their heads, crying aloud in wild voices of grief and piercing the air with their screams, till they came to the tomb and stood round about it while the four men laid their master in his great coffin of black marble beneath the pines and the rhododendrons. And the pipers followed after, making shrill and dreadful music that sounded as though some supernatural beings added their voices to the universal wail of woe. And on either side of the body walked the women, the prophet's kinsfolk; but Nehushta walked by Zoroaster, and ever and anon, as the funeral procession wound through the myrtle walks of the deep gardens, her dark and heavy eyes stole a glance sidelong at her strong fair lover. His face was white as death and set sternly before him, and his dishevelled hair and golden beard flowed wildly over the rough coarseness of his long sackcloth garments. But his step never faltered, though he walked barefooted upon the hard gravel, and from the upper chamber of the tower whence they bore the corpse to the very moment when they laid it in the tomb, his face never changed, neither looked he to the right nor to the left. And then, at last, when they had lowered their beloved master with linen bands to his last resting-place, and the women came near with boxes of nard and ambergris and precious ointments, Zoroaster looked long and fixedly at the swathed head, and the tears rolled down his cheeks and dropped upon his beard and upon the marble of the coffin; till at last he turned in silence, and went away through the multitude that parted before him, as pale as the dead and answering no man's greeting, nor even glancing at Nehushta who had stood at his elbow. And he went away and hid himself for the rest of that day.

But in the evening, when the sun was gone down, he came and stood upon the terrace in the darkness, for there was no moon. He wore again his arms, and his purple cloak was about him, for he had his duty to perform in visiting the fortress. The starlight glimmered faintly on his polished helmet and duskily made visible his marble features and his beard. He stood with his back to the pillars of the balustrade, looking towards the myrtles of the garden, for he knew that Nehushta would come to the wonted tryst. He waited long, but at last he heard a step upon the gravel path and the rustle of the myrtles, and presently in the faint light he could see the white skirt of her garment beneath the dark mantle moving swiftly towards him. He sprang forward to meet her and would have taken her in his arms, but she put him back and looked away from him while she walked slowly to the front of the terrace. Even in the gloom of the starlight Zoroaster could see that something had offended her, and a cold weight seemed to fall upon his breast and chilled the rising words of loving greeting.

Zoroaster followed her and laid his hand upon her shoulder. Unresponsive, she allowed it to remain there.

"My beloved," he said at last, trying in vain to look into her averted face, "have you no word for me to-night?" Still she answered nothing. "Has your sorrow made you forget our love?" he murmured close to her ear. She started back from him a little and looked at him. Even in the dusk he could see her eyes flash as she answered:

"Had not your own sorrow so utterly got the mastery over you to-day that you even refused to look at me?" she asked. "In all that long hour when we were so near together, did you give me one glance? You had forgotten me in the extremity of your grief!" she cried, scornfully. "And now that the first torrent of your tears has dwindled to a little stream, you have time to remember me! I thank my lord for the notice he deigns to give his handmaiden, but—I need it not. Well—why are you here?"

Zoroaster stood up to his height and folded his arms deliberately, facing Nehushta, and he spoke calmly, though there was in his voice the dulness of a great and sudden pain. He knew men well enough, but he knew little of women.

"There is a time to be sorrowful and a time for joy," he said. "There is a time for weeping and a time for the glances of love. I did as I did, because when a man has a great grief for one dead and when he desires to show his sorrow in doing honour to one who has been as a father to him, it is not meet that other thoughts should be in his mind; not even those thoughts which are most dear to him and nearest to his heart. Therefore I looked not at you when we were burying our master, and though I love you and in my heart look ever on your face, yet to-day my eyes were turned from you and I saw you not. Wherefore are you angry with me?"

"I am not angry," said Nehushta, "but think you love me little that you turn from me so easily." She looked down, and her face was quite hidden in the dark shadow. Then Zoroaster put his arm about her neck and drew her to him, and, though she resisted a little, in a moment her head rested on his breast. Then she struggled again.

"Nay, let me go, for you do not love me!" she said, half in a whisper. But he held her close.

"Nay, but you shall not go, for I do love you," he answered tenderly.

"Shall not?" cried she, turning in his arms, half fiercely; then her voice sank and thrilled softly. "Say that I will not," she murmured, and her arms went round him and pressed him passionately to her. "Oh, my beloved, why do you ever seem so cold? so cold—when I so love you?"

"I am not cold," he said fondly, "and I love you beyond all power of words to tell. Said we not that you had your way and I mine? Who shall tell us which is the sweeter music when both unite in so grand a harmony? Only doubt not, for doubting is as the drop that falls from the eaves upon the marble corner-stone, and, by ever falling, wears furrows in the stone that the whole ocean could not soften."

"I will not doubt any more," said Nehushta suddenly, "only—can you not love me a little sometimes in the way I do you? It is so sweet,—my way of loving."

"Indeed I will try, for it is very sweet," answered Zoroaster, and, bending down, he kissed her lips. Far off from the tower the melancholy cry of an owl echoed sadly across the gardens, and a cool damp breeze sprang up suddenly, from the east. Nehushta shuddered slightly, and drew her cloak about her.

"Let us walk upon the terrace," she said, "it is cold to-night—is not this the last night here?"

"Yes; to-morrow we must go hence upon our journey. This is the last night."

Nehushta drew closer to her lover as they paced the terrace together, and each wound one arm about the other. For some minutes they walked in silence, each perhaps recalling the many meetings upon that very terrace since the first time their lips met in love under the ivory moonlight of the month Tammuz, more than a year ago. At last Nehushta spoke.

"Know you this new king?" she asked. "I saw him but for a few moments last year. He was a young prince, but he is not fair."

"A young prince with an old man's head upon his shoulders," answered Zoroaster. "He is a year younger than I—but I would not have his battles to fight; nor, if I had, would I have taken Atossa to be my wife."

"Atossa?" repeated Nehushta.

"Yes. The king has already married her—she was the wife of Cambyses, and also of the false Smerdis, the Magian, whom Darius has slain."

"Is she fair? Have I not seen her?" asked Nehushta quickly.

"Indeed, you must have seen her at the court in Shushan, before we came to Ecbatana. She was just married to Cambyses then, but he regarded her little, for he was ever oppressed with wine and feasting. But you were a child then, and were mostly with the women of your house, and you may not have seen her."

"Tell me—had she not blue eyes and yellow hair? Had she not a cruel face—very cold?"

"Aye, it may be that she had a hard look. I remember that her eyes were blue. She was very unhappy; therefore she helped the Magian. It was not she that betrayed him."

"You pitied her even then, did you not?" asked Nehushta.

"Yes—she deserved pity."

"She will have her revenge now. A woman with a face like hers loves revenge."

"Then she will deserve pity no longer," said Zoroaster, with a slight laugh.

"I hate her!" said the princess, between her teeth.

"Hate her? How can you hate a woman you have never more than seen, and she has done you no evil in the world?"

"I am sure I shall hate her," answered Nehushta. "She is not at all beautiful—only cold and white and cruel. How could the Great King be so foolish as to marry her?"

"May he live for ever! He marries whom he pleases. But I pray you, do not begin by hating the queen overmuch."

"Why not? What have I to gain from the queen?" asked the princess. "Am I not of royal blood as well as she?"

"That is true," returned Zoroaster. "Nevertheless there is a prudence for princesses as well as for other people."

"I would not be afraid of the Great King himself with you beside me," said Nehushta proudly. "But I will be prudent to please you. Only—I am sure I shall hate her."

Zoroaster smiled to himself in the dusk, but he would not have had the princess see he was amused.

"It shall be as you please," he said; "we shall soon know how it will end, for we must begin our journey to-morrow."

"It will need three weeks, will it not?" asked Nehushta.

"Yes—it is at least one hundred and fifty farsangs. It would weary you to travel more than seven or eight farsangs in a day's journey—indeed, that is a long distance for any one."

"We shall always be together, shall we not?" asked the princess.

"I will ride beside your litter, my beloved," said Zoroaster. "But it will be very tedious for you, and you will often be tired. The country is very wild in some parts, and we must trust to what we can take with us for our comfort. Do not spare the mules, therefore, but take everything you need."

"Besides, we may not return," said Nehushta thoughtfully.

Her companion was silent. "Do you think we shall ever come back?" she asked presently.

"I have dreamed of coming back," answered Zoroaster; "but I fear it is to be even as you say."

"Why say you that you fear it! Is it not better to live at the court than here in this distant fortress, so shut off from the world that we might almost as well be among the Scythians? Oh, I long for the palace at Shushan! I am sure it will seem tenfold more beautiful now than it did when I was a child."

Zoroaster sighed. In his heart he knew there was to be no returning to Media, and yet he had dreamed of marrying the princess and being made governor of the province, and bringing his wife home to this beautiful land to live out a long life of quiet happiness. But he knew it was not to be; and though he tried hard to shake off the impression, he felt in his inmost self that the words of the dying prophet foretold truly what would happen to him. Only he hoped that there was an escape, and the passion in his heart scorned the idea that in loving Nehushta he was being led astray, or made to abandon the right path.

The cold breeze blew steadily from the east, with a chill dampness in it, sighing wearily among the trees. The summer was not yet wholly come, and the after-breath of the winter still made itself felt from time to time. The lovers parted, taking leave of the spot they loved so well,—Zoroaster with a heavy foreboding of evil to come; Nehushta with a great longing for the morrow, a mad desire to be on the way to Shushan.

Something in her way of speaking had given Zoroaster a sense of pain. Her interest in the court and in the Great King, the strange capricious hatred that seemed already forming in her breast against Atossa, the evident desire she betrayed to take part in the brilliant life of the capital,—indeed, her whole manner troubled him. It seemed so unaccountable that she should be angry with him for his conduct at the burial of the prophet, that he almost thought she had wished to take advantage of a trifle for the sake of annoying him. He felt that doubt which never comes so suddenly and wounds so keenly as when a man feels the most certain of his position and of himself.

He retired to his apartment in the palace with a burden of unhappiness and evil presentiment that was new to him. It was very different from the sincere sorrow he had felt and still suffered for the death of his master and friend. That misfortune had not affected him as regarded Nehushta. But now he had been separated from her during all the week by the exigencies of the funeral ceremonies, and he had looked forward to meeting her this evening as to a great joy after so much mourning, and he was disappointed. She had affected to be offended with him, yet his reason told him that he had acted naturally and rightly. Could he, the bearer of the prophet's body, the captain of all the fortress, the man of all others upon whom all eyes were turned, have exchanged love glances or spoken soft words to the princess by his side at such a time? It was absurd; she had no right to expect such a thing.

However, he reflected that a new kind of life was to begin on the morrow. For the best part of a month he would ride by her litter all day long, and sit at her table at noonday and evening; he would watch over her and take care of her, and see that her slightest wants were instantly supplied; a thousand incidents would occur whereby he might re-establish all the loving intimacy which seemed to have been so unexpectedly shaken. And so, consoling himself with the hopes of the future, and striving to overlook the present, he fell asleep, wearied with the fatigues and sorrows of the day.

But Nehushta lay all night upon her silken cushions, and watched the flickering little lamp and the strange shadows it cast among the rich, painted carvings of the ceiling. She slept little, but waking she dreamed of the gold and the glitter of Shushan, of the magnificence of the young king, and of the brilliant hard-featured beauty of Atossa, whom she already hated or had determined to hate. The king interested her most. She tried to recall his features and manner as he had appeared when he tarried one night in the fortress a year previous. She remembered a black-browed man in the prime of youth, with heavy brows and an eagle nose; his young beard growing black and square about his strong dark features, which would have seemed coarse saving for his bright eyes that looked every man fearlessly in the face. A short man he seemed in her memory, square built and powerful as a bloodhound, of quick and decisive speech, expecting to be understood before he had half spoken his thoughts; a man, she fancied, who must be untiring and violent of temper, inflexible and brave in the execution of his purpose—a strong contrast outwardly to her tall and graceful lover. Zoroaster's faultless beauty was a constant delight to her eyes; his soft deep voice sounded voluptuously passionate when he spoke to herself, coldly and deliberately dominating when addressing others. He moved with perfect certainty and assurance of purpose, his whole presence breathed a high and superior wisdom and untainted nobility of mind; he looked and acted like a god, like a being from another world, not subject to mortal passions, nor to the temptations of common mankind. She gloried in his perfection and in the secret knowledge that to her alone he was a man simply and utterly dominated by love. As she thought of him she grew proud and happy in the idea that such a man should be her lover, and she reproached herself for doubting his devotion that evening. After all, she had only complained that he had neglected her—as he had really done, she added. She wondered in her heart whether other men would have done the same in his place, or whether this power of coldly disregarding her presence when he was occupied with a serious matter were not due to a real and unconquerable hardness in his nature.

But as she lay there, her dark hair streaming over the yellow silk of her pillows, her mind strayed from her lover to the life before her, and the picture rose quickly in her imagination. She even took up the silver mirror that lay beside her and looked at herself by the dim light of the little lamp, and said to herself that she was beautiful, and that many in Shushan would do her homage. She was glad that Atossa was so fair—it would be a better contrast for her own dark southern beauty.

Towards morning she slept, and dreamed of the grand figure of the prophet, as she had seen him stretched upon his death-bed in the upper chamber of the tower; she thought the dead man stirred and opened his glazed eyes and pointed at her with his bony fingers, and spoke words of anger and reproach. Then she woke with a short cry in her terror, and the light of the dawn shone gray and clear through the doorway of the corridor at the end of her room, where two of her handmaids slept across the threshold, their white cloaks drawn over their heads against the chill air of the night.

Then the trumpets rang out in long-drawn clanging rhythm through the morning air, and Nehushta heard the trampling of the beasts that were being got ready for the journey, in the court without, and the cries of the drivers and of the serving-men. She rose quickly from her bed—a lithe white-clad figure in the dawn light—and pushed the heavy curtains aside and looked out through the lattice; and she forgot her evil dream, for her heart leaped again at the thought that she should no more be shut up in Ecbatana, and that before another month was over she would be in Shushan, in the palace, where she longed to be.

The sun was almost setting, and his light was already turning to a golden glow upon the vast plain of Shushan, as the caravan of travellers halted for the last time. A few stades away the two mounds rose above the royal city like two tables out of the flat country; the lower one surmounted by the marble columns, the towers and turrets and gleaming architraves of the palace; and in front, upon the right, the higher elevation crowned by the dark and massive citadel of frowning walls and battlements. The place chosen for the halt was the point where the road from Nineveh, into which they had turned when about half-way from Ecbatana, joined the broad road from Babylon, near to the bridge. For some time they had followed the quiet stream of the Choaspes, and, looking across it, had watched how the fortress seemed to come forward and overhang the river, while the mound of the palace fell away to the background. The city itself was, of course, completely hidden from their view by the steep mounds, that looked as inaccessible as though they had been built of solid masonry.

Everything in the plain was green. Stade upon stade, and farsang upon farsang, the ploughed furrows stretched away to the west and south; the corn standing already green and high, and the fig-trees putting out their broad green leaves. Here and there in the level expanse of country the rays of the declining sun were reflected from the whitewashed walls of a farmhouse; or in the farther distance lingered upon the burnt-brick buildings of an outlying village. Beyond the river, in the broad meadow beneath the turret-clad mound, half-naked, sunburnt boys drove home the small humped cows to the milking, scaring away, as they went, the troops of white horses that pastured in the same field, clapping their hands and crying out at the little black foals that ran and frisked by the side of their white dams. Here and there a broad-shouldered, bearded fisherman angled in the stream, or flung out a brown casting-net upon the placid waters, drawing it slowly back to the bank, with eyes intent upon the moving cords.

The caravan halted on the turf by the side of the dusty road; the mounted guards, threescore stalwart riders from the Median plains, fell back to make room for the travellers, and, springing to the ground, set about picketing and watering their horses—their brazen armour and scarlet and blue mantles blazing in a mass of rich colour in the evening sun; while their wild white horses, untired by the day's march, plunged and snorted, and shook themselves, and bit each other in play by mane and tail, in the delight of being at least half free.

Zoroaster himself—his purple mantle somewhat whitened with the dust, and his fair face a little browned by the three weeks' journey—threw the bridle of his horse to a soldier and ran quickly forward. A magnificent litter, closed all around with a gilded lattice, and roofed with three awnings of white linen, one upon the other, as a protection against the sun, was being carefully unyoked from the mules that had borne it. Tall Ethiopian slaves lifted it, and carried it to the greenest spot of the turf by the softly flowing river; and Zoroaster himself pushed back the lattice and spread a rich carpet before it. Nehushta took his proffered hand and stepped lightly out, and stood beside him in the red light. She was veiled, and her purple cloak fell in long folds to her feet, and she stood motionless, with her back to the city, looking towards the setting sun.

"Why do we stop here?" she asked suddenly.

"The Great King, may he live for ever, is said not to be in the city," answered Zoroaster, "and it would ill become us to enter the palace before him." He spoke aloud in the Median language that the slaves might hear him; then he added in Hebrew and in a lower voice, "It would be scarcely wise, or safe, to enter Shushan when the king is away. Who can tell what may have happened there in these days? Babylon has rebelled; the empire is far from settled. All Persia may be on the very point of a revolt."

"A fitting time indeed for our journey—for me and my women to be travelling abroad with a score of horsemen for a guard! Why did you bring me here? How long are we to remain encamped by the roadside, waiting the pleasure of the populace to let us in, or the convenience of this new king to return?"

Nehushta turned upon her companion as she spoke, and there was a ring of mingled scorn and disappointment in her voice. Her dark eyes stated coldly at Zoroaster from the straight opening between her veils, and before he could answer, she turned her back upon him and moved a few steps away, gazing out at the setting sun across the fertile meadows. The warrior stood still, and a dark flush overspread his face. Then he turned pale, but whatever were the words that rose to his lips, he did not speak them, but occupied himself with superintending the pitching of the women's tents. The other litters were brought, and set down with their occupants; the long file of camels, some laden with baggage and provisions, some bearing female slaves, kneeled down to be unloaded upon the grass, anxiously craning their long necks the while in the direction of the stream; the tent-pitchers set to work; and at the last another score of horsemen, who had formed the rear-guard of the caravan, cantered up and joined their companions who had already dismounted. With the rapid skill of long practice, all did their share, and in a few minutes all the immense paraphernalia of a Persian encampment were spread out and disposed in place for the night. Contrary to the usual habit Zoroaster had not permitted the tent-pitchers and other slaves to pass on while he and his charges made their noonday halt; for he feared some uprising in the neighbourhood of the city in the absence of the king, and he wished to keep his whole company together as a measure of safety, even at the sacrifice of Nehushta's convenience.

She herself still stood apart, and haughtily turned away from her serving-women, giving them no answer when they saluted her and offered her cushions and cooling drinks. She drew her cloak more closely about her and tightened her veil upon her face. She was weary, disappointed, almost angry. For days she had dreamed of the reception she would have at the palace, of the king and of the court; of the luxury of rest after her long journey, and of the thousand diversions and excitements she would find in revisiting the scenes of her childhood. It was no small disappointment to find herself condemned to another night in camp; and her first impulse was to blame Zoroaster.

In spite of her love for him, her strong and dominating temper often chafed at his calmness, and resented the resolute superiority of his intelligence; and then, being conscious that her own dignity suffered by the storms of her temper, she was even more angry than before, with herself, with him, with every one. But Zoroaster was as impassive as marble, saving that now and then his brow flushed, and paled quickly; and his words, if he spoke at all, had a chilled icy ring in them. Sooner or later, Nehushta's passionate temper cooled, and she found him the same as ever, devoted and gentle and loving; then her heart went out to him anew, and all her being was filled with the love of him, even to overflowing.

She had been disappointed now, and would speak to no one. She moved still farther from the crowd of slaves and tent-pitchers, followed at a respectful distance by her handmaidens, who whispered together as they went; and again she stood still and looked westward.

As the sun neared the horizon, his low rays caught upon a raising cloud of dust, small and distant as the smoke of a fire, in the plain towards Babylon, but whirling quickly upwards. Nehushta's eye rested on the far-off point, and she raised one hand to shade her sight. She remembered how, when she was a girl, she had watched the line of that very road from the palace above, and had seen a cloud of dust arise out of a mere speck, as a body of horsemen galloped into view. There was no mistaking what it was. A troop of horse were coming—perhaps the king himself. Instinctively she turned and looked for Zoroaster, and started, as she saw him standing at a little distance from her, with folded arms, his eyes bent on the horizon. She moved towards him in sudden excitement.

"What is it?" she asked in low tones.

"It is the Great King—may he live for ever!" answered Zoroaster. "None but he would ride so fast along the royal road."

For a moment they stood side by side, watching the dust cloud; and as they stood, Nehushta's hand stole out from her cloak and touched the warrior's arm, softly, with a trembling of the fingers, as though she timidly sought something she would not ask for. Zoroaster turned his head and saw that her eyes were moistened with tears; he understood, but he would not take her hand, for there were many slaves near, besides Nehushta's kinsfolk, and he would not have had them see; but he looked on her tenderly, and on a sudden, his eyes grew less sad, and the light returned in them.

"My beloved!" he said softly.

"I was wrong, Zoroaster—forgive me," she murmured. She suffered him to lead her to her tent, which was already pitched; and he left her there, sitting at the door and watching his movements, while he called together his men and drew them up in a compact rank by the roadside, to be ready to salute the king.

Nearer and nearer came the cloud; and the red glow turned to purple and the sun went out of sight; and still it came nearer, that whirling cloud-canopy of fine powdered dust, rising to right and left of the road in vast round puffs, and hanging overhead like the smoke from some great moving fire. Then, from beneath it, there seemed to come a distant roar like thunder, rising and falling on the silent air, but rising ever louder; and a dark gleam of polished bronze, with something more purple than the purple sunset, took shape slowly; then with the low roar of sound, came now and then, and then more often, the clank of harness and arms; till at last, the whole stamping, rushing, clanging crowd of galloping horsemen seemed to emerge suddenly from the dust in a thundering charge, the very earth shaking beneath their weight, and the whole air vibrating to the tremendous shock of pounding hoofs and the din of clashing brass.

A few lengths before the serried ranks rode one man alone,—a square figure, wrapped in a cloak of deeper and richer purple than any worn by the ordinary nobles, sitting like a rock upon a great white horse. As he came up, Zoroaster and his fourscore men threw up their hands.

"Hail, king of kings! Hail, and live for ever!" they cried, and as one man, they prostrated themselves upon their faces on the grass by the roadside.

Darius drew rein suddenly, bringing his steed from his full gallop to his haunches in an instant. After him the rushing riders threw up their right hands as a signal to those behind; and with a deafening concussion, as of the ocean breaking at once against a wall of rock, those matchless Persian horsemen halted in a body in the space of a few yards, their steeds plunging wildly, rearing to their height and struggling on the curb; but helpless to advance against the strong hands that held them. The blossom and flower of all the Persian nobles rode there,—their purple mantles flying with the wild motion, their bronze cuirasses black in the gathering twilight, their bearded faces dark and square beneath their gilded helmets.

"I am Darius, the king of kings, on whom ye call," cried the king, whose steed now stood like a marble statue, immovable in the middle of the road. "Rise, speak and fear nothing,—unless ye speak lies."

Zoroaster rose to his feet, then bent low, and taking a few grains of dust from the roadside, touched his mouth with his hand and let the dust fall upon his forehead.

"Hail, and live for ever! I am thy servant, Zoroaster, who was captain over the fortress and treasury of Ecbatana. According to thy word I have brought the kinsfolk of Jehoiakim, king of Judah,—chief of whom is Nehushta, the princess. I heard that thou wast absent from Shushan, and here I have waited for thy coming. I also sent thee messengers to announce that Daniel, surnamed Belteshazzar, who was Satrap of Media from the time of Cambyses, is dead; and I have buried him fittingly in a new tomb in the garden of the palace of Ecbatana."

Darius, quick and impulsive in every thought and action, sprang to the ground as Zoroaster finished speaking, and coming to him, took both his hands and kissed him on both cheeks.

"What thou hast done is well done,—I know thee of old. Auramazda is with thee. He is also with me. By his grace I have slain the rebels at Babylon. They spoke lies, so I slew them. Show me Nehushta, the daughter of the kings of Judah."

"I am thy servant. The princess is at hand," answered Zoroaster; but as he spoke, he turned pale to the lips.

By this time it had grown dark, and the moon, just past the full, had not yet risen from behind the mound of the fortress. The slaves brought torches of mingled wax and fir-gum, and their black figures shone strangely in the red glare, as they pressed toward the door of Nehushta's tent, lighting the way for the king.

Darius strode quickly forward, his gilded harness clanging as he walked, the strong flaring light illuminating his bold dark features. Under the striped curtain, drawn up to form the entrance of the tent, stood Nehushta. She had thrown aside her veil and her women had quickly placed upon her head the linen tiara, where a single jewel shown like a star in the white folds. Her thick black hair fell in masses upon her shoulders, and her mantle was thrown back, displaying the grand proportions of her figure, clad in tunic and close-fitting belt. As the king came near, she kneeled and prostrated herself before him, touching her forehead to the ground, and waiting for him to speak.

He stood still a full minute and his eyes flashed fire, as he looked on her crouching figure, in very pride that so queenly a woman should be forced to kneel at his feet—but more in sudden admiration of her marvellous beauty. Then he bent down, and took her hand and raised her to her feet. She sprang up, and faced him with glowing cheeks and flashing eyes; and as she stood she was nearly as tall as he.

"I would not that a princess of thy line kneeled before me," said he; and in his voice there was a strange touch of softness. "Wilt thou let me rest here awhile before I go up to Shushan? I am weary of riding and thirsty from the road."

"Hail, king of the world! I am thy servant. Rest thee and refresh thee here," answered Nehushta, drawing back into the tent. The king beckoned to Zoroaster to follow him and went in.

Darius sat upon the carved folding-chair that stood in the midst of the tent by the main pole, and eagerly drained the huge golden goblet of Shiraz wine which Zoroaster poured for him. Then he took off his headpiece, and his thick, coarse hair fell in a mass of dark curls to his neck, like the mane of a black lion. He breathed a long breath as of relief and enjoyment of well-earned repose, and leaned back in his chair, letting his eyes rest on Nehushta's face as she stood before him looking down to the ground. Zoroaster remained on one side, holding the replenished goblet in his hand, in case the king's thirst were not assuaged by a single draught.

"Thou art fair, daughter of Jerusalem," said the king presently. "I remember thy beauty, for I saw thee in Ecbatana. I sent for thee and thy kinsfolk that I might do thee honour; and I will also fulfil my words. I will take thee to be my wife."

Darius spoke quietly, in his usual tone of absolute determination. But if the concentrated fury of a thousand storms had suddenly broken loose in the very midst of the tent, the effect could not have been more terrible on his hearers.

Nehushta's face flushed suddenly, and for a moment she trembled in every joint; then she fell on her knees, prostrate before the king's feet, all the wealth of her splendid hair falling loose about her. Darius sat still, as though watching the result of his speech. He might have sat long, but in an instant, Zoroaster sprang between the king and the kneeling woman; and the golden goblet he had held rolled across the thick carpet on the ground, while the rich red wine ran in a slow stream towards the curtains of the door. His face was livid and his eyes like coals of blue fire, his fair locks and his long golden beard caught the torchlight and shone about him like a glory, as he stood up to his grand height and faced the king. Darius never quailed nor moved; his look met Zoroaster's with fearless boldness. Zoroaster spoke first, in low accents of concentrated fury:

"Nehushta the princess is my betrothed bride. Though thou wert king of the stars as well as king of the earth, thou shalt not have her for thy wife."

Darius smiled, not scornfully, an honest smile of amusement, as he stared at the wrathful figure of the northern man before him.

"I am the king of kings," he answered. "I will marry this princess of Judah to-morrow, and thee I will crucify upon the highest turret of Shushan, because thou speakest lies when thou sayest I shall not marry her."

"Fool! tempt not thy God! Threaten not him who is stronger than thou, lest he slay thee with his hands where thou sittest." Zoroaster's voice sounded low and distinct as the knell of relentless fate, and his hand went out towards the king's throat.

Until this moment, Darius had sat in his indifferent attitude, smiling carelessly, though never taking his eye from his adversary. Brave as the bravest, he scorned to move until he was attacked, and he would have despised the thought of calling to his guards. But when Zoroaster's hand went out to seize him, he was ready. With a spring like a tiger, he flew at the strong man's throat, and sought to drag him down, striving to fasten his grip about the collar of his cuirass, but Zoroaster slipped his hand quickly under his adversary's, his sleeve went back and his long white arm ran like a fetter of steel about the king's neck, while his other hand gripped him by the middle; so they held each other like wrestlers, one arm above the shoulder and one below, and strove with all their might.

The king was short, but in his thick-set broad shoulders and knotted arms there lurked the strength of a bull and the quickness of a tiger. Zoroaster had the advantage, for his right arm was round Darius's neck, but while one might count a score, neither moved a hairbreadth, and the blue veins stood out like cords on the tall man's arm. The fiery might of the southern prince was matched against the stately strength of the fair northerner, whose face grew as white as death, while the king's brow was purple with the agony of effort. They both breathed hard between their clenched teeth, but neither uttered a word.

Nehushta had leaped to her feet in terror at the first sign of the coming strife, but she did not cry out, nor call in the slaves or guards. She stood, holding the tent-pole with one hand, and gathering her mantle to her breast with the other, gazing in absolute fascination at the fearful life and death struggle, at the unspeakable and tremendous strength so silently exerted by the two men before her.

Suddenly they moved and swayed. Darius had attempted to trip Zoroaster with one foot, but slipping on the carpet wet with wine, had been bent nearly double to the ground; then by a violent effort, he regained his footing. But the great exertion had weakened his strength. Nehushta thought a smile nickered on Zoroaster's pale face and his flashing dark blue eyes met hers for a moment, and then the end began. Slowly, and by imperceptible degrees, Zoroaster forced the king down before him, doubling him backwards with irresistible strength, till it seemed as though bone and sinew and muscle must be broken and torn asunder in the desperate resistance. Then, at last, when his head almost touched the ground, Darius groaned and his limbs relaxed. Instantly Zoroaster threw him on his back and kneeled with his whole weight upon his chest,—the gilded scales of the corselet cracking beneath the burden, and he held the king's hands down on either side, pinioned to the floor. Darius struggled desperately twice and then lay quite still. Zoroaster gazed down upon him with blazing eyes.

"Thou who wouldst crucify me upon Shushan," he said through his teeth. "I will slay thee here even as thou didst slay Smerdis. Hast thou anything to say? Speak quickly, for thy hour is come."

Even in the extremity of his agony, vanquished and at the point of death, Darius was brave, as brave men are, to the very last. He would indeed have called for help now, but there was no breath in him. He still gazed fearlessly into the eyes of his terrible conqueror. His voice came in a hoarse whisper.

"I fear not death. Slay on if thou wilt—thou—hast—conquered."

Nehushta had come near. She trembled now that the fight was over, and looked anxiously to the heavy curtains of the tent-door.

"Tell him," she whispered to Zoroaster, "that you will spare him if he will do no harm to you, nor to me."

"Spare him!" echoed Zoroaster scornfully. "He is almost dead now—why should I spare him?"

"For my sake, beloved," answered Nehushta, with a sudden and passionate gesture of entreaty. "He is the king—he speaks truth; if he says he will not harm you, trust him."

"If I slay thee not, swear thou wilt not harm me nor Nehushta," said Zoroaster, removing one knee from the chest of his adversary.

"By the name of Auramazda," gasped Darius, "I will not harm thee nor her."

"It is well," said Zoroaster. "I will let thee go. And as for taking her to be thy wife, thou mayest ask her if she will wed thee," he added. He rose and helped the king to his feet. Darius shook himself and breathed hard for a few minutes. He felt his limbs as a man might do who had fallen from his horse, and then he sat down upon the chair, and broke into a loud laugh.

Darius was well known to all Persia and Media before the events of the last two months, and such was his reputation for abiding by his promise that he was universally trusted by those about him. Zoroaster had known him also, and he remembered his easy familiarity and love of jesting, so that even when he held the king at such vantage that he might have killed him by a little additional pressure of his weight, he felt not the least hesitation in accepting his promise of safety. But remembering what a stake had been played for in the desperate issue, he could not join in the king's laugh. He stood silently apart, and looked at Nehushta who leaned back against the tent-pole in violent agitation; her hands wringing each other beneath her long sleeves, and her eyes turning from the king to Zoroaster, and back again to the king, in evident distress and fear.

"Thou hast a mighty arm, Zoroaster," cried Darius, as his laughter subsided, "and thou hadst well-nigh made an end of the Great King and of Persia, Media, Babylon and Egypt in thy grip."

"Let the king pardon his servant," answered Zoroaster, "if his knee was heavy and his hand strong. Had not the king slipped upon the spilt wine, his servant would have been thrown down."

"And thou wouldst have been crucified at dawn," added Darius, laughing again. "It is well for thee that I am Darius and not Cambyses, or thou wouldst not be standing there before me while my guards are gossiping idly in the road. Give me a cup of wine since thou hast spared my life!" Again the king laughed as though his sides would break. Zoroaster hastily filled another goblet and offered it, kneeling before the monarch. Darius paused before he took the cup, and looked at the kneeling warrior's pale proud face. Then he spoke and his voice dropped to a less mirthful key, as he laid his hand on Zoroaster's shoulder.

"I love thee, prince," he said, "because thou art stronger than I; and as brave and more merciful. Therefore shalt thou stand ever at my right hand and I will trust thee with my life in thy hand. And in pledge hereunto I put my own chain of gold about thy neck, and I drink this cup to thee; and whosoever shall harm a hair of thine head shall perish in torments."

The king drank; and Zoroaster, overcome with genuine admiration of the great soul that could so easily forgive so dire an offence, bent and embraced the king's knees in token of adherence, and as a seal of that friendship which was never to be broken until death parted the two men asunder.

Then they arose, and at Zoroaster's order, the princess's litter was brought, and leaving the encampment to follow after them, they went up to the palace. Nehushta was borne between the litters of her women and her slaves on foot, but Zoroaster mounted his horse and rode slowly and in silence by the right side of the Great King.

CHAPTER VI

Athwart the gleaming colonnades of the eastern balcony, the early morning sun shone brightly, and all the shadows of the white marble cornices and capitals and jutting frieze work were blue with the reflection of the cloudless sky. The swallows now and then shot in under the overhanging roof and flew up and down the covered terrace; then with a quick rush, they sped forth again into the dancing sunshine with clean sudden sweep, as when a sharp sword is whirled in the air. Far below, the soft mist of the dawn still lay upon the city, whence the distant cries of the water-carriers and fruitsellers came echoing up from the waking streets, the call of the women to one another from the housetops, and now and then the neighing of a horse far out upon the meadows; while the fleet swallows circled over all in swift wide curves, with a silvery fresh stream of unceasing twittering music.

Zoroaster paced the balcony alone. He was fully armed, with his helmet upon his head; the crest of the winged wheels was replaced by the ensign Darius had chosen for himself,—the half-figure of a likeness of the king with long straight wings on either side, of wrought gold and very fine workmanship. The long purple mantle hung to his heels and the royal chain of gold was about his neck. As he walked the gilded leather of his shoes was reflected in the polished marble pavement and he trod cautiously, for the clean surface was slippery as the face of a mirror. At one end of the terrace a stairway led down to the lower story of the palace, and at the other end a high square door was masked by a heavy curtain of rich purple and gold stuff, that fell in thick folds to the glassy floor. Each time his walk brought him to this end Zoroaster paused, as though expecting that some one should come out. But as it generally happens when a man is waiting for something or some one that the object or person appears unexpectedly, so it occurred that as he turned back from the staircase towards the curtain, he saw that some one had already advanced half the length of the balcony to meet him—and it was not the person for whom he was looking.

At first, he was dazzled for a moment, but his memory served him instantly and he recognised the face and form of a woman he had known and often seen before. She was not tall, but so perfectly proportioned that it was impossible to wish that she were taller. Her close tunic of palest blue, bordered with a gold embroidery at the neck, betrayed the matchless symmetry of her figure, the unspeakable grace of development of a woman in the fullest bloom of beauty. From her knees to her feet, her under tunic showed the purple and white bands that none but the king might wear, and which even for the queen was an undue assumption of the royal insignia. But Zoroaster did not look at her dress, nor at her mantle of royal sea-purple, nor at the marvellous white hands that held together a written scroll. His eyes rested on her face, and he stood still where he was.

He knew those straight and perfect features, not large nor heavy, but of such rare mould and faultless type as man has not seen since, neither will see. The perfect curve of the fresh mouth; the white forward chin with its sunk depression in the midst, the deep-set, blue eyes and the straight pencilled brows; the broad smooth forehead and the tiny ear half hidden in the glory of sun-golden hair; the milk-white skin just tinged with the faint rose-light that never changed or reddened in heat or cold, in anger or in joy—he knew them all; the features of royal Cyrus made soft and womanly in substance, but unchanging still and faultlessly cold in his great daughter Atossa, the child of kings, the wife of kings, the mother of kings.

The heavy curtains had fallen together behind her, and she came forward alone. She had seen Zoroaster before he had seen her, and she moved on without showing any surprise, the heels of her small golden shoes clicking sharply on the polished floor. Zoroaster remained standing for a moment, and then, removing his helmet in salutation, went to one side of the head of the staircase and waited respectfully for the queen to pass. As she came on, passing alternately through the shadow cast by the columns, and the sunlight that blazed between, her advancing figure flashed with a new illumination at every step. She made as though she were going straight on, but as she passed over the threshold to the staircase, she suddenly stopped and turned half round, and looked straight at Zoroaster.

"Thou art Zoroaster," she said in a smooth and musical voice, like the ripple of a clear stream flowing through summer meadows.

"I am Zoroaster, thy servant," he answered, bowing his head. He spoke very coldly.

"I remember thee well," said the queen, lingering by the head of the staircase. "Thou art little changed, saving that thou art stronger, I should think, and more of a soldier than formerly."

Zoroaster stood turning his polished helmet in his hands, but he answered nothing; he cared little for the queen's praises. But she, it seemed, was desirous of pleasing him in proportion as he was less anxious to be pleased, for she turned again and walked forward upon the terrace.

"Come into the sunlight—the morning air is cold," she said, "I would speak with thee awhile."

A carved chair stood in a corner of the balcony. Zoroaster moved it into the sunshine, and Atossa sat down, smiling her thanks to him, while he stood leaning against the balustrade,—a magnificent figure as the light caught his gilded harness and gold neckchain, and played on his long fair beard and nestled in the folds of his purple mantle.

"Tell me—you came last night?" she asked, spreading her dainty hands in the sunshine as though to warm them. She never feared the sun, for he was friendly to her nativity and never seemed to scorch her fair skin like that of meaner women.

"Thy servant came last night," answered the prince.

"Bringing Nehushta and the other Hebrews?" added the queen.

"Even so."

"Tell me something of this Nehushta," said Atossa. She had dropped into a more familiar form of speech. But Zoroaster was careful of his words and never allowed his language to relapse from the distant form of address of a subject to his sovereign.

"The queen knoweth her. She was here as a young child a few years since," he replied. He chose to let Atossa ask questions for all the information she needed.

"It is so long ago," she said, with a little sigh. "Is she fair?"

"Nay, she is dark, after the manner of the Hebrews."

"And the Persians too," she interrupted.

"She is very beautiful," continued Zoroaster. "She is very tall." Atossa looked up quickly with a smile. She was not tall herself, with all her Beauty.

"You admire tall women?"

"Yes," said Zoroaster calmly—well knowing what he said. He did not wish to flatter the queen; and besides he knew her too well to do so if he wished to please her. She was one of those women who are not accustomed to doubt their own superiority over the rest of their sex.

"Then you admire this Hebrew princess?" said she, and paused for an answer. But her companion was as cold and calm as she. Seeing himself directly pressed by a suspicion, he changed his tactics and flattered Atossa for the sake of putting a stop to her questions.

"Height is not of itself beauty," he answered with a courteous smile. "There is a kind of beauty which no height can improve,—a perfection which needs not to be set high for all men to acknowledge it."

The queen simply took no notice of the compliment, but it had its desired effect, for she changed the tone of her talk a little, speaking more seriously.

"Where is she? I will go and see her," she said.

"She rested last night in the upper chambers in the southern part of the palace. Thy servant will bid her come if it be thy desire."

"Presently, presently," answered the queen. "It is yet early, and she was doubtless weary of the journey."

There was a pause. Zoroaster looked down at the beautiful queen as she sat beside him, and wondered whether she had changed; and as he gazed, he fell to comparing her beauty with Nehushta's, and his glance grew more intent than he had meant it should be, so that Atossa looked up suddenly and met his eyes resting on her face.

"It is long since we have met, Zoroaster," she said quickly. "Tell me of your life in that wild fortress. You have prospered in your profession of arms—you wear the royal chain." She put up her hand and touched the links as though to feel them. "Indeed it is very like the chain Darius wore when he went to

Babylon the other day." She paused a moment as though trying to recall something; then continued: "Yes—now I think of it, he had no chain when he came back. It is his—of course—why has he given it to you?" Her tones had a tinge of uncertainty in the question,—half imperious, as demanding an answer, half persuading, as though not sure the answer would be given. Zoroaster remembered that intonation of her sweet voice, and he smiled in his beard.

"Indeed," he answered, "the Great King who liveth for ever, put this chain about my neck with his own hands last night, when he halted by the roadside, as a reward, I presume, for certain qualities he believeth his servant Zoroaster to possess."

"Qualities—what qualities?"

"Nay, the queen cannot expect me to sing faithfully my own praises. Nevertheless, I am ready to die for the Great King. He knoweth that I am. May he live for ever!"

"It may be that one of the qualities was the successful performance of the extremely difficult task you have lately accomplished," said Atossa, with a touch of scorn.

"A task?" repeated Zoroaster.

"Yes—have you not brought a handful of Hebrew women all the way from Ecbatana to Shushan, through numberless dangers and difficulties, safe and sound, and so carefully prudent of their comfort that they are not even weary, nor have they once hungered or thirsted by the way, nor lost the smallest box of perfume, nor the tiniest of their golden hair-pins? Surely you have deserved to have a royal chain hung about your neck and to be called the king's friend."

"The reward was doubtless greater than my desert. It was no great feat of arms that I had to perform; and yet, in these days a man may leave Media under one king, and reach Shushan under another. The queen knoweth better than any one what sudden changes may take place in the empire," answered Zoroaster, looking calmly into her face as he stood; and she who had been the wife of Cambyses and the wife of the murdered Gomata-Smerdis, and who was now the wife of Darius, looked down and was silent, turning over in her beautiful hands the sealed scroll she bore.

The sun had risen higher while they talked, and his rays were growing hot in the clear air. The mist had lifted from the city below, and all the streets and open places were alive with noisy buyers and sellers, whose loud talking and disputing came up in a continuous hum to the palace on the hill, like the drone of a swarm of bees. The queen rose from her seat.

"It is too warm here," she said, and she once more moved toward the stairway. Zoroaster followed her respectfully, still holding his helmet in his hand. Atossa did not speak till she reached the threshold. Then, as Zoroaster bowed low before her, she paused and looked at him with her clear, deep-blue eyes.

"You have grown very formal in four years," she said softly. "You used to be more outspoken and less of a courtier. I am not changed—we must be friends as we were formerly."

Zoroaster hesitated a moment before he answered:

"I am the Great King's man," he said slowly. "I am, therefore, also the queen's servant."

Atossa raised her delicate eyebrows a little and a shade of annoyance passed for the first time over her perfect face, which gave her a look of sternness.

"I am the queen," she said coldly. "The king may take other wives, but I am the queen. Take heed that you be indeed my servant." Then, as she gathered her mantle about her and put one foot upon the stairs, she touched his shoulder gently with the tips of her fingers and added with a sudden smile, "And I will be your friend." So she passed down the stairs out of sight, leaving Zoroaster alone.

Slowly he paced the terrace again, reflecting profoundly upon his situation. Indeed he had no small cause for anxiety; it was evident that the queen suspected his love for Nehushta, and he was more than half convinced that there were reasons why such an affection would inevitably meet with her disapproval. In former days, before she was married to Cambyses, and afterwards, before Zoroaster had been sent into Media, Atossa had shown so marked a liking for him, that a man more acquainted with the world, would have guessed that she loved him. He had not suspected such a thing, but with a keen perception of character, he had understood that beneath the beautiful features and the frank gentleness of the young princess, there lurked a profound intelligence, an unbending ambition and a cold selfishness without equal; he had mistrusted her, but he had humoured her caprices and been in truth a good friend to her, without in the least wishing to accept her friendship for himself in return. He was but a young captain of five hundred then, although he was the favourite of the court; but his strong arm was dreaded as well as the cutting force of his replies when questioned, and no word of the court gossip had therefore reached his ears concerning Atossa's admiration for him. It was, moreover, so evident that he cared nothing for her beyond the most unaffected friendliness, that her disappointment in not moving his heart was a constant source of satisfaction to her enemies. There had reigned in those days a great and unbridled license in the court, and the fact of the daughter of Cyrus loving and being loved by the handsomest of the king's guards, would not of itself have attracted overmuch notice. But the evident innocence of Zoroaster in the whole affair, and the masterly fashion in which Atossa concealed her anger, if she felt any, caused the matter to be completely forgotten as soon as Zoroaster left Shushan, and events had, since then, succeeded each other too rapidly to give the courtiers leisure for gossiping about old scandals. The isolation in which Gomata had lived during the seven months while he maintained the popular impression that he was not Gomata-Smerdis, but Smerdis the brother of Cambyses, had broken up the court; and the strong, manly character of Darius had checked the license of the nobles suddenly, as a horse-breaker brings up an unbroken colt by flinging the noose about his neck. The king permitted that the ancient custom of marrying as many as four wives should be maintained, and he himself soon set an example by so doing; but he had determined that the whole corrupt fabric of court life should be shattered at one blow; and with his usual intrepid disregard of consequences and his iron determination to maintain his opinions, he had suffered no contradiction of his will. He had married Atossa,—in the first place, because she was the most beautiful woman in Persia; and secondly, because he comprehended her great intelligence and capacity for affairs, and believed himself able to make use of her at his pleasure. As for Atossa herself, she had not hesitated a moment in concurring in the marriage,—she had ruled her former husbands, and she would rule Darius in like manner, she thought, to her own complete aggrandisement and in the face of all rivals. As yet, the king had taken no second wife, although he looked with growing admiration upon the maiden Artystoné, who was then but fifteen years of age, the youngest daughter of Cyrus and own sister to Atossa.

All this Zoroaster knew, and he recognised, also from the meeting he had just had with the queen, that she was desirous of maintaining her friendship with himself. But since the violent scene of the previous night, he had determined to be the king's man in truest loyalty, and he feared lest Atossa's plans might, before long, cross her husband's. Therefore he accepted her offer of friendship coldly, and treated her with the most formal courtesy. On the other hand, he understood well enough that if she resented his manner of acting towards her, and ascertained that he really loved Nehushta, it would be in her power to produce difficulties and complications which he would have every cause for fearing. She would certainly discover the king's admiration for Nehushta. Darius was a man almost incapable of concealment; with whom to think was to act instantly and without hesitation. He generally acted rightly, for his instincts were noble and kingly, and his heart as honest and open as the very light of day. He said what he thought and instantly fulfilled his words. He hated a lie as poison, and the only untruth he had ever been guilty of was told when, in order to gain access to the dwelling of the false Smerdis, he had declared to the guards that he brought news of importance from his father. He had justified this falsehood by the most elaborate and logical apology to his companions, the six princes, and had explained that he only lied for the purpose of saving Persia; and when the lot fell to himself to assume the royal authority, he fulfilled most amply every promise he had given of freeing the country from tyranny, religious despotism and, generally, from what he termed "lies." As for the killing of Gomata-Smerdis, it was an act of public justice, approved by all sensible persons as soon as it was known by what frauds that impostor had seized the kingdom.

With regard to Atossa, Darius had abstained from asking her questions about her seven months of marriage with the usurper. She must have known well enough who the man was, but Darius understood her character well enough to know that she would marry whomsoever she saw in the chief place, and that her counsel and courage would be of inestimable advantage to a ruler. She herself never mentioned the past events to the king, knowing his hatred of lies on the one hand, and that on the other, the plain truth would redound to her discredit. He had given her to understand as much from the first, telling her that he took her for what she was, and not for what she had been. Her mind was at rest about the past, and as for the future, she promised herself her full share in her husband's success, should he succeed, and unbounded liberty in the choice of his successor, should he fail.

But all these considerations did not tend to clear Zoroaster's vision in regard to his own future. He saw himself already placed in a position of extreme difficulty between Nehushta and the king. On the other hand, he dreaded lest he should before long fall into disgrace with the king on account of Atossa's treatment of himself, or incur Atossa's displeasure through the great favour he received from Darius. He knew the queen to be an ambitious woman, capable of the wildest conceptions, and possessed of the utmost skill for their execution.

He longed to see Nehushta and talk with her at once,—to tell her many things and to warn her of many possibilities; above all, he desired to discuss with her the scene of the previous night and the strangely sudden determination the king had expressed to make her his wife.

But he could not leave his post. His orders had been to await the king in the morning upon the eastern terrace; and there he must abide until it pleased Darius to come forth; and he knew Nehushta would not venture down into that part of the palace. He wondered that the king did not come, and he chafed at the delay as he saw the sun rising higher and higher, and the shadows deepening in the terrace. Weary of waiting he sat down at last upon the chair where Atossa had rested, and folded his hands over his sword-hilt,—resigning himself to the situation with the philosophy of a trained soldier.

Sitting thus alone, he fell to dreaming. As he gazed out at the bright sky, he forgot his life and his love, and all things of the present; and his mind wandered away among the thoughts most natural and most congenial to his profound intellect. His attention became fixed in the contemplation of a larger dimension of intelligences,—the veil of darkness parted a little, and for a time he saw clearly in the light of a Greater Universe.

Atossa quitted the terrace where she had been talking with Zoroaster, in the full intention of returning speedily, but as she descended the steps, a plan formed itself in her mind, which she determined to put into immediate execution. Instead, therefore, of pursuing her way into the portico of the inner court, when she reached the foot of the staircase, she turned into a narrow passage that led into a long corridor, lighted only by occasional small openings in the wall. A little door gave access to this covered way, and when she entered, she closed it behind her, and tried to fasten it. But the bolt was rusty, and in order to draw it, she laid down the scroll she carried, upon a narrow stone seat by the side of the door; and then, with a strong effort of both her small white hands, she succeeded in moving the lock into its place. Then she turned quickly and hastened down the dusky corridor. At the opposite end a small winding stair led upwards into darkness. There were stains upon the lowest steps, just visible in the half light. Atossa gathered up her mantle and her under tunic, and trod daintily, with a look of repugnance on her beautiful face. The stains were made by the blood of the false Smerdis, her last husband, slain in that dark stairway by Darius, scarcely three months before.

Cautiously the queen felt her way upward till she reached a landing, where a narrow aperture admitted a little light. Higher up there were windows, and she looked carefully to her dress, and brushed away a little dust that her mantle had swept from the wall in passing; and once or twice, she looked back at the dark staircase with an expression of something akin to disgust. At last she reached a door which opened upon a terrace, much like the one where she had left Zoroaster a few moments before, saving that the floor was less polished, and that the spaces between the columns were half filled with hanging plants and creepers. Upon the pavement at one end were spread rich carpets, and half a dozen enormous cushions of soft-coloured silk were thrown negligently one upon the other. Three doors, hung with curtains, opened upon the balcony,—and near to the middle one, two slave-girls, clad in white, crouched upon their heels and talked in an undertone.

Atossa stepped forward upon the marble, and the rustle of her dress and the quick short sound of her heeled shoes, roused the two slave-girls to spring to their feet. They did not know the queen, but they thought it best to make a low obeisance, while their dark eyes endeavoured quickly to scan the details of her dress, without exhibiting too much boldness. Atossa beckoned to one of them to come to her, and smiled graciously as the dark-skinned girl approached.

"Is not thy mistress Nehushta?" she inquired; but the girl looked stupidly at her, not comprehending her speech. "Nehushta," repeated the queen, pronouncing the name very distinctly with a questioning intonation, and pointing to the curtained door. The slave understood the name and the question, and quick as thought, she disappeared within, leaving Atossa in some hesitation. She had not intended to send for the Hebrew princess, for she thought it would be a greater compliment to let Nehushta find her waiting; but since the barbarian slave had gone to call her mistress, there was nothing to be done but to abide the result.

Nehushta, however, seemed in no hurry to answer the summons, for the queen had ample time to examine the terrace, and to glance through the hanging plants at the sunlit meadows and the flowing stream to southward, before she heard steps behind the curtain, and saw it lifted to allow the princess to pass.

The dark maiden was now fully refreshed and rested from the journey, and she came forward to greet her guest in her tunic, without her mantle, a cloud of soft white Indian gauze loosely pinned upon her black hair and half covering her neck. Her bodice-like belt was of scarlet and gold, and from one side there hung a rich-hilted knife of Indian steel in a jewelled sheath. The long sleeves of her tunic were drawn upon her arms into hundreds of minute folds, and where the delicate stuff hung in an oblong lappet over her hands, there was fine needlework and embroidery of gold. She moved easily, with a languid grace of secure motion; and she bent her head a little as Atossa came quickly to meet her.

The queen's frank smile was on her face as she grasped both Nehushta's hands in cordial welcome, and for a moment, the two women looked into each other's eyes. Nehushta had made up her mind to hate Atossa from the first, but she did not belong to that class of women who allow their feelings to show themselves, and afterwards feel bound by the memory of what they have shown. She, too, smiled most sweetly as she surveyed the beautiful fair queen from beneath her long drooping lids, and examined her appearance with all possible minuteness. She remembered her well enough, but so warm was the welcome she received, that she almost thought she had misjudged Atossa in calling her hard and cold. She drew her guest to the cushions upon the carpets, and they sat down side by side.

"I have been talking about you already this morning, my princess," began Atossa, speaking at once in familiar terms, as though she were conversing with an intimate friend. Nehushta was very proud; she knew herself to be of a race as royal as Atossa, though now almost extinct; and in answering, she spoke in the same manner as the queen; so that the latter was inwardly amused at the self-confidence of the Hebrew princess.

"Indeed?" said Nehushta, "there must be far more interesting things than I in Shushan. I would have talked of you had I found any one to talk with."

The queen laughed a little.

"As I was coming out this morning, I met an old friend of mine upon the balcony before the king's apartment,—Zoroaster, the handsome captain. We fell into conversation, how handsome he has grown since I saw him last!" The queen watched Nehushta closely while affecting the greatest unconcern, and she thought the shadows about the princess's eyes turned a shade darker at the mention of the brilliant warrior. But Nehushta answered calmly enough:

"He took the most excellent care of us. I should like to see him to-day, to thank him for all he did. I was tired last night and must have seemed ungrateful."

"What need is there of ever telling men we are grateful for what they do for us?" returned the queen. "I should think there were not a noble in the Great King's guard who would not give his right hand to take care of you for a month, even if you never so much as noticed his existence."

Nehushta laughed lightly at the compliment.

"You honour me too much," she said, "but I suppose it is because most women think as you do that men call us so ungrateful. I think you judge from the standpoint of the queen, whereas I—"

"Whereas you look at things from the position of the beautiful princess, who is worshipped for herself alone, and not for the bounty and favour she may, or may not, dispense to her subjects."

"The queen is dispensing much bounty and favour to one of her subjects at this very moment," answered Nehushta quietly, as though deprecating further flattery.

"How glad you must be to have left that dreadful fortress at last!" cried the queen sympathetically. "My father used to go there every summer. I hated the miserable place, with those tiresome mountains and those endless gardens without the least variety in them. You must be very glad to have come here!"

"It is true," replied Nehushta, "I never ceased to dream of Shushan. I love the great city, and the people, and the court. I thought sometimes that I should have died of the weariness of Ecbatana. The winters were unbearable!"

"You must learn to love us, too," said Atossa, very sweetly. "The Great King wishes well to your race, and will certainly do much for your country. There is, moreover, a kinsman of yours, who is coming soon, expressly to confer with the king concerning the further rebuilding of the temple and the city of Jerusalem."

"Zorobabel?" asked Nehushta, quickly.

"Yes—that is his name, I believe. Do you say Zerub-Ebel, or Zerub-Abel? I know nothing of your language."

"His name is Zorob-Abel," answered Nehushta. "Oh, I wish he might persuade the Great King to do something for my people! Your father would have done so much if he had lived."

"Doubtless the Great King will do all that is possible for establishing the Hebrews and promoting their welfare," said the queen; but a distant look in her eyes showed that her thoughts were no longer concentrated on the subject. "Your friend Zoroaster," she added presently, "could be of great service to you and your cause, if he wished."

"I would that he were a Hebrew!" exclaimed Nehushta, with a little sigh, which did not escape Atossa.

"Is he not? I always thought that he had secretly embraced your faith. With his love of study and with his ideas, it seemed so natural."

"No," replied Nehushta, "he is not one of us, nor will he ever be. After all, though, it is perhaps of little moment what one believes when one is so just as he."

"I have never been able to understand the importance of religion," said the beautiful queen, spreading her white hand upon the purple of her mantle, and contemplating its delicate outline tenderly. "For my own part, I am fond of the sacrifices and the music and the chants. I love to see the priests go up to the altar, two and two, in their white robes,—and then to see how they struggle to hold up the bullock's head, so that his eyes may see the sun,—and how the red blood gushes out like a beautiful fountain. Have you ever seen a great sacrifice?"

"Oh yes! I remember when I was quite a little girl, when Cambyses—I mean—when the king came to the throne—it was magnificent!" Nehushta was not used to hesitate in her speech, but as she recalled the day when Cambyses was made king, it suddenly came over her that any reminiscences of the past might be painful to the extraordinary woman by her side. But Atossa showed no signs of being disturbed. On the contrary, she smiled more sweetly than ever, though there was perhaps a slight affectation of sadness in her voice as she answered:

"Do not fear to hurt me by referring to those times, dear princess. I am accustomed to speak of them well enough. Yes, indeed I remember that great day, with the bright sun shining upon the procession, and the cars with four horses that they dedicated to the sun, and the milk-white horse that they slaughtered upon the steps of the temple. How I cried for him, poor beast! It seemed so cruel to sacrifice a horse! Even a few black slaves would have been a more natural offering, or a couple of Scythians."

"I remember," said Nehushta, somewhat relieved at the queen's tone. "Of course I have now and then seen processions in Ecbatana, but Daniel would not let me go to the temple. They say Ecbatana is very much changed since the Great King has not gone there in summer. It is very quiet—it is given over to horse-merchants and grain-sellers, and they bring all the salted fish there from the Hyrcanian sea, so that some of the streets smell horribly."

Atossa laughed at the description, more out of courtesy than because it amused her.

"In my time," she answered, "the horse-market was in the meadow by the road toward Zagros, and the fish-sellers were not allowed to come within a farsang of the city. The royal nostrils were delicate. But everything is changed—here, everywhere. We have had several—revolutions—religious ones, I mean of course, and so many people have been killed that there is a savour of death in the air. It is amazing how much trouble people will give themselves about the question of sacrificing a horse to the sun, or a calf to Auramazda, or an Ethiopian to Nabon or Ashtaroth! And these Magians! They are really no more descendants of the priests in the Aryan home than I am a Greek. Half of them are nearly black—they are Hindus and speak Persian with an accent. They believe in a vast number of gods of all sizes and descriptions, and they sing hymns, in which they say that all these gods are the same. It is most confusing, and as the principal part of their chief sacrifice consists in making themselves exceedingly drunk with the detestable milkweed juice of which they are so fond, the performance is disgusting. The Great King began by saying that if they wished to sacrifice to their deities, they might do so, provided no one could find them doing it; and if they wished to be drunk, they might be drunk when and where they pleased; but that if they did the two together, he would crucify every Magian in Persia. His argument was very amusing. He said that a man who is drunk naturally speaks the truth, whereas a man who sacrifices to false gods inevitably tells lies; wherefore a man who sacrifices to false gods when he is drunk, runs the risk of telling lies and speaking the truth at the same time, and is consequently a creature revolting to logic, and must be immediately destroyed for the good of the whole race of mankind."

Nehushta had listened with varying attention to the queen's account of the religious difficulties in the kingdom, and she laughed at the Megoeric puzzle by which Darius justified the death of the Magians. But in her heart she longed to see Zoroaster, and was weary of entertaining her royal guest. By way of diversion she clapped her hands, and ordered the slaves who came at her summons to bring sweetmeats and sherbet of crushed fruit and snow.

"Are you fond of hunting?" asked Atossa, delicately taking a little piece of white fig-paste.

"I have never been allowed to hunt," answered Nehushta. "Besides, it must be very tiring."

"I delight in it—the fig-paste is not so good as it used to be—there is a new confectioner. Darius considered that the former one had religious convictions involving the telling of lies—and this is the result! We are fallen low indeed when we cannot eat a Magian's pastry! I am passionately fond of hunting, but it is far from here to the desert and the lions are scarce. Besides, the men who are fit for lion-hunting are generally engaged in hunting their fellow-creatures."

"Does the Great King hunt?" inquired Nehushta, languidly sipping her sherbet from a green jade goblet, as she lay among her cushions, supporting herself upon one elbow.

"Whenever he has leisure. He will talk of nothing else to you—"

"Surely," interrupted Nehushta, with an air of perfect innocence, "I shall not be so far honoured as that the Great King should talk with me?"

Atossa raised her blue eyes and looked curiously at the dark princess. She knew nothing of what had passed the night before, save that the king had seen Nehushta for a few moments, but she knew his character well enough to imagine that his frank and, as she thought, undignified manner might have struck Nehushta even in that brief interview. The idea that the princess was already deceiving her flashed across her mind. She smiled more tenderly than ever, with a little added air of sadness that gave her a wonderful charm.

"Yes, the Great King is very gracious to the ladies of the court," she said. "You are so beautiful and so different from them all that he will certainly talk long with you after the banquet this evening—when he has drunk much wine." The last words were added with a most special sweetness of tone.

Nehushta's face flushed a little as she drank more sherbet before she answered. Then, letting her soft dark eyes rest, as though in admiration, upon the queen's face, she spoke in a tone of gentle deprecation:

"Shall a man prefer the darkness of night to the glories of risen day?

Or shall a man turn from the lilies to pluck the lowly flower of the field?"

"You know our poets, too?" exclaimed Atossa, pleased with the graceful tone of the compliment, but still looking at Nehushta with curious eyes. There was a self-possession about the Hebrew princess that she did not like; it was as though some one had suddenly taken a quality of her own and made it theirs and displayed it before her eyes. There was indeed this difference, that while Atossa's calm and undisturbed manner was generally real, Nehushta's was assumed, and she herself felt that, at any moment, it might desert her at her utmost need.

"So you know our poets?" repeated the queen, and this time she laughed lightly. "Indeed I fear the king will talk to you more than ever, for he loves poetry, I daresay Zoroaster, too, has repeated many verses to you in the winter evenings at Ecbatana. He used to know endless poetry when he was a boy."

This time Nehushta looked at the queen, and wondered how she, who could not be more than two or three and twenty years old, although now married to her third husband, could speak of having known Zoroaster as a boy, seeing that he was past thirty years of age. She turned the question upon the queen.

"You must have seen Zoroaster very often before he left Shushan," she said. "You know him so well."

"Yes—every one knew him. He was the favourite of the court, with his beauty and his courage and his strange affection for that old—for the old Hebrew prophet. That is why Cambyses sent them both away," added she with a light laugh. "They were far too good, both of them, to be endured among the doings of those times."

Atossa spoke readily enough of Cambyses. Nehushta wondered whether she could be induced to speak of Smerdis. Her supposed ignorance of the true nature of what had occurred in the last few months would permit her to speak of the dead usurper with impunity.

"I suppose there have been great changes lately in the manners of the court—during this last year," suggested Nehushta carelessly. She pulled a raisin from the dry stem, and tried to peel it with her delicate fingers.

"Indeed there have been changes," answered Atossa, calmly. "A great many things that used to be tolerated will never be heard of now. On the whole, the change has been rather in relation to religion than otherwise. You will understand that in one year we have had three court religions. Cambyses sacrificed to Ashtaroth—and I must say he made a most appropriate choice of his tutelary goddess. Smerdis"—continued the queen in measured tones and with the utmost calmness of manner—"Smerdis devoted himself wholly to the worship of Indra, who appeared to be a convenient association of all the most agreeable gods; and the Great King now rules the earth by the grace of Auramazda. I, for my part, have always inclined to the Hebrew conception of one God—perhaps that is much the same as Auramazda, the All-Wise. What do you think?"

Nehushta smiled at the deft way in which the queen avoided speaking of Smerdis by turning the conversation again to religious topics. But fearing another lecture on the comparative merits of idolatry, human sacrifice, and monotheism, she manifested very little interest in the subject.

"I daresay it is the same. Zoroaster always says so, and that was the one point that Daniel could never forgive him. The sun is coming through those plants upon your head—shall we not have our cushions moved into the shade at the other end?" She clapped her hands and rose languidly, offering her hand to Atossa. But the queen sprang lightly to her feet.

"I have stayed too long," she said. "Come with me, dearest princess, and we will go out into the orange gardens upon the upper terrace. Perhaps," she added, adjusting the folds of her mantle, "we shall find Zoroaster there, or some of the princes, or even the Great King himself. Or, perhaps, it would amuse you to see where I live?"

Nehushta received her mantle from her slaves, and one of them brought her a linen tiara in place of the gauze veil she had twisted about her hair. But Atossa would not permit the change.

"It is too beautiful!" she cried enthusiastically. "So new! you must really not change it."

She put her arm around Nehushta affectionately and led her towards the door of the inner staircase. Then suddenly she paused, as though recollecting herself.

"No," she said, "I will show you the way I came. It is shorter and you should know it. It may be of use to you."

So they left the balcony by the little door that was almost masked by one of the great pillars, and descended the dark stairs. Nehushta detested every sort of bodily inconvenience, and inwardly wished the queen had not changed her mind, but had led her by an easier way.

"It is not far," said the queen, descending rapidly in front of her.

"It is dreadfully steep," objected Nehushta, "and I can hardly see my way at all. How many steps are there?"

"Only a score more," answered the queen's voice, farther down. She seemed to be hurrying, but Nehushta had no intention of going any faster, and carefully groped her way. As she began to see a glimmer of light at the last turn of the winding stair, she heard loud voices in the corridor below. With the cautious instinct of her race, she paused and listened. The hard, quick tones of an angry man dominated the rest.

CHAPTER VIII

Zoroaster had sat for nearly an hour, his eyes fixed on the blue sky, his thoughts wandering in contemplation of things greater and higher than those of earth, when he was roused by the measured tread of armed men marching in a distant room. In an instant he stood up, his helmet on his head,—the whole force of military habit bringing him back suddenly to the world of reality. In a moment the same heavy curtain, from under which Atossa had issued two hours before, was drawn aside, and a double file of spearmen came out upon the balcony, ranging themselves to right and left with well-drilled precision. A moment more, and the king himself appeared, walking alone, in his armour and winged helmet, his left hand upon the hilt of his sword, his splendid mantle hanging to the ground behind his shoulders. As he came between the soldiers, he walked more slowly, and his dark, deep-set eyes seemed to scan the bearing and accoutrements of each separate spearman. It was rarely indeed, in those early days of his power, that he laid aside his breastplate for the tunic, or his helmet for the tiara and royal crown. In his whole air and gait the character of the soldier dominated, and the look of the conqueror was already in his face.

Zoroaster strode forward a few paces, and stood still as the king caught sight of him, preparing to prostrate himself, according to the ancient custom. But Darius checked him by a gesture; turning half round, he dismissed the guard, who filed back through the door as they had come, and the curtain fell behind them.

"I like not these elaborate customs," said the king. "A simple salutation, the hand to the lips and forehead—it is quite enough. A man might win a battle if he had all the time that it takes him to fall down at my feet and rise up again, twenty times in a day."

As the king's speech seemed to require no answer, Zoroaster stood silently waiting for his orders. Darius walked to the balustrade and stood in the full glare of the sun for a moment, looking out. Then he came back again.

"The town seems to be quiet this morning," he said. "How long did the queen tarry here talking with thee, Zoroaster?"

"The queen talked with her servant for the space of half an hour," answered Zoroaster, without hesitation, though he was astonished at the suddenness and directness of the question.

"She is gone to see thy princess," continued the king.

"The queen told her servant it was yet too early to see Nehushta," remarked the warrior.

"She is gone to see her, nevertheless," asserted Darius, in a tone of conviction. "Now, it stands in reason that when the most beautiful woman in the world has been told that another woman is come who is more beautiful than she, she will not lose a moment in seeing her." He eyed Zoroaster curiously for a moment, and his thick black beard did not altogether hide the smile on his face. "Come," he added, "we shall find the two together."

The king led the way and Zoroaster gravely followed. They passed down the staircase by which the queen had gone, and entering the low passage, came to the small door which she had bolted behind her with so much difficulty. The king pushed his weight against it, but it was still fastened.

"Thou art stronger than I, Zoroaster," he said, with a deep laugh. "Open the door."

The young warrior pushed heavily against the planks, and felt that one of them yielded. Then, standing back, he dealt a heavy blow on the spot with his clenched fist; a second, and the plank broke in. He put his arm through the aperture, and easily slipped the bolt back, and the door flew open. The blood streamed from his hand.

"That is well done," said Darius as he entered. His quick eye saw something white upon the stone bench in the dusky corner by the door. He stooped and picked it up quickly. It was the sealed scroll Atossa had left there when she needed both her hands to draw the bolt. Darius took it to one of the narrow windows, looked at it curiously and broke the seal. Zoroaster stood near and wiped the blood from his bruised knuckle.

The contents of the scroll were short. It was addressed to one Phraortes, of Ecbatana in Media, and contained the information that the Great King had returned in triumph from Babylon, having subdued the rebels and slain many thousands in two battles. Furthermore, that the said Phraortes should give instant information of the queen's affairs, and do nothing in regard to them until further intimation arrived.

The king stood a moment in deep thought. Then he walked slowly down the corridor, holding the scroll loose in his hand. Just at that instant Atossa emerged from the dark staircase, and as she found herself face to face with Darius, she uttered an exclamation and stood still.

"This is very convenient place for our interview," said Darius quietly. "No one can hear us. Therefore speak the truth at once." He held up the scroll to her eyes.

Atossa's ready wit did not desert her, nor did she change colour, though she knew her life was in the balance with her words. She laughed lightly as she spoke:

"I came down the stairs this morning—"

"To see the most beautiful woman in the world," interrupted Darius, raising his voice. "You have seen her. I am glad of it. Why did you bolt the door of the passage?"

"Because I thought it unfitting that the passage to the women's apartments should be left open when so many in the palace know the way," she answered readily enough.

"Where were you taking this letter when you left it at the door?" asked the king, beginning to doubt whether there were anything wrong at all.

"I was about to send it to Ecbatana," answered Atossa with perfect simplicity.

"Who is this Phraortes?"

"He is the governor of the lands my father gave me for my own in Media. I wrote him to tell him of the Great King's victory, and that he should send me information concerning my affairs, and do nothing further until he hears from me."

"Why not?"

"Because I thought it possible that the Great King would spend the summer in Ecbatana, and that I should therefore be there myself to give my own directions. I forgot the letter because I had to take both hands to draw the bolt, and I was coming back to get it. Nehushta the princess is with me—she is now upon the staircase."

The king looked thoughtfully at his wife's beautiful face.

"You have evidently spoken the truth," he said slowly. "But it is not always easy to understand what your truth signifies. I often think it would be much wiser to strangle you. Say you that Nehushta is near? Call her, then. Why does she tarry?"

In truth Nehushta had trembled as she crouched upon the stairs, not knowing whether to descend or to fly up the steps again. As she heard the queen pronounce her name, however, she judged it prudent to seem to have been out of earshot, and with quick, soft steps, she went up till she came to the lighted part, and there she waited.

"Let the Great King go himself and find her," said Atossa proudly, "if he doubts me any further." She stood aside to let him pass. But Darius beckoned to Zoroaster to go. He had remained standing at some distance, an unwilling witness to the royal altercation that had taken place before him; but as he passed the queen, she gave him a glance of imploring sadness, as though beseeching his sympathy in what she was made to suffer. He ran quickly up the steps in spite of the darkness, and found Nehushta waiting by the window higher up. She started as he appeared, for he was the person she least expected. But he took her quickly in his arms, and kissed her passionately twice.

"Come quickly, my beloved," he whispered. "The king waits below."

"I heard his voice—and then I fled," she whispered hurriedly; and they began to descend again. "I hate her—I knew I should," she whispered, as she leaned upon his arm. So they emerged into the corridor, and met Darius waiting for them. The queen was nowhere to be seen, and the door at the farther extremity of the narrow way was wide open.

The king was as calm as though nothing had occurred; he still held the open letter in his hand as Nehushta entered the passage, and bowed herself before him. He took her hand for a moment, and then dropped it; but his eyes flashed suddenly and his arm trembled at her touch.

"Thou hadst almost lost thy way," he said. "The palace is large and the passages are many and devious. Come now, I will lead thee to the gardens. There thou canst find friends among the queen's noble women, and amusements of many kinds. Let thy heart delight in the beauty of Shushan, and if there is anything that thou desirest, ask and I will give it thee."

Nehushta bent her head in thanks. The only thing she desired was to be alone for half an hour with Zoroaster; and that seemed difficult.

"Thy servant desireth what is pleasant in thy sight," she answered. And so they left the passage by the open door, and the king himself conducted Nehushta to the entrance of the garden, and bade the slave-woman who met them to lead her to the pavilion where the ladies of the palace spent the day in the warm summer weather. Zoroaster knew that whatever liberty his singular position allowed him in the quarter of the building where the king himself lived, he was not privileged to enter that place which was set apart for the noble ladies. Darius hated to be always surrounded by guards and slaves, and the terraces and staircases of his dwelling were generally totally deserted,—only small detachments of spearmen guarding jealously the main entrances. But the remainder of the palace swarmed with the gorgeously dressed retinue of the court, with slaves of every colour and degree, from the mute smooth-faced Ethiopian to the accomplished Hebrew scribes of the great nobles; from the black and scantily-clad fan-girls to the dainty Greek tirewomen of the queen's toilet, who loitered near the carved marble fountain at the entrance to the gardens; and in the outer courts, detachments of the horsemen of the guard rubbed their weapons, or reddened their broad leather bridles and trappings with red chalk, or groomed the horse of some lately arrived officer or messenger, or hung about and basked in the sun, with no clothing but their short-sleeved linen tunics and breeches, discussing the affairs of the nation with the certainty of decision peculiar to all soldiers, high and low. There was only room for a squadron of horse in the palace; but though they were few, they were the picked men of the guard, and every one of them felt himself as justly entitled to an opinion concerning the position of the new king, as though he were at least a general.

But Darius allowed no gossiping slaves nor wrangling soldiers in his own dwelling. There all was silent and apparently deserted, and thither he led Zoroaster again. The young warrior was astonished at the way in which the king moved about unattended, as carelessly as though he were a mere soldier himself; he was not yet accustomed to the restless independence of character, to the unceasing activity and perfect personal fearlessness of the young Darius. It was hard to realise that this simple, hard-handed, outspoken man was the Great King, and occupied the throne of the magnificent and stately Cyrus, who never stirred abroad without the full state of the court about him; or that he reigned in the stead of the luxurious Cambyses, who feared to tread upon uncovered marble, or to expose himself to the draught of a staircase; and who, after seven years of caring for his body, had destroyed himself in a fit of impotent passion. Darius succeeded to the throne of Persia as a lion coming into the place of jackals, as an eagle into a nest of crows and carrion birds—untiring, violent, relentless and brave.

"Knowest thou one Phraortes, of Ecbatana?" the king asked suddenly when he was alone with Zoroaster.

"I know him," answered the prince. "A man rich, and powerful, full of vanity as a peacock, and of wiles like a serpent. Not noble. He is the son of a fish-vendor, grown rich by selling salted sturgeons in the market-place. He is also the overseer of the queen's farmlands in Media, and of the Great King's horse-breeding stables."

"Go forth and bring him to me," said the king shortly. Without a word, Zoroaster made a brief salute and turned upon his heel to go. But it was as though a man had thrust him through with a knife. The king gazed after him in admiration of his magnificent obedience.

"Stay!" he called out. "How long wilt thou be gone?"

Zoroaster turned sharply round in military fashion, as he answered:

"It is a hundred and fifty farsangs to Ecbatana. By the king's relays I can ride there in six days, and I can bring back Phraortes in six days more—if he die not of the riding," he added, with a grim smile.

"Is he old, or young? Fat, or meagre?" asked the king, laughing.

"He is a man of forty years, neither thin nor fat—a good horseman in his way, but not as we are."

"Bind him to his horse if he falls off from weariness. And tell him he is summoned to appear before me. Tell him the business brooks no delay. Auramazda be with thee and bring thee help. Go with speed."

Again Zoroaster turned and in a moment he was gone. He had sworn to be the king's faithful servant, and he would keep his oath, cost what it might, though it was bitterness to him to leave Nehushta without a word. He bethought him as he hastily put on light garments for the journey, that he might send her a letter, and he wrote a few words upon a piece of parchment, and folded it together. As he passed by the entrance of the garden on his way to the stables, he looked about for one of Nehushta's slaves; but seeing none, he beckoned to one of the Greek tirewomen, and giving her a piece of gold, bade her take the little scroll to Nehushta, the Hebrew princess, who was in the gardens. Then he went quickly on, and mounting the best horse in the king's stables, galloped at a break-neck pace down the steep incline. In five minutes he had crossed the bridge, and was speeding over the straight, dusty road toward Nineveh. In a quarter of an hour, a person watching him from the palace would have seen his flying figure disappearing as in a tiny speck of dust far out upon the broad, green plain.

But the Greek slave-woman stood with Zoroaster's letter in her hand and held the gold piece he had given her in her mouth, debating what she should do. She was one of the queen's women, as it chanced, and she immediately reflected that she might turn the writing to some better account than by delivering it to Nehushta, whom she had seen for a moment that morning as she passed, and whose dark Hebrew face displeased the frivolous Greek, for some hidden reason. She thought of giving the scroll to the queen, but then she reflected that she did not know what it contained. The words were written hastily and in the Chaldean character. Their import might displease her mistress. The woman was not a newcomer, and she knew Zoroaster's face well enough from former times; she knew also, or suspected, that the queen secretly loved him, and she argued from the fact of Zoroaster, who was dressed for a journey, sending so hastily a word to Nehushta, that he loved the Hebrew princess. Therefore, if the letter were a mere love greeting, with no name written in it, the queen might apply it to herself, and she would be pleased; whereas, if it were in any way clear that the writing was intended for Nehushta, the queen would certainly be glad that it should never be delivered. The result of this cunning argument was that the Greek woman thrust the letter into her bosom, and the gold piece into her girdle; and went to seek an opportunity of seeing the queen alone.

That day, towards evening, Atossa sat in an inner chamber before her great mirror; the table was covered with jade boxes, silver combs, bowls of golden hair-pins, little ivory instruments, and all the appurtenances of her toilet. Two or three magnificent jewels lay among the many articles of use, gleaming in the reflected light of the two tall lamps that stood on bronze stands beside her chair. She was fully attired and had dismissed her women; but she lingered a moment, poring over the little parchment scroll her chief hairdresser had slipped into her hand when they were alone for a moment. Only a black fan-girl stood a few paces behind her, and resting the stem of the long palm against one foot thrust forward, swung the broad round leaf quickly from side to side at arm's length, sending a constant stream of fresh air upon her royal mistress, just below the level of the lamps which burned steadily above.

The queen turned the small letter again in her hand, and smiled to herself as she looked into the great burnished sheet of silver that surmounted the table. With some difficulty she had mastered the contents, for she knew enough of Hebrew and of the Chaldean character to comprehend the few simple words.

"I go hence for twelve days upon the king's business. My beloved, my soul is with thy soul and my heart with thy heart. As the dove that goeth forth in the morning and returneth in the evening to his mate, so I will return soon to thee."

Atossa knew well enough that the letter had been intended for Nehushta. The woman had whispered that Zoroaster had given it to her, and Zoroaster would never have written those words to herself; or, writing anything, would not have written in the Hebrew language.

But as the queen read, her heart rose up in wrath against the Persian prince and against the woman he loved. When she had talked with him that morning, she had felt her old yearning affection rising again in her breast. She had wondered at herself, being accustomed to think that she was beyond all feeling for man, and the impression she had received from her half-hour's talk with him was so strong, that she had foolishly delayed sending her letter to Phraortes, in order to see the woman Zoroaster admired, and had, in her absence of mind, forgotten the scroll upon the seat in the corridor, and had brought herself into such desperate danger through the discovery of the missive, that she hardly yet felt safe. The king had dismissed her peremptorily from his presence while he waited for Nehushta, and she had not seen him during the rest of the day. As for Zoroaster, she had soon heard from her women that he had taken the road towards Nineveh before noon, alone and almost unarmed, mounted upon one of the fleetest horses in Persia. She had not a doubt that Darius had despatched him at once to Ecbatana to meet Phraortes, or at least to inquire into the state of affairs in the city. She knew that no one could outride

Zoroaster, and that there was nothing to be done but to await the issue. It was not possible to send a word of warning to her agent—he must inevitably take his chance, and if his conduct attracted suspicion, he would, in all probability, be at once put to death. She believed that, even in that event, she could easily clear herself; but she resolved, if possible, to warn him as soon as he reached Shushan, or even to induce the king to be absent from the palace for a few days at the time when Phraortes might be expected. There was plenty of time—at least eleven days.

Meanwhile, a desperate struggle was beginning within her, and the letter her woman had brought her hastened the conclusion to which her thoughts were rapidly tending.

She felt keenly the fact that Zoroaster, who had been so cold to her advances in former days, had preferred before her a Hebrew woman, and was now actually so deeply in love with Nehushta, that he could not leave the palace for a few days without writing her a word of love—he, who had never loved any one! She fiercely hated this dark woman, who was preferred before her by the man she secretly loved, and whom the king had brutally declared to be the most beautiful woman in the world. She longed for her destruction as she had never longed for anything in her life. Her whole soul rose in bitter resentment; not only did Zoroaster love this black-eyed, dark-browed child of captivity, but the king, who had always maintained that Atossa was unequalled in the world, even when he coldly informed her that he would never trust her, now dared to say before Zoroaster, almost before Nehushta herself, that the princess was the more beautiful of the two. The one man wounded her in her vanity, the other in her heart.

It would not be possible at present to be revenged upon the king. There was little chance of eluding his sleepless vigilance, or of leading him into any rash act of self-destruction. Besides, she knew him too well not to understand that he was the only man alive who could save Persia from further revolutions, and keep the throne against all comers. She loved power and the splendour of her royal existence, perhaps more than she loved Zoroaster. The idea of another change in the monarchy was not to be thought of, now that Darius had subdued Babylon. She had indeed a half-concerted plan with Phraortes to seize the power in Media in case the king were defeated in Babylonia, and the scroll she had so imprudently forgotten that very morning was merely an order to lay aside all such plans for the present, since the king had returned in triumph.

As far as her conscience was concerned, Atossa would as soon have overthrown and murdered the king to gratify the personal anger she felt against him at the present moment, as she would have wrecked the universe to possess a jewel she fancied. There existed in her mind no idea of proportion between the gratification of her passions and the means she might employ thereto; provided one gratification did not interfere with another which she always saw beyond. Nothing startled her on account of its mere magnitude; no plan was rejected by her merely because it implied ruin to a countless number of human beings who were useless to her. She coldly calculated the amount of satisfaction she could at any time obtain for her wishes and desires, so as not to prejudice the gratification of all the possible passions she might hereafter experience.

As for injuring Zoroaster, she would not have thought of it. She loved him in a way peculiar to herself, but it was love, nevertheless,—and she had no idea of wreaking her disappointment upon the object on which she had set her heart. As a logical consequence, she determined to turn all her anger against Nehushta, and she pictured to herself the delicious pleasure of torturing the young princess's jealousy to desperation. To convince Nehushta that Zoroaster was deceiving her, and really loved herself, the queen; to force Zoroaster into some position where he must either silently let Nehushta believe that he was attached to Atossa, or, as an alternative, betray the king's secrets by speaking the truth; to let Nehushta's vanity be flattered by the king's admiration,—nay, even to force her into a marriage with Darius, and then by suffering her again to fall into her first love for Zoroaster, bring her to a public disgrace by suddenly unmasking her to the king—to accomplish these things surely and quickly, reserving for herself the final delight of scoffing at her worsted rival—all this seemed to Atossa to constitute a plan at once worthy of her profound and scheming intelligence, and most sweetly satisfactory to her injured vanity and rejected love.

It would be hard for her to see Nehushta married to the king, and occupying the position of chief favourite even for a time. But the triumph would be the sweeter when Nehushta was finally overthrown, and meanwhile there would be much daily delight in tormenting the princess's jealousy. Chance, or rather the cunning of her Greek tirewoman, had thrown a weapon in her way which could easily be turned into an instrument of torture, and as she sat before her mirror, she twisted and untwisted the little bit of parchment, and smiled to herself, a sweet bright smile—and leaned her head back to the pleasant breeze of the fan.

CHAPTER IX

The noonday air was hot and dry in the garden of the palace, but in the graceful marble pavilion there was coolness and the sound of gently plashing water. Rose-trees and climbing plants screened the sunlight from the long windows, and gave a soft green tinge to the eight-sided hall, where a fountain played in the midst, its little jet falling into a basin hollowed in the floor. On the rippling surface a few water-lilies swayed gently with the constant motion, anchored by their long stems to the bottom. All was cool and quiet and restful, and Nehushta stood looking at the fountain.

She was alone and very unhappy. Zoroaster had left the palace without a word to her, and she knew only by the vague reports her slaves brought her, that he was gone for many days. Her heart sank at the thought of all that might happen before he returned, and the tears stood in her eyes.

"Are you here alone, dear princess?" said a soft, clear voice behind her. Nehushta started, as though something had stung her, as she recognised Atossa's tones. There was nothing of her assumed cordiality of the previous day as she answered. She was too unhappy, too weary of the thought that her lover was gone, to be able to act a part, or pretend a friendliness she did not feel.

"Yes—I am alone," she said quietly.

"So am I," answered Atossa, her blue eyes sparkling with the sunshine she brought in with her, and all her wonderful beauty beaming, as it were, with an overflowing happiness. "The ladies of the court are gone in state to the city, in the Great King's train, and you and I are alone in the palace. How deliciously cool it is in here."

She sat down upon a heap of cushions by one of the screened windows and contemplated Nehushta, who still stood by the fountain.

"You look sad—and tired, dearest Nehushta," said she presently. "Indeed you must not be sad here— nobody is sad here!"

"I am sad," repeated Nehushta, in a dreary, monotonous way, as though scarcely conscious of what she was saying. There was a moment's silence before Atossa spoke again.

"Tell me what it is," she said at last, in persuasive accents. "Tell me what is the matter. It may be that you lack something—that you miss something you were used to in Ecbatana. Will you not tell me, dearest?"

"Tell you what?" asked Nehushta, as though she had not heard.

"Tell me what it is that makes you sad," repeated the queen.

"Tell you?" exclaimed the princess, suddenly looking up, with flashing eyes, "tell you? oh no!"

Atossa looked a little sadly at Nehushta, as though hurt at the want of confidence she showed. But the Hebrew maiden turned away and went and looked through the hanging plants at the garden without. Then Atossa rose softly and came and stood behind her, and put her arm about her, and let her own fair cheek rest against the princess's dark face. Nehushta said nothing, but she trembled, as though something she hated were touching her.

"Is it because your friend has gone away suddenly?" asked Atossa almost in a whisper, with the sweetest accent of sympathy. Nehushta started a little.

"No!" she answered, almost fiercely. "Why do you say that?"

"Only—he wrote me a little word before he went. I thought you might like to know he was safe," replied the queen, gently pressing her arm about Nehushta's slender waist.

"Wrote to you?" repeated the princess, in angry surprise.

"Yes, dearest," answered the queen, looking down in well-feigned embarrassment. "I would not have told you, only I thought you would wish to hear of him. If you like, I will read you a part of what he says," she added, producing from her bosom the little piece of parchment carefully rolled together.

It was more than Nehushta could bear. Her olive skin turned suddenly pale, and she tore herself away from the queen.

"Oh no! no! I will not hear it! Leave me in peace—for your gods' sake, leave me in peace!"

Atossa drew herself up and stared coldly at Nehushta, as though she were surprised beyond measure and deeply offended.

"Truly, I need not be told twice to leave you in peace," she said proudly. "I thought to comfort you, because I saw you were sad—even at the expense of my own feelings. I will leave you now—but I bear no malice against you. You are very, very young, and very, very foolish."

Atossa shook her head, thoughtfully, and swept from the pavilion in stately and offended dignity. But as she walked alone through the garden, she smiled to herself and softly hummed a merry melody she had heard from an Egyptian actor on the previous evening. Darius had brought a company of Egyptians from Babylon, and after the banquet, had commanded that they should perform their music, and dancing, and mimicry, for the amusement of the assembled court.

Atossa's sweet voice echoed faintly among the orange trees and the roses, as she went towards the palace, and the sound of it came distantly to Nehushta's ears. She stood for a while where the queen had left her, her face pale and her hands wringing together; and then, with a sudden impulse, she went and threw herself upon the floor, and buried her head in the deep, soft cushions. Her hands wandered in the wealth of her black hair, and her quick, hot tears stained the delicate silk of the pillows.

How could he? How was it possible? He said he loved her, and now, when he was sent away for many days, his only thought had been to write to the queen—not to herself! An agony of jealousy overwhelmed her, and she could have torn out her very soul, and trampled her own heart under her feet in her anger. Passionately she clasped her hands to her temples; her head seemed splitting with a new and dreadful pain that swallowed all her thoughts for a moment, until the cold weight seemed again to fall upon her breast and all her passion gushed out in abundant tears. Suddenly a thought struck her. She roused herself, leaning upon one hand, and stared vacantly a moment at her small gilded shoe which had fallen from her bare foot upon the marble pavement. She absently reached forward and took the thing in her hand, and gravely contemplated the delicate embroidery and thick gilding, through her tears,—as one will do a foolish and meaningless thing in the midst of a great sorrow.

Was it possible that the queen had deceived her? How she wished she had let her read the writing as she had offered to do. She did not imagine at first that the letter was for herself and had gone astray. But she thought the queen might easily have pretended to have received something, or had even scratched a few words upon a bit of parchment, meaning to pass it off upon her as a letter from Zoroaster. She longed to possess the thing and to judge of it with her own eyes. It would hardly be possible to say whether it were written by him or not, as far as the handwriting was concerned; but Nehushta was sure she should recognise some word, some turn of language that would assure her that it was his. She could almost have risen and gone in search of the queen at once, to prove the lie upon her—to challenge her to show the writing. But her pride forbade her. She had been so weak—she should not have let Atossa see, even for a moment, that she was hurt, not even that she loved Zoroaster. She had tried to conceal her feelings, but Atossa had gone too far, had tortured her beyond all endurance, and she knew that, even if she had known what to expect, she could not have easily borne the soft, infuriating, deadly, caressing, goading taunts of that fair, cruel woman.

Then again, the whole possibility of Zoroaster's unfaithfulness came and took shape before her. He had known and loved Atossa of old, perhaps, and now the old love had risen up and killed the new—he had sworn so truly under the ivory moonlight in Ecbatana. And yet—he had written to this other woman and not to her. Was it true? Was it Atossa's cruel lie? In a storm of doubt and furious passion, her tears welled forth again; and once more she hid her face in the pale yellow cushions, and her whole beautiful body trembled and was wrung with her sobs.

Suddenly she was aware that some one entered the little hall and stood beside her. She dared not look up at first; she was unstrung and wretched in her grief and anger, and it was the strong, firm tread of a man. The footsteps ceased, and the intruder, whoever he might be, was standing still; she took courage and looked quickly up. It was the king himself. Indeed, she might have known that no other man would dare to penetrate into the recesses of the garden set apart for the ladies of the palace.

Darius stood quietly gazing at her with an expression of doubt and curiosity, that was almost amusing, on his stern, dark face. Nehushta was frightened, and sprang to her feet with the graceful quickness of a startled deer. She was indolent by nature, but as swift as light when she was roused by fear or excitement.

"Are you so unhappy in my palace?" asked Darius gently. "Why are you weeping? Who has hurt you?"

Nehushta turned her face away and dashed the tears from her eyes, while her cheeks flushed hotly.

"I am not weeping—no one—has hurt me," she answered, in a voice broken rather by embarrassment and annoyance, than by the sorrow she had nearly forgotten in her sudden astonishment at being face to face with the king.

Darius smiled, and almost laughed, as he stroked his thick beard with his broad brown hand.

"Princess," he said, "will you sit down again? I will deliver you a discourse upon the extreme folly of ever telling"—he hesitated—"of saying anything which is not precisely true."

There was something so simple and honest in his manner of speaking, that Nehushta almost smiled through her half-dried tears as she sat upon the cushions at the king's feet. He himself sat down upon the broad marble seat that ran round the eight-sided little building, and composing his face to a serious expression, that was more than half-assumed, began to deliver his lecture.

"I take it for granted that when one tells a lie, he expects to be believed. There must, then, be some thing or circumstance which can help to make his lies credible. Now, my dear princess, in the present instance, while I was looking you in the face and counting the tears upon your very beautiful cheeks, you deliberately told me that you were not weeping. There was, therefore, not even the shadow of a thing, or circumstance which could make what you said credible. It is evident that what you said was not true. Is it not so?"

Nehushta could not help smiling as she looked up and saw the kindly light in the king's dark eyes. She thought she understood he was amusing her for the sake of giving her time to collect herself, and in spite of the determined intention of marrying her he had so lately expressed, she felt safe with him.

"The king lives for ever," she answered, in the set phrase of assent common at the court.

"It is very probable," replied Darius gravely. "So many people say so, that I should have to believe all mankind liars if that were not true. But I must return to your own particular case. It would have been easy for you not to have said what you did. I must therefore suppose that in going out of the way to make an attempt to deceive me in the face of such evidence—by saying you were not weeping when the tears were actually falling from those very soft eyes of yours—you had an object to gain. Men employ truth and falsehood for much the same reason: A man who does not respect truth will, therefore, lie when he can hope to gain more by it. The man who lies expects to gain something by his lie, and the man who tells the truth hopes that, in so doing, he will establish himself a credit which he can use upon future occasions. But the object is the same. Tell me, therefore, princess, what did you hope to gain by trying to deceive me?" Darius laughed as he concluded his argument and looked at Nehushta to see what she would say—Nehushta laughed also, she could hardly tell why. The king's brilliant, active humour was catching. She reached out and thrust her foot into the little slipper that still lay beside her, before she answered.

"What I said was true in one way and not in another," she said. "I had been crying bitterly, but I stopped when I heard the king come and stand beside me. So it was only the tears the king saw and not the weeping. As for the object,"—she laughed a little,—"it was, perhaps, that I might gain time to dry my eyes."

Darius shifted his position a little.

"I know," he said gravely. "And I know why you were weeping, and it is my fault. Will you forgive me, princess? I am a hasty man, not accustomed to think twice when I give my commands."

Nehushta looked up suddenly with an expression of inquiry.

"I sent him away very quickly," continued the king. "If I had thought, I would have told him to come and bid you farewell. He would not have willingly gone without seeing you—it was my fault. He will return in twelve days."

Nehushta was silent and bit her lip as the bitter thought arose in her heart that it was not alone Zoroaster's sudden departure that had pained her. Then it floated across her mind that the king had purposely sent away her lover in order that he might himself try to win her heart.

"Why did you send him—and not another?" she asked, without looking up, and forgetting all formality of speech.

"Because he is the man of all others whom I can trust, and I needed a faithful messenger," answered Darius, simply.

Nehushta gazed into the king's face searching for some sign there, but he had spoken earnestly enough.

"I thought—" she began, and then stopped short, blushing crimson.

"You thought," answered Darius, "that I had sent him away never to return because I desire you for my wife. It was natural, but it was unjust. I sent him because I was obliged to do so. If you wish it, I will leave you now, and I will promise you that I will not look upon your face till Zoroaster returns."

Nehushta looked down and she still blushed. She could hardly believe her ears.

"Indeed," she faltered, "it were perhaps—best—I mean—" she could not finish the sentence. Darius rose quietly from his seat:

"Farewell, princess; it shall be as you desire," he said gravely, and strode towards the door. His face was pale and his lips set tight.

Nehushta hesitated and then, in a moment, she comprehended the whole nobility of soul of the young king,—a man at whose words the whole land trembled, who crushed his enemies like empty egg-shells beneath his feet, and yet who, when he held the woman he loved completely in his power, refused, even for a moment, to intrude his presence upon her against her wish.

She sprang from her seat and ran to him, and kneeled on one knee and took his hand. He did not look at her, but his own hand trembled violently in hers, and he made as though he would lift her to her feet.

"Nay," she cried, "let not my lord be angry with his handmaiden! Let the king grant me my request, for he is the king of men and of kings!" In her sudden emotion she spoke once more in the form of a humble subject addressing her sovereign.

"Speak, princess," answered Darius. "If it be possible, I will grant your request."

"I would—" she stopped, and again the generous blood overspread her dark cheek. "I would—I know not what I would, saving to thank thee for thy goodness and kindness—I was unhappy, and thou hast comforted me. I meant not that it was best that I should not look upon the king's face." She spoke the last words in so low a tone as she bent her head, that Darius could scarcely hear them. But his willing ears interpreted rightly what she said, and he understood.

"Shall I come to you to-morrow, princess, at the same hour?" he asked, almost humbly.

"Nay, the king knoweth that the garden is ever full of the women of the court," said Nehushta, hesitating; for she thought that it would be a very different matter to be seen from a distance by all the ladies of the palace in conversation with the king.

"Do not fear," answered Darius. "The garden shall be yours. There are other bowers of roses in Shushan whither the women can go. None but you shall enter here, so long as it be your pleasure. Farewell, I will come to you to-morrow at noon."

He turned and looked into her eyes, and then she took his hand and silently placed it upon her forehead in thanks. In a moment he was gone and she could hear his quick tread upon the marble of the steps outside, and in the path through the roses. When she knew that he was out of sight, Nehushta went out and stood in the broad blaze of the noonday sun. She passed her hand over her forehead, as though she had been dazed. It seemed as though a change had come over her and she could not understand it.

In the glad security of being alone, she ran swiftly down one of the paths, and across by another. Then she stopped short and bent down a great bough of blooming roses and buried her beautiful dark face in the sweet leaves and smelled the perfume, and laughed.

"Oh! I am so happy!" she cried aloud. But her face suddenly became grave, as she tried to understand what she felt. After all, Zoroaster was only gone for twelve days, and meanwhile she had secured her liberty, the freedom of wandering all day in the beautiful gardens, and she could dream of him to her heart's content. And the letter? It was a forgery, of course. That wicked queen loved Zoroaster and wished to make Nehushta give him up! Perhaps she might tell the king something of it when he came on the next day. He would be so royally angry! He would so hate the lie! And yet, in some way, it seemed to her that she could not tell Darius of this trouble. He had been so kind, so gentle, as though he had been her brother, instead of the Great King himself, who bore life and death in his right hand and his left, whose shadow was a terror to the world already, and at whose brief, imperious word a nation rose to arms and victory. Was this the terrible Darius? The man who had slain the impostor with his own sword?

who had vanquished rebel Babylon in a few days and brought home four thousand captives at his back? He was as gentle as a girl, this savage warrior—but when she recalled his features, she remembered the stern look that came into his face when he was serious, she grew thoughtful and wandered slowly down the path, biting a rose-leaf delicately with her small white teeth and thinking many things; most of all, how she might be revenged upon Atossa for what she had suffered that morning.

But Atossa herself was enjoying at that very moment the triumph of the morning and quietly planning how she might continue the torment she had imagined for Nehushta, without allowing its cruelty to diminish, while keeping herself amused and occupied to the fullest extent until Zoroaster should return. It was not long before she learned from her chief tirewoman that the king had been in the pavilion of the garden with Nehushta that morning, and it at once occurred to her that, if the king returned on the following day, it would be an easy thing to appear while he was with the princess, and by veiled words and allusions to Zoroaster, to make her rival suffer the most excruciating torments, which she would be forced to conceal from the king.

But, at the same time, the news gave her cause for serious thought. She had certainly not intended that Nehushta should be left alone for hours with Darius. She knew indeed that the princess loved Zoroaster, but she could not conceive that any woman should be insensible to the consolation the Great King could offer. If affairs took such a turn, she fully intended to allow the king to marry Nehushta, while she confidently believed it in her power to destroy her just when she had reached the summit of her ambition.

It chanced that the king chose that day to eat his evening meal in the sole company of Atossa, as he sometimes did when weary of the court ceremony. When, therefore, they reclined at sundown upon a small secluded terrace of the upper story, Atossa found an excellent opportunity of discussing Nehushta and her doings.

Darius lay upon a couch on one side of the low table, and Atossa was opposite to him. The air was dry and intensely hot, and on each side two black fan-girls plied their palm-leaves silently with all their might. The king lay back upon his cushions, his head uncovered, and all his shaggy curls of black hair tossed behind him, his broad, strong hand circling a plain goblet of gold that stood beside him on the table. For once, he had laid aside his breastplate, and a vest of white and purple fell loosely over his tunic; but his sword of keen Indian steel lay within reach upon the floor.

Atossa had raised herself upon her elbow, and her clear blue eyes were fixed upon the king's face, thoughtfully, as though expecting that he would say something. Contrary to all custom, she wore a Greek tunic with short sleeves caught at the shoulders by golden buckles, and her fair hair was gathered into a heavy knot, low down, behind her head. Her dazzling arms and throat were bare, but above her right elbow she wore a thick twisted snake of gold, her only ornament.

"The king is not athirst to-night," said Atossa at last, watching the full goblet that he grasped, but did not raise.

"I am not always thirsty," answered Darius moodily. "Would you have me always drunk, like a Babylonian dog?"

"No; nor always sober, like a Persian captain."

"What Persian captain?" asked the king, suddenly looking at her and knitting his brows.

"Why, like him, whom, for his sobriety you have sent to-day on the way to Nineveh," answered Atossa.

"I have sent no one to Nineveh to-day."

"To Ecbatana then, to inquire whether I told you the truth about my poor servant Phraortes—Fravartish, as you call him," said the queen, with a flash of spite in her blue eyes.

"I assure you," answered the king, laughing, "that it is solely on account of your remarkable beauty that I have not had you strangled. So soon as you grow ugly you shall surely die. It is very unwise of me, as it is!"

The queen, too, laughed, a low, silvery laugh.

"I am greatly indebted for my life," said she. "I am very beautiful, I am aware, but I am no longer the most beautiful woman in the world." She spoke without a trace of annoyance in her voice or face, as though it were a good jest.

"No," said Darius, thoughtfully. "I used to think that you were. It is in the nature of man to change his opinion. You are, nevertheless, very beautiful—I admire your Greek dress."

"Shall I send my tirewoman with one like it to Nehushta?" inquired Atossa, raising her delicate eyebrows, with a sweet smile.

"You will not need to improve her appearance in order that she may find favour in my eyes," answered Darius, laughing. "But the jest is good. You would rather send her an Indian snake than an ornament."

"Yes," returned the queen, who understood the king's strange character better than any one. "You cannot in honesty expect me not to hate a woman whom you think more beautiful than me! It would hardly be natural. It is unfortunate that she should prefer the sober Persian captain to the king himself."

"It is unfortunate—yes—fortunate for you, however."

"I mean, it will chafe sadly upon you when you have married her," said Atossa, calmly.

Darius raised the goblet he still held and setting it to his lips drank it at a draught. As he replaced it on the table, Atossa rose swiftly, and with her own hands refilled it from a golden ewer. The wine was of Shiraz, dark and sweet and strong. The king took her small white hand in his, as she stood beside him, and looked at it.

"It is a beautiful hand," he said. "Nehushta's fingers are a trifle shorter than yours—a little more pointed—a little less grasping. Shall I marry Nehushta, or not?" He looked up as he asked the question, and he laughed.

"No," answered Atossa, laughing too.

"Shall I marry her to Zoroaster?"

"No," she answered again, but her laugh was less natural.

"What shall I do with her?" asked the king.

"Strangle her!" replied Atossa, with a little fierce pressure on his hand as he held hers, and without the least hesitation.

"There would be frequent sudden deaths in Persia, if you were king," said Darius.

"It seems to me there are enough slain, as it is," answered the queen. "There are, perhaps, one—or two—"

Suddenly the king's face grew grave, and he dropped her hand.

"Look you!" he said, "I love jesting. But jest not overmuch with me. Do no harm to Nehushta, or I will make an end of your jesting for ever, by sure means. That white throat of yours would look ill with a bow-string about it."

The queen bit her lip. The king seldom spoke to her in earnest, and she was frightened.

On the following day, when she went to the garden, two tall spearmen guarded the entrance, and as she was about to go in, they crossed their lances over the marble door and silently barred the way.

CHAPTER X

Atossa started back in pure astonishment and stared for a moment at the two guards, looking from one to the other, and trying to read their stolid faces. Then she laid her hand on their spears, and would have pushed them aside; but she could not.

"Whose hounds are ye?" she said angrily. "Know ye not the queen? Make way!"

But the two strong soldiers neither answered nor removed their weapons from before the door.

"Dog-faced slaves!" she said between her teeth. "I will crucify you both before sundown!" She turned and went away, but she was glad that no one was there in the narrow vestibule before the garden to see her discomfiture. It was the first time in her life she had ever been resisted by an inferior, and she could not bear it easily. But when she discovered, half an hour later, that the guards were obeying the Great King's orders, she bowed her head silently and went to her apartments to consider what she should do.

She could do nothing. There was no appeal against the king's word. He had distinctly commanded that no one save Nehushta, not even Atossa herself, was to be allowed to enter; he had placed the guards there himself the previous day, and had himself given the order.

For eleven days the door was barred; but Atossa did not again attempt to enter. Darius would have visited roughly such an offence, and she knew how delicate her position was. She resigned herself and occupied her mind with other things. Daily, an hour before noon, Nehushta swept proudly through the gate, and disappeared among the roses and myrtles of the garden; and daily, precisely as the sun reached the meridian, the king went in between the spearmen, and disappeared in like manner.

Darius had grown so suddenly stern and cold in manner towards the queen, that she dared not even mention the subject of the garden to him, fearing a sadden outburst of his anger, which would surely put an end to her existence in the court, and very likely to her life.

As for Nehushta, she had plentiful cause for reflection and much time for dreaming. If the days were not happy, they were at least made bearable for her by the absolute liberty she enjoyed. The king would have given her slaves and jewels and rich gifts without end, had she been willing to accept them. She said she had all she needed—and she said it a little proudly; only the king's visits grew to be the centre of the day, and each day the visit lengthened, till it came to be nearly evening when Darius issued from the gate.

She always waited for him in the eight-sided pavilion, and as their familiarity grew, the king would not even permit her to rise when he came, nor to use any of those forms of the court speech which were so distasteful to him. He simply sat himself down beside her, and talked to her and listened to her answers, as though he were one of his own subjects, no more hampered by the cares and state of royalty than any soldier in the kingdom.

It was a week since Zoroaster had mounted to ride to Ecbatana, and Darius sat as usual upon the marble bench by the side of Nehushta, who rested among the cushions, talking now without constraint upon all matters that chanced to occur as subjects of conversation. She thought Darius was more silent than usual, and his dark face was pale. He seemed weary, as though from some great struggle, and presently Nehushta stopped speaking and waited to see whether the king would say anything.

During the silence nothing was heard saving the plash of the little fountain, and the low soft ripple of the tiny waves that rocked themselves against the edge of the basin.

"Do you know, Nehushta," he said at last, in a weary voice, "that I am doing one of the worst actions of my life?"

Nehushta started, and the shadows in her face grew darker.

"Say rather the kindest action you ever did," she murmured.

"If it is not bad, it is foolish," said Darius, resting his chin upon his hand and leaning forward. "I would rather it were foolish than bad—I fear me it is both."

Nehushta could guess well enough what it was he would say. She knew she could have turned the subject, or laughed, or interrupted him in many ways; but she did none of these things. An indescribable longing seized her to hear him say that he loved her. What could it matter? He was so loyal and good that he could never be more than a friend. He was the king of the world—had he not been honest and kind, he would have needed no wooing to do as he pleased to do, utterly and entirely. A word from his lips and the name of Zoroaster would be but the memory of a man dead; and again a word, and

Nehushta would be the king's wife! What need had he of concealment, or of devious ways? He was the king of the earth, whose shadow was life and death, whose slightest wish was a law to be enforced by hundreds of thousands of warriors! There was nothing between him and his desires—nothing but that inborn justice and truth, in which he so royally believed. Nehushta felt that she could trust him, and she longed—out of mere curiosity, she thought—to hear him speak words of love to her. It would only be for a moment—they would be so soon spoken; and at her desire, he would surely not speak them again. It seemed so sweet, she knew not why, to make this giant of despotic power do as she pleased; to feel that she could check him, or let him speak—him whom all obeyed and feared, as they feared death itself.

She looked up quietly, as she answered:

"How can it be either bad or foolish of you to make others so happy?"

"It seems as though it could be neither—and yet, all my reason tells me it is both," replied the king earnestly. "Here I sit beside you, day after day, deceiving myself with the thought that I am making your time pass pleasantly till—"

"There is not any deception in that," interrupted Nehushta gently. Somehow she did not wish him to pronounce Zoroaster's name. "I can never tell you how grateful I am—"

"It is I who am grateful," interrupted the king in his turn. "It is I who am grateful that I am allowed to be daily with you, and that you speak with me, and seem glad when I come—" He hesitated and stopped.

"What is there that is bad and foolish in that?" asked Nehushta, with a sudden smile, as she looked up into his face.

"There is more than I like to think," answered the king. "You say the time passes pleasantly for you. Do you think it is less pleasant for me?" His voice sank to a deep, soft tone, as he continued: "I sit here day after day, and day after day I love you more and more. I love you—where is the use of concealing that—if I could conceal it? You know it. Perhaps you pity me, for you do not love me. You pity me who hold the whole earth under my feet as an Egyptian juggler stands upon a ball, and rolls it whither he will." He ceased suddenly.

"Indeed I would that you did not love me," said Nehushta very gravely. She looked down. The pleasure of hearing the king's words was indeed exquisite, and she feared that her eyes might betray her. But she did not love him. She wondered what he would say next.

"You might as well wish that dry pastures should not burn when the sun shines on them, and there is no rain," he answered with a passing bitterness. "It is at least a satisfaction that my love does not harm you—that you are willing to have me for your friend—"

"Willing! Your friendship is almost the sweetest thing I know," exclaimed the princess. The king's eyes flashed darkly.

"Almost! Yes, truly—my friendship and another man's love are the sweetest things! What would my friendship be without his love? By Auramazda and the six Amshaspands of Heaven, I would it were my love and his friendship! I would that Zoroaster were the king, and I Zoroaster, the king's servant! I would give all Persia and Media, Babylon and Egypt, and all the uttermost parts of my kingdom, to hear your sweet voice say: 'Darius, I love thee!' I would give my right hand, I would give my heart from my breast and my soul from my body—my life and my strength, and my glory and my kingdom would I give to hear you say: 'Come, my beloved, and put thine arms about me!' Ah, child! you know not what my love is—how it is higher than the heavens in worshipping you, and broader than the earth to be filled with you, and deeper than the depths of the sea, to change not, but to abide for you always."

The king's voice was strong, and the power of his words found wings in it, and seemed to fly forth irresistibly with a message that demanded an answer. Nehushta regretted within herself that she had let him speak—but for all the world she could not have given up the possession of the words he had spoken. She covered her eyes with one hand and remained silent—for she could say nothing. A new emotion had got possession of her, and seemed to close her lips.

"You are silent," continued the king. "You are right. What should you answer me? My voice sounds like the raving of a madman, chained by a chain that he cannot break. If I had the strength of the mountains, I could not move you. I know it. All things I have but this—this love of yours that you have given to another. I would I had it! I should have the strength to surpass the deeds of men, had I your love! Who is this whom you love? A captain? A warrior? I tell you because you have so honoured him, so raised him upon the throne of your heart, I will honour him too, and I will raise him above all men, and all the nation shall bow before him. I will make a decree that he shall be worshipped as a god—this man whom you have made a god of by your love. I will build a great temple for you two, and I will go up with all the people, and fall down and bow before you, and worship you, and love you with every sinew and bone of my body, and with every hope and joy and sorrow of my soul. He whom you love shall ask, and whatsoever he asks I will give to him and to you. There shall not be anything left in the whole world that you desire, but I will give it to you. Am I not the king of the whole earth—the king of all living things but you?"

Darius breathed savagely hard through his clenched teeth, and rising suddenly, paced the pavement between Nehushta and the fountain. She was silent still, overcome with a sort of terror at his words—words, every one of which he was able to fulfil, if he so chose. Presently he stood still before her.

"Said I not well, that I rave as a madman—that I speak as a fool without understanding? What can I give you that you want? Or what thing can I devise that you have need of? Have you not all that the world holds for mortal woman and living man? Do you not love, and are you not loved in return? Have you not all—all—all? Ah! woe is me that I am lord over the nations, and have not a drop of the waters of peace wherewith to quench the thirst of my tormented soul! Woe is me that I rule the world and trample the whole earth beneath my feet, and cannot have the one thing that all the earth holds which is good! Woe is me, Nehushta, that you have cruelly stolen my peace from me, and I find it not—nor shall find it for evermore!"

The strong dark man stood wringing his hands together; his face was pale as the dead, his black eyes were blazing with a mad fire. Nehushta dared not look on the tempest she had roused, but she trembled and clasped her hands to her breast and looked down.

"Nay, you are right," he cried bitterly. "Answer me nothing, for you can have nothing to answer! Is it your fault that I am mad? Or is it your doing that I love you so? Has any one sinned in this? I have seen you—I saw you for a brief moment standing in the door of your tent—and seeing, I loved you, and love you, and shall love you till the heavens are rolled together and the scroll of all death is full! There is nothing, nothing that you can say or do. It is not your fault—it is not your sin; but it is by you and through you that I am undone,—broken as the tree in the storm of the mountains, burned up and parched as the beast perishing in the sun of the desert for lack of water, torn asunder and rent into pieces as the rope that breaks at the well! By you, and for you, and through you, I am ruined and lost—lost—lost for ever in the hell of my wretched greatness, in the immeasurable death of my own horrible despair!"

With a wild movement of agony, Darius fell at Nehushta's feet, prostrate upon the marble floor, and buried his face in the skirts of her mantle, utterly over-mastered and broken down by the tumult of his passion.

Nehushta was not heartless. Of a certainty she would have pitied any one in such distress and grief, even had the cause thereof come less near to herself. But, in all the sudden emotion she felt, the pity, the fear, and the self-reproach, there was joined a vague feeling that no man ever spoke as this man, that no lover ever poured forth such abundant love before, and in the dim suspicion of something greater than she had ever known, her fear and her pity grew stronger, and strove with each other.

At first she could not speak, but she put forth her delicate hand and laid it tenderly on the king's thick black hair, as gently as a mother might soothe a passionate child; and he suffered it to rest there. And presently she raised his head and laid it in her lap, and smoothed his forehead with her soft fingers, and spoke to him.

"You make me very sad," she almost whispered. "I would that you might be loved as you deserve love—that one more worthy than I might give you all I cannot give."

He opened his dark eyes that were now dull and weary, and he looked up to her face.

"There is none more worthy than you," he answered in low and broken tones.

"Hush," she said gently, "there are many. Will you forgive me—and forget me? Will you blot out this hour from your remembrance, and go forth and do those great and noble deeds which you came into the world to perform? There is none greater than you, none nobler, none more generous."

Darius lifted his head from her knee, and sprang to his feet.

"I will do all things, but I will not forget," he said. "I will do the great and the good deeds,—for you. I will be generous, for you; noble, for you; while the world lasts my deeds shall endure; and with them, the memory that they were done for you! Grant me only one little thing."

"Ask anything—everything," answered Nehushta, in troubled tones.

"Nehushta, you know how truly I love you—nay, I will not be mad again; fear not! Tell me this—tell me that if you had not loved Zoroaster, you would have loved me."

Nehushta blushed deeply and then turned pale. She rose to her feet, and took the king's outstretched hands.

"Indeed, indeed, you are most worthy of love—Darius, I could have loved you well." Her voice was very low, and the tears stood in her eyes.

"The grace of the All-Wise God bless thee!" cried the king, and it was as though a sudden bright light shone upon his face. Then he kissed her two hands fervently, and with one long look into her sorrowful eyes, he turned and left her.

But no man saw the king that day, nor did any know where he was, saving the two spearmen who stood at the door of his chamber. Within, he lay upon his couch, dry-eyed and stark, staring at the painted carvings of the ceiling.

CHAPTER XI

The time passed, and it was eleven days since Zoroaster had set out. The king and Nehushta had continued to meet in the garden as before, and neither had ever referred to the day when the torrent of his heart had been suddenly let loose. The hours sped quietly and swiftly, without any event of importance. Only the strange bond, half friendship and half love, had grown stronger than before; and Nehushta wondered how it was that she could love two men so well, and yet so differently. Indeed they were very different men. She loved Zoroaster, and yet it sometimes seemed as though he would more properly have filled the place of a friend than of a lover. Darius she had accepted as her friend, but there were moments when she almost forgot that he was not something more. She tried to think of her meeting with Zoroaster, whether it would be like former meetings,—whether her heart would beat more strongly, or not beat at all when her lips touched his as of old. Her judgment was utterly disturbed and her heart no longer knew itself. She gave herself over to the pleasure of the king's society in the abandonment of the moment, half foreseeing that some great change was at hand, over which she could exercise no control.

The sun was just risen, but the bridge over the quickly flowing Choaspes was still in the shadow cast over the plain by the fortress and the palace, when two horsemen appeared upon the road from Nineveh, riding at full gallop, and, emerging from the blue mist that still lay over the meadows, crossed the bridge and continued at full speed towards the ascent to the palace.

The one rider was a dark, ill-favoured man, whose pale flaccid cheeks and drooping form betrayed the utmost fatigue. A bolster was bound across the withers of his horse and another on the croup, so that he sat as in a sort of chair, but he seemed hardly able to support himself even with this artificial assistance, and his body swayed from side to side as his horse bounded over the sharp curve at the foot of the hill. His mantle was white with dust, and the tiara upon his head was reduced to a shapeless and dusty piece of crumpled linen, while his uncurled hair and tangled beard hung forward together in disorderly and dust-clotted ringlets.

His companion was Zoroaster, fair and erect upon his horse, as though he had not ridden three hundred farsangs in eleven days. There was dust indeed upon his mantle and garments, as upon those of the man he conducted, but his long fair hair and beard blew back from his face as he held his head erect to the breeze he made in riding, and the light steel cap was bright and burnished on his forehead. A slight flush reddened his pale cheeks as he looked upward to the palace, and thought that his ride was over and his errand accomplished. He was weary, almost to death; but his frame was elastic and erect still.

As they rode up the steep, the guards at the outer gate, who had already watched them for twenty minutes as they came up the road, mere moving specks under the white mist, shouted to those within that Zoroaster was returning, and the officer of the gate went at once to announce his coming to the king. Darius himself received the message, and followed the officer down the steps to the tower of the gateway, reaching the open space within, just as the two riders galloped under the square entrance and drew rein upon the pavement of the little court. The spearmen sprang to their feet and filed into rank as the cry came down the steps that the king was approaching, and Zoroaster leaped lightly from his horse, and bid Phraortes do likewise; but the wretched Median could scarce move hand or foot without help, and would have fallen headlong, had not two stout spearmen lifted him to the ground, and held him upon his legs.

Darius marched quickly up to the pair and stood still, while Zoroaster made his brief salutation. Phraortes, who between deadly fatigue and deadly fear of his life, had no strength left in him, fell forward upon his knees as the two soldiers relaxed their hold upon his arms.

"Hail, king of kings! Live for ever!" said Zoroaster. "I have fulfilled thy bidding. He is alive."

Darius laughed grimly as he eyed the prostrate figure of the Median.

"Thou art a faithful servant, Zoroaster," he answered, "and thou ridest as the furies that pursue the souls of the wicked—as the devils of the mountains after a liar. He would not have lasted much farther, this bundle of sweating dust. Get up, fellow!" he said, touching Phraortes's head with his toe. "Thou liest grovelling there like a swine in a ditch."

The soldiers raised the exhausted man to his feet. The king turned to Zoroaster.

"Tell me, thou rider of whirlwinds," he said, laughing, "will a man more readily tell the truth, or speak lies, when he is tired?"

"A man who is tired will do whichever will procure him rest," returned Zoroaster, with a smile.

"Then I will tell this fellow that the sooner he speaks the truth the sooner he may sleep," said the king. Going near to Zoroaster, he added in an undertone: "Before thou thyself restest, go and tell the queen privately that she send away her slaves, and await me and him thou hast brought in a few minutes. This fellow must have a little refreshment, or he will die upon the steps."

Zoroaster turned and went up the broad stairs, and threaded the courts and passages, and mounted to the terrace where he had first met Atossa before the king's apartments. There was no one there, and he was about to enter under the great curtain, when the queen herself came out and met him face to face. Though it was yet very early, she was attired with more than usual care, and the faint colours of her dress and the few ornaments she wore, shone and gleamed brightly in the level beams of the morning sun. She had guessed that Zoroaster would return that day, and she was prepared for him.

As she came suddenly upon him, she gave a little cry, that might well have been feigned.

"What! Are you already returned?" she asked, and the joy her voice expressed was genuine. He looked so godlike as he stood there in the sunlight—her heart leaped for joy of only seeing him.

"Yes—I bear this message from the Great King to the queen. The Great King commands that the queen send away her slaves, and await the king and him I have brought with me, in the space of a few minutes."

"It is well," answered Atossa, "There are no slaves here and I await the king." She was silent a moment. "Are you not glad to have come back?" she asked, presently.

"Yes," said Zoroaster, whose face brightened quickly as he spoke. "I am indeed glad to be here again. Would not any one be glad to have finished such a journey?"

The queen stood with her back to the curtained doorway and could see down the whole length of the balcony to the head of the staircase. Zoroaster faced her and the door. As he spoke, Atossa's quick eyes caught sight of a figure coming quickly up the last steps of the stairway. She recognised Nehushta instantly, but no trembling of her lids or colouring of her cheek, betrayed that she had seen the approach of her enemy. She fixed her deep-blue eyes upon Zoroaster's, and gazing somewhat sadly, she spoke in low and gentle tones:

"The time has seemed long to me since you rode away, Zoroaster," she said.

Zoroaster, astonished at the manner in which she spoke, turned pale, and looked down coldly at her beautiful face. At that moment Nehushta stepped upon the smooth marble pavement of the balcony.

Still Atossa kept her eyes fixed on Zoroaster's.

"You answer me nothing?" she said in broken tones. Then suddenly, as though acting under an irresistible impulse, she threw her arms wildly about his neck and kissed him passionately again and again.

"Oh Zoroaster, Zoroaster, my beloved!" she cried, "you must never, never leave me again!" And again she kissed him, and fell forward upon his breast, holding him so tightly that, for a moment, he did not know which way to move. He put his hands upon her shoulders, to her waist—to try to push her from him. But it was in vain; she clung to him desperately and sobbed upon his breast.

In the sudden and fearful embarrassment in which he was placed, he did not hear a short, low groan far off behind him, nor the sound of quickly retreating steps upon the stairs. But Atossa heard and rejoiced fiercely; and when she looked up, Nehushta was gone, with the incurable wound in her breast.

Atossa suddenly let her arms fall from the warrior's neck, looked into his eyes once, and then, with a short, sharp cry, she buried her face in her hands and leaned back against the door-post by the heavy striped curtain.

"Oh, my God! What have I done?" she moaned.

Zoroaster stood for one moment in hesitation and doubt. It seemed as though he had received a sudden revelation of numberless things he had never understood. He spoke quietly, at last, with a great effort, and his voice sounded kindly.

"I thank the good powers that I do not love thee—and I would that thou didst not love me. For I am the Great King's servant, faithful to death—and if I loved thee I should be a liar, and a coward, and the basest of all mankind. Forget, I pray thee, that thou hast spoken, and let me depart in peace. For the Great King is at hand, and thou must not suffer that he find thee weeping, lest he think thou fearest to meet Phraortes the Median face to face. Forget, I pray thee—and forgive thy servant if he have done anything amiss."

Atossa looked up suddenly. Her eyes were bright and clear, and there was not a trace of tears in them. She laughed harshly.

"I—weep before the king! You do not know me. Go, if thou wilt. Farewell, Zoroaster,"—her voice softened a little,—"farewell. It may be that you shall live, but it may be that you shall die, because I love you."

Zoroaster bent his head in respectful homage, and turned and went his way. The queen looked after him, and as he disappeared upon the staircase, she began to smooth her head-dress and the locks of her golden hair, and for a moment, she smiled sweetly to herself.

"That was a mortal wound, well dealt," she said aloud. But as she gazed out over the city, her face grew grave and thoughtful. "But I do love him," she added softly, "I do—I do—I loved him long ago." She turned quickly, as though fearing some one had overheard her. "How foolish I am!" she exclaimed impatiently; and she turned and passed away under the heavy curtain, leaving the long balcony once more empty,—save for the rush of a swallow that now and then flew in between the pillars, and hovered for a moment high up by the cornice, and sped out again into the golden sunshine of the summer morning.

Zoroaster left Atossa with the hope of finding some means of seeing Nehushta. But it was impossible. He knew well that he could not so far presume as to go to her apartment by the lower passage where he had last seen her on the day of his departure for Ecbatana, and the slave whom he despatched from the main entrance of the women's part of the palace returned with the brief information that Nehushta was alone in her chamber, and that no one dared disturb her.

Worn out with fatigue and excitement, and scarcely able to think connectedly upon the strange event of the morning, Zoroaster wearily resigned himself to seeing Nehushta at a later hour, and entering his own cool chamber, lay down to rest. It was evening when he awoke.

Meanwhile the king commanded that Phraortes should be fed and refreshed, and immediately brought to the queen's apartment. Half an hour after Zoroaster had left her, Atossa was in the chamber which was devoted to her toilet. She sat alone before her great silver mirror, calmly awaiting the turn of events. Some instinct had told her that she would feel stronger to resist an attack in the sanctuary of her small inner room, where every object was impregnated with her atmosphere, and where the lattices of the two windows were so disposed that she would be able to see the expression of her adversaries without exposing her own face to the light.

She leaned forward and looked closely at herself in the glass, and with a delicate brush of camel's hair smoothed one eyebrow that was a little ruffled. It had touched Zoroaster's tunic when she threw herself upon his breast; she looked at herself with a genuine artistic pleasure, and smiled.

Before long she heard the sound of leathern shoes upon the pavement outside, and the curtain was suddenly lifted. Darius pushed Phraortes into the room by the shoulders and made him stand before the queen. She rose and made a salutation, and then sat down again in her carved chair. The king threw himself upon a heap of thick, hard cushions that formed a divan on one side of the room, and prepared to watch attentively the two persons before him.

Phraortes, trembling with fear and excessive fatigue, fell upon his knees before Atossa, and touched the floor with his forehead.

"Get upon thy feet, man," said the king shortly, "and render an account of the queen's affairs."

"Stay," said Atossa, calmly; "for what purpose has the Great King brought this man before me?"

"For my pleasure," answered Darius. "Speak fellow! Render thy account, and if I like not the manner of thy counting, I will crucify thee."

"The king liveth for ever," said Phraortes feebly, his flaccid cheeks trembling, as his limbs moved uneasily.

"The queen also liveth for ever," remarked Darius. "What is the state of the queen's lands at Ecbatana?"

At this question Phraortes seemed to take courage, and began a rapid enumeration of the goods, cattle and slaves.

"This year I have sown two thousand acres of wheat which will soon be ripe for the harvest. I have sown also a thousand acres with other grain. The fields of water-melons are yielding with amazing abundance since I caused the great ditches to be dug last winter towards the road. As for the fruit trees and the vinelands, they are prospering; but at present we have not had rain to push the first budding of the grapes. The olives will doubtless be very abundant this year, for last year there were few, as is the manner with that fruit. As for the yielding of these harvests of grain and wine and oil and fruit, I doubt not that the whole sales will amount to an hundred talents of gold."

"Last year they only yielded eighty-five," remarked the queen, who had affected to listen to the whole account with the greatest interest. "I am well pleased, Phraortes. Tell me of the cattle and sheep—and of the slaves; whether many have died this year."

"There are five hundred head of cattle, and one hundred calves dropped in the last two months. From the scarcity of rain this year, the fodder has been almost destroyed, and there is little hay from the winter. I have, therefore, sent great numbers of slaves with camels to the farther plains to eastward, whence they return daily with great loads of hay—of a coarse kind, but serviceable. As for the flocks, they are now pasturing for the summer upon the slopes of the Zagros mountains. There were six thousand head of sheep and two thousand head of goats at the shearing in the spring, and the wool is already sold for eight talents. As for the slaves, I have provided for them after a new fashion. There were many young men from the captives that came after the war two years ago. For these I have purchased wives of the dealers from Scythia. These Scythians sell all their women at a low price. They are hideous barbarians, speaking a strange tongue, but they are very strong and enduring, and I doubt not they will multiply exceedingly and bring large profits—"

"Thou art extraordinarily fluent in thy speech," interrupted the king. "But there are details that the queen wishes to know. Thou art aware that in a frontier country like the province of Ecbatana, it is often necessary to protect the crops and the flocks from robbers. Hast thou therefore thought of arming any of these slaves for this purpose?"

"Let not the king be angry with his servant," returned Phraortes, without hesitation. "There are many thousand soldiers of the king in Echatana, and the horsemen traverse the country continually. I have not armed any of the slaves, for I supposed we were safe in the protection of the king's men. Nevertheless, if the Great King command me—"

"Thou couldst arm them immediately, I suppose?" interrupted Darius. He watched Atossa narrowly; her face was in the shadow.

"Nay," replied Phraortes, "for we have no arms. But if the king will give us swords and spearheads—"

"To what end?" asked Atossa. She was perfectly calm since she saw that there was no fear of Phraortes making a mistake upon this vital point. "What need have I of a force to protect lands that are all within a day's journey of the king's fortress? The idea of carrying weapons would make all the slaves idle and quarrelsome. Leave them their spades and their ploughs, and let them labour while the soldiers fight. How many slaves have I now, Phraortes?"

"There were, at the last return, fourteen thousand seven hundred and fifty-three men, ten thousand two hundred and sixteen women, and not less than five thousand children. But I expect—"

"What can you do with so many?" asked Darius, turning sharply to the queen.

"Many of them work in the carpet-looms," answered Phraortes. "The queen receives fifty talents yearly from the sales of the carpets."

"All the carpets in the king's apartments are made in my looms," said Atossa, with a smile. "I am a great merchant."

"I have no doubt I paid you dearly enough for them, too," said the king, who was beginning to be weary of the examination. He had firmly expected that either the Median agent, or the queen herself, would betray some emotion at the mention of arming the slaves, for he imagined that if Atossa had really planned any outbreak, she would undoubtedly have employed the large force of men she had at her disposal, by finding them weapons and promising them their liberty in the event of success.

He was disappointed at the appearance of the man Phraortes. He had supposed him a strong, determined, man of imperious ways and turbulent instincts, who could be easily led into revolution and sedition from the side of his ambition. He saw before him the traditional cunning, quick-witted merchant of Media, pale-faced and easily frightened; no more capable of a daring stroke of usurpation than a Jewish pedlar of Babylon. He was evidently a mere tool in the hands of the queen; and Darius stamped impatiently upon the floor when he thought that he had perhaps been deceived after all—that the queen had really written to Phraortes simply on account of her property, and that there was no revolution at all to be feared. Impulsive to the last degree, when the king had read the letter to Phraortes, his first thought had been to see the man for himself, to ask him a few questions and to put him at once to death if he found him untruthful. The man had arrived, broken with excessive fatigue and weak from the fearful journey; but under the very eye of the king, he had nevertheless given a clear and concise account of himself; and, though he betrayed considerable fear, he gave no reason for supposing that what he said was not true. As for the queen, she sat calmly by, polishing her nails with a small instrument of ivory, occasionally asking a question, or making a remark, as though it were all the most natural occurrence in the world.

Darius was impetuous and fierce. His intuitive decisions were generally right, and he acted upon them instantly, without hesitation; but he had no cunning and little strategy. He was always for doing and never for waiting; and to the extreme rapidity of his movements he owed the success he had. In the first three years of his reign he fought nineteen battles and vanquished nine self-styled kings; but he never, on any occasion, detected a conspiracy, nor destroyed a revolution before it had broken out openly. He was often, therefore, at the mercy of Atossa and frequently found himself baffled by her power of concealing a subtle lie under the letter of truth, and by her supreme indifference and coldness of manner under the most trying circumstances. In his simple judgment it was absolutely impossible for any one to lie directly without betraying some hesitation, and each time he endeavoured to place Atossa in some difficult position, when she must, he thought, inevitably betray herself, he was met by her inexplicable calm; which he was forced to attribute to the fact that she was in the right—no matter how the evidence might be against her.

The king decided that he had made a mistake in the present instance and that Phraortes was innocent of any idea of revolution. He could not conceive how such a man should be capable of executing a daring stroke of policy. He determined to let him go.

"You ought to be well satisfied with the result of these accounts," he said, staring hard at Atossa. "You see you know more of your affairs, and sooner, than you could have known if you had sent your letter. Let this fellow go, and tell him to send his accounts regularly in future, or he will have the pains of riding hither in haste to deliver them. Thou mayest go now and take thy rest," he added, rising and pushing the willing Phraortes before him out of the room.

"Thou hast done well. I am satisfied with thee, Phraortes," said Atossa coldly.

Once more the beautiful queen was left alone, and once more she looked at herself in the silver mirror, somewhat more critically than before. It seemed to her as she gazed and turned first one side of her face to the light and then the other, that she was a shade paler than usual. The change would have been imperceptible to any one else, but she noticed it with a little frown of disapproval. But presently she smoothed her brow and smiled happily to herself. She had sustained a terrible danger successfully.

She had hoped to have been able to warn Phraortes how to act; but, partly because the meeting had taken place so soon after his arrival, and partly because she had employed a portion of that brief interval with Zoroaster and in the scene she had suddenly invented and acted, she had been obliged to meet her chief agent without a moment's preparation, and she knew enough of his cowardly character to fear lest he should betray her and throw himself upon the king's mercy as a reward for the information he could give. But the crucial moment had passed successfully and there was nothing more to fear. Atossa threw herself upon the couch where the king had sat, and abandoned herself to the delicious contemplation of the pain she must have given in showing herself to Nehushta in Zoroaster's arms. She was sure that as the princess could not have seen Zoroaster's face, she must have thought that it was he who was embracing the queen. She must have suffered horribly, if she really loved him!

CHAPTER XII

When Darius left the queen, he gave over the miserable Phraortes to the guards, to be cared for, and bent his steps towards the gardens. It was yet early, but he wished to be alone, and he supposed that Nehushta would come there before noon, as was her wont. Meanwhile, he wished to be free of the court and of the queen. Slowly he entered the marble gate and walked up the long walk of roses, plucking a leaf now and then, and twisting it in his fingers, scenting the fresh blossoms with an almost boyish gladness, and breathing in all the sweet warmth of the summer morning. He had made a mistake, and he was glad to be away, where he could calmly reflect upon the reason of his being deceived.

He wandered on until he came to the marble pavilion, and would have gone on to stray farther into the gardens, but that he caught sight of a woman's mantle upon the floor as he passed by the open doorway. He went up the few steps and entered.

Nehushta lay upon the marble pavement at her full length, her arms extended above her head. Her face was ghastly pale and her parted lips were white. She looked as one dead. Her white linen tiara had almost fallen from her heavy hair, and the long black locks streamed upon the stone in thick confusion. Her fingers were tightly clenched, and on her face was such an expression of agony, as Darius had never dreamed of, nor seen in those dead in battle.

The king started back in horror as he caught sight of the prostrate figure. He thought she was dead—murdered, perhaps—until, as he gazed, he saw a faint movement of breathing. Then he sprang forward, and kneeled, and raised her head upon his knee, and chafed her temples and her hands. He could reach the little fountain as he knelt, and he gathered some water in his palm and sprinkled it upon her face.

At last she opened her eyes—then closed them wearily again—then opened them once more in quick astonishment, and recognised the king. She would have made an effort to rise, but he checked her, and she let her head sink back upon his knee. Still he chafed her temples with his broad, brown hand, and gazed with anxious tenderness into her eyes, that looked at him for a moment, and then wandered and then looked again.

"What is this?" she asked, vacantly, at last.

"I know not," answered the king. "I found you here—lying upon the floor. Are you hurt?" he asked tenderly.

"Hurt? No—yes, I am hurt—hurt even to death," she added suddenly. "Oh, Darius, I would I could tell you! Are you really my friend?"

She raised herself without his help and sat up. The hot blood rushed back to her cheeks and her eyes regained their light.

"Can you doubt that I am your friend, your best friend?" asked the king.

Nehushta rose to her feet and paced the little hall in great emotion. Her hands played nervously with the golden tassels of her mantle, her head-dress had fallen quite back upon her shoulders, and the masses of her hair were let loose. From time to time she glanced at the king, who eyed her anxiously as he stood beside the fountain.

Presently she stopped before him, and very gravely fixed her eyes on him.

"I will tell you something," she said, beginning in low tones. "I will tell you this—I cannot tell you all. I have been horribly deceived, betrayed, made a sport of. I cannot tell you how—you will believe me, will you not? This man I loved—I love him not—has cast me off as an old garment, as a thing of no price—as a shoe that is worn out and that is not fit for his feet to tread upon. I love him not—I hate him—oh, I love him not at all!"

Darius's face grew dark and his teeth ground hard together, but he stood still, awaiting what she should say. But Nehushta ceased, and suddenly she began again to walk up and down, putting her hand to her temples, as though in pain. Once more she paused, and, in her great emotion laid her two hands upon the shoulder of the king, who trembled at her touch, as though a strong man had struck him.

"You said you loved me, once," said Nehushta, in short, nervous tones, almost under her breath. "Do you love me still?"

"Is it so long since I told you I loved you?" asked Darius, with a shade of bitterness. "Ah! do not tempt me—do not stir my sickness. Love you? Yea—as the earth loves the sun—as man never loved woman. Love you? Ay! I love you, and I am the most miserable of men." He shook from head to foot with strong emotion, and the stern lines of his face darkened as he went on speaking. "Yet, though I love you so, I cannot harm him,—for my great oath's sake I cannot—yet for you, almost I could. Ah Nehushta, Nehushta!" he cried passionately, "tempt me not! Ask me not this, for you can almost make a liar of the Great King if you will!"

"I tempt you not," answered the princess. "I will not that you harm a hair of his head. He is not worthy that you should lift the least of your fingers to slay him. But this I tell you—" she hesitated. The king in his violent excitement, as though foreseeing what she would say, seized her hands and held them tightly while he gazed into her eyes.

"Darius," she said, almost hurriedly, "if you love me, and if you desire it, I will be your wife."

A wild light broke from the king's eyes. He dropped her hands and stepped backwards from her, staring hard. Then, with, a quick motion, he turned and threw himself upon the marble seat that ran around the hall, and buried his face and sobbed aloud.

Nehushta seemed to regain some of her calmness, when once she had said the fatal words. She went and knelt beside him and smoothed his brow and wild, rough hair. The great tears stained his dark cheek. He raised himself and looked at her and put one arm about her neck.

"Nehushta," he whispered, "is it true?"

She bowed her head silently. Darius drew her towards him and laid her cheek upon his breast. His face bent down to hers, most tenderly, as though he would have kissed her. But suddenly he drew back, and turned his eyes away.

"No," he said, as though he had regained the mastery over himself. "It is too much to ask—that I might kiss you! It is too much—too much—that you give me. I am not worthy that you should be my wife. Nay!" he cried, as she would not let him rise from his seat. "Nay, let me go, it is not right—it is not worthy—I must not see you any more. Oh, you have tempted me till I am too weak—"

"Darius, you are the noblest of men, the best and bravest." Then with a sudden impulse it seemed to Nehushta that she really loved him. The majestic strength of Zoroaster seemed cold and meaningless beside the fervour of the brave young king, striving so hard to do right under the sorest temptation, striving to leave her free, even against her will. For the moment she loved him, as such women do, with a passionate impulse. She put her arms about him and drew him down to her.

"Darius, it is truth—I never loved you, but I love you now, for, of all living men, you have the bravest heart." She pressed a kiss hotly upon his forehead and her head sank upon his shoulder. For one moment the king trembled, and then, as though all resistance were gone from him, his arms went round her, locking with hers that held him, and he kissed her passionately.

When Zoroaster awoke from his long sleep it was night. He had dreamed evil dreams, and he woke with a sense of some great disaster impending. He heard unwonted sounds in the hall outside his chamber, and he sprang to his feet and called one of the soldiers of his guard.

"What is happening?" asked Zoroaster quickly.

"The Great King, who lives for ever, has taken a new wife to-day," answered the soldier, standing erect, but eyeing Zoroaster somewhat curiously. Zoroaster's heart sank within him.

"What? Who is she?" he asked, coming nearer to the man.

"The new queen is Nehushta—the Hebrew princess," answered the spearman. "There is a great banquet, and a feast for the guard, and much food and wine for the slaves—"

"It is well," answered Zoroaster. "Go thou, and feast with the rest."

The man saluted, and left the room. Zoroaster remained standing alone, his teeth chattering together and his strong limbs shaking beneath him. But he abandoned himself to no frenzy of grief, nor weeping; one seeing him would have said he was sick of a fever. His blue eyes stared hard at the lamp-light and his face was white, but he did not so much as utter an exclamation, nor give one groan. He went and sat down upon a chair and folded his hands together, as though waiting for some event. But nothing happened; no one came to disturb him in his solitude, though he could hear the tramping feet and the unceasing talk of the slaves and soldiers without. In the vast palace, where thousands dwelt, where all were feasting or talking of the coming banquet, Zoroaster was utterly alone.

At last he rose, slowly, as though with an effort, and paced twice from one end of the room to the other. Upon a low shelf on one side, his garments were folded together, while his burnished cuirass and helmet and other arms which he had not worn upon his rapid journey to Ecbatana, hung upon nails in the wall above. He looked at all these things and turned the clothes over piece by piece, till he had found a great dark mantle and a black hood such as was worn in Media. These he put on, and beneath the cloak he girded a broad, sharp knife about him. Then wrapping himself closely round with the dark-coloured stuff and drawing the hood over his eyes, he lifted the curtain of his door and went out, without casting a look behind him.

In the crowd of slaves he passed unnoticed; for the hall was but dimly lighted by a few torches, and every one's attention was upon the doings of the day and the coming feast.

Zoroaster soon gathered from the words he heard spoken, that the banquet had not yet begun, and he hastened to the columned porch through which the royal party must pass on the way to the great hall which formed the centre of the main building. Files of spearmen, in their bronze breastplates and scarlet and blue mantles, lined the way, which was strewn with yellow sand and myrtle leaves and roses. At every pillar stood a huge bronze candlestick, in which a torch of wax and fir-gum burned, and flared, and sent up a cloud of half pungent, half aromatic smoke. Throngs of slaves and soldiers pressed close behind the lines of spearmen, elbowing each other with loud jests and surly complaints, to get a better place, a sea of moving, shouting, gesticulating humanity. Zoroaster's great height and broad shoulders enabled him easily to push to the front, and he stood there, disguised and unknown, peering between the heads of two of his own soldiers to obtain the first view of the procession as it came down the broad staircase at the end of the porch.

Suddenly the blast of deep-toned trumpets was heard in the distance, and silence fell upon the great multitude. With a rhythmic sway of warlike tone the clangour rose and fell, and rose again as the trumpeters came out upon the great staircase and began to descend. After them came other musicians, whose softer instruments began to be heard in harmony with the resounding bass of the horns, and then, behind them, came singers, whose strong, high voices completed the full burst of music that went before the king.

With measured tread the procession advanced. There were neither priests, nor sacrificers, nor any connected with any kind of temple; but after the singers came two hundred noble children clad in white, bearing long garlands of flowers that trailed upon the ground, so that many of the blossoms were torn off and strewed the sand.

But Zoroaster looked neither on the singers, nor on the children. His eyes were fixed intently on the two figures that followed them—Darius, the king, and Nehushta, the bride. They walked side by side, and the procession left an open spaced ten paces before and ten paces behind the royal pair. Darius wore the tunic of purple and white stripes, the mantle of Tyrian purple on his shoulders and upon his head the royal crown of gold surrounded the linen tiara; his left hand, bare and brown and soldier-like, rested upon the golden hilt of his sword, and in his right, as he walked, he carried a long golden rod surmounted by a ball, twined with myrtle from end to end. He walked proudly forward, and as he passed, many a spearman thought with pride that the Great King looked as much a soldier as he himself.

By his left side came Nehushta, clad entirely in cloth of gold, while a mantle of the royal purple hung down behind her. Her white linen tiara was bound round with myrtle and roses, and in her hands she bore a myrtle bough.

Her face was pale in the torchlight, but she seemed composed in manner, and from time to time she glanced at the king with a look which was certainly not one of aversion.

Zoroaster felt himself growing as cold as ice as they approached, and his teeth chattered in his head. His brain reeled with the smoke of the torches, the powerful, moving tones of the music and the strangeness of the whole sight. It seemed as though it could not be real. He fixed his eyes upon Nehushta, but his face was shaded all around by his dark hood. Nevertheless, so intently did he gaze upon her that, as she came near, she felt his look, as it were, and, searching in the crowd behind the soldiers, met his eyes. She must have known it was he, even under the disguise that hid his features, for, though she walked calmly on, the angry blood rushed to her face and brow, overspreading her features with a sudden, dark flush.

Just as she came up to where Zoroaster stood, he thrust his covered head far out between the soldiers. His eyes gleamed like coals of blue fire and his voice came low, with a cold, clear ring, like the blade of a good sword striking upon a piece of iron.

"Faithless!"

That was all he said, but all around heard the cutting tone, that neither the voices of the singers, nor the clangour of the trumpets could drown.

Nehushta drew herself up and paused for one moment, and turned upon the dark-robed figure a look of such unutterable loathing and scorn as one would not have deemed could be concentrated in a human face. Then she passed on.

The two spearmen turned quickly upon the man between them, who had uttered the insult against the new queen, and laid hold of him roughly by the shoulders. A moment more and his life would have been ended by their swords. But his strong, white hands stole out like lightning, and seized each soldier by the wrist, and twisted their arms so suddenly and with such furious strength, that they cried aloud with pain and fell headlong at his feet. The people parted for a space in awe and wonder, and Zoroaster turned, with his dark mantle close drawn around him, and strode out through the gaping crowd.

"It is a devil of the mountains!" cried one.

"It is Ahriman himself!" said another.

"It is the soul of the priest of Bel whom the king slew at Babylon!"

"It is the Evil Sprit of Cambyses!"

"Nay," quoth one of the spearmen, rubbing his injured hand, "it was Zoroaster, the captain. I saw his face beneath that hood he wore."

"It may be," answered his fellow. "They say he can break a bar of iron, as thick as a man's three fingers, with his hand. But I believe it was a devil of the mountains."

But the procession marched on, and long before the crowd had recovered enough from its astonishment to give utterance to these surmises, Zoroaster had passed out of the porch and back through the deserted courts, and down the wide staircase to the palace gate, and out into the quiet, starlit night, alone and on foot.

He would have no compromise with his grief; he would be alone with it. He needed not mortal sympathy and he would not have the pity of man. The blow had struck home with deadly certainty and the wound was such as man cannot heal, neither woman. The fabric of happiness, which in a year he had built himself, was shattered to its foundation, and the fall of it was fearful. The ruin of it reached over the whole dominion of his soul and rent all the palace of his body. The temple that had stood so fair, whither his heart had gone up to worship his beloved one, was destroyed and utterly beaten to pieces; and the ruin of it was as a heap of dead bones, so loathsome in decay, that the eyes of his spirit turned in horror and disgust from the inward contemplation of so miserable a sight.

Alone and on foot, he went upon his dreary way, dry-eyed and calm. There was nothing left of all his past life that he cared for. His armour hung in his chamber in the palace and with it he left the Zoroaster he had known—the strong, the young, the beautiful; the warrior, the lover, the singer of sweet songs, the smiter of swift blows, the peerless horseman, the matchless man. He who went out alone into the great night, was a moving sorrow, a horror of grief made visible as a walking shadow among things real, a man familiar already with death as with a friend, and with the angel of death as with a lover.

Alone—it was a beginning of satisfaction to be away from all the crowd of known and unknown faces familiar to his life—but the end and attainment of satisfaction could only come when he should be away from himself, from the heavy body that wearied him, and from the heavier soul that was crushed with itself as with a burden. For sorrow was his companion from that day forth, and grief undying was his counsellor.

Ah God! She was so beautiful and her love was so sweet and strong! Her face had been as the face of an angel, and her virgin-heart as the innermost leaves of the rose that are folded together in the bud before the rising of the sun. Her kiss was as the breath of spring that gladdens the earth into new life, her eyes as crystal wells, from the depths whereof truth rose blushing to the golden light of day. Her lips were so sweet that a man wondered how they could ever part, till, when they parted, her gentle breath bore forth the music of her words, that was sweeter than all created sounds. She was of all earthly women the most beautiful—the very most lovely thing that God had made; and of all mortal women that have loved, her love had been the purest, the gentlest, the truest. There was never woman like to her, nor would be again.

And yet—scarce ten days had changed her, had so altered and disturbed the pure elements of her wondrous nature that she had lied to herself and lied to her lover the very lie of lies—for what? To wear a piece of purple of a richer dye than other women wore, to bind her hair with a bit of gold, to be called a queen—a queen forsooth! when she had been from her birth up the sovereign queen of all created women!

The very lie of lies! Was there ever such a monstrous lie since the world first learned the untruths of the serpent's wisdom? Had she not sworn and promised, by the holiness of her God, to love Zoroaster for ever? For ever. O word, that had meant heaven, and now meant hell!—that had meant joy without any end and peace and all love!—that meant now only pain eternal, and sorrow, and gnawing torment of a wound that would never heal! O Death, that yesterday would have seemed Life for her! O Life, that to-day, by her, was made the Death of deaths!

Emptiness of emptiness—the whole world one hollow cavern of vanity—lifeless and lightless, where the ghosts of the sorrows of men moan dismally, and the shadows of men's griefs scream out their wild agony upon the ghastly darkness! Night, through which no dawn shall ever gleam, fleet and fair, to touch with rosy fingers the eyes of a dead world and give them sight! Winter, of unearthly cold, that through all the revolving ages of untiring time, shall never see the face of another spring, nor feel its icy veins thawing with the pulses of a forgotten life, quickened from within with the thrilling hope of a new and glorious birth!

Far out upon the southern plain Zoroaster lay upon the dew-wet ground and gazed up into the measureless depths of heaven, where the stars shone out like myriads of jewels set in the dark mantle of night!

Gradually, as he lay, the tempest of his heart subsided, and the calm of the vast solitude descended upon him, even as the dew had descended upon the earth. His temples ceased to throb with the wild pulse that sent lightnings through his brain at every beat, and from the intensity of his sorrow, his soul seemed to float upwards to those cool depths of the outer firmament where no sorrow is. His eyes grew glassy and fixed, and his body rigid in the night-dews; and his spirit, soaring beyond the power of earthly forces to weigh down its flight, rose to that lofty sphere where the morning and the evening are but one eternal day, where the mighty unison of the heavenly chorus sends up its grand plain-chant to God Most High.

CHAPTER XIII

Far in the wild mountains of the south, where a primeval race of shepherds pastures its flocks of shaggy goats upon the scanty vegetation of rocky slopes, there is a deep gorge whither men seldom penetrate, and where the rays of the sun fall but for a short hour at noonday. A man may walk, or rather climb, along the side of the little stream that rushes impetuously down among the black rocks, for a full hour and a half before he reaches the end of the narrow valley. Then he will come upon a sunken place, like a great natural amphitheatre, the steep walls of boulders rising on all sides to a lofty circle of dark crags. In the midst of this open space a spring rises suddenly from beneath a mass of black stone, with a rushing, gurgling sound, and makes a broad pool, whence the waters flow down in a little torrent through the gorge till they emerge far below into the fertile plain and empty themselves into the Araxes, which flows by the towers and palaces of lordly Stakhar, more than two days' journey from the hidden circle in the mountains.

It would have been a hard thing to recognise Zoroaster in the man who sat day after day beside the spring, absorbed in profound meditation. His tall figure was wasted almost to emaciation by fasting and exposure; his hair and beard had turned snow-white, and hung down in abundant masses to his waist, and his fair young face was pale and transparent. But in his deep blue eyes there was a light different from the light of other days—the strange calm fire of a sight that looks on wondrous things, and sees what the eyes of men may not see, and live.

Nearly three years had passed since he went forth from the palace of Shushan, to wander southwards in search of a resting-place, and he was but three-and-thirty years of age. But between him and the past there was a great gulf—the interval between the man and the prophet, between the cares of mortality and the divine calm of the higher life.

From time to time indeed, he ascended the steep path he had made among the stones and rocks, to the summit of the mountain; and there he met one of the shepherds of the hills, who brought him once every month a bag of parched grain and a few small, hard cheeses of goats' milk; and in return for these scanty provisions, he gave the man each time a link from the golden chain he had worn and which was still about his neck when he left the palace. Three-and-thirty links were gone since he had come there, and the chain was shorter by more than half its length. It would last until the thousand days were accomplished, and there would still be much left. Auramazda, the All-Wise, would provide.

Zoroaster sat by the spring and watched the crystal waters sparkle in the brief hour of sunshine at noonday, and turn dark and deep again when the light was gone. He moved not through the long hours of day, sitting as he had sat in that place now for three years neither scorched by the short hours of sunlight, nor chilled by winter's frost and snow. The wild long-haired sheep of the mountain came down to drink at noon, and timidly gazed with their stupid eyes at the immovable figure; and at evening the long-bodied, fierce-eyed wolves would steal stealthily among the rocks and come and snuff the ground about his feet, presently raising their pointed heads with a long howl of fear, and galloping away through the dusk in terror, as though at something unearthly.

And when at last the night was come, Zoroaster arose and went to the spot where the rocks, overhanging together, left a space through which one might enter; and the white-haired man gave one long look at the stars overhead, and disappeared within.

There was a vast cave, the roof reaching high up in a great vault; the sides black and polished, as though smoothed by the hands of cunning workmen; the floor a bed of soft, black sand, dry and even as the untrodden desert. In the midst, a boulder of black rock lay like a huge ball, and upon its summit burned a fire that was never quenched, and that needed no replenishing with fuel. The tall pointed flame shed a strangely white light around, that flashed and sparkled upon the smooth black walls of the cavern, as though they were mirrors. The flame also was immovable; it neither flickered, nor rose, nor fell; but stood as it were a spear-head of incandescent gold upon the centre of the dark altar. There was no smoke from that strange fire, nor any heat near it, as from other fires.

Then Zoroaster bent and put forth his forefinger and traced a figure upon the sand, which was like a circle, save that it was cut from north-west to south-east by two straight lines; and from north-east to south-west by two straight lines; and at each of the four small arcs, where the straight lines cut the circumference of the great circle, a part of a smaller circle outside the great one united the points over each other. And upon the east side, toward the altar, the great circle was not joined, but open for a short distance.

When the figure was traced, Zoroaster came out from it and touched the black rock whereon the fire burned; and then he turned back and entered the circle, and with his fingers joined it where it was open on the east side through which he had entered. And immediately, as the circle was completed, there sprung up over the whole line he had traced a soft light; like that of the fire, but less strong. Then Zoroaster lay down upon his back, with his feet to the west and his head toward the altar, and he folded his hands upon his breast and closed his eyes. As he lay, his body became rigid and his face as the face of the dead; and his spirit was loosed in the trance and freed from the bonds of earth, while his limbs rested.

Lying there, separated from the world, cut off within the circle of a symbolised death by the light of the universal agent, Zoroaster dreamed dreams and saw visions.

His mind was first opened to the understanding of those broader conceptions of space and time of which he had read in the books of Daniel, his master. He had understood the principles then, but he had not realised their truth. He was too intimately connected with the life around him, to be able to see in the clearer light which penetrates with universal truth all the base forms of perishable matter.

Daniel had taught him the first great principles. All men, in their ignorance, speak of the infinities of space and time as being those ideas which man cannot of himself grasp or understand. Man, they say, is limited in capacity; he can, therefore, not comprehend the infinite. A greater fault than this could not be committed by a thinking being. For infinity being unending, it is incapable of being limited; it rejects definition, which belongs, by its nature, to finite things. For definition means the placing of bounds, and that which is infinite can have no bounds. The man, therefore, who seeks to bound what has no bounds, endeavours to define what is, by its nature, undefinable; and finding that the one poor means which he has of conveying fallacious impressions of illusory things to his mind through his deadened senses, is utterly insufficient to give him an idea of what alone is real, he takes refuge in his cross ignorance and coarse grossness of language, and asserts boldly that the human mind is too limited in its nature to conceive of infinite space, or of infinite time.

Not only is the untrammelled mind of man capable of these bolder conceptions, but even the wretched fool who sees in the material world the whole of what man can know, could never get so far as to think even of the delusive objects on which he pins his foolish faith, unless the very mind which he insults and misunderstands, had by its nature that infinite capacity of comprehension which, he says, exists not. For otherwise, if the mind be limited, there must be a definite limit to its comprehensive faculty, and it is easy to conceive that such a limit would soon become apparent to every student; as apparent as it is that a being, confined within three dimensions of space, cannot, without altering his nature, escape from these three dimensions, nor from the laws which govern matter having length, breadth and thickness alone, without the external fourth dimension, with its interchangeability of exterior and interior angles.

The very thought that infinite space cannot be understood, is itself a proof that the mind unconsciously realises the precise nature of such infinity, in attributing to it at once the all-comprehensiveness from which there is no escape, in which all dimensions exist, and by virtue of which all other conceptions become possible; since this infinite space contains in itself all dimensions of existence—transitory, real and potential; and if the capacity of the mind is co-extensive with the capacity of infinite space, since it feels itself undoubtedly capable of grasping any limited idea contained in any portion of the illimitable whole, it follows that the mind is of itself as infinite as the space in which all created things have their transitory form of being, and in which all uncreated truths exist eternally. The mind is aware of infinity by that true sort of knowledge which is an intimate conviction not dependent upon the operation of the senses.

Gradually, too, as Zoroaster fixed his intuition upon the first main principle of all possible knowledge, he became aware of the chief cause—of the universal principal of vivifying essence, which pervades all things, and in which arises motion as the original generator of transitory being. The great law of division became clear to him—the separation for a time of the universal agent into two parts, by the separation and reuniting of which comes light and heat and the hidden force of life, and the prime rules of attractive action; all things that are accounted material. He saw the division of darkness and light, and how all things that are in the darkness are reflected in the light; and how the light which we call light is in reality darkness made visible, whereas the true light is not visible to the eyes that are darkened by the gross veil of transitory being. And as from the night of earth, his eyes were gradually opened to the astral day, he knew that the forms that move and have being in the night are perishable and utterly unreal; whereas the purer being which is reflected in the real light is true and endures for ever.

Then, by his knowledge and power, and by the light that was in him, he divided the portion of the universal agent that was in the cave where he dwelt into two portions, and caused them to reunite in the midst upon the stone that was there; and the flame burned silently and without heat upon his altar, day and night, without intermission; and by the division of the power within him, he could divide the power also that was latent in other transitory beings, according to those laws which, being eternal, are manifested in things not eternal, but perishable.

And further, he meditated upon the seven parts of man, and upon their separation, and upon the difference of their nature.

For the first element of man is perishable matter.

And the second element of man is the portion of the universal agent which gives him life.

And the third element of man is the reflection of his perishable substance in the astral light, coincident with him, but not visible to his earthly eye.

The fourth element of man is made up of all the desires he feels by his material senses. This part is not real being, nor transitory being, but a result.

The fifth element of man is that which says: "I am," whereby a man knows himself from other men; and with it there is an intelligence of lower things, but no intelligence of things higher.

The sixth element is the pure understanding, eternal and co-extensive with all infinity of time and space—real, imperishable, invisible to the eye of man.

The seventh element is the soul from God.

Upon these things Zoroaster meditated long, and as his perishable body became weakened and emaciated with fasting and contemplation, he was aware that, at times, the universal agent ceased to be decomposed and recomposed in the nerves of his material part, so that his body became as though dead, and with, it the fourth element which represents the sense of mortal desires; and he himself, the three highest elements of him,—his individuality, his intelligence and his soul,—became separated for a time from all that weighed them down; and his mind's eyes were opened, and he saw clearly in the astral light, with an intuitive knowledge of true things, and false.

And so, night after night, he lay upon the floor of his cavern, rigid and immovable; his body protected from all outer harmful influences by the circle of light he had acquired the power of producing. For though there was no heat in the flame, no mortal breathing animal could so much as touch it with the smallest part of his body without being instantly destroyed as by lightning. And so he was protected from all harm in his trances; and he left his body at will and returned to it, and it breathed again, and was alive.

So he saw into the past and into the present and into the future, and his soul was purified beyond the purity of man, and soared upwards, and dreamed of the eternal good and of the endless truth; and at last it seemed to him that he should leave his body in its trance, and never return to it, nor let it breathe again. For since it was possible thus to cast off mortality and put on immortality, it seemed to him that it was but a weariness to take up the flesh and wear it, when it was so easy to lay it down. Almost he had determined that he would then let death come, as it were unawares, upon his perishable substance, and remain for ever in the new life he had found.

But as his spirit thought in this wise, he heard a voice speaking to him, and he listened.

"One moment is as another, and there is no difference between one time and another time."

"One moment in eternity is of as great value as another moment, for eternity changes not, neither is one part of it better than another part."

"Though man be immortal as to his soul, he is mortal as to his body, and the time which his soul shall spend in his body is of as great worth to him as the time which he shall spend without it."

"Think not that by wilfully abandoning the body, even though you have the power and the knowledge to do so, you will escape from the state in which it has pleased God to put you."

"Rather shall your pain and the time of your suffering be increased, because you have not done with the body that which the body shall do."

"The life of the soul while it is in the body, has as much value as when it has left it. You shall not shorten the time of dwelling in the flesh."

"Though you know all things, you know not God. For though you know your body which is in the world, and the world which is in time, and time which is in space, yet your knowledge goeth no farther, for space and all that therein is, is in God."

"You have learned earthly things and heavenly things. Learn then that you shall not escape the laws of earth while you are on earth, nor the laws of heaven when you are in heaven. Lift up your heart to God, but do in the body those things which are of the body."

"There are other men put into the world besides you. If you leave the world, what does your knowledge profit other men? And yet it is to profit other men that God has put you into the world."

"And not you only, but every man. The labour of man is to man, and the labour of angels to angels. But the time of man is as valuable in the sight of God, as the time of angels."

"All things that are not accomplished in their time shall be left unaccomplished for ever and ever. If while you are in the flesh, you accomplish not the things of the flesh after the manner of your humanity, you shall enter into the life of the spirit as one blind, or maimed; for your part is not fulfilled."

"Wisdom is this. A man shall not care for the things of the world for himself, and his soul shall be lifted and raised above all that is mean and perishable; but he shall perform his part without murmuring. He shall not forget the perishable things, though he soar to the imperishable."

"For man is to man as one portion of eternity to another; and as eternity would be imperfect if one moment could be removed, so also the earth would be imperfect if one man should be taken from it before his appointed time."

"If a man therefore take himself out of the world, he causes imperfection, and sins against perfection, which is the law of God."

"Though the world be in darkness, the darkness is necessary to the light. Though the world perish, and heaven perish not for ever, yet is the perishable necessary to the eternal."

"For the transitory and the unchangeable exist alike in eternity and are portions of it. And one moment is as another, and there is no difference between one time and another time."

"Go, therefore, and take up your body, and do with it the deeds of the body among men; for you have deeds to do, and unless they are done in their time, which is now, they will be unfulfilled for ever, and you will become an imperfect spirit."

"The imperfect spirit shall be finally destroyed, for nothing that is imperfect shall endure. To be perfect all things must be fulfilled, all deeds done, in the season while the spirit is in darkness with the body. The deeds perish, and the body which doeth them, but the soul of the perfect man is eternal, and the reflection of what he has done, abides for ever in the light."

"Hasten, for your time is short. You have learned all things that are lawful to be learnt, and your deeds shall be sooner accomplished."

"Hasten, for one moment is as another, and there is no difference between the value of one time and of another time."

"The moment which passes returns not, and the thing which a man should do in one time cannot be done in another time."

The voice ceased, and the spirit of Zoroaster returned to his body in the cave, and his eyes opened. Then he rose, and standing within the circle, cast sand upon the portion towards the east; and so soon as the circle was broken, it was extinguished and there remained nothing but the marks Zoroaster had traced with his fingers upon the black sand.

He drew his tattered mantle around him, and went to the entrance of the cave, and passed out. And it was night.

Overhead, the full moon cast her broad rays vertically into the little valley, and the smooth black stones gleamed darkly. The reflection caught the surface of the little pool by the spring, and it was turned to a silver shield of light.

Zoroaster came forward and stood beside the fountain, and the glory of the moon fell upon his white locks and beard and on the long white hand he laid upon the rock.

His acute senses, sharpened beyond those of men by long solitude and fasting, distinguished the step of a man far up the height on the distant crags, and his keen sight soon detected a figure descending cautiously, but surely, towards the deep abyss where Zoroaster stood. More and more clearly he saw him, till the man was near, and stood upon an overhanging boulder within speaking distance. He was the shepherd who, from time to time, brought food to the solitary mystic; and who alone, of all the goatherds in those hills, would have dared to invade the sacred precincts of Zoroaster's retreat. He was a brave fellow, but the sight of the lonely man by the fountain awed him; it seemed as though his white hair emitted a light of its own under the rays of the moon, and he paused in fear lest the unearthly ascetic should do him some mortal hurt.

"Wilt thou harm me if I descend?" he called out timidly.

"I harm no man," answered Zoroaster. "Come in peace."

The active shepherd swung himself from the boulder, and in a few moments he stood among the stones at the bottom, a few paces from the man he sought. He was a dark fellow, clad in goat-skins, with pieces of leather bound around his short, stout legs. His voice was hoarse, perhaps with some still unconquered fear, and his staff rattled as he steadied himself among the stones.

"Art not thou he who is called Zoroaster?" he asked.

"I am he," answered the mystic. "What wouldest thou?"

"Thou knowest that the Great King with his queens and his court are at the palace of Stakhar," replied the man. "I go thither from time to time to sell cheeses to the slaves. The Great King has made a proclamation that whosoever shall bring before him Zoroaster shall receive a talent of gold and a robe of purple. I am a poor shepherd—fearest thou to go to the palace?"

"I fear nothing. I am past fear these three years."

"Will the Great King harm thee, thinkest thou? Thou hast paid me well for my pains since I first saw thee, and I would not have thee hurt."

"No man can harm me. My time is not yet come."

"Wilt thou go with me?" cried the shepherd, in sudden delight. "And shall I have the gold and the robe?"

"I will go with thee. Thou shalt have all thou wouldest," answered Zoroaster. "Art thou ready? I have no goods to burden me."

"But thou art old," objected the shepherd, coming nearer. "Canst thou go so far on foot? I have a beast; I will return with him in the morning, and meet thee upon the height. I came hither in haste, being but just returned from Stakhar with the news."

"I am younger than thou, though my hair is white. I will go with thee. Lead the way."

He stooped and drank of the fountain in the moonlight, from the hollow of his hand. Then he turned, and began to ascend the steep side of the valley. The shepherd led the way in silence, overcome between his awe of the man and his delight at his own good fortune.

CHAPTER XIV

It was now three years since Nehushta had been married to Darius, and the king loved her well. But often, in that time, he had been away from her, called to different parts of the kingdom by the sudden outbreaks of revolution which filled the early years of his reign. Each time he had come back in triumph, and each time he had given her some rich gift. He found indeed that he had no easy task to perform in keeping the peace between his two queens; for Atossa seemed to delight in annoying Nehushta and in making her feel that she was but the second in the king's favour, whatever distinctions might be offered her. But Darius was just and was careful that Atossa should receive her due, neither more nor less.

Nehushta was glad when Zoroaster was gone. She had suffered terribly in that moment when he had spoken to her out of the crowd, and the winged word had made a wound that rankled still. In those three years that passed, Atossa never undeceived her concerning the sight she had seen, and she still believed that Zoroaster had basely betrayed her. It was impossible, in her view, that it could be otherwise. Had she not seen him herself? Could any man do such an action who was not utterly base and heartless? She had, of course, never spoken to Darius of the scene upon the terrace. She did not desire the destruction of Atossa, nor of her faithless lover. Amid all the tender kindness the king lavished upon her, the memory of her first love endured still, and she could not have suffered the pain of going over the whole story again. He was gone, perhaps dead, and she would never see him again. He would not dare to set foot in the court. She remembered the king's furious anger against him, when he suspected that the hooded man in the procession was Zoroaster. But Darius had afterwards said, in his usual careless way, that he himself would have done as much, and that for his oath's sake, he would never harm the young Persian. By the grace of Auramazda he swore, he was the king of kings and did not make war upon disappointed lovers!

Meanwhile, Darius had built himself a magnificent palace, below the fortress of Stakhar, in the valley of the Araxes, and there he spent the winter and the spring, when the manifold cares of the state would permit him. He had been almost unceasingly at war with the numerous pretenders who set themselves up for petty kings in the provinces. With unheard-of rapidity, he moved from one quarter of his dominions to another, from east to west, from north to south; but each time that he returned, he found some little disturbance going on at the court, and he bent his brows and declared that a parcel of women were harder to govern than all Media, Persia, and Babylon together.

Atossa wearied him with her suggestions.

"When the king is gone upon an expedition," she said, "there is no head in the palace. Otanes is a weak man. The king will not give me the control of the household, neither will he give it to any one else."

"There is no one whom I can trust," answered Darius. "Can you not dwell together in peace for a month?"

"No," answered Atossa, with her winning smile, "it is impossible; the king's wives will never agree among themselves. Let the king choose some one and make a head over the palace."

"Whom shall I choose?" asked Darius, moodily.

"The king had a faithful servant once," suggested Atossa.

"Have I none now?"

"Yea, but none so faithful as this man of whom I speak, nor so ready to do the king's bidding. He departed from Shushan when the king took Nehushta to wife—"

"Mean you Zoroaster?" asked Darius, bending his brows, and eyeing Atossa somewhat fiercely. But she met his glance with indifference.

"The same," she answered. "Why not send for him and make him governor of the palace? He was indeed a faithful servant—and a willing one."

Still the king gazed hard at her face, as though trying to fathom the reason of her request, or at least to detect some scornful look upon her face to agree with her sneering words. But he was no match for the unparalleled astuteness of Atossa, though he had a vague suspicion that she wished to annoy him by calling up a memory which she knew could not be pleasant, and he retorted in his own fashion.

"If Zoroaster be yet alive I will have him brought, and I will make him governor of the palace. He was indeed a faithful servant—he shall rule you all and there shall be no more discord among you."

And forthwith the king issued a proclamation that whosoever should bring Zoroaster before him should receive a talent of gold and a robe of purple as a reward.

But when Nehushta heard of it she was greatly troubled; for Atossa began to tell her that Zoroaster was to return and to be made governor of the palace; but Nehushta rose and left her forthwith, with such a look of dire hatred and scorn that even the cold queen thought she had, perhaps, gone too far.

There were other reasons why the king desired Zoroaster's return. He had often wondered secretly how the man could so have injured Nehushta as to turn her love into hate in a few moments; but he had never questioned her. It was a subject neither of them could have approached, and Darius was far too happy in his marriage to risk endangering that happiness by any untoward discovery. Nehushta's grief and anger had been so genuine when she told him of Zoroaster's treachery that it had never occurred to him that he might be injuring the latter in marrying the princess, though his generous heart had told him more than once, that Nehushta had married him half from gratitude for his kindness, and half out of anger with her false lover; but, capricious as she was in all other things, towards the king she was always the same, gentle and affectionate, though there was nothing passionate in her love. And now, the idea of seeing the man who had betrayed her installed in an official position in the palace, was terrible to her pride. She could not sleep for thinking how she should meet him, and what she should do. She grew pale and hollow-eyed with the anticipation of evil and all her peace went from her. Deep down in her heart there was yet a clinging affection for the old love, which she smothered and choked down bravely; but it was there nevertheless, a sleeping giant, ready to rise and overthrow her whole nature in a moment, if only she could wash away the stain of faithlessness which sullied his fair memory, and lift the load of dishonour which had crushed him from the sovereign place he had held in the dominion of her soul.

Darius was himself curious to ascertain the truth about Zoroaster's conduct. But another and a weightier reason existed for which he wished him to return. The king was disturbed about a matter of vital importance to his kingdom, and he knew that, among all his subjects, there was not one more able to give him assistance and advice than Zoroaster, the pupil of the dead prophet Daniel.

The religion of the kingdom was of a most uncertain kind. So many changes had passed over the various provinces which made up the great empire that, for generations, there had been almost a new religion for every monarch. Cyrus, inclining to the idolatry of the Phoenicians, had worshipped the sun and moon, and had built temples and done sacrifice to them and to a multitude of deities. Cambyses had converted the temples of his father into places of fire-worship, and had burnt thousands of human victims; rejoicing in the splendour of his ceremonies and in the fierce love of blood that grew upon him as his vices obtained the mastery over his better sense. But under both kings the old Aryan worship of the Magians had existed among the people, and the Magians themselves had asserted, whenever they dared, their right to be considered the priestly caste, the children of the Brahmins of the Aryan house. Gomata—the false Smerdis—was a Brahmin, at least in name, and probably in descent; and during his brief reign the only decrees he issued from his retirement in the palace of Shushan, were for the destruction of the existing temples and the establishment of the Magian worship throughout the kingdom. When Darius had slain Smerdis, he naturally proceeded to the destruction of the Magi, and the streets of Shushan ran with their blood for many days. He then restored the temples and the worship of Auramazda, as well as he was able; but it soon became evident that the religion was in a disorganised state and that it would be no easy matter to enforce a pure monotheism upon a nation of men who, in their hearts, were Magians, nature-worshippers; and who, through successive reigns, had been driven by force to the adoration of strange idols. It followed that the people resisted the change and revolted whenever they could find a leader. The numerous revolutions, which cost Darius no less than nineteen battles, were, almost without exception, brought about in the attempt to restore the Magian worship in various provinces of the kingdom, and it may well be doubted whether, at any time in the world's history, an equal amount of blood was ever shed in so short a period in the defence of religious convictions.

Darius himself was a man who had the strongest belief in the power of Auramazda, the All-Wise God, and who did not hesitate to attribute all the evil in the world to Ahriman, the devil. He had a bitter contempt for all idolatry, nature-worship and superstition generally, and he adhered in his daily life to the simple practices of the ancient Mazdayashnians. But he was totally unfitted to be the head of a religious movement; and, although he had collected such of the priesthood as seemed most worthy, and had built them temples and given them privileges of all kinds, he was far from satisfied with their mode of worship. He could not frame a new doctrine, but he had serious doubts whether the ceremonies his priests performed were as simple and religious as he wished them to be. The chants, long hymns of endless repetition and monotony, were well enough, perhaps; the fire that was kept burning perpetually was a fitting emblem of the sleepless wisdom and activity of the Supreme Being in overcoming darkness with light. But the boundless intoxication into which the priests threw themselves by the excessive drinking of the Haoma, the wild and irregular acts of frenzy by which they expressed their religious fervour when under the influence of the subtle drink, were adjuncts to the simple purity of the bloodless sacrifice which disgusted the king, and he hesitated long as to some reform in these matters. The oldest Mazdayashnians declared that the drinking of Haoma was an act, at once pleasing to God and necessary to stimulate the zeal of the priests in the long and monotonous chanting, which would otherwise soon sink to a mere perfunctory performance of a wearisome task. The very repetition which the hymns contained seemed to prove that they were not intended to be recited by men not under some extraordinary influence. Only the wild madness of the Haoma drinker could sustain such an endless series of repeated prayers with fitting devotion and energy.

All this the king heard and was not satisfied. He attended the ceremonies with becoming regularity and sat through the performance of the rites with exemplary patience. But he was disgusted, and he desired a reform. Then he remembered how Zoroaster himself was a good Mazdayashnian, and how he had occupied himself with religious studies from his youth up, and how he had enjoyed the advantage of being the companion of Daniel, the Hebrew governor, whose grand simplicity of faith had descended, to some degree, upon his pupil. The Hebrews, Darius knew, were a sober people of the strongest religious convictions, and he had heard that, although eating formed, in some way, a part of their ceremonies, there was no intoxication connected with their worship. Zoroaster, he thought, would be able to give him advice upon this point, which would be good. In sending for the man he would fulfil the double purpose of seeming to grant the queen's request, and at the same time, of providing himself with a sage counsellor in his difficulties. With his usual impetuosity, he at once fulfilled his purpose, assuring himself that Zoroaster must have forgotten Nehushta by this time, and that he, the king, was strong enough to prevent trouble if he had not.

But many days passed, and though the proclamation was sent to all parts of the kingdom, nothing was heard of Zoroaster. His retreat was a sure one and there was no possibility of his being found.

Atossa, who in her heart longed for Zoroaster's return, both because by his means she hoped to bring trouble upon Nehushta, and because she still felt something akin to love for him, began to fear that he might be dead, or might have wandered out of the kingdom; but Nehushta herself knew not whether to hope that he would return, or to rejoice that she was to escape the ordeal of meeting him. She would have given anything to see him for a moment, to decide, as it were, whether she wished to see him, or not. She was deeply disturbed by the anxiety she felt and longed to know definitely what she was to expect.

She began to hate Stakhar with its splendid gardens and gorgeous colonnades, with its soft southern air that blew across the valley of roses all day long, wafting up a wondrous perfume to the south windows. She hated the indolent pomp in which she lived and the idle luxury of her days. Something in her hot-blooded Hebrew nature craved for the blazing sun and the sand-wastes of Syria, for the breath of the desert and for the burning heat of the wilderness. She had scarcely ever seen these things, for she had sojourned during the one-and-twenty years of her life, in the most magnificent palaces of the kingdom, and amid the fairest gardens the hand of man could plant. But the love of the sun and of the sand was bred in the blood. She began to hate the soft cushions and the delicate silks and the endless flowers scenting the heavy air.

Stakhar itself was a mighty fortress, in the valley of the Araxes, rising dark and forbidding from the banks of the little river, crowned with towers and turrets and massive battlements, that overlooked the fertile extent of gardens, as a stern schoolmaster frowning over a crowd of fair young children. But Darius had chosen the site of his palace at some distance from the stronghold; where the river bent suddenly round a spur of the mountain, and watered a wider extent of land. The spur of the hill ran down, by an easy gradation, into the valley; and beyond it the hills separated into the wide plain of Merodasht that stretched southward many farsangs to the southern pass. Upon this promontory the king had caused to be built a huge platform which was ascended by the broadest flight of steps in the whole world, so easy of gradation that a man might easily have ridden up and then down again without danger to his horse. Upon the platform was raised the palace, a mighty structure resting on the vast columned porticoes and halls, built entirely of polished black marble, that contrasted strangely with the green slopes of the hills above and with the bright colours of the rose-gardens. Endless buildings rose behind the palace, and stretched far down towards the river below it. Most prominent of those above was the great temple of Auramazda, where the ceremonies were performed which gave Darius so much anxiety. It was a massive, square building, lower than the palace, consisting of stone walls surrounded by a deep portico of polished columns. It was not visible from the great staircase, being placed immediately behind the palace and hidden by it.

The walls and the cornices and the capitals of the pillars were richly sculptured with sacrificial processions, and long trains of soldiers and captives, with great inscriptions of wedge-shaped letters, and with animals of all sorts. The work was executed by Egyptian captives; and so carefully was the hard black marble carved and polished, that a man could see his face in the even surfaces, and they sent back the light like dark mirrors.

The valley above Stakhar was grand in its great outlines of crags and sharp, dark peaks, and the beetling fortress upon its rocky base, far up the gorge, seemed only a jutting fragment of the great mountain, thrown off and separated from the main chain by an earthquake, or some vast accident of nature. But from the palace itself the contrast of the views was great. On one side, the rugged hills, crag-crowned and bristling black against the north-western sky; on the other, the great bed of rose-gardens and orangeries and cultivated enclosures filled the plain, till in the dim distance rose the level line of the soft blue southern hills, blending mistily in the lazy light of a far-off warmth. It seemed as though on one side of the palace were winter, and on the other summer; on the one side cold, and on the other heat; on the one side rough strength, and on the other gentle rest.

But Nehushta gazed northward and was weary of the cold, and southward, and she wearied of the heat. There was nothing—nothing in it all that was worth one moment of the old sweet moonlit evenings among the myrtles at Ecbatana. When she thought, there was nothing of all her royal state and luxury that she would not readily give to have had Zoroaster remain faithful to her. She had put him away from her heart, driven him out utterly, as she believed; but now that he was spoken of again, she knew not whether she loved him a little in spite of all his unfaithfulness, or whether it was only the memory of the love she had felt before which stirred in her breast, and made her unconsciously speak his name when she was alone.

She looked back over the three years that were passed, and she knew that she had done her duty by the king. She knew also that she had done it willingly, and that there had been many moments when she said to herself that she loved Darius dearly. Indeed, it was not hard to find a reason for loving him, for he was brave and honest and noble in all his thoughts and ways; and whatever he had been able to do to show his love for Nehushta, he had done. It was not the least of the things that had made her life pass so easily, that she felt daily how she was loved before her rival, and how, in her inmost heart, Atossa chafed at seeing Darius forsake her society for that of the Hebrew princess. If the king had wearied of her, Nehushta would very likely have escaped from the palace, and gone out to face any misfortunes the world might hold for her, rather than remain to bear the scoffing of the fair smiling woman she so hated. Or, she would have stolen in by night to where Atossa slept, and the wicked-looking Indian knife she wore, would have gone down, swift and sure, to the very haft, into the queen's heart. She would not have borne tamely any slight upon her beauty or her claims. But, as it was, she reigned supreme. The king was just, and showed no difference in the state and attendance of the two queens, but it was to Nehushta he turned, when he drank deep at the banquet and pledged the loving cup. It was to Nehushta that he went when the cares of state were heavy and he needed counsel; and it was upon her lap he laid his weary head, when he had ridden far and fast for many days, returning from some hard-fought field.

But the queens hated each other with a fierce hatred, and when Darius was absent, their divisions broke out sometimes into something like open strife. Their guards buffeted each other in the courts, and their slave-women tore out each other's hair upon the stairways. Then, when the king returned, there reigned an armed peace for a time, which none dared break. But rumours of the disturbances that had taken place often reached the royal ears, and Darius was angry and swore great oaths, but could do nothing; being no wiser than many great men who have had to choose between the caprices of two women who hated each other.

Now the rumour went abroad that Zoroaster would return to the court; and for a space, the two queens kept aloof, for both knew that if he came back, some mortal conflict would of necessity arise between them; and each watched the other, and was cautious.

The days passed by, but no one answered the proclamation. No one had seen or heard of Zoroaster, since the night when he left the palace at Shushan. He had taken nothing with him, and had left no trace behind to guide the search. Many said he had left the kingdom; some said he was dead in the wilderness. But Nehushta sighed and took little rest, for do what she would, she had hoped to see him once more.

CHAPTER XV

The interior of the temple was lighted with innumerable lamps, suspended from the ceiling, of bronze and of the simplest workmanship, like everything which pertained to the worship of Auramazda. In the midst, upon a small altar of black stone, stood a bronze brazier, shaped like a goblet, wherein a small fire of wood burned quietly, sending up little wreaths of smoke, which spread over the flat ceiling and hung like a mist about the lamps; before the altar lay a supply of fuel—fine, evenly-cut sticks of white pine-wood, piled in regular order in a symmetrical heap. At one extremity of the oblong hall stood a huge mortar of black marble, having a heavy wooden pestle, and standing upon a circular base, in which was cut a channel all around, with an opening in the front from which the Haoma juice poured out abundantly when the fresh milkweed was moistened and pounded together in the mortar. A square receptacle of marble received the fluid, which remained until it had fermented during several days, and had acquired the intoxicating strength for which it was prized, and to which it owed its sacred character. By the side of this vessel, upon a low marble table, lay a huge wooden ladle; and two golden cups, short and wide, but made smaller in the middle like a sand-glass, stood there also.

At the opposite end of the temple, before a marble screen which shielded the doorway, was placed a great carved chair of ebony and gold and silver, raised upon a step above the level of the floor.

It was already dark when the king entered the temple, dressed in his robes of state, with his sword by his side, his long sceptre tipped with the royal sphere in his right hand, and the many-pointed crown upon his head. His heavy black beard had grown longer in the three years that had passed, and flowed down over his vest of purple and white half-way to his belt. His face was stern, and the deep lines of his strong features had grown more massive in outline. With the pride of every successive triumph had come also something more of repose and conscious power. His step was slower, and his broad brown hand grasped the golden sceptre with less of nervous energy and more unrelenting force. But his brows were bent, and his expression, as he took his seat before the screen, over against the altar of the fire, was that of a man who was prepared to be discontented and cared little to conceal what he felt.

After him came the chief priest, completely robed in white, with a thick, white linen sash rolled for a girdle about his waist, the fringed ends hanging stiffly down upon one side. Upon his head he wore a great mitre, also of white linen, and a broad fringed stole of the same material fell in two wide bands from each side of his neck to his feet. His beard was black and glossy, fine as silk, and reached almost to his waist. He came and stood with his back to the king and his face to the altar, ten paces from the second fire.

Then, from behind the screen and from each side of it, the other priests filed out, two and two, all clad in white like the chief priest, save that their mitres were smaller and they wore no stole. They came out and ranged themselves around the walls of the temple, threescore and nine men, of holy order, trained in the ancient chanting of the Mazdayashnian hymns; men in the prime and strength of life, black-bearded and broad-shouldered, whose massive brows and straight features indicated noble powers of mind and body.

The two who stood nearest to the chief priest came forward, and taking from his hands a square linen cloth he bore, bound it across his mouth and tied it behind his neck in a firm knot by means of strings. Then, one of them put into his left hand a fan of eagles' feathers, and the other gave him a pair of wrought-iron pincers. Then they left him to advance alone to the altar.

He went forward till he was close to the bronze brazier, and stooping down, he took from the heap of fuel a clean white stick, with the pincers, which he carefully laid upon the fire. Then with his left hand he gently fanned the flames, and his mouth being protected by the linen cloth in such a manner that his breath could not defile the sacred fire, he began slowly and in a voice muffled by the bandage he wore, to recite the beginning of the sacrificial hymn:

"Best of all goods is purity.
Glory, glory to him
Who is best and purest in purity.
For he who ruleth from purity, he abideth according to the will of the Lord.
The All-Wise giveth gifts for the works which man doeth in the world for the Lord.
He who protecteth the poor giveth the kingdom to Ahura."

Then all the priests repeated the verses together in chorus, their voices sounding in a unison which, though not precisely song, seemed tending to a musical cadence as the tones rose and fell again upon the last two syllables of each verse. And then again, the chief priest and the other priests together repeated the hymn, many times, in louder and louder chorus, with more and more force of intonation; till the chief priest stepped back from the fire, and delivering up the pincers and the fan, allowed the two assistants to unbind the cloth from his mouth.

He walked slowly up the temple on the left side, and keeping his right hand toward the altar, he walked seven times around it, repeating a hymn alone in low tones; till, after the seventh time, he went up to the farther end of the hall, and stood before the black marble trough in which the fermented Haoma stood ready, having been prepared with due ceremony three days before.

Then, in a loud voice, he intoned the chant in praise of Zaothra and Bareshma, holding high in his right hand the bundle of sacred stalks; which he, from time to time, moistened a little in the water from a vessel which stood ready, and sprinkled to the four corners of the temple. The priests again took up the strain in chorus, repeating over and over the burden of the song.

"Zaothra, I praise thee and desire thee with praise!
Bareshma, I praise thee and desire thee with praise!
Zaothra, with Bareshma united, I praise you and desire you with praise!
Bareshma, with Zaothra united, I praise you and desire you with praise!"

Suddenly the chief priest laid down the Bareshma, and seizing one of the golden goblets, filled it, with the wooden ladle, from the dark receptacle of the juice. As he poured it high, the yellow light of the lamp caught the transparent greenish fluid, and made it sparkle strangely. He put the goblet to his lips and drank.

The king, sitting in silence upon his carved throne at the other extremity of the temple, bent his brows in a dark frown as he saw the hated ceremony begin. He knew how it ended, and grand as the words were which they would recite when the subtle fluid had fired their veins, he loathed to see the intoxication that got possession of them; and the frenzy with which they howled the sacred strains seemed to him to destroy the solemnity and dignity of a hymn, in which all that was solemn and high would otherwise have seemed to be united.

The chief priest drank and then, filling both goblets, gave them to the priests at his right and left hand; who, after drinking, passed each other, and made way for those next them; and so the whole number filed past the Haoma vessel and drank their share till they all had changed places, and those who had stood upon the right, now stood upon the left; and those who were first upon the left hand, were now upon the right. And when all had drunk, the chief priest intoned the great hymn of praise, and all the chorus united with him in high, clear tones:

"The All-Wise Creator, Ahura Mazda, the greatest, the best, the most fair in glory and majesty,"

"The mightiest in his strength, the wisest in his wisdom, the holiest in his holiness, whose power is of all power the fairest,"

"Who is very wise, who maketh all things to rejoice afar,"

"Who hath made us and formed us, who hath saved us, the holiest among the heavenly ones,"

"Him I adore and praise, unto him I declare the sacrifice, him I invite,"

"I declare the sacrifice to the Protector, the Peace-maker, who maketh the fire to burn, who preserveth the wealth of the earth; the whole earth and the wisdom thereof, the seas and the waters, the land and all growing things, I invite to the sacrifice."

"Cattle and living things, and the fire of Ahura, the sure helper, the lord of the archangels,"

"The nights and the days, I call upon, the purity of all created light,"

"The Lord of light, the sun in his glory, glorious in name and worthy of honour,"

"Who giveth food unto men, and multiplieth the cattle upon the earth, who causeth mankind to increase, I call upon and invite to the sacrifice,"

"Water, and the centre of all waters, given and made of God, that refresheth all things and maketh all things to grow, I call upon and invite."

"The souls of the righteous and pure, the whole multitude of living men and women upon earth, I call upon and invite."

"I call upon the triumph and the mighty strength of God,"

"I call upon the archangels who keep the world, upon the months, upon the pure, new moon, the lordship of purity in heaven,"

"I call upon the feasts of the years and the seasons, upon the years and the months and days,"

"I call upon the star Ahura, and upon the one great and eternal in purity, and upon all the stars, the works of God,"

"Upon the star Tistrya I call, the far-shining, the magnificent—upon the fair moon that shineth upon the young cattle, upon the glorious sun swift in the race of his flight, the eye of the Lord."

"I call upon the spirits and souls of the righteous, on the fire-begotten of the Lord, and upon all fires."

"Mountains and all hills, lightened and full of light."

"Majesty of kingly honour, the Majesty of the king which dieth not, is not diminished,"

"All wisdom and blessings and true promises, all men who are full of strength and power and might,"

"All places and lands and countries beneath the heavens, and above the heavens, light without beginning, existing, and without end,"

"All creatures pure and good, male and female upon the earth."

"All you I invite and call upon to the sacrifice."

"Havani, pure, lord of purity!"

"Shavanghi, pure, lord of purity!"

"Rapithwina, pure, lord of purity!"

"Uzayêirina, pure, lord of purity!"

"Aiwishruthrema, Aibigaya, pure, lord of purity!"

"Ushahina, pure, lord of purity!"

"To Havani, Shavanghi and Vishya, the pure, the lords of purity most glorious, be honour and prayer and fulfilment and praise."

"To the days, and the nights, and the hours, the months and the years and the feasts of years, be honour and prayer and fulfilment and praise before Auramazda, the All-Wise, for ever and ever and ever."

As the white-robed priests shouted the verses of the long hymn, their eyes flashed and their bodies moved rhythmically from side to side with an ever-increasing motion. From time to time, the golden goblets were filled with the sweet Haoma juice, and passed rapidly from hand to hand along the line, and as each priest drank more freely of the subtle fermented liquor, his eyes gained a new and more unnatural light, and his gestures grew more wild, while the whole body of voices rose together from an even and dignified chant to an indistinguishable discord of deafening yells.

Ever more and more they drank, repeating the verses of the hymn without order or sequence. One man repeated a verse over and over again in ear-piercing shrieks, swaying his body to and fro till he dropped forward upon the ground, foaming at the mouth, his features distorted with a wild convulsion, and his limbs as rigid as stone. Here, a band of five locked their arms together, and, back to back, whirled madly round, screaming out the names of the archangels, in an indiscriminate rage of sound and broken syllables. One, less enduring than the rest, relaxed his hold upon his fellow's arm and fell headlong on the pavement, while the remaining four were carried on by the force of their whirling, and fell together against others who steadied themselves against the wall, swaying their heads and arms from side to side. Overthrown by the fall of their companions, these in their turn fell forward upon the others, and in a few moments, the whole company of priests lay grovelling one upon the other, foaming at the mouth, but still howling out detached verses of their hymn—a mass of raging, convulsed humanity, tearing each other in the frenzy of drunkenness, rolling over and over each otter in the twisted contortions of frenzied maniacs. The air grew thick with the smoke of the fire and of the lamps, and the unceasing, indescribable din of the hoarsely howling voices seemed to make the very roof rock upon the pillars that held it up, as though the stones themselves must go mad and shriek in the universal fury of sound. The golden goblets rolled upon the marble pavement, and the sweet green juice ran in slimy streams upon the floor. The high priest himself, utterly intoxicated and screaming with a voice like a wild beast in agony, fell backwards across the marble vase at the foot of the mortar and his hand and arm plashed into the dregs of the fermented Haoma.

Never had the drunken frenzy reached such a point before. The king had sat motionless and frowning upon his seat until he saw the high priest fall headlong into the receptacle of the sacred Haoma. Then, with a groan, he laid his two hands upon the arms of his carved chair, and rose to his feet in utter disgust and horror. But, as he turned to go, he stood still and shook from head to foot, for he saw beside him a figure that might, at such a moment, have startled the boldest.

A tall man of unearthly looks stood there, whose features he seemed to know, but could not recognise. His face was thin to emaciation, and his long, white hair fell in tangled masses, with his huge beard, upon his half-naked shoulders and bare chest. The torn, dark mantle he wore was falling to the ground as he faced the drunken herd of howling priests and lifted up his thin blanched arms and bony fingers, as though in protest at the hideous sight. His deep-set eyes were blue and fiery, flashing with a strange light. He seemed not to see Darius, but he gazed in deepest horror upon the writhing mass of bestial humanity below.

Suddenly his arms shook, and standing there, against the dark marble screen, like the very figure and incarnation of fate, he spoke in a voice that, without effort, seemed to dominate the hideous din of yelling voices—a voice that was calm and clear as a crystal bell, but having that in it which carried instantly the words he spoke to the ears of the very most besotted wretch that lay among the heaps upon the floor—a voice that struck like a sharp steel blade upon iron.

"I am the prophet of the Lord. Hold ye your peace."

As a wild beast's howling suddenly diminishes and grows less and dies away to silence, when the hunter's arrow has sped close to the heart with a mortal wound, so in one moment, the incoherent din sank down, and the dead stillness that followed was dreadful by contrast. Darius stood with his hand upon the arm of his chair, not understanding the words of the fearful stranger; still less the mastering power those words had upon the drunken priests. But his courage did not desert him, and he feared not to speak.

"How sayest thou that thou art a prophet? Who art thou?" he asked.

"Thou knowest me and hast sent for me," answered the white-haired man, in his calm tones; but his fiery eyes rested on the king's, and Darius almost quailed under the glance. "I am Zoroaster; I am come to proclaim the truth to thee and to these miserable men, thy priests."

The fear they felt had restored the frenzied men to their senses. One by one, they rose and crept back towards the high priest himself, who had struggled to his feet, and stood upon the basement of the mortar above all the rest.

Then Darius looked, and he knew that it was Zoroaster, but he knew not the strange look upon his face, and the light in his eyes was not as the light of other days. He turned to the priests.

"Ye are unworthy priests," he cried angrily, "for ye are drunk with your own sacrifice, and ye defile God's temple with unseemly cries. Behold this man—can ye tell me whether he be indeed a prophet?" Darius, whose anger was fast taking the place of the awe he had felt when he first saw Zoroaster beside him, strode a step forward, with his hand upon his sword-hilt, as though he would take summary vengeance upon the desecrators of the temple.

"He is surely a liar!" cried the high priest from his position beyond the altar, as though hurling defiance at Zoroaster through the flames.

"He is surely a liar!" repeated all the priests together, following their head.

"He is a Magian, a worshipper of idols, a liar and the father of lies! Down with him! Slay him before the altar; destroy the unbeliever that entereth the temple of Ahura Mazda!"

"Down with the Magian! Down with the idolater!" cried the priests, and moved forward in a body toward the thin white-haired man who stood facing them, serene and high.

Darius drew his short sword and rushed before Zoroaster to strike down the foremost of the priests. But Zoroaster seized the keen blade in the air as though it had been a reed, and wrenched it from the king's strong grip, and broke it in pieces like glass, and cast the fragments at his feet. Darius staggered back in amazement, and the herd of angry men, in whose eyes still blazed the drunkenness of the Haoma, huddled together for a moment like frightened sheep.

"I have no need of swords," said Zoroaster, in his cold, clear voice.

Then the high priest cried aloud, and ran forward and seized a brand from the sacred fire.

"It is Angramainyus, the Power of Evil," he yelled fiercely. "He is come to fight with Auramazda in his temple! But the fire of the Lord shall destroy him!"

As the priest rushed upon him, with the blazing brand raised high to strike, Zoroaster faced him and fixed his eyes upon the angry man. The priest suddenly stood still, his hand in mid-air, and the stout piece of burning wood fell to the floor, and lay smouldering and smoking upon the pavement.

"Tempt not the All-Wise Lord, lest he destroy thee," said Zoroaster solemnly. "Harken, ye priests, and obey the word from heaven. Take the brazier from your altar, and scatter the embers upon the floor, for the fire is defiled."

Silent and trembling, the priests obeyed, for they were afraid; but the high priest stood looking in amazement upon Zoroaster.

When the brazier was gone, and the coals were scattered out upon the pavement, and the priests had trodden out the fire with their leathern shoes, Zoroaster went to the black marble altar, and faced the east, looking towards the stone mortar at the end. He laid his long, thin hands upon the flat surface and drew them slowly together; and, in the sight of the priests, a light sprang up softly between his fingers; gradually at first, then higher and higher, till it stood like a blazing spear-head in the midst, emitting a calm, white effulgence that darkened the lamps overhead, and shed an unearthly whiteness on Zoroaster's white face.

He stepped back from the altar, and a low murmur of astonishment rose from all the crowd of white-robed men. Darius stood in silent wonder, gazing alternately upon the figure of Zoroaster, and upon the fragments of his good sword that lay scattered upon the pavement.

Zoroaster looked round upon the faces of the priests with blazing eyes:

"If ye be true priests of Ahura Mazda, raise with me the hymn of praise," he said. "Let it be heard in the heavens, and let it echo beyond the spheres!"

Then his voice rose calm and clear above all the others, and lifting up his eyes and hands, he intoned the solemn chant:

"He, who by truth ruleth in purity, abideth according to the will of the Lord."

"The Lord All-Wise is the giver of gifts to men for the works which men in the world shall do in the truth of the Lord."

"He who protecteth the poor giveth the kingdom to God."

"Best of all earthly goods is truth."

"Glory, glory on high for ever to him who is best in heaven, and truest in truth on earth!"

Zoroaster's grand voice rang out, and all the priests sang melodiously together; and upon the place which had been the scene of such frenzy and fury and drunkenness, there descended a peace as holy and calm as the quiet flame that burned without fuel upon the black stone in the midst. One by one, the priests came and fell at Zoroaster's feet; the chief priest first of all.

"Thou art the prophet and priest of the Lord," each said, one after another. "I acknowledge thee to be the chief priest, and I swear to be a true priest with thee."

And last of all, the king, who had stood silently by, came and would have kneeled before Zoroaster. But Zoroaster took his hands, and they embraced.

"Forgive me the wrong I did thee, Zoroaster," said Darius. "For thou art a holy man, and I will honour thee as thou wast not honoured before."

"Thou hast done me no wrong," answered Zoroaster. "Thou hast sent for me, and I am come to be thy faithful friend, as I swore to thee, long ago, in the tent at Shushan."

Then they took Zoroaster's torn clothes, and they clad him in white robes and set a spotless mitre upon his head; and the king, for the second time, took his golden chain from his own neck, and put it about Zoroaster's shoulders. And they led him away into the palace.

CHAPTER XVI

When it was known that Zoroaster had returned, there was some stir in the palace. The news that he was made high priest soon reached Nehushta's ears, and she wondered what change had come over him in three years that could have made a priest of such a man. She remembered him young and marvellously fair, a warrior at all points, though at the same time an accomplished courtier. She could not imagine him invested with the robes of priesthood, leading a chorus of singers in the chanting of the hymns.

But it was not only as a chief priest that Darius had reinstalled Zoroaster in the palace. The king needed a counsellor and adviser, and the learned priest seemed a person fitted for the post.

On the following day, Nehushta, as was her wont, went out, in the cool of the evening, to walk in the gardens, attended by her maidens, her fan-girls and the slaves who bore her carpet and cushions in case she wished to sit down. She walked languidly, as though she hardly cared to lift her delicate slippered feet from the smooth walk, and often she paused and plucked a flower, and all her train of serving-women stopped behind her, not daring even to whisper among themselves, for the young queen was in no gentle humour of mind. Her face was pale and her eyes were heavy, for she knew the man she had so loved in other days was near, and though he had so bitterly deceived her, the sound of his sweet promises was yet in her ears; and sometimes, in her dreams, she felt the gentle breath of his mouth upon her sleeping lips, and woke with a start of joy that was but the forerunner of a new sadness.

Slowly she paced the walks of the rose-gardens, thinking of another place in the far north, where there had been roses, and myrtles too, upon a terrace where the moonlight was very fair.

As she turned a sharp corner where the overhanging shrubbery darkened the declining light to a dusky shade, she found herself face to face with the man of whom she was thinking. His tall thin figure, clad in spotless white robes, seemed like a shadow in the gloom, and his snowy beard and hair made a strange halo about his young face, that was so thin and worn. He walked slowly, his hands folded together, and his eyes upon the ground; while a few paces behind him two young priests followed with measured steps, conversing in low tones, as though fearing to disturb the meditations of their master.

Nehushta started a little and would have passed on, although she recognised the face of him she had loved. But Zoroaster lifted his eyes, and looked on her with so strange an expression that she stopped short in the way. The deep, calm light in his eyes awed her, and there was something in his majestic presence that seemed of another world.

"Hail, Nehushta!" said the high priest quietly.

But, at the sound of his voice, the spell was broken. The Hebrew woman lifted her head proudly, and her black eyes flashed again.

"Greet me not," she answered, "for the greeting of a liar is like the sting of the serpent that striketh unawares in the dark."

Zoroaster's face never changed, only his luminous eyes gazed on hers intently, and she paused again, as though riveted to the spot.

"I lie not, nor have lied to thee ever," he answered calmly. "Go thou hence, ask her whom thou hatest, whether I have deceived thee. Farewell."

He turned his gaze from her and passed slowly on, looking down to the ground, his hands folded before him. He left her standing in the way, greatly troubled and not understanding his saying.

Had she not seen with her eyes how he held Atossa in his arms on that evil morning in Shushan? Had she not seen how, when he was sent away, he had written a letter to Atossa and no word to herself? Could these things which she had seen and known, be untrue? The thought was horrible—that her whole life had perhaps been wrecked and ruined by a mistake. And yet there was not any mistake, she repeated to herself. She had seen; one must believe what one sees. She had heard Atossa's passionate words of love, and had seen Zoroaster's arms go round her drooping body; one must believe what one sees and hears and knows!

But there was a ringing truth in his voice just now when he said: "I lie not, nor have lied to thee ever." A lie—no, not spoken, but done; and the lie of an action is greater than the lie of a word. And yet, his voice sounded true just now in the dusk, and there was something in it, something like the ring of a far regret. "Ask her whom thou hatest," he had said. That was Atossa. There was no other woman whom she hated—no man save him.

She had many times asked herself whether or no she loved the king. She felt something for him that she had not felt for Zoroaster. The passionate enthusiasm of the strong, dark warrior sometimes carried her away and raised her with it; she loved his manliness, his honesty, his unchanging constancy of purpose. And yet Zoroaster had had all these, and more also, though they had shown themselves in a different way. She looked back and remembered how calm he had always been, how utterly superior in his wisdom. He seemed scarcely mortal, until he had one day fallen—and fallen so desperately low in her view, that she loathed the memory of that feigned calmness and wisdom and parity. For it must have been feigned. How else could he have put his arms about Atossa, and taken her head upon his breast, while she sobbed out words of love?

But if he loved Atossa, she loved him as well. She said so, cried it aloud upon the terrace where any one might have heard it. Why then had he left the court, and hidden himself so long in the wilderness? Why, before going out on his wanderings, had he disguised himself, and gone and stood where the procession passed, and hissed out a bitter insult as Nehushta went by? For her sake he had abandoned his brilliant life these three years, to dwell in the desert, to grow so thin and miserable of aspect that he looked like an old man. And his hair and beard were white—she had heard that a man might turn white from sorrow in a day. Was it grief that had so changed him? Grief to see her wedded to the king before his eyes? His voice rang so true: "Ask her whom thou hatest," he had said. In truth she would ask. It was all too inexplicable, and the sudden thought that she had perhaps wronged him three long years ago—even the possibility of the thought that seemed so little possible to her yesterday—wrought strangely in her breast, and terrified her. She would ask Atossa to her face whether Zoroaster had loved her. She would tell how she had seen them together upon the balcony, and heard Atossa's quick, hot words. She would threaten to tell the king; and if the elder queen refused to answer truth, she would indeed tell him and put her rival to a bitter shame.

She walked more quickly upon the smooth path, and her hands wrung each other, and once she felt the haft of that wicked Indian knife she ever wore. When she turned back and went up the broad steps of the palace, the moon was rising above the far misty hills to eastward, and there were lights beneath the columned portico. She paused and looked back across the peaceful valley, and far down below, a solitary nightingale called out a few melancholy notes, and then burst forth into glorious song.

Nehushta turned again to go in, and there were tears in her dark eyes, that had not stood there for many a long day. But she clasped her hands together, and went forward between the crouching slaves, straight to Atossa's apartment. It was not usual for any one to gain access to the eider queen's inner chambers without first obtaining permission, from Atossa herself, and Nehushta had never been there. They met rarely in public, and spoke little, though each maintained the appearances of courtesy; but Atossa's smile was the sweeter of the two. In private they never saw each other; and the queen's slaves would perhaps have tried to prevent Nehushta from entering, but her black eyes flashed upon them in such dire wrath as she saw them before her, that they crouched away and let her pass on unmolested.

Atossa sat, as ever at that hour in her toilet-chamber, surrounded by her tirewomen. The room was larger than the one at Shushan, for she had caused it to be built after her own plans; but her table was the same as ever, and upon it stood the broad silver mirror, which she never allowed to be left behind when she travelled.

Her magnificent beauty had neither changed nor faded in three years. Such strength as hers was not to be broken, nor worn out, by the mere petty annoyances of palace life. She could sustain the constant little warfare she waged against the king, without even so much as looking careworn and pale for a moment, though the king himself often looked dark and weary, and his eyes were heavy with sleeplessness for the trouble she gave him. Yet he could new determine to rid himself of her, even when he began to understand the profound badness of her character. She exercised a certain fascination over him, as a man grows fond of some beautiful, wicked beast he has half-tamed, though it turn and show its teeth at him sometimes, and be altogether more of a care than a pastime. She was so fair and evil that he could not hurt her; it would have seemed a crime to destroy anything so wondrously made. Moreover, she could amuse him and make many an hour pass pleasantly when she was so disposed.

She was fully attired for the banquet that was to take place late in the evening, but her women were still about her, and she looked at herself critically in the mirror, and would have changed the pinning of her tiara, so that her fair hair should fall forward upon one side, instead of backwards over her shoulder. She tried the effect of the change upon her face, and peered into the mirror beneath the bright light of the tall lamps; when, on a sudden, as she looked, she met the reflection of two angry dark eyes, and she knew that Nehushta was behind her.

She rose to her feet, turning quickly, and the sweep of her long robe overthrew the light carved chair upon the marble floor. She faced Nehushta with a cold smile that betrayed surprise at being thus interrupted in her toilet rather than any dread of the interview. Her delicate eyebrows arched themselves in something of scorn, but her voice came low and sweet as ever.

"It is rarely indeed that the queen Nehushta deigns to visit her servant," she said. "Had she sent warning of her coming, she would have been more fittingly received."

Nehushta stood still before her. She hated that cool, still voice that choked her like a tightening bow-string about her neck.

"We have small need of court formalities," answered the Hebrew woman, shortly. "I desire to speak with you alone upon a matter of importance."

"I am alone," returned Atossa, seating herself upon the carved chair, which one of the slaves had instantly set up again, and motioning to Nehushta to be seated. But Nehushta glanced at the serving-women and remained standing.

"You are not alone," she said briefly.

"They are not women—they are slaves," answered Atossa, with a smile.

"Will you not send them away?"

"Why should I?"

"You need not—I will," returned Nehushta. "Begone, and quickly!" she added, turning to the little group of women and slave-girls who stood together, looking on in wonder. At Nehushta's imperious command, they hurried through the door, and the curtains fell behind them. They knew Nehushta's power in the palace too well to hesitate to obey her, even in the presence of their own mistress.

"Strange ways you have!" exclaimed Atossa, in a low voice. She was fiercely angry, but there was no change in her face. She dangled a little chain upon her finger, and tapped the ground with her foot as she sat. That was all.

"I am not come here to wrangle with you about your slaves. They will obey me without wrangling. I met Zoroaster in the gardens an hour since."

"By a previous arrangement, of course?" suggested Atossa, with a sneer. But her clear blue eyes fixed themselves upon Nehushta with a strange and deadly look.

"Hold your peace and listen to me," said Nehushta in a fierce, low voice, and her slender hand stole to the haft of the knife by her side.

Atossa was a brave woman, false though she was; but she saw that the Hebrew princess had her in her power—she saw the knife and she saw the gleam in those black eyes. They were riveted on her face, and she grew grave and remained silent.

"Tell me the truth," pursued Nehushta hurriedly. "Did Zoroaster love you three years ago—when I saw you in his arms upon the terrace the morning when he came back from Ecbatana?"

But she little knew the woman with whom she had to deal. Atossa had found time in that brief moment to calculate her chances of safety. A weaker woman would have lied; but the fair queen saw that the moment had come wherein she could reap a rich harvest of vengeance upon her rival, and she trusted to her coolness and strength to deliver her if Nehushta actually drew the knife she wore.

"I loved him," she said slowly. "I love him yet, and I hate you more than I love him. Do you understand?"

"Speak—go on!" cried Nehushta, half breathless with anger.

"I loved him, and I hated you. I hate you still," repeated the queen slowly and gravely. "The letter I had from him was written to you—but it was brought to me. Nay—be not so angry, it was very long ago. Of course you can murder me, if you please—you have me in your power, and you are but a cowardly Jew, like twenty of my slave-women. I fear you not. Perhaps you would like to hear the end?"

Nehushta had come nearer and stood looking down at the beautiful woman, her arms folded before her. Atossa never stirred as Nehushta approached, but kept her eye steadily fixed on hers. Nehushta's arms were folded, and the knife hung below her girdle in its loose sheath.

Atossa's white arm went suddenly out and laid hold of the haft, and the keen blue steel flashed out of its scabbard with a sheen like dark lightning on a summer's evening.

Nehushta started back as she saw the sharp weapon in her enemy's hand. But Atossa laughed a low sweet laugh of triumph.

"You shall hear the end now," she said, holding the knife firmly in her hand. "You shall not escape hearing the end now, and you shall not murder me with your Indian poisoner here." She laughed again as she glanced at the ugly curve of the dagger. "I was talking with Zoroaster," she continued, "when I saw you upon the stairs, and then—oh, it was so sweet! I cried out that he should never leave me again, and I threw my arms about his neck—his lordly neck that you so loved!—and I fell, so that he had to hold me up. And you saw him. Oh, it was sweet! It was the sweetest moment of my life when I heard you groan and hurry away and leave us! It was to hurt you that I did it—that I humbled my queenliness before him; but I loved him, though—and he, he your lover, whom you despised then and cast away for this black-faced king of ours—he thrust me from him, and pushed me off, and drove me weeping to my chamber, and he said he loved me not, nor wished my love. Ay, that was bitter, for I was ashamed—I who never was shamed of man or woman. But there was more sweetness in your torment than bitterness in my shame. He never knew you were there. He screamed out to you from the crowd in the procession his parting curse on your unfaithfulness and went out—but he nearly killed those two strong spearmen who tried to seize him. How strong he was then, how brave! What a noble lover for any woman! So tall and delicate and fair with all his strength! He never knew why you left him—he thought it was to wear the king's purple, to thrust a bit of gold in your hair! He must have suffered—you have suffered too—such delicious torture, I have often soothed myself to sleep with the thought of it. It is very sweet for me to see you lying there with my wound in your heart. It will rankle long; you cannot get it out—you are married to the king now, and Zoroaster has turned priest for love of you. I think even the king would hardly love you if he could see you now—you look so pale. I will send for the Chaldean physician—you might die. I should be sorry if you died, you could not suffer any more then. I could not give up the pleasure of hurting you—you have no idea how delicious it is. Oh, how I hate you!"

Atossa rose suddenly to her feet, with flashing eyes. Nehushta, in sheer horror of such hideous cruelty, had fallen back against the door-post, and stood grasping the curtain with one hand while the other was pressed to her heart, as though to control the desperate agony she suffered. Her face was paler than the dead, and her long, black hair fell forward over her ghastly cheeks.

"Shall I tell you more?" Atossa began again. "Should you like to hear more of the truth? I could tell you how the king—"

But as she spoke, Nehushta threw up her hands and pressed them to her throbbing temples; and with a low wail, she turned and fled through the doorway between the thick curtains, that parted with her weight and fell together again when she had passed.

"She will tell the king," said Atossa aloud, when she was gone. "I care not—but I will keep the knife," she added, laying the keen blade upon the table, amid the little instruments of her toilet.

But Nehushta ran fast through the corridors and halls till she came to her slaves who had waited for her at the entrance to the queen's apartment. Then she seemed to recollect herself, and slackened her pace, and went on to her own chambers. But, her women saw her pale face, and whispered together as they cautiously followed her.

She was wretched beyond all words. In a moment, her doubts and her fears had all been realised, and the stain of unfaithfulness had been washed from the memory of her lover. But it was too late to repent her hastiness. She had been married to Darius now for nearly three years, and Zoroaster was a man so changed that she would hardly have recognised him that evening, had she not known that he was in the palace. He looked more like the aged Daniel whom he had buried at Ecbatana than like the lordly warrior of three years ago. She wondered, as she thought of the sound of his voice in the, garden, how she could ever have doubted him, and the remembrance of his clear eyes was both bitter and sweet to her.

She lay upon her silken pillows and wept hot tears for him she had loved long ago, for him and for herself—most of all for the pain she had made him suffer, for that bitter agony that had turned his young, fair locks to snowy white; she wept the tears for him that she could fancy he must have shed in those long years for her. She buried her face and sobbed aloud, so that even the black fan-girl who stood waving the long palm-leaf over her in the dim light of the bedchamber—even the poor black creature from the farther desert, whom her mistress did not half believe human, felt pity for the royal sorrow she saw, and took one hand from the fan to brush the tears from her small red eyes.

Nehushta's heart was broken, and from that day none saw her smile. In one hour the whole misery of all possible miseries came upon her, and bowed her to the ground, and crushed out the life and the light of her nature. As she lay there, she longed to die, as she had never longed for anything while she lived, and she would have had small hesitation in killing the heart that beat with such agonising pain in her breast—saving that one thought prevented her. She cared not for revenge any more. What was the life of that cold, cruel thing, the queen, worth, that by taking it, she could gain comfort? But she felt and knew that, before she died, she must see Zoroaster once more, and tell him that she knew all the truth—that she knew he had not deceived her, and that she implored his forgiveness for the wrong she had done him. He would let her rest her head upon his breast and weep out her heartful of piteous sorrow once before she died. And then—the quiet stream of the Araxes flowed softly, cold and clear, among the rose-gardens below the palace. The kindly water would take her to its bosom, beneath the summer's moon, and the nightingales she loved would sing her a gentle good-night—good-night for ever, while the cool wave flowed over her weary breast and aching head.

CHAPTER XVII

On the next day, in the cool of the evening, Nehushta walked again in the garden. But Zoroaster was not there. And for several days Nehushta came at that hour, and at other hours in the day, but found him not. She saw him indeed from time to time in public, but she had no opportunity of speaking with him as she desired. At last, she determined to send for him, and to see whether he would come, or not.

She went out, attended only by two slaves; the one bearing a fan and the other a small carpet and a cushion—black women from the southern parts of Syria, towards Egypt, who would not understand the high Persian she would be likely to speak with Zoroaster, though her own Hebrew tongue was intelligible to them. When she reached a quiet spot, where one of the walks ended suddenly in a little circle among the rose-trees, far down from the palace, she had her carpet spread, and her cushion was placed upon it, and she wearily sat down. The fan-girl began to ply her palm-leaf, as much to cool the heated summer air as to drive away the swarms of tiny gnats which abounded in the garden. Nehushta rested upon one elbow, her feet drawn together upon the carpet of dark soft colours and waited a few minutes as though in thought. At last she seemed to have decided, and turned to the slave who had brought her cushion, as she stood at a little distance, motionless, her hands folded and hidden under the thickness of the broad sash that girded her tunic at the waist.

"Go thou," said the queen, "and seek out the high priest Zoroaster, and bring him hither quickly."

The black woman turned and ran like a deer down the narrow path, disappearing in a moment amongst the shrubbery.

The breeze of the swinging fan blew softly on Nehushta's pale face and stirred the locks of heavy hair that fell from her tiara about her shoulders. Her eyes were half closed as she leaned back, and her lips were parted in a weary look of weakness that was new to her. Nearly an hour passed and the sun sank low, but Nehushta hardly stirred from her position.

It seemed very long before she heard steps upon the walk—the quick soft step of the slave-woman running before, barefooted and fleet, and presently the heavier tread of a man's leather shoe. The slave stopped at the entrance to the little circle of rose-trees, and a moment later, Zoroaster strode forward, and stood still and made a deep obeisance, a few steps from Nehushta.

"Forgive me that I sent for thee, Zoroaster," said the queen in quiet tones. But, as she spoke, a slight blush overspread her face, and relieved her deadly pallor. "Forgive me—I have somewhat to say which thou must hear."

Zoroaster remained standing before her as she spoke, and his luminous eyes rested upon her quietly.

"I wronged thee three years ago, Zoroaster," said the queen in a low voice, but looking up at him. "I pray thee, forgive me—I knew not what I did."

"I forgave thee long ago," answered the high priest.

"I did thee a bitter wrong—but the wrong I did myself was even greater. I never knew till I went and asked—her!" At the thought of Atossa, the Hebrew woman's eyes flashed fire, and her small fingers clenched upon her palm. But, in an instant, her sad, weary look returned.

"That is all—if you forgive me," she said, and turned her head away. It seemed to her that there was nothing more to be said. He did not love her—he was far beyond love.

"Now, by Ahura Mazda, I have indeed forgiven thee. The blessing of the All-Wise be upon thee!" Zoroaster bent again, as though to take his leave, and he would have gone from her.

But when she heard his first footsteps, Nehushta raised herself a little and turned quickly towards him. It seemed as though the only light she knew were departing from her day.

"You loved me once," she said, and stopped, with an appealing look on her pale face. It was very, weak of her; but oh! she was far spent with sorrow and grief. Zoroaster paused, and looked back upon her, very calmly, very gently.

"Ay—I loved you once—but not now. There is no more love in the earth for me. But I bless you for the love you gave me."

"I loved you so well," said Nehushta. "I love you still," she added, suddenly raising herself and gazing on him with a wild look in her eyes. "Oh, I love you still!" she cried passionately. "I thought I had put you away—forgotten you—trodden out your memory that I so hated I could not bear to hear your name! Ah! why did I do it, miserable woman that I am! I love you now—I love you—I love you with my whole heart—and it is too late!" She fell back upon her cushion, and covered her face with her hands, and her breast heaved with passionate, tearless sobbing.

Zoroaster stood still, and a deep melancholy came over his beautiful, ethereal face. No regret stirred his breast, no touch of the love that had been waked his heart that slept for ever in the peace of the higher life. He would not have changed from himself to the young lover of three years ago, if he had been able. But he stood calm and sorrowful, as an angel from heaven gazing on the grief of the world—his thoughts full of sympathy for the pains of men, his soul still breathing the painless peace of the outer firmament whence he had come and whither he would return.

"Nehushta," he said at last, seeing that her sobbing did not cease, "it is not meet that you should thus weep for anything that is past. Be comforted; the years of life are few, and you are one of the great ones of the earth. It is needful that all should suffer. Forget not that although your heart be heavy, you are a queen, and must bear yourself as a queen. Take your life strongly in your hands and live it. The end is not far and your peace is at hand."

Nehushta looked up suddenly and grew very grave as he spoke. Her heavy eyes rested on his, and she sighed—but the sigh was still broken, by the trembling of her past sobs.

"You, who are a priest and a prophet," she said,—"you, who read the heaven as it were a book—tell me, Zoroaster, is it not far? Shall we meet beyond the stars, as you used to tell me—so long ago?"

"It is not far," he answered, and a gentle smile illuminated his pale face. "Take courage—for truly it is not far."

He gazed into her eyes for a moment, and it seemed as though some of that steadfast light penetrated into her soul, for as he turned and went his way among the roses, a look of peace descended on her tired face, and she fell back upon her cushion and closed her eyes, and let the breeze of the palm-fan play over her wan cheeks and through her heavy hair.

But Zoroaster returned into the palace, and he was very thoughtful. He had many duties to perform, besides the daily evening sacrifice in the temple, for Darius consulted him constantly upon many matters connected with the state; and on every occasion Zoroaster's keen foresight and knowledge of men found constant exercise in the development of the laws and statutes Darius was forming for his consolidated kingdom. First of all, the question of religion seemed to him of paramount importance; and here Zoroaster displayed all his great powers of organisation, as well as the true and just ideas he held upon the subject. Himself an ascetic mystic, he foresaw the danger to others of attempting to pursue the same course, or even of founding a system of mystical study. The object of mankind must be the welfare of mankind, and a set of priests who should shut themselves off from their fellow-men to pursue esoteric studies and to acquire knowledge beyond the reach of common humanity, must necessarily forget humanity itself in their effort to escape from it. The only possible scheme upon which a religion for the world could be based—especially for such a world as the empire of Darius—must be one where the broad principle of common good living stood foremost, and where the good of all humanity should be the good of each man's soul.

The vast influence of Zoroaster's name grew day by day, as from the palace of Stakhar he sent forth priests to the various provinces, full of his own ideas, bearing with them a simple form of worship and a rigid rule of life, which the iron laws of Darius began at once to enforce to the letter. The vast body of existing hymns, of which many were by no means distinctly Mazdayashnian, were reduced to a limited number containing the best and purest; and the multifarious mass of conflicting caste practices, partly imported from India, and partly inherited by the pure Persians from the Aryan home in Sogdiana, was simplified and reduced to a plain rule. The endless rules of purification were cut down to simple measures of health; the varying practices in regard to the disposal of the dead were all done away with by a great royal edict commanding the building of Dakhmas, or towers of death, all over the kingdom; within which the dead were laid by persons appointed for the purpose, and which were cleansed by them, at stated intervals. Severe measures were taken to prevent the destruction of cattle, for there were evident signs of the decrease of the beasts of the field in consequence of the many internal wars that had waged of late; and special laws were provided for the safety of dogs, which were regarded, for all reasons, as the most valuable companions of men in those times, as a means of protection to the flocks in the wilderness, and as the scavengers and cleansers of the great cities. Human life was protected by the most rigorous laws, and the utmost attention was given to providing for the treatment of women of all classes. It would have been impossible to conceive a system better fitted to develop the resources of a semi-pastoral country, to preserve peace and to provide for the increasing wants and the public health of a multiplying people.

As for the religious rites, they assumed a form and a character which made them seem like simplicity itself by the side of the former systems; and which, although somewhat complicated by the additions and alterations of a later and more superstitious, generation, have still maintained the noble and honourable characteristics imparted to them by the great reformer and compiler of the Mazdayashnian religion.

The days flew quickly by, and Zoroaster's power grew apace. It was as though the whole court and kingdom had been but waiting for him to come and be the representative of wisdom and justice beside the conquering king, who had in so short a time reduced so many revolutions and fought so many fields in the consolidation of his empire. Zoroaster laid hold of all the existing difficulties with a master-hand. His years of retirement seemed to have given him the accumulated force of many men, and the effect of his wise measures was quickly felt in every quarter of the provinces; while his words went forth like fire in the mouths of the priests he sent from Stakhar. He had that strange and rare gift, whereby a man inspires in his followers the profoundest confidence and the greatest energy to the performance of his will. He would have overthrown a world had he found himself resisted and oppressed, but every one of his statutes and utterances was backed by the royal arms and enforced by decrees against which there was no appeal. In a few months his name was spoken wherever the Persian rule was felt, and spoken everywhere with a high reverence; in which there was no fear mixed, such as people felt when they mentioned the Great King, and added quickly: "May he live for ever!"

In a few months the reform was complete, and the half-clad ascetic had risen by his own wisdom and by the power of circumstances into the chiefest position in all Persia. Loaded with dignities, treated as the next to the Great King in all things, wearing the royal chain of office over his white priest's robes, and sitting at the right hand of Darius at the feast, Zoroaster nevertheless excited no envy among the courtiers, nor encroached in any way upon their privileges. The few men whom Darius trusted were indeed rarely at Stakhar,—the princes who had conspired against Smerdis, and Hydarnes and a few of the chief officers of the army,—they were mostly in the various provinces, in command of troops and fortresses, actively employed in enforcing the measures the king was framing with Zoroaster, and which were to work such great changes in the destinies of the empire. But when any of the princes or generals were summoned to the court by the king and learned to know what manner of man this Zoroaster was, they began to love him and to honour him also, as all those did who were near him. And they went away, saying that never king had so wise and just a counsellor as he was, nor one so worthy of trust in the smallest as in the greatest things.

But the two queens watched him, and watched his growing power, with different feelings. Nehushta scarcely ever spoke to him, but gazed at him from her sad eyes when none saw her; pondering over his prophecy that foretold the end so near at hand. She had a pride in seeing her old lover the strongest in the whole land, holding the destinies of the kingdom as in a balance; and it was a secret consolation to her to know that he had been faithful to her after all, and that it was for her sake that he had withdrawn into the desert and given himself to those meditations from which he had only issued to enjoy the highest power. And as she looked at him, she saw how he was much changed, and it hardly seemed as though in his body he were the same man she had so loved. Only when he spoke, and she heard the even, musical tones of his commanding voice, she sometimes felt the blood rise to her cheeks with the longing to hear once more some word of tender love, such as he had been used to speak to her. But though he often looked at her and greeted her ever kindly, his quiet, luminous eyes changed not when they gazed on her, nor was there any warmer touch of colour in the waxen whiteness of his face. His youth was utterly gone, as the golden light had faded from his hair. He was not like an old man—he was hardly like a man at all; but rather like some beautiful, strange angel from another world, who moved among men and spoke with them, but was not of them. She seemed to look upon a memory, to love the shadow cast on earth by a being that was gone. But she loved the memory and the shadow well, and month by month, as she gazed, she grew more wan and weary.

It would not have been like Darius to take any notice of a trouble that did not present itself palpably before him and demand his attention. Nehushta scarcely ever spoke of Zoroaster, and when the king mentioned him to her, it was always in connection with affairs of state. She seemed cold and indifferent, and the hot-blooded soldier monarch no longer looked on Zoroaster as a possible rival. He had white hair—he was therefore an old man, out of all questions of love. But Darius was glad that the Hebrew queen never referred to former times, nor ever seemed to regret her old lover. Had he known of that night meeting in Atossa's toilet chamber, and of what Atossa had said then, his fury would probably have had no bounds. But he never knew. Nehushta was too utterly broken-hearted by the blow she had received to desire vengeance, and though she quietly scorned all intercourse with the woman who had injured her, she cared not to tell the king of the injury. It was too late. Had she known of the cruel deception that had been practised on her, one hour before she had married Darius, Atossa would have been in her grave these three years, and Nehushta would not have been queen. But the king knew none of these things, and rejoiced daily in the wisdom of his chief counsellor and in the favour Auramazda had shown in sending him such a man in his need.

Meanwhile, Atossa's hatred grew apace. She saw with anger that her power of tormenting Nehushta was gone from her, that the spirit she had loved to torture was broken beyond all sensibility, and that the man who had scorned her love was grown greater than she. Against his wisdom and the king's activity, she could do little, and her strength seemed to spend itself in vain. Darius laughed mercilessly at her cunning objections to Zoroaster's reforms; and Zoroaster himself eyed hear coldly, and passed her by in silence when they met.

She bethought herself of some scheme whereby to destroy Zoroaster's power by a sudden and violent shock; and for a time, she affected at more than usual serenity of manner, and her smile was sweeter than ever. If it were possible, she thought, to attract the king's attention and forces to some distant point, it would not be a difficult matter to produce a sudden rising or disturbance in Stakhar, situated as the place was upon the very extreme border of the kingdom, within a few hours' march across the hills from the uncivilised desert country, which was infested at that time with hostile and turbulent tribes. She had a certain number of faithful retainers at her command still, whom she could employ as emissaries in both directions, and in spite of the scene that had taken place at Shushan when Phraortes was brought to her by the king, she knew she could still command his services for a revolution. He was a Magian at heart, and hated the existing monarchy. He was rich and powerful, and unboundedly vain—he could easily be prevailed upon to accept the principality of Media as a reward for helping to destroy the Persian kingdom; and indeed the matter had been discussed between him and the queen long ago.

Atossa revolved her scheme in her mind most carefully for two whole months, and at last she resolved to act. Eluding all vigilance of the king, and laughing to herself at the folly of Darius and Zoroaster in allowing her such liberty, she succeeded without much trouble in despatching a letter to Phraortes, inquiring whether her affairs were now in such a prosperous condition as to admit of their being extended.

On the other hand, she sent a black slave she owned, with gifts, into the country of the barbarian tribes beyond the hills, to discover whether they could be easily tempted. This man she bribed with the promise of freedom and rich possessions, to undertake the dangerous mission. She knew him to be faithful, and able to perform the part he was to play.

In less than two months Phraortes sent a reply, wherein he stated that the queen's affairs were so prosperous that they might with safety be extended as she desired, and that he was ready to undertake any improvements provided she sent him the necessary directions and instructions.

The slave returned from the land of the dwellers in tents, with the information that they were numerous as the sands of the sea, riding like the whirlwinds across the desert, keen as a race of eagles for prey, devouring as locusts spreading over a field of corn, and greedy as jackals upon the track of a wounded antelope. Nothing but the terror of the Great King's name restrained them within their boundaries; which they would leave at a moment's notice, as allies of any one who would pay them. They dwelt mostly beyond the desert to eastward in the low hill country; and they shaved their beards and slept with their horses in their tents. They were more horrible to look upon than the devils of the mountains, and fiercer than wolves upon the mountain paths.

Allowing for the imagery of her slave's account, Atossa comprehended that the people described could be easily excited to make a hostile descent upon the southern part of the kingdom, and notably upon the unprotected region about Stakhar, where the fortress could afford shelter to a handful of troops and fugitives, but could in no wise defend the whole of the fertile district from a hostile incursion.

Atossa spent much time in calculating the distance from the palace to the fortress, and she came to the conclusion that a body of persons moving with some encumbrance might easily reach the stronghold in half a day. Her plan was a simple one, and easy of execution; though there was no limit to the evil results its success might have upon the kingdom.

She intended that a revolution should break out in Media, not under the leadership of Phraortes, lest she herself should perish, having been already suspected of complicity with him. But a man could be found—some tool of her powerful agent, who could be readily induced to set himself up as a pretender to the principality of the province, and he could easily be crushed at a later period by Phraortes, who would naturally furnish the money and supplies for the insurrection.

As soon as the news reached Stakhar, Darius would, in all probability, set out for Media in haste to arrive at the scene of the disturbance. He would probably leave Zoroaster behind to manage the affairs of state, which had centred in Stakhar during the last year and more. If, however, he took him with him, and left the court to follow on as far as Shushan, Atossa could easily cause an incursion of the barbarous tribes from the desert. The people of the south would find themselves abandoned by the king, and would rise against him, and Atossa could easily seize the power. If Zoroaster remained behind, the best plan would be to let the barbarians take their own course and destroy him. Separated from any armed force of magnitude sufficient to cope with a sudden invasion, he would surely fall in the struggle, or take refuge in an ignominious flight. With the boldness of her nature, Atossa trusted to circumstances to provide her with an easy escape for herself; and in the last instance, she trusted, as she had ever done, to her marvellous beauty to save her from harm. To her beauty alone she owed her escape from many a fit of murderous anger in the time of Cambyses, and to her beauty she owed her salvation when Darius found her at Shushan, the wife and accomplice of the impostor Smerdis. She might again save herself by that means, if by no other, should she, by any mischance, fall into the hands of the barbarians. But she was determined to overthrow Zoroaster, even if she had to destroy her husband's kingdom in the effort. It was a bold and simple plan, and she doubted not of being successful.

During the months while she was planning these things, she was very calm and placid; her eyes met Zoroaster's with a frank and friendly glance that would have disarmed one less completely convinced of her badness; and her smile never failed the king when he looked for it. She bore his jests with unfailing equanimity and gentleness, for she felt that she should not have to bear them long. Even to Nehushta she gave an occasional glance as though of hurt sympathy—a look that seemed to say to the world that she regretted the Hebrew queen's sullen temper and moody ways, so different from her own, but regarded them all the while as the outward manifestation of some sickness, for which she was to be pitied rather than blamed.

But, as the time sped, her heart grew more and more glad, for the end was at hand, and there was a smell of death in the air of the sweet rose-valley.

CHAPTER XVIII

Once more the spring months had come, and the fields grew green and the trees put forth their leaves. Four years had passed since Daniel had died in Ecbatana, leaving his legacy of wisdom to Zoroaster; and almost a year had gone by since Zoroaster had returned to the court at Stakhar. The time had sped very swiftly, except for Nehushta, whose life was heavy with a great weariness and her eyes hollow with suffering sleeplessness. She was not always the same, saving that she was always unhappy. There were days when she was resigned to her lot and merely hoped that it would soon be over; and she wondered how it was that she did not slip out of the gardens at evening, and go and sink her care and her great sorrow in the cool waves of the Araxes, far down below. But then the thought came over her that she must see his face once more; and it was always once more, so that the last time never came. And again, there were days when she hoped all things, madly, indiscriminately, without sequence—the king might die, Zoroaster might again love her, all might be well. But the mood of a hope that is senseless is very fleet, and despair follows close in its footsteps. Nehushta grew each time more sad, as she grew more certain that for her there was no hope.

At least it seemed as though Atossa had given up loving Zoroaster and thought no more of him than of another. Indeed Atossa seemed more anxious to please the king than formerly, in proportion as Darius seemed less easily pleased by her. But over all, Zoroaster's supremacy was felt in the palace, and though he was never known to be angry with any one, he was more feared than the fierce king himself, for his calm clear eyes were hard to meet and the words that fell from his lips had in them the ring of fate. Moreover, he was known and his power was dreaded from one end of the kingdom to the other, and his name was like the king's signet, which sealed all things, and there was no appeal.

Upon a fair morning in the spring-time, when the sun was shining outside upon the roses still wet with dew, the king sat in an inner hall, half lying upon a broad couch, on which the warm rays of the sun fell through an upper window. He was watching with absorbed attention the tricks of an Indian juggler who had lately arrived at the court, and whom he had summoned that morning to amuse a leisure hour, for when the king was not actively engaged in business, or fighting, he loved some amusement, being of a restless temper and mind that needed constant occupation.

Atossa sat near him, upon a carved chair, turning over and over in her fingers a string of pearls as she gazed at the performances of the juggler. Two spearmen, clad in blue and scarlet and gold, stood motionless by the door, and Darius and Atossa watched the sleight-handed Indian alone.

The man tossed a knife into the air and caught it, then two, then three, increasing the number in rapid succession till a score of bright blades made a shining circle in the air as he quickly tossed them up and passed them from hand to hand and tossed them again. Darius laughed at the man's skill, and looked up at the queen.

"You remind me of that fellow," said Darius.

"The king is very gracious to his handmaiden," answered Atossa, smiling, "I think I am less skilful, but more fair."

"You are fairer, it is true," returned the king; "but as for your skill, I know not. You seem always to be playing with knives, but you never wound yourself any more than he does."

The queen looked keenly at Darius, but her lips smiled gently. The thought crossed her mind that the king perhaps knew something of what had passed between her and Nehushta nearly a year before, with regard to a certain Indian dagger. The knives the juggler tossed in the air reminded her of it by their shape. But the king laughed gaily and she answered without hesitation:

"I would it were true, for then I could be not only the king's wife, but the king's juggler!"

"I meant not so," laughed Darius. "The two would hardly suit one another."

"And yet, I need more skill than this Indian fellow, to be the king's wife," answered the queen slowly.

"Said I not so?"

"Nay—but you meant not so," replied Atossa, looking down.

"What I say, I mean," he returned. "You need all the fairness of your face to conceal the evil in your heart, as this man needs all his skill in handling those sharp knives, that would cut off his fingers if, unawares, he touched the wrong edge of them."

"I conceal nothing," said the queen, with a light laugh. "The king has a thousand eyes—how should I conceal anything from him?"

"That is a question which I constantly ask myself," answered Darius. "And yet, I often think I know your thoughts less well than those of the black girl who fans you when you are hot, and whose attention is honestly concentrated upon keeping the flies from your face—or of yonder stolid spearmen at the door, who watch us, and honestly wish they were kings and queens, to lie all day upon a silken couch, and watch the tricks of a paid conjurer."

As Darius spoke, the guards he glanced at turned suddenly and faced each other, standing on each side of the doorway, and brought their heavy spears to the ground with a ringing noise. In a moment the tall, thin figure of Zoroaster, in his white robes, appeared between them. He stopped respectfully at the threshold, waiting for the king to notice him, for, in spite of his power and high rank, he chose to maintain rigidly the formalities of the court.

Darius made a sign and the juggler caught his whirling knives, one after the other, and thrust them into his bag, and withdrew.

"Hail, Zoroaster!" said the king. "Come near and sit beside me, and tell me your business."

Zoroaster came forward and made a salutation, but he remained standing, as though the matter on which he came were urgent.

"Hail, king, and live for ever!" he said. "I am a bearer of evil news. A rider has come speeding from Ecbatana, escaped from the confusion. Media has revolted, and the king's guards are besieged within the fortress of Ecbatana."

Darius sat upright upon the edge of his couch; the knotted veins upon his temples swelled with sudden anger and his brow flushed darkly.

"Doubtless it is Phraortes who has set himself up as king," he said. Then, suddenly and fiercely, he turned upon Atossa. "Now is your hour come," he cried in uncontrollable anger. "You shall surely die this day, for you have done this, and the powers of evil shall have your soul, which is of them, and of none other."

Atossa, for the first time in her whole life, turned pale to the lips and trembled, for she already seemed to taste death in the air. But even then, her boldness did not desert her, and she rose to her feet with a stateliness and a calmness that almost awed the king's anger to silence.

"Slay me if thou wilt," she said in a low voice, but firmly. "I am innocent of this deed." The great lie fell from her lips with a calmness that a martyr might have envied. But Zoroaster stepped between her and the king. As he passed her, his clear, calm eyes met hers for a moment. He read in her face the fear of death, and he pitied her.

"Let the king hear me," he said. "It is not Phraortes who has headed the revolt, and it is told me that Phraortes has fled from Ecbatana. Let the king send forth his armies and subdue the rebels, and let this woman go; for the fear of death is upon her and it may be that she has not sinned in this matter. And if she have indeed sinned, will the king make war upon women, or redden his hands with the blood of his own wife?"

"You speak as a priest—I feel as a man," returned the king, savagely. "This woman has deserved death many times—let her die. So shall we be free of her."

"It is not lawful to do this thing," returned Zoroaster coldly, and his glance rested upon the angry face of Darius, as he spoke, and seemed to subdue his furious wrath. "The king cannot know whether she have deserved death or not, until he have the rebels of Ecbatana before him. Moreover, the blood of a woman is a perpetual shame to the man who has shed it."

The king seemed to waver, and Atossa, who watched him keenly, understood that the moment had come in which she might herself make an appeal to him. In the suddenness of the situation she had time to ask herself why Zoroaster, whom she had so bitterly injured, should intercede for her. She could not understand his nobility of soul, and she feared some trap, into which she should fall by and by. But, meanwhile, she chose to appeal to the king's mercy herself, lest she should feel that she owed her preservation wholly to Zoroaster. It was a bold thought, worthy of a woman of her strength, in a moment of supreme danger.

With a quick movement she tore the tiara from her head and let it fall upon the floor. The mass of her silken hair fell all about her like a vesture of gold, and she threw herself at the king's feet, embracing his knees with a passionate gesture of appeal. Her face was very pale, and the beauty of it seemed to grow by the unnatural lack of colour, while her soft blue eyes looked up into the king's face with such an expression of imploring supplication that he was fain to acknowledge to himself that she moved his heart, for she had never looked so fair before. She spoke no word, but held his knees, and as she gazed, two beautiful great tears rolled slowly from under her eyelids, and trembled upon her pale, soft cheeks, and her warm, quick breath went up to his face.

Darius tried to push her from him, but she would not go, and he was forced to look at her, and his anger melted, and he smiled somewhat grimly, though his brows were bent.

"Go to," he said, "I jested. It is impossible for a man to slay anything so beautiful as you."

Atossa's colour returned to her cheeks, and bending down, she kissed the king's knees and his hands, and her golden hair fell all about her and upon the king's lap. But Darius rose impatiently, and left her kneeling by the couch. He was already angry with himself for having forgiven her, and he hated his own weakness bitterly.

"I will myself go hence at once with the guards, and I will take half the force from the fortress of Stakhar and go to Shushan, and thence, with the army that is there, I will be in Ecbatana in a few days. And I will utterly crush out these rebels who speak lies and do not acknowledge me. Remain here, Zoroaster, and govern this province until I return in triumph."

Darius glanced once more at Atossa, who lay by the couch, half upon it and half upon the floor, seemingly dazed at what had occurred; and then he turned upon his heel and strode out of the room between the two spearmen of the guard, who raised their weapons as he passed, and followed him with a quick, rhythmical tread down the broad corridor outside.

Zoroaster was left alone with the queen.

As soon as Darius was gone, Atossa rose to her feet, and with all possible calmness proceeded to rearrange her disordered hair and to place her head-dress upon her head. Zoroaster stood and watched her; her hand trembled a little, but she seemed otherwise unmoved by what had occurred. She glanced up at him from under her eyelids as she stood with her head bent down and her hands raised, to arrange her hair.

"Why did you beg the king to spare my life?" she asked. "You, of all men, must wish me dead."

"I do not wish you dead," he answered coldly. "You have yet much evil to do in the world, but it will not be all evil. Neither did I need to intercede for you. Your time is not come, and though the king's hand were raised to strike you, it would not fall upon you, for you are fated to accomplish many things."

"Do you not hate me, Zoroaster?"

It was one of the queen's chief characteristics that she never attempted concealment when it could be of no use, and in such cases affected an almost brutal frankness. She almost laughed as she asked the question—it seemed so foolish, and yet she asked it.

"I do not hate you," answered the priest. "You are beneath hatred."

"And I presume you are far above it?" she said very scornfully, and eyed him in silence for a moment. "You are a poor creature," she pursued, presently. "I heartily despise you. You suffered yourself to be deceived by a mere trick; you let the woman you loved go from you without an effort to keep her. You might have been a queen's lover, and you despised her. And now, when you could have the woman who did you a mortal injury be led forth to death before your eyes, you interceded for her and saved her life. You are a fool. I despise you."

"I rejoice that you do," returned Zoroaster coldly. "I would not have your admiration, if I might be paid for receiving it with the whole world and the wisdom thereof."

"Not even if you might have for your wife the woman you loved in your poor, insipid way—but you loved her nevertheless? She is pale and sorrowful, poor creature; she haunts the gardens like the shadow of death; she wearies the king with her wan face. She is eating her heart out for you—the king took her from you, you could take her from him to-morrow, if you pleased. The greater your folly, because you do not. As for her, her foolishness is such that she would follow you to the ends of the earth—poor girl! she little knows what a pale, wretched, sapless thing you have in your breast for a heart."

But Zoroaster gazed calmly at the queen in quiet scorn at her scoffing.

"Think you that the sun is obscured, because you can draw yonder curtain before your window and keep out his rays?" he asked. "Think you that the children of light feel pain because the children of darkness say in their ignorance that there is no light?"

"You speak in parables—having nothing plain to say," returned the queen, thrusting a golden pin through her hair at the back and through the folds of her linen tiara. But she felt Zoroaster's eyes upon her, and looking up, she was fascinated by the strange light in them. She strove to look away from him, but could not. Suddenly her heart sank within her. She had heard of Indian charmers and of Chaldean necromancers and wise men, who could perform wonders and slay their enemies with a glance. She struggled to take her eyes from his, but it was of no use. The subtle power of the universal agent had got hold upon her, and she was riveted to the spot so long as he kept his eyes upon her. He spoke again, and his voice seemed to come to her with a deafening metallic force, as though it vibrated to her very brain.

"You may scoff at me; shield yourself from me, if you can," said Zoroaster. "Lift one hand, if you are able—make one step from me, if you have the strength. You cannot; you are altogether in my power. If I would, I could kill you as you stand, and there would be no mark of violence upon you, that a man should be able to say you were slain. You boast of your strength and power. See, you follow the motion of my hand, as a dog would. See, you kneel before me, and prostrate yourself in the dust at my feet, at my bidding. Lie there, and think well whether you are able to scoff any more. You kneeled to the king of your own will; you kneel to me at mine, and though you had the strength of a hundred men, you must kneel there till I bid you rise."

The queen was wholly under the influence of the terrible power Zoroaster possessed. She was no more able to resist his will than a drowning man can resist the swift torrent that bears him down to his death. She lay at the priest's feet, helpless and nerveless. He gazed at her for a moment as she crouched before him.

"Rise," he said, "go your way, and remember me."

Relieved from the force of the subtle influence he projected, Atossa sprang to her feet and staggered back a few paces, till she fell upon the couch.

"What manner of man art thou?" she said, staring wildly before her, as though recovering from some heavy blow that had stunned her.

But she saw Zoroaster's white robes disappear through the door, even while the words were on her lips, and she sank back in stupefaction upon the cushions of the couch.

Meanwhile the trumpets sounded in the courts of the palace and the guards were marshalled out at the king's command. Messengers mounted and rode furiously up the valley to the fortress, to warn the troops there to make ready for the march; and before the sun reached the meridian, Darius was on horseback, in his armour, at the foot of the great staircase. The blazing noonday light shone upon his polished helmet and on the golden wings that stood out on either side of it, and the hot rays were sent flashing back from his gilded harness, and from the broad scales of his horse's armour.

The slaves of the palace stood in long ranks before the columns of the portico and upon the broad stairs on each side, and Zoroaster stood on the lowest step, attended by a score of his priests, to receive the king's last instructions.

"I go forth, and in two months I will return in triumph," said Darius. "Meanwhile keep thou the government in thy hand, and let not the laws be relaxed because the king is not here. Let the sacrifice be performed daily in the temple, and let all things proceed as though I myself were present. I will not that petty strifes arise because I am away. There shall be peace—peace—peace forever throughout my kingdom, though I shed much blood to obtain it. And all the people who are evildoers and makers of strife and sedition shall tremble at the name of Darius, the king of kings, and of Zoroaster, the high priest of the All-Wise. In peace I leave you, to cause peace whither I go; and in peace I will come again to you. Farewell, Zoroaster, truest friend and wisest counsellor; in thy keeping I leave all things. Take thou the signet and bear it wisely till I come."

Zoroaster received the royal ring and bowed a low obeisance. Then Darius pressed his knees to his horse's sides and the noble steed sprang forward upon the straight, broad road, like an arrow from a bow. The mounted guards grasped their spears and gathered their bridles in their hands and followed swiftly, four and four, shoulder to shoulder, and knee to knee, their bronze cuirasses and polished helmets blazing in the noonday sun and dashing as they galloped on; and in a moment there was nothing seen of the royal guard but a tossing wave of light far up the valley; and the white dust, that had risen, as they plunged forward, settled slowly in the still, hot air upon the roses and shrubs that hung over the enclosure of the garden at the foot of the broad staircase.

Zoroaster gazed for a moment on the track of the swift warriors; then went up the steps, followed by his priests, and entered the palace.

Atossa and Nehushta had watched the departure of the king from their upper windows, at the opposite ends of the building, from behind the gilded lattices. Atossa had recovered somewhat from the astonishment and fear that had taken possession of her when she had found herself under Zoroaster's strange influence, and as she saw Darius ride away, while Zoroaster remained standing upon the steps, her courage rose. She resolved that nothing should induce her again to expose herself to the chief priest's unearthly power, and she laughed to herself as she thought that she might yet destroy him, and free herself from him for ever. She wondered how she could ever have given a thought of love to such a man, and she summoned her black slave, and sent him upon his last errand, by which he was to obtain his freedom.

But Nehushta gazed sadly after the galloping guards, and her eye strove to distinguish the king's crest before the others, till all was mingled in the distance, in an indiscriminate reflection of moving light, and then lost to view altogether in the rising dust. Whether she loved him truly, or loved him not, he had been true and kind to her, and had rested his dark head upon her shoulder that very morning before he went, and had told her that, of all living women, he loved her best. But she had felt a quick sting of pain in her heart, because she knew that she would give her life to lie for one short hour on Zoroaster's breast and sob out all her sorrow and die.

CHAPTER XIX

Four days after the king's departure, Nehushta was wandering in the gardens as the sun was going down, according to her daily custom. There was a place she loved well—a spot where the path widened to a circle, round which the roses grew, thick and fragrant with the breath of the coming summer, and soft green shrubs and climbing things that twisted their tender arms about the myrtle trees. The hedge was so high that it cut off all view of the gardens beyond, and only the black north-western hills could just be seen above the mass of shrubbery; beyond the mountains and all over the sky, the glow of the setting sun spread like a rosy veil; and the light tinged the crests of the dark hills and turned the myrtle leaves to a strange colour, and gilded the highest roses to a deep red gold.

The birds were all singing their evening song in loud, happy chorus, as only Eastern birds can sing; the air was warm and still, and the tiny gnats chased each other with lightning quickness in hazy swarms overhead, in the reflected glow.

Nehushta loved the little open space, for it was there that, a year ago, she had sent for Zoroaster to come to her that she might tell him she knew the truth at last. She stood still and listened to the singing of the birds, gazing upwards at the glowing sky, where the red was fast turning to purple; she breathed in the warm air and sighed softly; wishing, as she wished every night, that the sunset might fade to darkness, and there might be no morning for her any more.

She had lived almost entirely alone since Darius had gone to Shushan; she avoided Atossa, and she made no effort to see Zoroaster, who was entirely absorbed by the management of the affairs of the state. In the king's absence there were no banquets, as there used to be when he was in the palace, and the two queens were free to lead whatever life seemed best to them, independently of each other and of the courtiers. Atossa had chosen to shut herself up in the seclusion of her own apartments, and Nehushta rarely left her own part of the palace until the evening. But when the sun was low, she loved to linger among the roses in the garden, till the bright shield of the moon was high in the east, or till the faint stars burned in their full splendour, and the nightingales began to call and trill their melancholy song from end to end of the sweet valley.

So she stood on this evening, looking up into the sky, and her slaves waited her pleasure at a little distance. But while she gazed, she heard quick steps along the walk, and the slave-women sprang aside to let some one pass. Nehushta turned and found herself face to face with Atossa, who stood before her, wrapped in a dark mantle, a white veil of Indian gauze wound about her head, and half-concealing her face. It was a year since they had met in private, and Nehushta drew herself suddenly to her height, and the old look of scorn came over her dark features. She would have asked haughtily what brought Atossa there, but the fair queen was first in her speech. There was hardly even the affectation of friendliness in her tones, as she stood there alone and unattended, facing her enemy.

"I came to ask if you wished to go with me," said Atossa.

"Where? Why should I go with you?"

"I am weary of the palace. I think I will go to Shushan to be nearer the king. To-night I will rest at the fortress."

Nehushta stared coldly at the fair woman, muffled in her cloak and veil.

"What is it to me whether you go to the ends of the earth, or whether you remain here?" she asked.

"I wished to know whether you desired to accompany me, else I should not have asked you the question. I feared that you might be lonely here in Stakhar—will you not come?"

"Again I say, why do you ask me? What have I to do with you?" returned Nehushta, drawing her mantle about her as though to leave Atossa.

"If the king were here, he would bid you go," said Atossa, looking intently upon her enemy.

"It is for me to judge what the king would wish me to do—not for you. Leave me in peace. Go your way if you will—it is nothing to me."

"You will not come?" Atossa's voice softened and she smiled serenely. Nehushta turned fiercely upon her.

"No! If you are going—go! I want you not!"

"You are glad I am going, are you not?" asked Atossa, gently.

"I am glad—with a gladness only you can know. I would you were already gone!"

"You rejoice that I leave you alone with your lover. It is very natural—"

"My lover!" cried Nehushta, her wrath rising and blazing in her eyes.

"Ay, your lover! the thin, white-haired priest, that once was Zoroaster—your old lover—your poor old lover!"

Nehushta steadied herself for a moment. She felt as though she must tear this woman in pieces. But she controlled her anger by a great effort, though she was nearly choking as she drew herself up and answered.

"I would that the powers of evil, of whom you are, might strangle the thrice-accursed lie in your false throat!" she said, in low fierce tones, and turned away.

Still Atossa stood there, smiling as ever. Nehushta looked back as she reached the opposite end of the little plot.

"Are you not yet gone? Shall I bid my slaves take you by the throat and force you from me?" But, as she spoke, she looked beyond Atossa, and saw that a body of dark men and women stood in the path. Atossa had not come unprotected.

"I see you are the same foolish woman you ever were," answered the older queen. Just then, a strange sound echoed far off among the hills above, strange and far as the scream of a distant vulture sailing its mate to the carrion feast—an unearthly cry that rang high in the air from side to side of the valley, and struck the dark crags and doubled in the echo, and died away in short, faint pulsations of sound upon the startled air.

Nehushta started slightly. It might have been the cry of a wolf, or of some wild beast prowling upon the heights, but she had never heard such a sound before. But Atossa showed no surprise, and her smile returned to her lips more sweetly than ever—those lips that had kissed three kings, and that had never spoken truly a kind or a merciful word to living man, or child, or woman.

"Farewell, Nehushta," she said, "if you will not come, I will leave you to yourself—and to your lover. I daresay he can protect you from harm. Heard you that sound? It is the cry of your fate. Farewell, foolish girl, and may every undreamed-of quality of evil attend you to your dying day—"

"Go!" cried Nehushta, turning and pointing to the path with a gesture of terrible anger. Atossa moved back a little.

"It is no wonder I linger awhile—I thought you were past suffering. If I had time, I might yet find some way of tormenting you—you are very foolish—"

Nehushta walked rapidly forward upon her, as though to do her some violence with her own hands. But Atossa, as she gave way before the angry Hebrew woman, drew from beneath her mantle the Indian knife she had once taken from her. Nehushta stopped short, as she saw the bright blade thrust out against her bosom. But Atossa held it up one moment, and then threw it down upon the grass at her feet.

"Take it!" she cried, and in her voice, that had been so sweet and gentle a moment before, there suddenly rang out a strange defiance and a bitter wrath. "Take what is yours—I loathe it, for it smells of you—and you, and all that is yours, I loathe and hate and scorn!"

She turned with a quick movement and disappeared amongst her slaves, who closed in their ranks behind her, and followed her rapidly down the path. Nehushta remained standing upon the grass, peering after her retreating enemy through the gloom; for the glow had faded from the western sky while they had been speaking, and it was now dusk.

Suddenly, as she stood, almost transfixed with the horror of her fearful anger, that strange cry rang again through the lofty crags and crests of the mountains, and echoed and died away.

Nehushta's slave-women, who had hung back in fear and trembling during the altercation between the two queens, came forward and gathered about her.

"What is it?" asked the queen in a low voice, for her own heart beat with the anticipation of a sudden danger. "It is the cry of your fate," Atossa had said—verily it sounded like the scream of a coming death.

"It is the Druksh of the mountains!" said one.

"It is the howling of wolves," said another, a Median woman from the Zagros mountains.

"The war-cry of the children of Anak is like that," said a little Syrian maid, and her teeth chattered with fear.

As they listened, crouching and pressing about their royal mistress in their terror, they heard below in the road, the sound of horses and men moving quickly past the foot of the gardens. It was Atossa and her train, hurrying along the highway in the direction of the fortress.

Nehushta suddenly pushed the slaves aside, and fled down the path towards the palace, and the dark women hurried after. One of them stooped and picked up the Indian knife and hid it in her bosom as she ran.

The whole truth had flashed across Nehushta's mind in an instant. Some armed force was collecting upon the hills to descend in a body upon the palace, to accomplish her destruction. Atossa had fled to a place of safety, after enjoying the pleasure of tormenting her doomed enemy to the last moment, well knowing that no power would induce Nehushta to accompany her. But one thought filled Nehushta's mind in her instantaneous comprehension of the truth; she must find Zoroaster, and warn him of the danger. They would have time to fly together, yet. Atossa must have known how to time her flight, since the plot was hers, and she had not yet been many minutes upon the road.

Through the garden she ran, and up the broad steps to the portico. Slaves were moving about under the colonnade, leisurely lighting the great torches that burned there all night. They had not heard the strange cries from the hills; or, hearing only a faint echo, had paid no attention to the sound.

Nehushta paused, breathless with running. As she realised the quiet that reigned in the palace, where the slaves went about their duties as though nothing had occurred, or were likely to occur, it seemed to her as though she must have been dreaming. It was impossible that if there were any real danger, it should not have become known at least to some one of the hundreds of slaves who thronged the outer halls and corridors. Moreover there were numerous scribes and officers connected with the government; some few nobles whom Darius had left behind when he went to Shushan; there were their wives and families residing in various parts, of the palace and in the buildings below it, and there was a strong detachment of Persian guards. If there were danger, some one must have known it.

She did not know that at that moment the inhabitants of the lower palace were already alarmed, while some were flying, leaving everything behind, in their haste to reach the fortress higher up the valley. Everything seemed quiet where she was, and she determined to go alone in search of Zoroaster, without raising any alarm. Just as she entered the doorway of the great hall, she heard the cry again echoing behind her through the valley. It was as much as she could do to control the terror that again took hold of her at the dreaded sound, as she passed the files of bowing slaves, and went in between the two tall spearmen who guarded the inner entrance, and grounded their spears with military precision as she went by.

She had one slave whom she trusted more than the rest. It was the little Syrian maid, who was half a Hebrew.

"Go," she said quickly, in her own tongue. "Go in one direction and I will go in another, and search out Zoroaster, the high priest, and bring him to my chamber. I also will search, but if I find him not, I will wait for thee there."

The dark girl turned and ran through the halls, swift as a startled fawn, to fulfil her errand, and Nehushta went another way upon her search. She was ashamed to ask for Zoroaster. The words of her enemy were still ringing in her ears—"alone with your lover;" it might be the common talk of the court for all she knew. She went silently on her way. She knew where Zoroaster dwelt. The curtain of his simple chamber was thrown aside and a faint light burned in the room. It was empty; a scroll lay open upon the floor beside a purple cushion, as he had left it, and his long white mantle lay tossed upon the couch which served him for a bed.

She gazed lovingly for one moment into the open chamber, and then went on through the broad corridor, dimly lighted everywhere with small oil lamps. She looked into the council chamber and it was deserted. The long rows of double seats were empty, and gleamed faintly in the light. High upon the dais at the end, a lamp burned above the carved chair of ivory and gold, whereon the king sat when the council was assembled. There was no one there. Farther on, the low entrance to the treasury was guarded by four spearmen, whose arms clanged upon the floor as the queen passed. But she saw that the massive bolts and the huge square locks upon them were in their places. There was no one within. In the colonnade beyond, a few nobles stood talking carelessly together, waiting for their evening meal to be served them in a brightly illuminated hall, of which the doors stood wide open to admit the cool air of the coming night. The magnificently-arrayed courtiers made a low obeisance and then stood in astonishment as the queen went by. She held up her head and nodded to them, trying to look as though nothing disturbed her.

On and on she went through the whole wing, till she came to her own apartment. Not so much as one white-robed priest had she seen upon all her long search. Zoroaster was certainly not in the portion of the palace through, which she had come. Entering her own chambers, she looked round for the little Syrian maid, but she had not returned.

Unable to bear the suspense any longer, she hastily despatched a second slave in search of the chief priest—a Median woman, who had been with her in Ecbatana.

It seemed as though the minutes were lengthened to hours. Nehushta sat with her hands pressed to her temples, that throbbed as though the fever would burst her brain, and the black fan-girl plied the palm-leaf with all her might, thinking that her mistress suffered from the heat. The other women she dismissed; and she sat waiting beneath the soft light of the perfumed lamp, the very figure and incarnation of anxiety.

Something within her told her that she was in great and imminent danger, and the calm she had seen in the palace could not allay in her mind the terror of that unearthly cry she had heard three times from the hills. As she thought of it, she shuddered, and the icy fear seemed to run through all her limbs, chilling the marrow in her bones, and freezing her blood suddenly in its mad course.

"Left alone with your lover"—"it is the cry of your fate"—Atossa's words kept ringing in her ears like a knell—the knell of a shameful death; and as she went over the bitter taunts of her enemy, her chilled pulses beat again more feverishly than before. She could not bear to sit still, but rose and paced the room in intense agitation. Would they never come back, those dallying slave-women?

The fan-girl tried to follow her mistress, and her small red eyes watched cautiously every one of Nehushta's movements. But the queen waved her off and the slave went and stood beside the chair where she had sat, her fan hanging idly in her hand. At that moment, the Median woman entered the chamber.

"Where is he?" asked Nehushta, turning suddenly upon her.

The woman made a low obeisance and answered in trembling tones:

"They say that the high priest left the palace two hours ago, with the queen Atossa. They say—"

"Thou liest!" cried Nehushta vehemently, and her face turned white, as she stamped her foot upon the black marble pavement. The woman sprang back with a cry of terror, and ran towards the door. She had never seen her mistress so angry. But Nehushta called her back.

"Come hither—what else do they say?" she asked, controlling herself as best she could.

"They say that the wild riders of the eastern desert are descending from the hills," answered the slave hurriedly and almost under her breath. "Every one is flying—everything is in confusion—I hear them even now, hurrying to and fro in the courts, the soldiers—"

But, even as she spoke, an echo of distant voices and discordant cries came through the curtains of the door from without, the rapid, uneven tread of people running hither and thither in confusion, the loud voices of startled men and the screams of frightened women—all blending together in a wild roar that grew every moment louder.

Just then, the little Syrian maid came running in, almost tearing the curtains from their brazen rods as she thrust the hangings aside. She came and fell breathless at Nehushta's feet and clasped her knees.

"Fly, fly, beloved mistress," she cried, "the devils of the mountains are upon us—they cover the hills—they are closing every entrance—the people in the lower palace are all slain—"

"Where is Zoroaster?" In the moment of supreme danger, Nehushta grew calm, and her senses were restored to her again.

"He is in the temple with the priests—by this time he is surely slain—he could know of nothing that is going on—fly, fly!" cried the poor Syrian girl in an agony of terror.

Nehushta laid her hand kindly upon the head of the little maid, and turning in the pride of her courage, now that she knew the worst, she spoke calmly to the other slaves who thronged in from the outer hall, some breathless with fear, others screaming in an agony of acute dread.

"On which side are they coming?" she asked.

"Prom the hills, from the hills they are descending in thousands," cried half a dozen of the frightened women at once, the rest huddled together like sheep, moaning in their fear.

"Go you all to the farther window," cried Nehushta, in commanding tones. "Leap down upon the balcony—it is scarce a man's height—follow it to the end and past the corner where it joins the main wall of the garden. Run along upon the wall till you find a place where you can descend. Through the gardens you can easily reach the road by the northern gate. Fly and save yourselves in the darkness. You will reach the fortress before dawn if you hasten. You will hasten," she added with something of disdain in her voice, for before she had half uttered her directions, the last of the slave-women, mad with terror, disappeared through the open window, and she could hear them drop, one after the other, in quick succession upon the marble balcony below. She was alone.

But, looking down, she saw at her feet the little Syrian maid, looking with imploring eyes to her face.

"Why do you not go with the rest?" asked Nehushta, stooping down and laying one hand upon the girl's shoulder.

"I have eaten thy bread—shall I leave thee in the hour of death?" asked the little slave, humbly.

"Go, child," replied Nehushta, very kindly. "I have seen thy devotion and truth—thou must not perish."

But the Syrian leaped to her feet, and there was pride in her small face, as she answered:

"I am a bondwoman, but I am a daughter of Israel, even as thou art. Though all the others leave thee, I will not. It may be I can help thee."

"Thou art a brave child," said Nehushta; and she drew the girl to her and pressed her kindly. "I must go to Zoroaster—stay thou here, hide thyself among the curtains—escape by the window, if any come to harm thee." She turned and went rapidly out between the curtains, as calm and as pale as death.

The din in the palace had partially subsided, and new and strange cries re-echoed through the vast halls and corridors. An occasional wild scream—a momentary distant crash as of a door breaking down and thundering upon the marble pavement; and then again, the long, strange cries, mingled with a dull, low sound as of a great moaning—all came up together, and seemed to meet Nehushta as she lifted the curtains and went out.

But the little Syrian maid grasped the Indian knife in her girdle, and stole stealthily upon her mistress's steps.

CHAPTER XX

Nehushta glided like a ghost along the corridors and dimly-lighted halls. As yet, the confusion seemed to be all in the lower story of the palace, but the roaring din rose louder every moment—the shrieks of wounded women with the moaning of wounded men, the clash of swords and arms, and, occasionally, a quick, loud rattle, as half a dozen arrows that had missed their mark struck the wall together.

Onward she flew, not pausing to listen, lest in a moment more the tide of fight should be forced up the stairs and overtake her. She shuddered as she passed the head of the great staircase and heard, as though but a few steps from her, a wild shriek that died suddenly into a gurgling death hiss.

She passed the treasury, whence the guards had fled, and in a moment more she was above the staircase that led down to the temple behind the palace. There was no one there as yet, as far as she could see in the starlight. The doors were shut, and the massive square building frowned through the gloom, blacker than its own black shadow.

Nehushta paused as she reached the door, and listened. Very faintly through the thick walls she could hear the sound of the evening chant. The priests were all within with Zoroaster, unconscious of their danger and of all that was going on in the palace, singing the hymns of the sacrifice before the sacred fire,—chanting, as it were, a dirge for themselves. Nehushta tried the door. The great bronze gates were locked together, and though she pushed, with her whole strength, they would not move a hair's breadth.

"Press the nail nearest the middle," said a small voice behind her. Nehushta started and looked round. It was the little Syrian slave, who had followed her out of the palace, and stood watching her in the dark. Nehushta put her hand upon the round head of the nail and pressed, as the slave told her to do. The door opened, turning slowly and noiselessly upon its hinges. Both women entered; the Syrian girl looked cautiously back and pushed the heavy bronze back to its place. The Egyptian artisan who had made the lock, had told one of the queen's women whom he loved the secret by which it was opened, and the Syrian had heard it repeated and remembered it.

Once inside, Nehushta ran quickly through the corridor between the walls and rushing into the inner temple, found herself behind the screen and in a moment more she stood before all the priests and before Zoroaster himself. But even as she entered, the Syrian slave, who had lingered to close the gates, heard the rushing of many feet outside, and the yelling of hoarse voices, mixed with the clang of arms.

Solemnly the chant rose around the sacred fire that seemed to burn by unearthly means upon the black stone altar. Zoroaster stood before it, his hands lifted in prayer, and his waxen face and snow-white beard illuminated by the dazzling effulgence.

The seventy priests, in even rank, stood around the walls, their hands raised in like manner as their chief priest's; their voices going up in a rich chorus, strong and tuneful, in the grand plain-chant. But Nehushta broke upon their melody, with a sudden cry, as she rushed before them.

"Zoroaster—fly—there is yet time. The enemy are come in thousands—they are in the palace. There is barely time!" As she cried to him and to them all, she rushed forward and laid one hand upon his shoulder.

But the high priest turned calmly upon her, his face unmoved, although all the priests ceased their chanting and gathered about their chief in sudden fear. As their voices ceased, a low roar was heard from without, as though the ocean were beating at the gates.

Zoroaster gently took Nehushta's hand from his shoulder.

"Go thou, and save thyself," he said kindly. "I will not go. If it be the will of the All-Wise that I perish, I will perish before this altar. Go thou quickly, and save thyself while there is yet time."

But Nehushta took his hand in hers, that trembled with the great emotion, and gazed into his calm eyes as he spoke—her look was very loving and very sad.

"Knowest thou not, Zoroaster, that I would rather die with thee than live with any other? I swear to thee, by the God of my fathers, I will not leave thee." Her soft voice trembled—for she was uttering her own sentence of death.

"There is no more time!" cried the voice of the little Syrian maid, as she came running into the temple. "There is no more time! Ye are all dead men! Behold, they are breaking down the doors!"

As she spoke, the noise of some heavy mass striking against the bronze gates echoed like thunder through the temple, and at each blow a chorus of hideous yells rose, wild and long-drawn-out, as though the fiends of hell were screaming in joy over the souls of the lost.

The priests drew together, trembling with fear, brave and devoted though they were. Some of them would have run towards the door, but the Syrian maid stood before them.

"Ye are dead men and there is no salvation—ye must die like men," said the little maid, quietly. "Let me go to my mistress." And she pushed through the crowd of white-robed men, who surged together in their sudden fear, like a white-crested wave heaved up from the deep by a fierce wind.

Nehushta still held Zoroaster's hand and stared wildly upon the helpless priests. Her one thought was to save the man she loved, but she saw well enough that it was too late. Nevertheless she appealed to the priests.

"Can none of you save him?" she cried.

Foremost in the little crowd was a stern, dark man—the same who had been the high priest before Zoroaster came, the same who had first hurled defiance at the intruder, and then had given him his whole allegiance. He spoke out loudly:

"We will save him and thee if we are able," he cried in brave enthusiasm for his chief. "We will take you between us and open the doors, and it may be that we can fight our way out—though we are all slain, he may be saved." He would have laid hold on Zoroaster, and there was not one of the priests who would not have laid down his life in the gallant attempt. But Zoroaster gently put him back.

"Ye cannot save me, for my hour is come," he said, and a radiance of unearthly glory stole upon his features, so that he seemed transfigured and changed before them all. "The foe are as a thousand men against one. Here we must die like men, and like priests of the Lord before His altar."

The thundering at the doors continued to echo through the whole temple, almost drowning every other sound as it came; and the yells of the infuriated besiegers rose louder and louder between.

Zoroaster's voice rang out clear and strong and the band of priests gathered more and more closely about him. Nehushta still held his hand tightly between her own, and, pale as death, she looked up to him as he spoke. The little Syrian girl stood, beside her mistress, very quite and grave.

"Hear me, ye priests of the Lord," said Zoroaster. "We are doomed men and must surely die, though we know not by whose hand we perish. Now, therefore, I beseech you to think not of this death which we must suffer in our mortal bodies, but to open your eyes to the things which are not mortal and which perish not eternally. For man is but a frail and changing creature as regards his mortality, seeing that his life is not longer than the lives of other created things, and he is delicate and sickly and exposed to manifold dangers from his birth. But the soul of man dieth not, neither is there any taint of death in it, but it liveth for ever and is made glorious above the stars. For the stars, also, shall have an end, and the earth—even as our bodies must end here this night; but our soul shall see the glory of God, the All-Wise, and shall live."

"The sun riseth and the earth is made glad, and it is day; and again he setteth and it is night, and the whole earth is sorrowful. But though our sun is gone down and we shall see him rise no more, yet shall we see a sun which setteth not for ever, and of whose gladness there is no end. The morning cometh, after which there shall be no evening. The Lord Ahura Mazda, who made all things, made also these our bodies, and put us in them to live and move and have being for a space on earth. And now he demands them again; for he gave them and they are his. Let us give them readily as a sacrifice, for he who knoweth all things, knoweth also why it is meet that we should die. And he who hath created all things which we see and which perish quickly, hath created also the things which we have not seen, but shall see hereafter;—and the time is at hand when our eyes shall be opened to the world which endureth, though they be closed in death upon the things which perish. Raise then a hymn of thanks with me to the All-Wise God, who is pleased to take us from time into eternity, from darkness into light, from change to immortality, from death by death to life undying."

"Praise we the All-Wise God, who hath made and created the years and the ages;
Praise him who in the heavens hath sown and hath scattered the seed of the stars;
Praise him who moves between the three ages that are, and that have been, and shall be;
Praise him who rides on death, in whose hand are all power and honour and glory;
Praise him who made what seemeth, the image of living, the shadow of life;
Praise him who made what is, and hath made it eternal for ever and ever,
Who made the days and nights, and created the darkness to follow the light,
Who made the day of life, that should rise up and lighten the shadow of death."

Zoroaster raised one hand to heaven as he chanted the hymn, and all the priests sang with him in calm and holy melody, as though death were not even then with them. But Nehushta still held his other hand fast, and her own were icy cold.

With a crash, as though the elements of the earth were dissolving into primeval confusion, the great bronze doors gave way, and fell clanging in—and the yells of the besiegers came to the ears of the priests, as though the cover had been taken from the caldron of hell, suffering the din of the damned and their devils to burst forth in demoniac discord.

In an instant the temple was filled with a swarm of hideous men, whose eyes were red with the lust of blood and their hands with slaughter. Their crooked swords gleamed aloft as they pressed forward in the rush, and their yells rent the very roof.

They had hoped for treasure,—they saw but a handful of white-robed unarmed men, standing around one taller than the rest; and in the throng they saw two women. Their rage knew no bounds, and their screams rose more piercing than ever, as they surrounded the doomed band, and overwhelmed them, and dyed their misshapen blades in the crimson blood that flowed so red and strong over the fair white vestures.

The priests struggled like brave men to the last. They grasped their hideous foes by arm and limb and neck, and tossed some of them back upon their fellows; fighting desperately with their bare hands against the armed murderers. But the foe were a hundred to one, and the priests fell in heaps upon each other while the blood flowed out between the feet of the wild, surging throng, who yelled and slew, and yelled again, as each priest tottered back and fell, with the death-wound in his breast.

At last, one tall wretch, with bloodied eyes and distorted features, leaped across a heap of slain and laid hold of Nehushta by the hair with his reeking hand, and strove to drag her out. But Zoroaster's thin arms went round her like lightning and clasped her to his breast. Then the little Syrian maid raised her Indian knife, with both hands, high above her head, and smote the villain with all her might beneath the fifth rib, that he died in the very act; but ere he had fallen, a sharp blade fell swiftly, like a crooked flash of light, and severed the small hands at the wrist; and the brave, true-hearted little maid fell shrieking to the floor. One shriek—and that was all; for the same sword smote her again as she lay, and so she died.

But Nehushta's head fell forward on the high priest's breast, and her arms clasped him wildly as his clasped her.

"Oh, Zoroaster, my beloved, my beloved! Say not any more that I am unfaithful, for I have been faithful even unto death, and I shall be with you beyond the stars for ever!"

He pressed her closer still, and in that awful moment, his white face blazed with the radiant light of the new life that comes by death alone.

"Beyond the stars and for ever!" he cried. "In the light of the glory of God most high!"

The keen sword flashed out once more and severed Nehushta's neck, and found its sheath in her lover's heart; and they fell down dead together, and the slaughter was done.

But on the third day, Darius the king returned; for a messenger met him, bringing news that his soldiers had slain the rebels in Echatana, though they were ten to one. And when he saw what things had been done in Stakhar, and looked upon the body of the wife he had loved, lying clasped in the arms of his most faithful and beloved servant, he wept most bitterly. And he rode forth and destroyed utterly the wild riders of the eastern hills, and left not one child to weep for its father that was dead. But two thousand of them he brought to Stakhar, and crucified them all upon the roadside, that their blood might avenge the blood of those he had loved so well.

And he took the bodies of Zoroaster the high priest, and of Nehushta the queen, and of the little Syrian maid, and he buried them with spices and fine linen, and in plates of pure gold, together in a tomb over against the palace, hewn in the rock of the mountain.

F. Marion Crawford – A Short Biography

Francis Marion Crawford was born in Bagni di Lucca, Italy on 2nd August, 1854, the only son of the American sculptor Thomas Crawford and Louisa Cutler Ward. His aunt was Julia Ward Howe, the American poet, most famous for the words to 'The Battle Hymn of the Republic'.

After his father's death in 1857, his mother remarried to Luther Terry, with whom she had Crawford's half-sister, Margaret Ward Terry.

Crawford's education began at St Paul's School, Concord, New Hampshire and then went on to Cambridge University, the University of Heidelberg and finally the University of Rome.

In 1879, Crawford went to India to study the ancient language of Sanskrit and to edit Allahabad, The Indian Herald.

Returning to America in February 1881, he enrolled at Harvard University for a year to continue his studies in Sanskrit. Crawford had no real career path at this time although for two years he contributed to various periodicals, mainly The Critic.

Early in 1882, Crawford established a close, lifelong friendship with Isabella Stewart Gardner, a noted and eccentric heiress from Boston who over the years built up a large and eclectic collection of art.

Crawford lived most of his time in Boston with his Aunt Julia and Uncle Sam. The family were concerned by his lack of ambition, prospects in general, and his financial ones in particular.

His mother had hoped he might train in Boston for a career as an operatic baritone based on his private renditions of Schubert lieder. With that in mind it was, in January 1882, that George Henschel, the conductor of the Boston Symphony Orchestra, was called in to assess young Crawford's talents. Henschel was direct and to the point. Crawford would 'never be able to sing in perfect tune'. His Uncle Sam, knowing that Crawford was keen on literary pursuits, proposed that his years in India might be good source material to write about. Crawford agreed. He set to work. Uncle Sam also set about developing contacts with a number of New York publishers.

Events moved very quickly. By December of that year Crawford had completed his first novel, 'Mr Isaacs', based on modern Anglo-Indian life flavoured with a touch of Oriental mystery. It was an immediate success. Crawford set about writing a second novel and the result was 'Dr Claudius' in 1883.

In October 1884 he married Elizabeth Berdan, the daughter of the Civil War Union General Hiram Berdan. The marriage would produce two sons; Harold and Bertram, and two daughters; Eleanor and Clara.

Crawford, buoyed by his excellent start, now decided to return to Italy and to live there permanently. The couple initially went to Sorrento and lived at the historic Hotel Cocumella during 1885 before moving permanently to Sant' Agnello, where the purchase of the Villa Renzi would now be rededicated as Villa Crawford.

As a writer Crawford had more than his fair share of detractors but, perhaps due to the physical distance between author and these detractors, they did not distract from his prolific output.

Each year seemed to bring a new F. Marion Crawford novel. His popularity was evident although some works, such as 1896's offering 'Adam Johnstone's Son', was described by his left-wing English contemporary, George Gissing, as "rubbish". Over half of his novels are set in Italy. He also wrote three long historical studies of Italy and was nearing completion on a history of Rome in the Middle Ages when he died.

His 'Saracinesca' series are considered his best works. The third in the series, 'Don Orsino' (1892) was told against the background of a real estate bubble and is especially effective. The volume immediately after was 'Corleone' (1897), and the first major treatment of the Mafia in literature.

Crawford himself was fondest of 'Khaled: A Tale of Arabia' (1891), a story of a genie who becomes human. 'A Cigarette-Maker's Romance' (1890) was dramatized, and had considerable popularity on the stage as well as in its novel form.

Towards the end of the 1890's Crawford ventured down another path with his writing. He began his historical works. 'Ave Roma Immortalis' was published in 1898, followed by 'Rulers of the South' (1900), and 'Gleanings from Venetian History' (1905). Most were re-titled with longer more explanatory titles for the American market. Within them all his careful and precise knowledge of the local Italian history together with his literary talents combined to great effect.

Whilst on an American Lecture tour in the winter of 1897-1898 Crawford was researching and gathering technical information for his historical work 'Marietta' (published 1901), that describes glass-making in late medieval Venice. Whilst visiting a glass-smelting plant in Colorado he suffered a severe lung injury when he inhaled toxic gasses. This would eventually contribute to his death a decade or so later.

Crawford's commercial popularity and appeal at the time was such that in 1901, the American Macmillan firm began a deluxe uniform edition of his novels as his works came up for re-printing. In 1904 the P. F. Collier Company in New York was authorized to publish a 25-volume edition (which was later expanded to 32 volumes).

In 1902 he wrote a stage play 'Francesca da Rimini', that was produced in Paris by his friend and legendary actress Sarah Bernhardt.

Towards the end of his life Hollywood had begun to realise that his works were a valuable source of stories and ideas and several were turned into movies and continued to be so for decades after his death.

Crawford also had a gift for pulling off excellent short stories. Several, such as 'The Upper Berth' (1886), 'For the Blood Is the Life' (1905, a vampiress tale), 'The Dead Smile' (1899), and 'The Screaming Skull' (1908), are among the most anthologized classics of the horror genre. After his death several collected volumes were published from various sources.

After most of his fictional works had been published, most had the view that he was a gifted narrator; and his books of fiction, were full of historic vitality and energy as well as dramatic characterization. He was widely popular among readers to whom literature was more for escapism than a confrontation with reality or pages of subjective analysis. In 'The Novel: What It Is' (1893), Crawford was both resolute and disarming in defending his literary approach, self-conceived as a combination of romanticism and realism, defining the art form in terms of its marketplace and audience. The novel, he wrote, is "a marketable commodity" and "intellectual artistic luxury" that "must amuse, indeed, but should amuse reasonably, from an intellectual point of view .... Its intention is to amuse and please, and certainly not to teach and preach; but in order to amuse well it must be a finely-balanced creation ...."

Francis Marion Crawford died at Sorrento on Good Friday 1909 at Villa Crawford of a heart attack.

F. Marion Crawford – A Concise Bibliography

Novels

Mr. Isaacs: A Tale of Modern India (1882)
Dr. Claudius (1883)
To Leeward (1884)
A Roman Singer (1884)
An American Politician (1884)

Zoroaster (1885)
A Tale of a Lonely Parish (1886)
Saracinesca (1887)
Marzio's Crucifix (1887)
Paul Patoff (1887)
With the Immortals (1888)
Greifenstein (1889)
Sant' Ilario (1889); sequel to Saracinesca
A Cigarette-Maker's Romance (1890)
Khaled: A Tale of Arabia (1891)
The Witch of Prague (1891)
The Three Fates (1892)
Don Orsino (1892); sequel to Sant' Ilario
The Children of the King (1893)
Pietro Ghisleri (1893)
Marion Darche (1893)
Katharine Lauderdale (1894)
The Upper Berth (1894); with "By the Waters of Paradise"
Love in Idleness (1894)
The Ralstons (1894); sequel to Katharine Lauderdale
Casa Braccio (1895); related to Katharine Lauderdale and The Ralstons.
Adam Johnstone's Son (1896)
Taquisara (1896)
A Rose of Yesterday (1897)
Corleone (1897)
Via Crucis (1899)
In the Palace of the King (1900)
Marietta (1901)
Cecilia (1902)
Man Overboard! (1903)
The Heart of Rome (1903)
Whosoever Shall Offend (1904)
Soprano (1905); U.S. title: Fair Margaret.
A Lady of Rome (1906)
Arethusa (1907)
The Little City of Hope (1907)
The Primadonna (1908); sequel to Soprano/Fair Margaret
The Diva's Ruby (1908); sequel to The Primadonna
The White Sister (1909)
Stradella (1909)
The Undesirable Governess (1910)
Wandering Ghosts; British title: Uncanny Tales.

Non-fiction

Our Silver (1881)
The Novel: What It Is (1893)

Constantinople (1895)
Bar Harbor (1896)
Ave Roma Immortalis (1898)
Rulers of the South (1900; 1905 in the U.S. as Southern Italy and Sicily and The Rulers of the South)
Gleanings from Venetian History (1905; in the U.S. as Salvae Venetia and in 1909 as Venice; the People and the Place)

Drama

In the Palace of the King (1900) with Lorrimer Stoddard.
Francesca da Rimini (1902) The piece was adapted into an opera by Franco Leoni in 1904.
Evelyn Hastings (1902) Unpublished typescript discovered in 2008.
The White Sister (1909) with Walter C. Hackett.

Filmography

A Cigarette-Maker's Romance, directed by Frank Wilson (UK, 1913, based on the novella)
The White Sister, directed by Fred E. Wright [it] (1915, based on the novel)
In the Palace of the King [it], directed by Fred E. Wright [it] (1915, based on the novel)
Whosoever Shall Offend, directed by Arrigo Bocchi (UK, 1919, based on the novel)
Il cuore di Roma, directed by Edoardo Bencivenga (Italy, 1919, based on the novel)
A Cigarette-Maker's Romance, directed by Tom Watts (UK, 1920, based on the novella)
Saracinesca [it], directed by Gaston Ravel (Italy, 1921, based on the novel)
Sant' Ilario [it], directed by Henry Kolker (Italy, 1923, based on the novel)
The White Sister, directed by Henry King (1923, based on the novel)
In the Palace of the King, directed by Emmett J. Flynn (1923, based on the novel)
Son of India, directed by Jacques Feyder (1931, based on the novel Mr. Isaacs)
The White Sister, directed by Victor Fleming (1933, based on the novel)
The Screaming Skull, directed by Alex Nicol (1958, named after the short story)
The White Sister, directed by Tito Davison (Mexico, 1960, based on the novel)